CHRISTOPHER & DANA REEVE FOUNDATION
PARALYSIS RESOURCE CENTER

Paralysis Resource Guide

Third Edition

by Sam Maddox

Paralysis Resource Guide
Third Edition

by Sam Maddox

This project was supported, in part by grant number 90PR3001, from the U.S. Administration for Community Living, Department of Health and Human Services, Washington, D.C. 20201. Grantees undertaking projects under government sponsorship are encouraged to express freely their findings and conclusions. Points of view or opinions do not, therefore, necessarily represent official Administration for Community Living policy.

Cover photograph by Timothy Greenfield-Sanders
Book design by Michael Kellner

The material contained in this book is presented for the purpose of educating and informing readers about paralysis and its effects. Nothing contained herein should be construed as medical diagnosis or treatment advice. This information should not be used in place of the advice of a physician or other qualified healthcare provider. If any questions arise while reading this book, the PRC strongly recommends contacting a physician or the appropriate healthcare provider.

ISBN 978-0-9726831-3-5

For information or to request additional copies of this book:
Paralysis Resource Center
636 Morris Turnpike, Suite 3A
Short Hills, New Jersey 07078
Toll-free 1-800-539-7309
email c/o infospecialist@ChristopherReeve.org

Acknowledgements

WELCOME TO THE THIRD EDITION of the *Paralysis Resource Guide*—it's up-to-date, bigger, deeper and here's hoping, more useful than ever.

Allow me to recognize key people at the Christopher & Dana Reeve Foundation, including Executive VP/Director of Research Susan Howley and VP, Policy and Programs Maggie Goldberg. PRC Senior Director Sheila Fitzgibbon and Director of Special Initiatives Douglas Landsman helped fact-check and bulletproof the text. Foundation staffers Rebecca Sultzbaugh, Donna Valente, Jenn Hatfield, Beth Eisenbud, Kathy McArthur, Patricia Stush, Katie Spiegel, Bernadette Mauro and the PRC team of Information Specialists also helped with the revision.

Very special thanks and kudos to Christopher Voelker, whose portraits grace this edition with personality and purpose. Mr. V is indeed a master of light, shadow and stagecraft. And thanks to Melanie Manson, who is married to Chris, for the art and craft of hair and makeup.

Thanks very much to Michael Kellner for the coherent and accommodating book design. Thank you Kate Lapin for editorial services.

This book is made possible by the support of the Department of Health and Human Services (HHS), Administration for Community Living (ACL), National Center on Birth Defects and Developmental Disabilities (NCBDDD). Many organizations in the disability community provided resources as we reach for the highest standards of verisimilitude.

The Paralysis Resource Guide is dedicated to the memories of Christopher Reeve and Dana Morosini Reeve. They lived life fully and fearlessly, with purpose and passion. The spirit of Chris and Dana is embodied in the pages of this book: Life is dear, choice is good, hope is irrepressible.

SM
Thousand Oaks, California

Table of Contents

KEN REGAN/CAMERA 5

PRC Welcome

HELLO, AND WELCOME TO THE PARALYSIS RESOURCE GUIDE. This book, created by the Christopher & Dana Reeve Foundation Paralysis Resource Center (PRC), offers comprehensive information and connections. Our goal is to help you find what you need to stay as healthy, as active and as independent as possible. The book serves the full community of people affected by paralysis, including of course loved ones and caregivers—people who know how paralysis can be a family issue.

Our founders, Christopher and Dana, understood how frightening it is to suddenly become paralyzed. Being active one day and immobile the next thrusts you suddenly into an entirely new existence. The changes are enormous and often overwhelming.

First, let us assure you that you are not alone. In the United States, there are 1.25 million people living with paralysis caused by spinal cord injury, and hundreds of thousands of others with paralysis caused by other types of trauma or disease. Although it's a club no one would choose to join, there are people who have gone through similar situations who are eager to help you maximize your health and well-being.

The PRC was created to provide information services and resources on the full range of topics related to paralysis, including specific health and clinical information on the various conditions that cause paralysis, whether by stroke, trauma or disease. We have strong ties with many national organizations to make sure you get the most relevant and reliable information.

Paralysis is much more than a medical issue, of course. The PRC hopes to encourage you to be active and to participate in your community as much on your own terms as possible. We have resources available on travel and recreation, specialized assistive equipment and automobiles, and key information to help navigate the healthcare and insurance systems.

You'll also find information on a multitude of organizations around the country that offer programs to promote independent living for children and adults with paralysis. You will find numerous listings in this book devoted to accessibility, health promotion, advocacy, research, and more. We have funded numerous Quality of Life grants through the PRC and the Christopher & Dana Reeve Foundation to support such organizations around the country.

If you don't find what you need here in the book, be sure and visit the PRC Website, **www.paralysis.org**. If you prefer to speak to a trained information specialist, please contact us by phone (toll-free 1-800-539-7309) or email (*infospecialist@ChristopherReeve.org*) and we will research your question for you.

Finally, and perhaps most importantly, we want you to know that paralysis is not a hopeless condition. Scientists are making steady progress in deciphering the complexities of diseases and injuries to the brain and spinal cord; we are convinced that they will succeed in developing treatments for acute and chronic paralysis. To learn even more about promising research, and how to support the Foundation's mission, visit the website **www.ChristopherReeve.org**

—The PRC Staff

Message From the President and CEO

WELCOME TO THE PARALYSIS RESOURCE GUIDE, a one-stop handbook to help you and your loved ones through the often bewildering world of paralysis.

The goals of this book and of the Christopher & Dana Reeve Foundation Paralysis Resource Center are to improve the lives of millions of people living with paralysis. We offer information you can trust in order to make the best choices for a fulfilling and active life.

The Reeve Foundation has over the years invested millions of dollars to support research to restore function in the damaged spinal cord. While we expect the long-term payoff of treatments and cures, we understand the day-to-day challenges of living with paralysis. That's why we offer tools, services and resources, here and now, through our Quality of Life grants and the Paralysis Resource Center.

We also advocate for the rights of people with disabilities; we want you to be armed with the information and knowledge you need to face the world of paralysis with the fierce determination and courage of our namesakes.

We have a wonderful, dedicated team here at the Foundation carrying on Christopher and Dana's vision and keeping their legacy of hope and perseverance alive. But we all know there is much work ahead of us; we have yet to reach our goal of mobility, full participation and independence for all citizens. Until that day, we will continue to pursue today's care and tomorrow's cure.

PETER WILDEROTTER
President and CEO
Christopher & Dana Reeve Foundation

Message From the PRC Director

WINFIELD WETHERBEE

THE PARALYSIS RESOURCE CENTER was created in 2002 to provide a comprehensive, national resource to promote health, foster community involvement and improve quality of life for people living with paralysis, their caregivers and loved ones. Our staff is dedicated to providing a roadmap to navigate the inevitable chaos of paralysis.

Our message, like that of our founders, Christopher and Dana, is full of hope. It is upbeat and encouraging, credible and realistic. Paralysis can be a devastating occurrence—for the affected individual, of course, but also for families and friends.

The Paralysis Resource Center, formed through a cooperative agreement with the Centers for Disease Control and Prevention, offers information (in English, Spanish and several Asian languages, including Chinese, Vietnamese and Korean) directly by telephone from our team of information specialists (toll-free 1-800-539-7309), by e-mail (*infospecialist@ ChristopherReeve.org*) or online at **www.paralysis.org**, and in print here in the Paralysis Resource Guide. The Reeve Foundation's Resource Center offers a variety of services and programs:

Peer & Family Support: This is a national peer-to-peer mentoring program providing critical emotional support as well as local and national information and resources to people living with paralysis, and their families and caregivers. The peer mentoring program is founded on the notion that you should not be alone. For more see page 172.

Information Specialist Services: Our seasoned specialists, several of whom live with spinal cord injury, answer questions regarding paralysis by providing reliable information and referral to local, state, and national resources. We answer questions on all topics from insurance

Continued on next page

Continued from previous page

reimbursement, equipment needs to health information and home modifications. Through interpreter services, our team can provide free information in over 150 languages.

Library: A free lending library of over 5,000 books and videos on paralysis which are loaned through national interlibrary program or directly to one's home. The library is open to the public in Short Hills, NJ.

Quality of Life Grants: This program provides financial support to organizations that serve people with disabilities, their families and caregivers. The Quality of Life program awards grants to a wide range of nonprofit organizations that offer accessible playgrounds, wheelchair sports, therapeutic riding, emergency services after natural disasters, and much more.

Military and Veterans: This Reeve Foundation initiative addresses the needs of service members, whether they are paralyzed through combat-related, service-related, or non-service related events. We help with navigating the military and veterans systems and also with the transition back to the community. See Chapter 8, page 318.

Multicultural Outreach: This program serves diverse populations across the United States and partners with organizations to improve the quality of life for people living with paralysis in underserved communities.

Online Community: The Foundation's website, **www.paralysis.org**, is a rich depository of connection and camaraderie. The online community enables people to connect and share solutions with others living with paralysis. The Reeve community is active, friendly and helpful, and features an expert team of contributors; the blog Life After Paralysis articulates self-reliance, resourcefulness and optimism. Our writers put a face on living well with paralysis.

We hope you find this book, and our other information services, to be beneficial. Remember, the Paralysis Resource Center is here for you; you don't have to be alone.

Maggie Goldberg
Vice President, Policy and Programs

Portraits

BY

CHRISTOPHER VOELKER

The portraits in the following pages, and others starting on page 352, celebrate the very human faces of people living with disability and paralysis. The galleries embody grace and composure, and perhaps a bit of whimsy. If you look closely in the shadows you might detect a hint of pathos. But there is no tragedy or regret: these people are alive and well, eager to share their stories, and happy, if asked, to offer advice or to inspire. The idea, says photographer Christopher Voelker, "is to capture persons living with a disability as creative works of art in themselves, while removing the stigma of illogical stereotyping." Voelker's own story informs his art; he joined the spinal cord injury community as a tetraplegic at 17, the result of a motocross accident. Voelker, an Ambassador for Reeve Foundation, says the assignment of photographing portraits for the *Paralysis Resource Guide* is "a dream come true. I am proud to work with the Reeve Foundation to help spread awareness of its mission. I hope my work opens the doors for people living with paralysis to jump into their own dreams."

Chelsie Hill

R O L L   M O D E L

In 2010, when I was 17, I was a passenger in a drunk driving accident, leaving me a T10 paraplegic. Growing up dancing, that was the worst possible news I thought I could ever hear. People would say, 'once a dancer always a dancer.' That made no sense at first. But I learned that 'giving up' is not in my vocabulary, that if you set your mind to it, you can do anything. I'm co-founder of Team Hotwheelz wheelchair dance team, and my dad and I started the Walk and Roll Foundation; we educate teens and adults about how to make responsible choices, especially in regards to driving under the influence of alcohol, substance abuse, or while distracted. By my example I hope to show that you are not defined by the physical—live your life the way that makes you happy because if you're not happy ... no one around you will be. Keep calm and push on! (*Chelsie appears regularly on the television series* Push Girls).

Ali Stroker

A C T R E S S & S I N G E R

Ali Stroker was spinal cord injured in a car accident when she was two. She was born singing, a talent that she has nurtured into a career. She was the first person in a wheelchair to be cast in a leading role in a professional music production (*The 25th Annual Putnam County Spelling Bee* at the Paper Mill Playhouse in Milburn, NJ). Ali is a longtime ambassador for the Reeve Foundation. A Jersey girl with a California look, she has a broad outlook about the greater scheme of things. Says she, "I've never seen my injury as a disability. Having a spinal cord injury and being in a wheelchair has always felt like an opportunity to see and do things a little differently. My advice to people is this: Always keep your mind and heart open. Any time a door closes know that another one is opening just around the corner. Find the gift in every moment. We are the lucky ones!" *www.alistroker.com*

Leon Bostick

S T R O N G M A N

L eon Bostick, a former Marine who holds degrees in chemical engineering, business and law, got hurt when a weight machine loaded with weight broke and landed on him, injuring his spinal cord. He stays strong; though unable to grip, he can still lift. He has two things to say to someone who might be new to the world of paralysis. "First, get out of the house and be sociable. It's too easy to be comfortable at home." Second, says Leon, "You have to try more things after your injury than you did before. I never went skiing before my injury. Never went surfing or scuba diving. I'm still doing things I never thought about doing before I used a wheelchair."

Patterson Grissom

SOLDIER — WWII

I grew up on a farm in Kansas. In 1944 I was in the Army, Third Infantry Division. We had just crossed the Rhine; at about 4:30 a.m. I stopped a bullet. My claim to fame is that I'm always going to be known as the guy who threw Marlon Brando out of the hospital. A bunch of us paraplegics were living at the Birmingham Hospital, that's in Van Nuys, California. One of the guys was friends with a girl who worked in a Hollywood studio and knew producer Stanley Kramer. He was famous for making *Home of the Brave*, a war movie, and *Champion*, which had just won an Oscar; he wanted to know more about us injured guys. Well, at the time director John Ford had an estate in nearby Reseda and hosted a weekly barbeque for vets who were the combat photographers. They had invited us guys from Birmingham, too, along with Kramer and screenwriter Carl Forman. We were told some Hollywood guys were thinking of making a movie about us. Not long after, we heard that Kramer would direct the picture; he had convinced Marlon Brando to come west—he was on Broadway starring in *A Streetcar Named Desire* and had never been west before. Brando went on to play Bud Wilcheck, a World War II paraplegic, with Jack Webb as another para. The movie was called *The Men*. Some of us in Birmingham got parts as extras and I got a speaking part. In the script, Brando was raising hell, came in drunk to the hospital, where we all lived, and started breaking windows and crashing his wheelchair around. I spoke up, saying, "He's married, he has a car, there is no reason he has to be here. I say we throw him out." And Brando did get booted out of the hospital. I thought the script was quite good, very realistic about what we were going through. It wasn't a documentary but it showed us guys in wheelchairs doing rehab, playing basketball. It changed the way people thought about paraplegia. (*Grissom, living with paralysis for nearly 70 years, makes his home in Northridge, CA*).

Lyena Strelkoff

M O M ,   S P E A K E R ,   W R I T E R

Let me be clear about something—paralysis sucks. The daily incontinence, the brittle and breaking bones, the amount of time and energy it takes to get dressed or get in and out of the car. You can be sure when my son pulls at my shirt and says, "Mama, up!" gratitude is the last thing on my mind. And yet, when I look at the greatest blessings of my life, the gems that live at the very heart of me, they ALL arrived through the doorway of paralysis. Falling taught me the most remarkable lessons, and somehow it fine-tuned my existing skills so that I could share those lessons, and teach others how to share their lessons, in life-changing ways. In my case, tragedy was a catalyst for extraordinary transformation. Paralysis definitely brought out the best in me. It's made me kinder, more compassionate, more generous. Goddess knows it's made me more patient. It's brought out my resilience, and shown me courage I did not know I had. It's made me more still, yes, in very painful ways, but also in the best possible way. I am so much more able to receive, to allow good things and good life to flow into me. And maybe most importantly, it's given me voice, and I am serving others with that voice. For all the pain and heartache and frustration, paralysis has brought out my brilliance, and I am shinier than I ever imagined I could be. (Excerpt from *www.itsnotaboutthechair.com*).

Alan Rucker

W R I T E R

I woke up from a nap one Tuesday afternoon, felt a nerve-induced ring of fire around my waist, and an hour and a half later was paralyzed for life. It was like an anvil had fallen out of the sky and hit me in the back. In reality, it was something called transverse myelitis, a kind of MS of the spine that usually strikes only once, but as in my case, can leave a lot of damage in its path. I was 51 at the time, my so-called career as a Hollywood writer had flat-lined, I had a mortgage the size of Montana, and my mother-in-law had just moved in to stay. As a good friend said, to have all of this misfortune at once, I must have really screwed someone over in a former life. It took me years to recover from this maelstrom, but I did. The good news for anyone struck down like this is that there is life after paralysis. You have to make it up as you go along and it takes years to work through it. Most people think they would turn into a pill-popping basket case if they became paralyzed. Some will, but most find they have more grit than they ever imagined. If there is a "lesson" to paralysis, it's this: you are not the weak sister you thought you were. And, by association, that applies to your worst fears and most intractable problems. Just recalibrate and move on. I write books and articles now, and have nothing to do with TV. That was my major recalibration. I'm already sitting—I might as well do it in front of a computer screen. Work got me through those early days of grief and doubt, but it is not as important anymore. Job #1 now is my health. Job #2: living life with my family and in George Carlin's words, "watching the carnival." Work now is writing about all of that. What else? Maybe going to Scotland someday. That's about it.

Rucker is a regular contributor to the blog "Life After Paralysis," online at www.ChristopherReeve.org

Angela Rockwood

P U S H   G I R L   &   M O D E L

A ngela Rockwood is one of the Push Girls. She's the model, the one who split with her husband. She became paralyzed in an auto accident in 2001. Though she can't fully move her fingers, Angela can work a phone and computer, push a manual chair, feed herself, paint and apply her own makeup. She is an Ambassador for the Christopher & Dana Reeve Foundation, and worked with the organization's Multicultural Outreach program in Asian-American communities. Angela lives in Los Angeles. and embraces a sort of sunny-side up personality to match the scene. "I had been transported to the realm of the paralyzed for a reason," she says. "I realized I had a huge choice to make: to go down the positive path, be an example for others in similar positions and be a voice." And the voice says: "Nothing in life is to be feared. It is only to be understood... It is confidence in our bodies, minds and spirits that allows us to keep looking for new adventures, new directions to grow in, and new lessons to learn. Just live life and lose the fear."

Christiaan Bailey

P R O S U R F E R

C hristiaan "Otter" Bailey sustained a spinal cord injury in 2006. "When people first get hurt, they initially feel as their life may be over to a certain extent, because they might not have the same physical abilities they once did," he says. "I prefer to look at this experience from the point of Spirit, Mind, Body. If you have the Spirit to pursue what you are passionate about, no matter the cost, and train your Mind to focus on your goals, no matter the distraction, then you can triumph over any challenge the Body can throw at you." These days Bailey is a professional surfer who travels the world. He helped create an adaptive adventure foundation, Ocean Healing Group, specifically tailored for youngsters who use wheelchairs, and their parents. They have programs in both Costa Rica and Australia and empower kids with disabilities by exposing them to a wide variety of adaptive adventure sports, including surfing, chairskating, scuba diving, ziplining and riding. Says Bailey, "We operate under the mantra of helping kids carve the 'dis' out of disability."

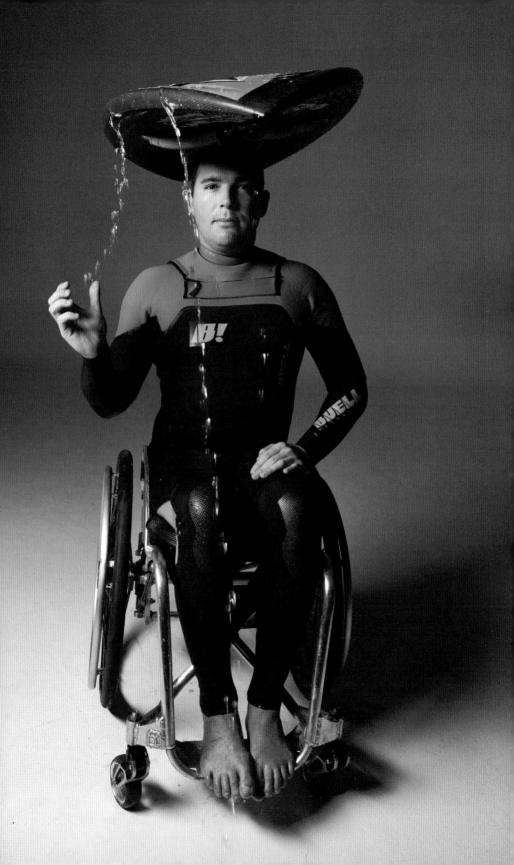

Zack Weinstein

A C T O R

When he was in college, Zack, a theater major, broke his neck. Thinking a tetraplegic is going to have a tough career road ahead, some of his professors tried to get him to change his major. He refused to take any of their advice. "I can still talk and express emotions, so why can't I continue to study acting?" That he has done, having moved with his wife to Los Angeles. It's a tough town to get a break in. Zack has tasted success with a nice singing part on the hit show *Glee*, and a part in *Criminal Minds*. Says Zack: "I sometimes meet resistance at auditions for parts that aren't necessarily written for somebody in a wheelchair, but I've also had casting directors and directors who are wonderful about that in the other direction. Like the great thing about *Criminal Minds* is that they brought me in for the part, and the part had nothing to do with being in a wheelchair. It was just a smart-ass kid in the classroom." He was awarded the Christopher & Dana Reeve Foundation Acting Scholarship at the 2012 Media Access Awards to pursue his craft. "The scholarship is a vote of confidence for me. I've had some success that I'm really proud of in this industry, and I'm just like any other actor in this town; I'm working really hard to continue to build on it." Zack was a beneficiary of other Reeve support: "My family and I were greatly assisted by the Paralysis Resource Center and its Information Specialists. This book, the PRG, was enormously helpful."

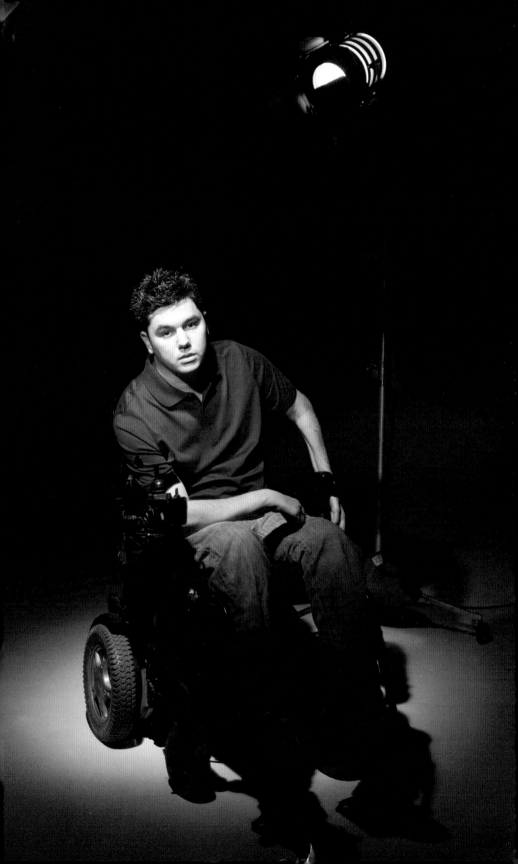

Danielle Sheypuk

T H E R A P I S T

Dating, relationships, and sexuality are fundamental to our health and happiness as human beings. Evidenced in the multitude of television shows and movies, pop culture tells us that it is a universal struggle of significant magnitude. But grappling with 'finding the one' and feeling fulfilled sexually is more than just the plot of a hit television show, it is essential to our emotional and physical well-being." That's from Danielle Sheypuk, a clinical psychologist who's on a mission to include people with disabilities into the dating mix. Danielle is employed full-time at the Bensonhurst Outpatient Clinic of South Beach Psychiatric Center, part of the New York State Office of Mental Health. "While there have been many campaigns designed to improve the lives of people with physical disabilities, very little attention has been paid to improving their romantic relationships. I advocate for the recognition and improvement of this important facet of our lives. Like those long ago arriving at Ellis Island, I came to Manhattan hoping for a land of opportunity and finding a freedom from the constraints of attempting to date with a physical disability. Since my arrival more than a decade ago, I have put myself out there on the dating scene. My experience and struggles with dating and relationships has taught me that this is a widespread problem, not one relegated to small towns like the one I left (Scranton, PA); this problem has become my passion."

Ellen Stohl

W I F E , M O M , T E A C H E R

Written in 1986: "My name is Ellen Stohl, I am a model/actress, who three years ago was injured in a tragic auto accident. At first, I had given up hope of pursuing my career, but after a few months and a lot of learning, I realized a wheelchair should not make a difference. Since that realization, I have been working twice as hard to achieve my career goals not only for myself but also to teach society that being disabled does not make a difference. The reason I choose *Playboy* for this endeavor is that sexuality is the hardest thing for disabled persons to hold onto. Not to say that they are not capable, but rather that society's emphasis on perfection puts this definitive damper on self-esteem. Well, I believe it is time to show society the real story. Anyone can be sexy; it is a matter of how a person feels about himself or herself, and personally I feel great."

Ellen was indeed selected to pose for the magazine. She says it helped change the cultural landscape to define women with disabilities as whole women. Today she is married, has a daughter and teaches a class on the principles of educational psychology at Cal State Northridge.

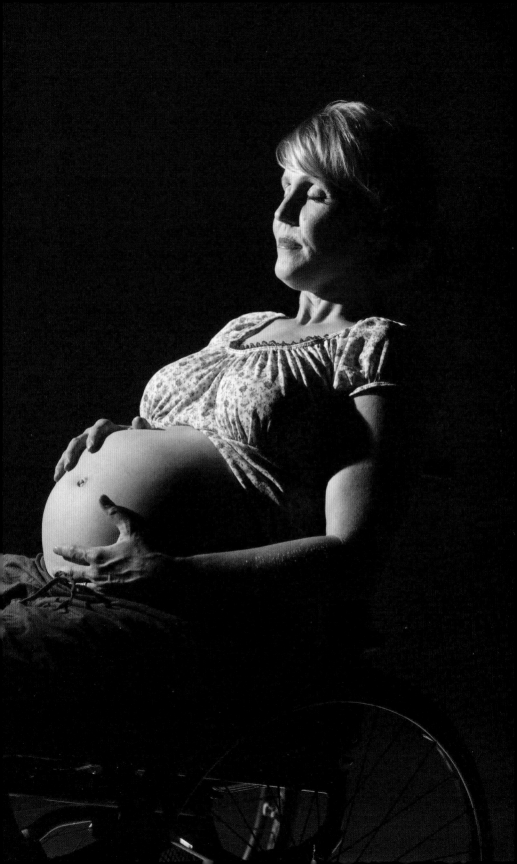

Geri Jewell

C O M E D I E N N E

In 1980, Geri Jewell was cast as Cousin Geri on the NBC sitcom *The Facts Of Life*. This was a breakthrough role—she was the first person with a disability to have a regular role on a prime-time series. She literally taught America about disability. Geri, who has cerebral palsy, broke into show business as a comedienne. Meanwhile, she has been on several other shows, most recently as Jewel in the HBO series *Deadwood*. Along the way, she's bumped up against abuse, discrimination and Hollywood backstabbing, chronicled in her autobiography *I'm Walking as Straight as I Can: Transcending Disability in Hollywood and Beyond*. How does Geri deal? With humor and honesty. And a lot of perseverance. Says she: "CP in itself has been the greatest blessing in my life. I don't look at cerebral palsy as a negative or a positive. I look at CP as a neutral. It's part of the human condition. We all have adversity so we can grow and evolve and learn. I believe that my success partially had to do with the theory of the bumblebee. Scientifically and technically, a bumblebee's body weight is too heavy to fly with those tiny little wings. But the bumblebee doesn't know any different. So she just flies away."

Jenni Gold

D I R E C T O R

I have spinal muscular atrophy and began using an electric wheelchair in the 6th grade. I went to film school at the University of Central Florida and directed my first feature in 1998--the indy action film *Ready, Willing and Able*, which cast an actress with a disability as our action hero and included never-before-seen wheelchair stunts. I am a proud member of the Directors Guild of America; I opened a production company, Gold Pictures, in 2001. I have done a number of video projects for the Reeve Foundation, including a series on driving and cars, and a 32-segment piece on power wheelchairs. I am married, I have a strong sense of faith, and I believe that there is no such word as "can't." I'm on the right path, but it is long and bumpy. But I like what director Billy Wilder said: "Trust your own instinct. Your mistakes might as well be your own, instead of someone else's." I like this quote too, from Winston Churchill: "Never, never, never give up."

Joseph Ogbomon

C O M P U T E R E N G I N E E R

I am so lucky to live in a digital age. Advanced digital technology enriches my daily life and makes my existence full of meaning. Without computers and the Internet, I cannot imagine how I could spend every day in my wheelchair. Disability is still a painful experience but the joy, opportunity and convenience that the Internet brings me is also unlimited. I earnestly wish that every disabled person and children from poor homes in the world will someday have a computer of their own so they can have the same chance to make full use of their talents and will feel the love and equality between human beings which I now experience every day of my life. Knowing that for people living with disabilities, computers and the Internet are nothing less than the very best of God's gifts. In cyberspace or on the Internet the differences between high and low, rich and poor, disabled and able-bodied all melt away."

(Joseph founded a charity, CompuTech For Humanity, which has received funding from the Reeve Foundation Quality of Life Grant program; he provides rebuilt computers free of charge to people with disabilities; see *www.computechforhumanity.org*).

Katie Sharify

S T E M   C E L L   P I O N E E R

Katie Sharify was the fifth and final person to get injected with embryonic stem cells in the now-defunct Geron trial in 2011. One might wonder, how does a person make the pressure-packed decision (within two weeks of injury) to participate in a high-profile clinical trial that may not help. In her case, Katie decided, against the wishes of her parents, to get the cells—not for herself, but in order to help the field of regenerative medicine. If you go into the trial for selfish reasons, she said, you will be disappointed. Katie was 23 at the time she was spinal cord injured in an auto accident in Northern California. She also had a brain injury and so for the first week in intensive care, she was in a drugged-up haze. When she came to her senses, her parents, who do not speak English well, told her she was paralyzed but that she was going to be in a clinical trial that would cure her. Her doctors had sized Katie up as a candidate for the Geron trial and had begun discussions with her parents. Once the medical team explained to Katie what stem cells were, and that she would be enrolled in a safety trial that would probably not lead to any recovery, she had to break this news to her parents; they immediately objected to any further participation. Katie thought about it, did her own research, asked a million questions and came to understand the risks. She knew she would be signing on for 15 years of follow-up. She finally said yes. So far, no recovery. And many months later, after some moments of regret and second guessing, Katie says she made the right decision and would do it again. "It's bigger than me," she says.

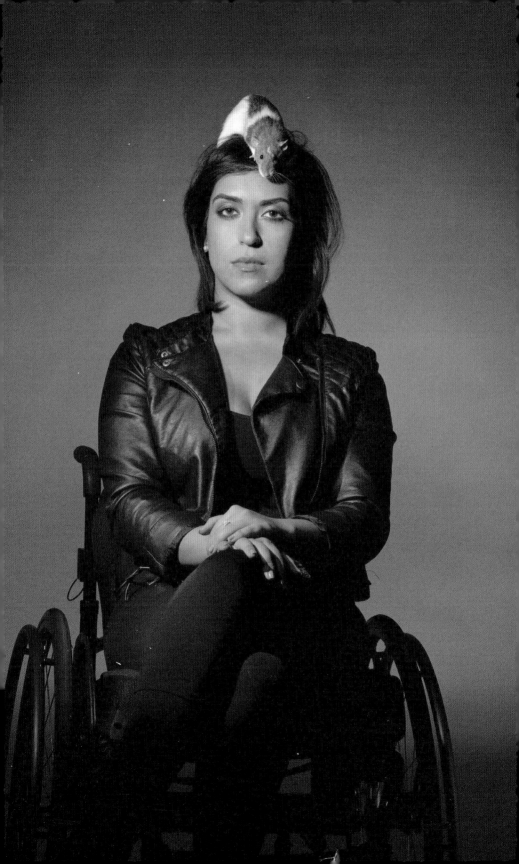

Tommy Hollenstein

P A I N T E R

Tommy Hollenstein's artwork is colorful and chaotic yet infused with the optimism and transformative drama that define the Southern California experience. He paints by joystick, that is, with the tires of his power wheelchair—rolling through paint spilled on the floor, or with a dab of color coated on the tires. He starts with a quarter-inch masonite board, which an assistant has prepped with a base color. He puts it on the floor and looks over the side of his power chair to master the paint hitting the board. Once he lays down a tone, even just a small patch, he stops to hose off the tires, lets the first paint dry then adds a new layer. A single painting may take as many as 50 layers of paint and several weeks to complete. Tommy's powerwheels story began in March 1985 after he crashed his mountain bike. He says he'd wanted to be an artist since he was five. But without any use of his hands, he didn't see how. The redemptive art story begins 12 years into quad-life with Weaver, a service dog. Man and dog had an almost psychic bond. As Weaver got old Tommy wanted to make a tribute: "I literally poured puddles of paint on a canvas so I could roll through it and Weaver could walk through it. I just wanted to see tire tracks and paw prints." The result was more than a keepsake. It was epiphanous. Tommy realized he had colors and shapes and feelings bubbling up. He experimented with paints and surfaces, developed the layered style that some regard as Jackson Pollock-like, rolled through many quarts of Disney-like paint, and he is indeed a serious painter now. His works are in the homes of actor Joachim Phoenix, writer Dean Koontz and rock guitarist Slash. Says Tommy, "I want people to go get a positive feeling, to move beyond their expectations, their limitations, including people who are not disabled. Go do something you dreamed about as a child. That's what I did." See the art at *www.tommyhollenstein.com*

Basics by Conditions

Paralysis is the result of nerve damage in the brain or spinal cord, due to trauma, disease, or birth condition. This chapter characterizes the primary causes.

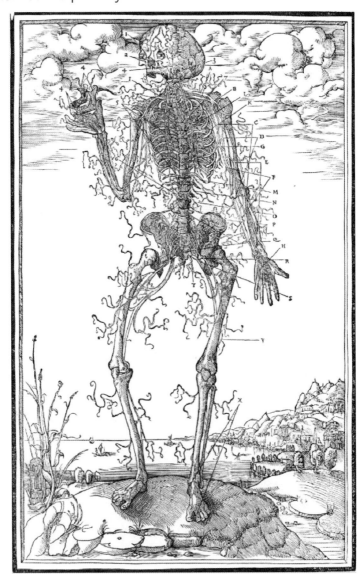

ALS

AMYOTROPHIC LATERAL SCLEROSIS (ALS), also known as Lou Gehrig's disease after the New York Yankee baseball player who was diagnosed with it, is a rapidly progressive neurological disease that affects as many as 30,000 Americans, with nearly 6,000 new cases occurring each year.

ALS belongs to a group of disorders known as motor neuron diseases. Motor neurons are nerve cells located in the brain, brainstem, and spinal cord that serve as control units and communication links between the nervous system and the voluntary muscles of the body. The loss of these cells causes the muscles under their control to weaken and waste away, leading to paralysis. ALS is often fatal within five years of diagnosis, mainly due to respiratory failure. People who opt for permanent use of a feeding tube and a ventilator after failure of swallowing and respiratory muscles can generally be kept alive for many more years.

ALS symptoms may include frequent tripping and falling; loss of control in hands and arms; difficulty speaking, swallowing, and/or breathing; persistent fatigue; and twitching and cramping. Typically, ALS strikes in midlife. For reasons unknown, men are about one-and-a-half times more likely to have the disease than women.

Because ALS affects motor neurons, the disease does not usually impair a person's mind, personality, or intelligence. It does not affect the ability to see, smell, taste, hear, or recognize touch. People with ALS usually maintain control of eye muscles and bladder and bowel function.

There is no known cure for ALS, nor is there a therapy to prevent or reverse its course. Riluzole is the only FDA-approved drug shown to prolong the survival of people with ALS—but only for a few extra months. Riluzole is believed to minimize damage to motor neurons due to the release of the neurotransmitter glutamate. ALS patients have raised levels of glutamate in the fluid bathing the brain and spinal cord. Riluzole may also extend the time before a person needs ventilation support. Riluzole does not reverse the damage already done to motor neurons however, and people taking the drug must be monitored for liver damage and other possible side effects.

In 2011, the FDA approved the NeuRx Diaphragm Pacing System (DPS) for ALS patients experiencing breathing issues. Clinical trials demonstrated that DPS neurostimulation helped ALS patients live longer and sleep better than with standard care. **www.synapsebiomedical.com** (see pages 152-153 for more).

ALS experts have identified numerous compounds that show promise for treating the disease. Several drugs and cell therapies are currently being tested in patients. A company called Neuralstem has enrolled several dozen patients in a clinical trial testing neural stem cells; there have been no safely issues and some indication that the cells are beneficial. See **www.neuralstem.com**

There is strong evidence that trophic factors, molecules that nurture and protect cells, can rescue dying neurons in animal models of ALS. Indeed, targeted delivery to a vulnerable cell may be beneficial. So far, human trials have failed to follow up on success in animals. This work is still in progress.

A drug called arimoclomol, originally developed to treat diabetic complications, inhibits progression of ALS in a mouse model of the disease. Arimoclomol is thought to amplify "molecular chaperone" proteins, normally found in all cells of the body; these cells may protect a motor nerve cell against toxic proteins, repairing those that are believed to cause diseases such as ALS. Arimoclomol appears to accelerate the regeneration of previously damaged nerves in animals. Early phase clinical trials have shown the drug to be safe in humans; more tests are ongoing for dose and treatment.

Drug cocktails: Recent mouse model studies of ALS showed dramatic benefits using a combination of drugs, including Riluzole, nimodipine (a calcium channel blocker used in the treatment of acute stroke and migraine headache) and minocycline (an antibiotic that may block inflammation). The compounds given together appear to delay cell death, prevent nerve cell loss, and reduce inflammation. For more on ALS clinical trials, see **www.clinicaltrials.gov**

Physical or occupational therapy and special equipment can enhance independence and safety throughout the course of ALS. Low-impact aerobic exercise such as walking, swimming, and stationary bicycling can strengthen unaffected muscles, prevent deconditioning, improve cardiovascular health, and help patients fight fatigue and depression. Range-of-motion and stretching exercises can help prevent painful spasticity and muscle contractures (shortening of muscles, limits joint movement). Occupational therapists can suggest devices such as ramps, braces, walkers, and wheelchairs that help people conserve energy and remain mobile, while making it easier to perform activities of daily living.

Respiratory weakness: People with ALS are at risk for pneumonia and pulmonary embolism. Indicators of deteriorating respiratory status can include difficulty breathing, especially when lying down or after meals; lethargy; drowsiness; confusion; anxiety; irritability; loss of appetite; fatigue; morning headaches; and depression. When the muscles that assist in breathing weaken, use of ventilatory assistance (intermittent positive pressure ventilation, IPPV; or bi-level positive airway pressure, BiPAP) may be used to aid breathing during sleep. When muscles are no longer able to maintain oxygen and carbon dioxide levels, these devices may be required full-time.

Another problem common to many people with ALS is the inability to cough forcefully enough to clear away even normal amounts of mucus. People are advised to make sure their fluid intake is sufficient to keep the secretions thin; some take an over-the-counter cough medicine containing the expectorant guaifenesin, a mucus thinner. A weak cough can be made more effective by quad coughing (assisting a cough by applying a sort of Heimlich-like maneuver as the patient coughs), supplying fuller breaths with an ambu-bag to improve the cough, or using a device such as a "cofflator" or "in-exsufflator" (delivers deep breaths through a mask and then quickly reverses to negative pressure to simulate a cough).

Drooling: While people with ALS do not overproduce saliva, their swallowing problems can create sialorrhea, or excess salivation and drooling. Sialorrhea can be undertreated—it may take trials of several medications until one provides relief without undesirable side effects.

Muscle problems: Spasticity is present in some people with ALS. It causes a tightening of muscles and a stiffening of the arms, legs, back, abdomen, or neck. It can be triggered by a simple touch and can be painful especially if it sets off muscle cramps, common in ALS because of muscle fatigue. Cramps can be very painful but become less severe with time—weakening muscles can't tighten into a cramp anymore. Fasciculation (muscle twitching) is common, too, though these are not painful so much as annoying.

Loss of communication: While the loss of the ability to communicate is not life-threatening or painful, being "locked-in" is a very frustrating aspect of ALS. Although assistive technology offers many solutions, it may be underutilized because people lack information about their options. Assistive devices range from simple call buttons and sensitive switches to small communication boards that speak pre-recorded words and messages. Also, equipment is available to magnify a weak whisper into audible speech. If a person can move nearly any body part, there is potential for some basic communication. Numerous communication devices are on the market and can be found in many home health dealers or Internet shopping sites. See **www.alsa.org** for a list of products and vendors.

In experiments using brain waves, people who are locked-in due to ALS have learned to communicate by way of a computer using only their thoughts. For example, trials of the BrainGate System, which implants a sensor in the brain to transmit, have shown that neural signals associated with the intent to move a limb can be "decoded" by a computer in real-time and used to operate external devices, including robot arms. Trials are ongoing; see **http://cyberkineticsinc.com**

There are other ways that computers can be used by people who are almost totally paralyzed. See page 276 for more information on hands-free control of cursors for communication, entertainment, and even work. Research holds great promise for treatments for ALS, including drugs, cell transplants, gene therapy, and immune system modulation.

SOURCES

National Institute on Neurological Disorders and Stroke, ALS Association

❧ **Below are links to resources.**

ALS Association (ALSA) features news, research support, and resources; it offers a national network of support groups, clinics, and specialty hospitals. ALSA has funded about $70 million to identify the cause and a cure for ALS. 202-407-8580; **www.alsa.org**

The ALS Therapy Development Foundation is a nonprofit biotechnology company working to discover treatments. 617-441-7200; **www.als.net**

Project ALS aligns researchers and doctors from many disciplines to collaborate and share data openly in four main areas: basic research, genetics, stem cells, and drug screening. 212-420-7382, toll-free 1-800-603-0270; **www.projectals.org**

ARTERIOVENOUS MALFORMATIONS

ARTERIOVENOUS MALFORMATIONS (AVMs) are defects of the circulatory system that are believed to arise during fetal development or soon after birth. They comprise snarled tangles of arteries and veins, disrupting the vital cycle that would normally carry oxygen-saturated blood in arteries away from the heart to the body's cells, and return oxygen-depleted blood by way of veins to the lungs and heart. An AVM directly connects arteries and veins, and thereby reduces oxygen to nervous system tissue and increases the risk of bleeding.

Arteriovenous malformations can form wherever arteries and veins exist. They occur most often without symptoms. However, AVMs that form in the brain or spinal cord can be especially problematic. Even in the absence of bleeding or significant oxygen loss, large AVMs can damage the brain or spinal cord by their presence. They can range in size from a fraction of an inch to more than 2.5 inches in diameter. The larger the lesion, the greater the amount of pressure there is on surrounding brain or spinal cord structures.

AVMs of the brain or spinal cord (neurological AVMs) affect approximately 300,000 Americans. They occur in males and females of all racial or ethnic backgrounds at roughly equal rates.

Common symptoms of AVMs are seizures and headaches. Other neurological symptoms may include muscle weakness or paralysis in one part of the body or loss of coordination (ataxia). Also, AVMs can cause pain or disturbances of vision or speech. Mental confusion or hallucination is also possible. There is evidence that AVMs may also cause subtle learning or behavioral disorders during childhood.

Diagnosis of AVM is by either computed axial tomography (CT) or magnetic resonance imaging (MRI) scans. Angiography is an accurate way to get the exact location of the malformation. A thin tube is inserted in a leg artery, threaded toward the brain, and then injected with a dye. The scans reveal the AVM tangle.

Arteriovenous malformations can put veins under great pressure since there are no capillaries to slow blood flow. Over time, the AVM may rupture and cause a hemorrhage. While the risk of hemorrhage is small, the risk increases over time; treatment is usually recommended.

Treatment: Advances in technique have made surgical treatment of most cases of AVM safe and effective. Surgery inside the skull may attempt to cut out or burn away the AVM with a laser. Another option for smaller AVMs is stereotactic radiosurgery, which focuses radiation on AVM blood vessels to slowly obliterate them. It may take from one to three years to remove the AVM.

A third treatment option is endovascular embolization, which is similar to an angiogram. A catheter is inserted into a leg artery and threaded through the body toward the affected arteries. A glue-like substance is injected to block key blood vessels leading to the AVM, thus reducing its size so radiosurgery or conventional surgery may treat it.

Surgery is a decision that must be made with full understanding of risks. Untreated, AVMs may lead to serious neurological deficits or death. Surgery on the central nervous system, however, has known risks as well; AVM surgery is invasive and can be quite complex.

SOURCES

National Institute of Neurological Disorders and Stroke, Mayo Clinic, National Organization for Rare Disorders

❧ **Below are links to resources.**

Mayo Clinic offers many educational materials about arteriovenous malformation and provides treatment at three centers. 507-284-2511; **www.mayoclinic.org,** search arteriovenous-malformation

The National Institute for Neurological Disorders and Stroke (NINDS) offers clinical detail and resources on AVM. 301-496-5751, toll-free 1-800-352-9424; **www.ninds.nih.gov/disorders/avms/avms.htm**

National Organization for Rare Disorders (NORD) includes AVM in its materials. 203-744-0100; toll-free 1-800-999-6673; **www.rarediseases.org**

BRACHIAL PLEXUS INJURY

BRACHIAL PLEXUS INJURIES are caused by excessive stretching, tearing, or other trauma to a network of nerves located between the spine and the shoulder, arm, and hand. Symptoms may include a limp or paralyzed arm and loss of muscle control or sensation in the arm, hand, or wrist. Chronic pain is often a concern. Injuries often occur due to vehicular accidents, sports mishaps, gunshot wounds, or surgeries; these injuries can also happen during the birth process if a baby's shoulders become impacted, causing the brachial plexus nerves to stretch or tear.

Some brachial plexus injuries may heal without treatment; many babies improve or recover by three to four months of age. Treatment for these injuries includes occupational or physical therapy and, in some cases, surgery. For avulsion (tears) and rupture injuries there is no potential for recovery unless surgical reconnection is made in a timely manner. For neuroma (scarring) and neuropraxia (stretching) injuries, the potential for recovery is encouraging; most people with neuropraxia injuries recover.

SOURCES

United Brachial Plexus Network, National Institute of Neurological
Disorders and Stroke

ɞ **Below is a link to resources.**

United Brachial Plexus Network provides support related
to brachial plexus injuries; toll-free 1-866-877-7004;
www.ubpn.org

BRAIN INJURY

THE BRAIN IS THE CONTROL CENTER for all of the body's functions,
including conscious activities (walking, talking) and unconscious ones
(breathing, digestion). The brain also controls thought, comprehension,
speech, and emotion. Injury to the brain, whether the result of severe
trauma to the skull or a closed injury in which there is no fracture or
penetration, can disrupt some or all of these functions.

Traumatic brain injury (TBI) is mainly the result of motor vehicle
accidents, falls, acts of violence, and sports injuries. It is more than twice
as likely in males than in females. The estimated incidence rate is 100
in 100,000 people. The Centers for Disease Control and Prevention
estimates that 5.3 million Americans are living with disabilities from
brain trauma, added to more than 50,000 deaths per year. The highest
incidence is among persons 15 to 24 years of age and 75 years and older.
Alcohol is associated with half of all brain injuries, either in the person
causing the injury or in the injured person.

People with spinal cord injury often have accompanying brain injury;
this is especially true for higher cervical injuries, close to the brain.

Enclosed within the bony framework of the skull, the brain is a
gelatinous material that floats in cerebrospinal fluid, which acts as a shock
absorber in rapid head movements. Injury to the brain can be caused
by a fracture or penetration of the skull (such as a vehicle accident, fall,
or gunshot wound), a disease process (including neurotoxins, infection,
tumors, or metabolic abnormalities), or a closed head injury such as

shaken baby syndrome or rapid acceleration/deceleration of the head. The outer surface of the skull is smooth, but the inner surface is jagged—this is the cause of significant damage in closed head injuries, as the brain tissue rebounds inside the skull over rough bony structures. With trauma, brain damage may occur at the time of impact or may develop later due to swelling (cerebral edema) and bleeding into the brain (intracerebral hemorrhage) or bleeding around the brain (epidural or subdural hemorrhage).

If the head is hit with sufficient force, the brain turns and twists on its axis (the brainstem), interrupting normal nerve pathways and causing a loss of consciousness. If this unconsciousness persists over a long period of time, the injured person is considered to be in a coma, a disruption of nerve messages going from the brainstem to the cortex.

A closed head injury often occurs without leaving obvious external signs, however other differences between closed and penetrating injuries can be significant. A bullet wound to the head, for example, might destroy a large area of the brain but the result may be minor if the area is not a critical one. Closed head injuries often result in more damage and extensive neurologic deficits, including partial to complete paralysis; cognitive, behavioral, and memory problems; and persistent vegetative state.

Injured brain tissue can recover over time. However, once brain tissue is dead or destroyed, there is no evidence that new brain cells form. The process of recovery usually continues even without new cells, perhaps as other parts of the brain take over the function of the destroyed tissue.

A concussion is a type of closed head injury; while most people fully recover from a concussion, there is evidence that accumulated injury to the brain, even moderate injury, causes long-term effects.

Brain injury can have serious and lifelong effects on physical and mental functioning, including loss of consciousness, altered memory and/or personality, and partial or complete paralysis. Common behavioral problems include verbal and physical aggression, agitation, learning difficulties, poor self-awareness, altered sexual functioning, impulsivity, and social disinhibition. Social consequences of mild, moderate, and severe TBI are numerous, including higher risk of suicide, divorce, chronic unemployment, and substance abuse. The annual cost of acute

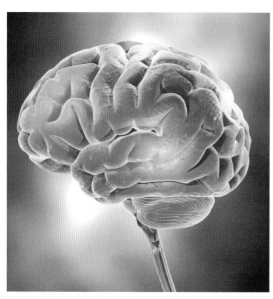

care and rehabilitation in the United States for new cases of TBI is enormous: $9 billion to $10 billion. Estimates for average lifetime cost of care for a person with severe TBI range from $600,000 to $2 million.

The rehabilitation process begins immediately after injury. Once memory begins to be restored, the rate of recovery often increases. However, many problems may persist, including those related to movement, memory, attention, complex thinking, speech and language, and behavioral changes; survivors often cope with depression, anxiety, loss of self-esteem, altered personality, and, in some cases, a lack of self-awareness of their deficits.

Rehab may include cognitive exercises to improve attention, memory, and executive skills. These programs are structured, systematic, goal-directed, and individualized; they involve learning, practice, and social contact. Sometimes memory books and electronic paging systems are used to improve particular functions and to compensate for deficits. Psychotherapy, an important component of a comprehensive rehabilitation program, treats depression and loss of self-esteem. Rehab may also include medications for behavioral disturbances associated with TBI. Some of these drugs have significant side effects in persons with TBI and are used only in compelling circumstances.

Behavior modification has been used to reduce personality and behavioral effects of TBI and to retrain social skills. Vocational training is also common to many rehab programs. According to a consensus statement on brain injury from the National Institutes of Health, persons with TBI and their families should play an integral role in the planning and design of their individualized rehabilitation programs.

SOURCES

National Institute of Neurological Disorders and Stroke, Brain Injury Resource Center

🐾 **Below are links to resources.**

Brain Injury Association of America (BIAA) features resources on living with brain injury, treatment, rehabilitation, research, prevention, etc. It also has state-by-state affiliates. 703-761-0750 or toll-free 1-800-444-6443; **www.biausa.org**

Brain Injury Resource Center/Head Injury Hotline (BIRC) operates a resource center "to empower you to have your needs met and avoid exploitation." 206-621-8558; **www.headinjury.com**

Defense and Veterans Brain Injury Center (DVBIC) serves active duty military, their dependents and veterans with traumatic brain injury. **www.dvbic.org**

Traumatic Brain Injury (TBI) Model Systems of Care are specialty head injury clinics with federal grants for developing and demonstrating expertise with TBI. The centers create and disseminate new knowledge about the course, treatment, and outcomes of these types of injuries, and demonstrate the benefits of a coordinated system of care. **www.tbindc.org**

Craig Hospital, Englewood, CO
Kessler Foundation Inc., West Orange, NJ
Albert Einstein Healthcare Network, Philadelphia, PA
The Ohio State University, Columbus, OH
University of Washington, Seattle, WA
Indiana University, Bloomington, IN
The Institute for Rehabilitation and Research, Houston, TX
Spaulding Rehabilitation Hospital, Boston, MA

New York University School of Medicine, New York, NY
Baylor Research Institute, Dallas, TX
Virginia Commonwealth University, Richmond, VA
Mount Sinai School of Medicine, New York, NY
University of Pittsburgh, Pittsburgh, PA
Mayo Clinic, Rochester, MN
University of Alabama, Birmingham, AL
University of Miami, Miami, FL

Traumatic Brain Injury Research: The brain is quite fragile, though it is protected by hair, skin, and skull, and a cushion of fluid. In the past, this protection was mostly adequate, until we developed more lethal weapons and new ways of hurtling along at high speeds.

Brain injuries vary, depending on which part of the brain is injured. A blow to the hippocampus causes memory loss. A brainstem injury is similar to a high spinal cord injury. Injury to the basal ganglia affects movement, and damage to the frontal lobes can lead to emotional problems. Injury to certain parts of the cortex affects speech and understanding. Each symptom may require specialized care and treatment.

A brain injury also involves many physiological processes, including nerve cell (axon) injury, contusions (bruises), hematomas (clots), and swelling. As in stroke, spinal cord injury, and other types of nerve trauma, brain injury is not an isolated process, it is a continuous event; waves of destruction can last days and even weeks after the initial damage. With currently available treatments, doctors are unable to fully repair the original injury, which may include massive loss of nerve cells.

The spread of secondary damage to the brain can be limited, however. Scientists have targeted some of these secondary factors, including cerebral ischemia (loss of blood), low cerebral blood flow, low oxygen levels, and the release of excitatory amino acid (e.g., glutamate). Edema, once thought to be the result of blood vessel leakage, is now believed to be due to continuing cell death in the injured tissue.

There have been numerous drug trials to control a wide range of secondary effects of brain trauma, including glutamate toxicity (selfotel, cerestat, dexanabinol), calcium damage (nimodipine), and cell membrane breakdown (tirilazad, PEG-SOD). Smaller clinical studies have investigated application of growth hormones, anticonvulsants, bradykinin (increases blood vessel permeability), and cerebral perfusion pressure (increases blood flow to the brain). Several trials have tested the effect of acute hypothermia (cooling) after brain trauma; while there are intensive care units that apply cooling, there are no specific recommendations for its use. Clinical trials of potential neuroprotective agents have generally not been successful, even though the various therapies seemed to work well in animals. Scientists say this is because the gap between animal models and human clinical practice is huge—human injury is widely variable and poorly demonstrated in a small lab animal. Also, it is often difficult to initiate treatment in humans within the proper therapeutic time frame. Animals don't always experience the same intolerable side effects to drugs as humans do, and animal models can't address the complicated and sometimes lifelong effects of brain trauma on human mind, memory, and behavior.

To be sure, the injured brain does have some capacity to recover. As scientists put it, the brain is "plastic"— that is, using nerve growth factors, tissue transplantation, or other techniques, the brain can be encouraged to remodel itself and thus restore function. Because different mechanisms are active at different times during recovery, interventions may work better at certain times. A series of timed medications might be used, each addressing specific biochemical processes in the wake of brain damage. While cell replacement (including stem cells) is theoretically possible, much research remains before application in humans.

CEREBRAL PALSY

CEREBRAL PALSY (CP) refers to a group of conditions that affect control of movement and posture. CP disorders are not caused by problems in the muscles or nerves. Instead, faulty development or damage to areas in the brain cause inadequate control of movement and posture. Symptoms range from mild to severe, including forms of paralysis.

Cerebral palsy does not always cause profound disability. While a child with severe CP might be unable to walk and may require extensive care, a child with mild cerebral palsy might only be slightly off-balance and require no special assistance. Cerebral palsy is not contagious, nor is it usually inherited. With treatment, most children significantly improve their abilities. While symptoms may change over time, cerebral palsy by definition is not progressive; if impairment does increase, it's usually due to a disease or condition other than CP.

Children with cerebral palsy often require treatment for intellectual disabilities, learning disabilities, and seizures, as well as vision, hearing and speech difficulties. Cerebral palsy is not usually diagnosed until a child is about two to three years old; it affects about two to three children out of 1,000 over the age of three; about 500,000 children and adults in the United States have CP. There are three major types:

Spastic cerebral palsy: About 70 to 80 percent of those affected have spastic cerebral palsy, in which muscles are stiff, making movement difficult. When both legs are affected (spastic diplegia), a child may have difficulty walking because tight muscles in the hips and legs cause the legs to turn inward and scissor at the knees. In other cases, only one side of the body is affected (spastic hemiplegia), often with the arm more severely affected than the leg. Most severe is spastic quadriplegia, in which all four limbs and the trunk are affected, often along with the muscles of the mouth and tongue.

Dyskinetic (athetoid) cerebral palsy: About 10 to 20 percent of people with CP have the dyskinetic form, which affects the entire body. It is characterized by fluctuations in muscle tone from too tight to too loose; dyskinetic CP is sometimes associated with uncontrolled movements (slow and writhing or rapid and jerky). Children often have trouble learning to control their bodies well enough to sit and walk. Because muscles of the face and tongue can be affected, swallowing and speech may be difficult.

Ataxic cerebral palsy: About 5 to 10 percent of people with CP have the ataxic form, which affects balance and coordination; they may walk with an unsteady gait and have difficulty with motions that require coordination, such as writing.

In the United States, about 10 to 20 percent of children who have CP acquired the disorder after birth, the result of brain damage in the first few months or years of life; brain infections, such as bacterial meningitis or viral encephalitis; or head injury. Cerebral palsy present at birth may not be detected for months. In most cases, the cause of congenital cerebral palsy is unknown. Scientists have pinpointed some specific events during pregnancy or around the time of birth that can damage motor centers in the developing brain. Until recently, doctors believed that a lack of oxygen during delivery was the primary cause of cerebral palsy. Studies show that this causes only about 10 percent of cases.

Hyperbaric oxygen continues to be explored for treatment of CP, stroke, or brain injury. Some clinics and manufacturers promote its use for CP but there is no consensus that it is effective.

A child with CP usually begins physical therapy to increase motor skills (sitting and walking), improve muscle strength, and help prevent contractures (shortening of muscles that limit joint movement). Sometimes braces, splints, or casts are used to improve function of the hands or legs. If contractures are severe, surgery may be recommended to lengthen affected muscles.

A newer technique called constraint-induced therapy (CIT) is a type of physical therapy used successfully with adult stroke survivors with a weak arm on one side of the body. The therapy restrains the stronger arm in a cast, forcing the weaker arm to perform activities. In a randomized, controlled study of children with cerebral palsy, one group of children went through conventional physical therapy and another group through 21 consecutive days of CIT. Researchers looked for evidence of improvement in the function of the disabled arm, whether the improvement lasted after the end of treatment, and if it was associated with significant gains in other areas, such as trunk control, mobility, communication, and self-help skills. Children receiving CIT outperformed the children receiving conventional physical therapy across all measures, and six months later they still had better control of their arm.

Researchers are developing new ways to target and strengthen spastic muscles. For example, with functional electrical stimulation (FES), a microscopic wireless device is inserted into specific muscles or nerves and is powered by remote control. This technique has been used to activate and strengthen muscles in the hand, shoulder, and ankle in people with cerebral palsy, as well as in stroke survivors. For more information on FES, see page 179.

Drugs may ease spasticity or reduce abnormal movement. In some cases, a small pump is implanted under the skin to continuously deliver an anti-spasm drug, such as baclofen. Success has been reported using Botox injections to quiet selective muscles. For younger children with spasticity affecting both legs, dorsal rhizotomy may permanently reduce spasticity and improve the ability to sit, stand, and walk. In this procedure, doctors cut some of the nerve fibers that contribute to spasticity.

As a child with cerebral palsy grows older, therapy and other support services will change. Physical therapy is supplemented by vocational training, recreation and leisure programs, and special education, when necessary. Counseling for emotional and psychological issues is important during adolescence.

SOURCES

United Cerebral Palsy, March of Dimes, Centers for Disease Control and Prevention, National Institute of Neurological Disorders and Stroke

> **Below are links to resources.**

United Cerebral Palsy (UCP) offers resources on CP health and wellness, plus lifestyle, education and advocacy resources. UCP advances full inclusion of people with disabilities; two-thirds of people served by UCP have disabilities other than cerebral palsy. UCP, 202-776-0406; **www.ucp.org**

The March of Dimes Birth Defects Foundation features resources and connections to address birth defects, infant mortality, low birth weight and lack of prenatal care. Toll-free 1-888-663-4637; **www.modimes.org**

The Cerebral Palsy International Research Foundation (CPIRF) funds research to discover the cause, cure and care for those with CP and related developmental disabilities. 609-452-1200; **www.cpirf.org**

FRIEDREICH'S ATAXIA

FRIEDREICH'S ATAXIA (FA) is an inherited disease that causes progressive damage to the nervous system. It can result in muscle weakness, speech difficulties, or heart disease. The first symptom is usually difficulty with walking; this gradually worsens and can spread to the arms and the trunk. Loss of sensation in the extremities may spread to other parts of the body. Other features include loss of tendon reflexes, especially in the knees and ankles. Most people with Friedreich's ataxia develop scoliosis (a curving of the spine to one side), which may require surgical intervention.

Other symptoms may include chest pain, shortness of breath, and heart palpitations. These symptoms are the result of various forms of heart disease that often accompany Friedreich's ataxia, such as hypertrophic cardiomyopathy (enlargement of the heart), myocardial fibrosis (formation of fiber-like material in the muscles of the heart), and cardiac failure.

Friedreich's ataxia is named after the physician Nicholas Friedreich, who first described the condition in the 1860s. "Ataxia" refers to coordination problems and unsteadiness and occurs in many diseases and conditions. Friedreich's ataxia is marked by degeneration of nerve tissue in the spinal cord and of nerves that control arm and leg movement. The spinal cord becomes thinner and nerve cells lose some of the myelin insulation that helps them conduct impulses.

Friedreich's ataxia is rare; it affects about 1 in 50,000 people in the United States. Males and females are affected equally. Symptoms usually begin between the ages of five and fifteen, but can appear as early as eighteen months or as late as age thirty.

There is currently no effective cure or treatment for Friedreich's ataxia. However, many of the symptoms and accompanying complications can be treated. Studies show that frataxin is an important mitochondrial protein for proper function of several organs. Yet in people with FA, the amount of frataxin in affected cells is severely reduced. This loss of frataxin may make the nervous system, heart, and pancreas particularly susceptible to damage from free radicals (produced when excess iron reacts with oxygen). Researchers have tried to reduce the levels of free radicals using treatment with antioxidants. Initial clinical studies in Europe suggested that antioxidants like coenzyme Q10, vitamin E, and idebenone may offer limited benefit. However, clinical trials in the United States have not revealed effectiveness of idebenone in people with Friedreich's ataxia; more powerful modified forms of this agent and other antioxidants are in trials at this time. Meanwhile, scientists also are exploring ways to increase frataxin levels and manage iron metabolism through drug treatments, genetic engineering, and protein delivery systems.

SOURCES

National Institute of Neurological Disorders and Stroke, National Organization for Rare Disorders, Friedreich's Ataxia Research Alliance, Muscular Dystrophy Association

ॐ **Below are links to resources.**

Friedreich's Ataxia Research Alliance (FARA) offers information on Friedreich's ataxia and the related ataxias, including current research, as well as information for researchers, patients, families and caregivers. FARA also offers support and information for the newly diagnosed. 703-413-4468; **www.curefa.org**

National Ataxia Foundation (NAF) supports research into hereditary ataxia, with numerous affiliated chapters and support groups in the United States and Canada. 763-553-0020; **www.ataxia.org**

National Organization for Rare Disorders (NORD) is committed to the identification and treatment of more than 6,000 rare disorders, including Friedreich's ataxia, through education, advocacy, research and service. **www.rarediseases.org**

Muscular Dystrophy Association (MDA) offers news and information about neuromuscular diseases, including ataxias. Toll-free 1-800-344-4863; **www.mdausa.org**

GUILLAIN-BARRÉ SYNDROME

GUILLAIN-BARRÉ (GHEE-YAN BAH-RAY) SYNDROME is a disorder in which the body's immune system attacks part of the peripheral nervous system. The first symptoms include varying degrees of weakness or tingling sensations in the legs, often spreading to the arms and upper body; these can increase in intensity until a person is totally paralyzed. Many people require intensive care during the early course of their illness, especially if a ventilator is required.

Guillain-Barré syndrome is rare. It usually occurs a few days or weeks after a person has had symptoms of a respiratory or gastrointestinal viral infection; while the most common related infection is bacterial, 60 percent of cases do not have a known cause. Some cases may be triggered by the influenza virus or by an immune reaction to the influenza virus. Occasionally, surgery or vaccinations will trigger it. The disorder can develop over the course of hours or days, or it may take three to four weeks. It is not known why Guillain-Barré strikes some people and not others. Most people recover from even the most severe cases of Guillain-Barré, although some continue to have a degree of weakness. There is no known cure for this syndrome, but therapies can reduce its severity and accelerate recovery. There are a number of ways to treat the complications. Plasmapheresis (also known as plasma exchange) mechanically removes autoantibodies from the bloodstream. High-dose immunoglobulin therapy is also used to boost the immune system. Researchers hope to understand the workings of the immune system to identify which cells are responsible for carrying out the attack on the nervous system.

SOURCE

The National Institute of Neurological Disorders and Stroke

❧ **Below is a link to resources.**

GBS/CIDP Foundation International offers information on Guillain-Barré and Chronic Inflammatory Demyelinating Polyneuropathy. 610-667-0131 or toll-free 1-866-224-3301; **www.gbs-cidp.org**

THE LEUKODYSTROPHIES

THE LEUKODYSTROPHIES ARE PROGRESSIVE, hereditary disorders that affect the brain, spinal cord, and peripheral nerves. Specific leukodystrophies include metachromatic leukodystrophy, Krabbe disease, adrenoleukodystrophy, Canavan disease, Alexander disease, Zellweger syndrome, Refsum disease, and cerebrotendinous xanthomatosis. Pelizaeus-Merzbacher disease can also lead to paralysis.

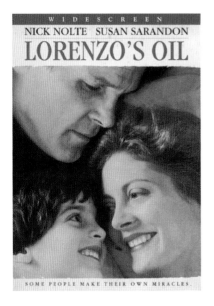

Adrenoleukodystrophy (ALD) affected the young boy Lorenzo Odone, whose story is told in the 1993 film "Lorenzo's Oil." In this disease, the fatty covering (myelin sheath) on nerve fibers in the brain is lost, and the adrenal gland degenerates, leading to progressive neurological disability. (See **www.myelin.org**, established in 1989 by Augusto and Michaela Odone with the goal of accelerating research on myelin repair.)

&** Below is a link to resources.**

United Leukodystrophy Foundation (ULF) raises funds, offers resources and clinical detail on the leukodystrophies. Toll-free 1-800-728-5483 or 815-748-3211; **www.ulf.org**

LYME DISEASE

LYME DISEASE IS A BACTERIAL (*Borrelia burgdorferi*) infection transmitted to humans by the bite of certain black-legged ticks, although fewer than 50 percent of all Lyme disease patients recall a tick bite. Typical symptoms include fever, headache, and fatigue. Lyme disease, which can lead to neurological symptoms, including loss of function in arms and legs, is often misdiagnosed as amyotrophic lateral sclerosis or multiple sclerosis. According to some Lyme disease experts, standard diagnostic methods fail to discover as many as 40 percent of cases. Most cases of Lyme disease can be treated successfully with antibiotics over several weeks. While some people with long-term Lyme disease take antibiotics over an extended course of time, most physicians do not consider Lyme to be a chronic infection. According to published medical literature, many patients diagnosed as having chronic Lyme disease demonstrate no evidence of prior infection; only 37 percent of patients in one referral center had current or previous infection with *B. burgdorferi* as the explanation for their symptoms. There are reports that hyperbaric oxygen and bee venom have

Borrelia burgdorferi

been effective for some in treating symptoms of the disease. A number people with chronic Lyme disease have traveled abroad for expensive, unauthorized stem cell therapies.

☙ **Below are links to resources.**

International Lyme and Associated Diseases Society, offers educational materials. **http://ilads.org**
American Lyme Disease Foundation, offers resources and treatment information. **www.aldf.com**
Lyme Disease Association, offers information and referral. **www.lymediseaseassociation.org**

MULTIPLE SCLEROSIS

MULTIPLE SCLEROSIS (MS) IS A CHRONIC and often disabling disease of the central nervous system. Symptoms may be episodic and mild, such as numbness in a limb, or severe, including paralysis, cognitive loss, or loss of vision. MS involves decreased nerve function associated with scar formation on myelin, the covering of nerve cells. Repeated episodes of inflammation destroy myelin, leaving multiple areas of scar tissue (sclerosis) along the covering of the nerve cells. This results in slowing or blockage of nerve impulse transmission in that area. Multiple sclerosis often progresses with episodes (called "exacerbations") that last days, weeks, or months. Exacerbations may alternate with times of reduced or no symptoms (remission). Recurrence (relapse) is common.

Symptoms of MS include weakness, tremor, or paralysis of one or more extremities; spasticity (uncontrollable spasms); movement problems; numbness; tingling; pain; loss of vision; loss of coordination and balance; incontinence; loss of memory or judgment; and, most commonly, fatigue.

Fatigue, occurring in about 80 percent of people with MS, can significantly interfere with a person's ability to work and function. It may be the most prominent symptom in a person who has otherwise been minimally affected by the disease. MS-related fatigue generally occurs on a daily basis and tends to worsen as the day progresses. It tends to be aggravated by heat and humidity. MS-related fatigue does not appear to be correlated with depression or the degree of physical impairment.

Multiple sclerosis varies greatly from person to person and in the severity and the course of the disease. A relapsing-remitting course, the most common form of MS, is characterized by partial or total recovery after attacks; about 75 percent of people with MS begin with a relapsing-remitting course.

Relapsing-remitting MS may become steadily progressive. Attacks and partial recoveries may continue to occur. This is called secondary-progressive MS. Of those who start with relapsing-remitting, more than half will develop secondary-progressive MS within ten years; 90 percent within 25 years.

A progressive course from onset of the disease is called primary-progressive MS. In this case, symptoms generally do not remit.

The exact cause of MS is unknown. Studies indicate an environmental factor may be involved. There is a higher incidence in northern Europe, northern United States, southern Australia, and New Zealand than in other areas of the world. Because people in sunnier climates are less likely to get MS, research has targeted vitamin D levels; indeed, there is some link between lower levels of vitamin D and MS. Vitamin D is synthesized naturally by the skin as it is exposed to sunlight. Studies show that people in northern climates often have reduced vitamin D levels; babies born in less sunny April have the highest risk of developing multiple sclerosis later in life while those born in sunnier October have the lowest risk.

There may also be a familial tendency toward the disorder. Most people with MS are diagnosed between the ages of 20 and 40. Women are more commonly affected than men. The progress, severity, and symptoms of MS in any individual cannot yet be predicted.

Multiple sclerosis is believed to be an abnormal immune response directed against the central nervous system (CNS). The cells and proteins of the body's immune system, which normally defend the body against infections, leave the blood vessels serving the CNS and turn against the brain and spinal cord, destroying myelin. The specific triggering mechanism that causes the immune system to attack its own myelin remains unknown, although a viral infection combined with an inherited genetic susceptibility is a leading suspect. While many different viruses have been thought to cause MS, there has been no definitive evidence linking its cause to any one virus.

Multiple sclerosis was among the first diseases to be described scientifically. Nineteenth-century doctors did not fully understand what they saw and recorded, but drawings from autopsies done as early as 1838 clearly show what is known today as MS. In 1868, Jean-Martin Charcot, a neurologist at the University of Paris, carefully examined a young woman with a tremor of a sort he had never seen before. He noted her other neurological problems, including slurred speech and abnormal eye movements, and compared them to other patients he had seen. When she died, he examined her brain and found the characteristic scars or "plaques" of MS.

Dr. Charcot wrote a complete description of the disease and the changes in the brain that accompany it. He was baffled by its cause and frustrated by its resistance to all of his treatments, including electrical stimulation and strychnine (a nerve stimulant and poison). He also tried injections of gold and silver (somewhat helpful in the other major nerve disorder common at that time, syphilis).

One century later, in 1969, the first successful scientific clinical trial was completed for a treatment of MS. A group of patients who were having MS exacerbations were given a steroid drug; steroids remain in use today for acute exacerbations.

Clinical trials since then have led to approvals of several drugs shown to affect immune response, and thus the course of MS. Betaseron helps reduce the severity and frequency of attacks. Avonex, approved in 1996, slows the development of disability and reduces the severity and frequency of attacks. Copaxone treats relapsing-remitting MS; Rebif reduces the number and frequency of relapses and slows the progression of disability; Novantrone treats advanced or chronic MS and reduces the number of relapses.

In 2006, Tysabri was approved for relapsing-remitting multiple sclerosis, with very restrictive prescription policies due to a high risk for immune-related side effects. The drug is a monoclonal antibody that appears to hamper movement of potentially damaging immune cells from the bloodstream, across the blood-brain barrier, and into the brain and spinal cord. FDA prescribing information about Tysabri includes a "black box" warning about the risk of PML (progressive multifocal leukoencephalopathy), an infection of the brain that usually leads to death or severe disability.

Recently, three oral medications have been approved for treating MS: Gilenya, for reducing the frequency of relapses and delaying physical disability in relapsing forms of MS; Aubagio, which inhibits the function of specific immune cells implicated in MS; and Tecfidera, shown to reduce relapses and development of brain lesions, and to slow disability progression over time.

A drug called Ampyra was approved to improve walking speed in people with MS. The active ingredient, 4AP, has been widely used for many years as a nerve stimulant by people with MS or spinal cord injury and is available by prescription from compounding pharmacies. Ampyra is a refined, time-release formulation.

There are many research efforts underway to treat MS:

- Antibiotics that fight infection may decrease MS disease activity. Various infectious agents have been proposed as potential causes for MS, including Epstein-Barr virus, herpes virus, and coronaviruses. Minocycline (an antibiotic) has showed promising results as an anti-inflammatory agent in trails with relapsing-remitting MS.
- Plasmapheresis is a procedure in which a person's blood is removed to separate plasma from other blood substances that may contain antibodies and other immune-sensitive products. The purified plasma is then transfused back into the patient. Plasmapheresis is used to treat myasthenia gravis, Guillain-Barré, and other demyelinating diseases. Studies of plasmapheresis in people with primary and secondary progressive MS have had mixed results.
- Bone marrow transplantation is being studied in MS. By wiping out the immune cells in a patient's bone marrow with chemotherapy and then repopulating it with healthy mesenchymal stem cells, researchers hope the rebuilt immune system will stop attacking its own nerves.
- There is excitement about other types of stem cells in treating MS. Experimental work is being done with embryonic stem cells, olfactory ensheathing glia (a type of adult stem cell), and with umbilical cord blood stem cells. A number of clinics outside the United States offer treatments with various cell lines; no data exists to evaluate these clinics and they should be approached with caution.
- Other MS research: Immune system defenders called T-cells erode myelin by producing small chemical signals (cytokines) that activate cells known as macrophages, which destroy the myelin. A man-made antibody called Zenapax (approved for use in people with kidney transplants) attaches itself to the rogue T-cells, blocking their role in the damage process. Results have been encouraging in early relapsing-remitting MS trials.

- A drug called Tcelna is in clinical trials as a sort of MS vaccine; it is manufactured from the blood of each MS patient and thus specifically tailored to each patient's immune response to myelin-reactive T-cells (MRTC), known to attack myelin.
- Rituxan, a drug that is already used to treat cancer and rheumatoid arthritis, reduced by more than half the chance that people with MS would have symptom flare-ups over a six-month period. Early studies also show that people taking Rituxan had fewer brain lesions than those on placebo. The drug probably won't get approved for MS: its patent protection will expire before Phase III trials can be completed.
- It may be possible to repair damage to myelin (a process called remyelinization). Various cell types, including Schwann cells, can migrate and remyelinate brain and spinal cord nerves after transplantation directly into experimental lesions.

Symptom management options: Medicines commonly used for MS symptoms include baclofen, tizanidine, or diazepam, often used to reduce muscle spasticity. Doctors prescribe anti-cholinergic medications to reduce urinary problems and antidepressants to improve mood or behavior symptoms. Amantadine (an antiviral drug) and pemoline (a stimulant usually prescribed to calm hyperactive children) are sometimes used to treat fatigue. There are many alternative medical treatments for MS, including acupuncture, bee venom, and dental amalgam removal. There are many diets that are promoted to treat MS.

Physical therapy, speech therapy, or occupational therapy may improve a person's outlook, reduce depression, maximize function, and improve coping skills. Exercise early in the course of MS helps to maintain muscle tone. It is helpful to avoid fatigue, stress, physical deterioration, temperature extremes, and illness to reduce factors that could trigger an MS attack. MS is chronic, unpredictable, and at this time incurable, but life expectancy can be normal or nearly so.

SOURCES:

National Institute of Neurological Disorders and Stroke, National Multiple Sclerosis Society, Consortium of MS Centers, Multiple Sclerosis Complementary and Alternative Medicine/Rocky Mountain MS Center

❧ **Below are links to resources.**

The National Multiple Sclerosis Society provides
information on living with MS, treatment, scientific
progress, MS specialty centers, clinical research funding,
local chapters, and resources for healthcare professionals.
Toll-free 1-800-344-4867; **www.nationalmssociety.org**

Multiple Sclerosis Complementary Care, a section of
the Rocky Mountain MS Center, provides information
and discussion of complementary and alternative medicine therapies commonly used by people with MS, such
as acupuncture, herbal medicine, and homeopathy.
http://livingwell.mscenter.org/complementary-care.html;
registration required.

**The Consortium of Multiple Sclerosis Centers/
North American Research Committee on MS** is
a rich repository of clinical and research information for
people with MS. Publishes the *International Journal of MS
Care*. **www.mscare.org**

The Multiple Sclerosis Society of Canada has
information about the disease, progress in MS research,
services, details about fundraising events, and donation
opportunities. **www.mssociety.ca**

Multiple Sclerosis Foundation offers an interactive, multimedia MS library, and online forum. **www.msfacts.org**

Multiple Sclerosis Association of America features
news, information, and community connections.
www.msaa.com

Acupuncture

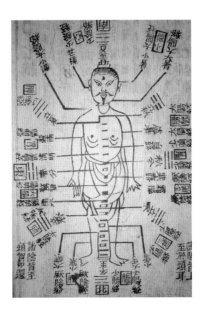

There is some evidence that the ancient Chinese practice of acupuncture may help people with MS. Acupuncture is a traditional Chinese medicine, based on a theory of body functioning that involves the flow of energy through 14 pathways (called meridians) throughout the body. Disease, as the theory goes, results from an imbalance or disruption in the flow of energy. A Canadian study of 217 people with MS who received acupuncture found that two-thirds reported some type of beneficial effect, including improvements in fatigue, pain, spasticity, walking, bowel and bladder difficulties, tingling and numbness, weakness, sleep disorders, loss of coordination, optic neuritis, and MS attacks. These results appear promising, but since this was a self-assessment survey, it lacks the rigorous elements of a formal clinical trial. According to the National MS Society, two studies showed that one in four respondents with MS had tried acupuncture for symptom relief. About 10 to 15 percent said they planned to continue using acupuncture. While there have been no controlled clinical trials to evaluate the safety and efficacy of acupuncture in people with MS, the practice is without side-effects and has no known risk factors. More research is needed. See National Multiple Sclerosis Society, *www.nationalmssociety.org*

NEUROFIBROMATOSIS

NEUROFIBROMATOSIS (NF) is a genetic, progressive and unpredictable disorder of the nervous system which causes tumors to form on the nerves anywhere in the body at any time. Although most NF-related tumors are not cancerous, they may cause problems by compressing the spinal cord and surrounding nerves; this can lead to paralysis. The most common tumors are neurofibromas, which develop in the tissue surrounding peripheral nerves. There are three types of neurofibromatosis: Type 1 causes skin changes and deformed bones, can affect the spinal cord and brain, often contributes to learning disabilities, and usually starts at birth. Type 2 causes hearing loss, ringing in the ears, and poor balance; it often starts in the teen years. Schwannomatosis, the rarest form, causes intense pain. As a group, the neurofibromatoses affect more than 100,000 Americans. There is no known cure for any form of NF, although the genes for both NF-1 and NF-2 have been identified.

SOURCES:

National Institute of Neurological Disorders and Stroke, Neurofibromatosis Network

Below are links to resources.

Neurofibromatosis Network advocates for NF research, disseminates medical and scientific information about NF, offers a national referral database for clinical care, and promotes awareness of NF. **www.nfnetwork.org**

Children's Tumor Foundation supports research and the development of treatments for neurofibromatosis, provides information, and helps in the development of clinical centers, best practices, and patient support mechanisms. **www.ctf.org**

Neurofibromatosis Inc. California offers medical symposiums, family support and patient advocacy, and supports NF research. **www.nfcalifornia.org**

POST-POLIO SYNDROME

POLIOMYELITIS IS A DISEASE caused by a virus that attacks nerves that control motor function. Polio (infantile paralysis) has nearly been eradicated from nearly every country in the world since the approval of the Salk (1955) and Sabin (1962) vaccines. In 2013, only three countries (Afghanistan, Nigeria, and Pakistan) remained polio-endemic, down from more than 125 in 1988.

The World Health Organization (WHO) estimates that 12 million people worldwide live with some degree of disability caused by poliomyelitis. The National Center for Health Statistics estimates about one million polio survivors in the United States, with almost half reporting paralysis resulting in some form of impairment. The last major outbreaks of polio in the United States were in the early 1950s.

For years, most polio survivors lived active lives, their memory of polio mainly forgotten, their health status stable. But by the late 1970s, survivors who were 20 or more years past their original diagnosis began noting new problems, including fatigue, pain, breathing or swallowing problems, and additional weakness—medical professionals called this post-polio syndrome (PPS).

Some people experience PPS-related fatigue as a flu-like exhaustion that worsens as the day progresses. This type of fatigue can also increase during physical activity, and it may cause difficulty with concentration and memory. Others experience muscle weakness that increases with exercise and improves with rest.

Research indicates that the length of time one has lived with the residuals of polio is as much of a risk factor as age. It also appears that individuals who experienced the most severe original paralysis with the greatest functional recovery have more problems with PPS than others with less severe original involvement.

Post-polio syndrome appears to be related to physical overuse and, perhaps, nerve stress. When the poliovirus destroyed or injured motor neurons, muscle fibers were orphaned and paralysis resulted. Polio survivors who regained movement did so because non-affected neighboring nerve cells began to "sprout" and reconnect to what might be considered orphaned muscles.

Survivors who have lived for years with this restructured neuromuscular system are now experiencing the consequences including overworked surviving nerve cells, muscles, and joints, compounded by the effects of growing older. There is no conclusive evidence to support the idea that post-polio syndrome is a reinfection of the poliovirus.

Polio survivors are urged to take care of their health in all the usual ways—by seeking periodic medical attention, being nutrition-wise, avoiding excessive weight gain, and by stopping smoking or overindulging in alcohol. Survivors are advised to listen to their body's warning signals, avoid activities that cause pain, prevent overuse of muscles, and conserve energy by avoiding tasks that are nonessential, and by using adaptive equipment when needed.

Post-polio syndrome is not typically a life-threatening condition, but it may cause significant discomfort and disability. The most common disability caused by PPS is deterioration of mobility. People with PPS may also experience difficulties performing daily activities such as cooking, cleaning, shopping, and driving. Energy-conserving assistive devices such as canes, crutches, walkers, wheelchairs, or electric scooters may be necessary for some people.

Living with post-polio syndrome often means adjusting to new disabilities; for some, reliving childhood experiences of coming to terms with polio can be difficult. For example, moving from a manual to a power chair can be tough. Fortunately, PPS is gaining increasing attention in the medical community, and there are many - professionals who understand it and can provide appropriate medical and psychological help. In addition, there are PPS support groups, newsletters, and educational networks that provide up-to-date information about PPS while assuring survivors that they are not alone in their struggle.

SOURCES

International Polio Network, Montreal Neurological Hospital Post-Polio Clinic

Franklin D. Roosevelt, seldom seen as a polio survivor, with Ruthie Bye and Fala, 1941

FRANKLIN D. ROOSEVELT PRESIDENTIAL LIBRARY AND MUSEUM/MARGARET SUCKLEY

🎗 **Below are links to resources.**

Post-Polio Health International offers information for
polio survivors and promotes networking among the post-
polio community. PPHI publishes numerous resources,
including the quarterly *Polio Network News*, the annual
Post-Polio Directory, and *The Handbook on the Late Effects of
Poliomyelitis for Physicians and Survivors*. PPHI is the evolu-
tion of the GINI organization, founded as a mimeograph
newsletter by Gini Laurie in St. Louis 50 years ago. 314-
534-0475; **www.post-polio.org**

Post-Polio Institute is the home of Richard Bruno, clinical psychologist specializing in fatigue, pain, and stress—
as well as PPS. **www.postpolioinfo.com**

SPINA BIFIDA

SPINA BIFIDA IS THE MOST COMMON permanently disabling birth defect. One out of 1,000 newborns in the United States is born with spina bifida; each year 4,000 pregnancies are affected by spina bifida. About 95 percent of babies with spina bifida are born to parents with no family history. While spina bifida appears to run in certain families, it does not follow any particular pattern of inheritance.

Spina bifida, a type of neural tube defect (NTD), means "cleft spine," or an incomplete closure in the spinal column. This birth defect occurs between the fourth and sixth weeks of pregnancy when the embryo is less than an inch long. Normally, a groove in the middle of the embryo deepens, allowing the sides to meet and enclose the tissue destined to be the spinal cord. In spina bifida, the sides of the embryo do not fully meet, resulting in a malformed neural tube that affects the spinal column and, in many cases, forms a spinal cord cleft, or lesion.

The most serious form of spina bifida may include muscle weakness or paralysis below the cleft area, loss of sensation, and loss of bowel and bladder control. There are three general types of spina bifida (listed below from mild to severe).

Spina bifida occulta: This is an opening in one or more of the vertebrae (bones) of the spinal column without apparent damage to the spinal cord. It is estimated that 40 percent of all Americans may have spina bifida occulta, but because they experience few or no symptoms, very few of them ever know that they have it.

Meningocele: The meninges, or the protective covering around the spinal cord, pushes out through the opening in the vertebrae in a sac called the meningocele. The spinal cord remains intact; this can be repaired with little or no damage to the nerve pathways.

Myelomeningocele: This is the most severe form of spina bifida, in which a portion of the spinal cord itself protrudes through the back. In some cases, sacs are covered with skin; in others, tissue and nerves are exposed. A common effect of myelomeningocele is a hydrocephalus. A large percentage of children born with myelomeningocele have a hydrocephalus, an accumulation of fluid in the brain that is controlled by a surgical procedure called shunting. This relieves the fluid build-up in the brain and reduces the risk of brain damage, seizures, or blindness. In some cases, children with spina bifida who also have a history of hydrocephalus experience learning problems. They may have difficulty paying attention, expressing or understanding language, and grasping reading and math. Early intervention with children who experience learning problems can help considerably to prepare them for school and life.

Examples of secondary conditions associated with spina bifida are orthopedic problems, latex allergy, tendinitis, obesity, skin breakdown, gastrointestinal disorders, learning disabilities, depression, and social and sexual issues.

Although spina bifida is relatively common, until recently most children born with a myelomeningocele died shortly after birth. Now that surgery to drain spinal fluid and protect against hydrocephalus can be performed in the first 24 hours of life, children with myelomeningocele are much more likely to survive. Quite often, however, they have a series of operations throughout childhood. Advances in surgery and urology make it possible for 90 percent of infants born with spina bifida to live full and active lives into adulthood. It is estimated that about 70,000 people are living with spina bifida in the United States today.

Birth defects can happen in any family. Women with certain chronic health problems, including diabetes and seizure disorders (treated with anticonvulsant medications), have an increased risk (approximately 1 out of 100) of having a baby with spina bifida. Many things can affect a pregnancy, including family genes and things women may be exposed to during pregnancy. Recent studies have shown that folic acid is one factor that may reduce the risk of having an NTD baby. Taking folic acid before and during early pregnancy reduces the risk of spina bifida and other neural tube defects. Folic acid, a common water-soluble B vitamin, is essential for the functioning of the human body. During periods of rapid growth, such as fetal development, the body's requirement for this vitamin increases. The average American diet does not supply the recommended level of folic acid; it can be found in multivitamins, fortified breakfast cereals, dark green leafy vegetables such as broccoli and spinach, egg yolks, and some fruits and fruit juices.

According to the Spina Bifida Association of America (SBAA), if all women who could become pregnant were to take a multivitamin with 400 micrograms of folic acid, the risk of neural tube defects could be reduced by up to 75 percent. There are three prenatal tests that usually detect spina bifida: a blood test for alpha-fetoprotein; ultrasound; and amniocentesis.

Children with spina bifida can achieve independence as they learn mobility skills with the use of crutches, braces, or wheelchairs. Many children can independently manage their bowel and bladder problems. According to SBAA, it is important that attention be focused on the psychological and social development of children and young adults with spina bifida. Many recent studies, including SBAA's Adult Network Survey, clearly indicate the presence of emotional problems that result from factors such as low self-esteem and lack of social skills training.

Researchers are looking for the genes linked to a predisposition to spina bifida. They are also exploring the complex mechanisms of normal brain development to see what goes wrong with the neural tube in spina bifida.

Since the 1930s, treatment of babies with this condition has been to surgically close the opening in their back within a few days of birth. This prevents further damage to the nervous tissue; it does not restore function to the already damaged nerves. In recent years, some doctors have begun operating on babies with spina bifida before they are born. Nerve function in babies with spina bifida seems to worsen through the course of pregnancy; this progressive pattern of damage to the spinal cord may be caused by contact with amniotic fluid and suggests intervention as early as possible.

Many children with spina bifida have symptoms related to a tethered cord (the cord and the membranes that line it stick together, restricting spinal cord growth and spinal fluid movement). Better surgical techniques are now available to treat this, thus reducing pain and weakness and improving bowel and bladder function.

SOURCES

Spina Bifida Association, National Institute of Neurological Disorders and Stroke, March of Dimes Birth Defects Foundation

ॐ **Below are links to resources.**

Spina Bifida Association (SBA) promotes the prevention
of spina bifida and works to enhance the lives of all affected. 202-944-3295 or toll-free 1-800-621-3141; or visit
www.sbaa.org

March of Dimes Birth Defects Foundation offers
information about the four major problems that threaten
the health of America's babies: birth defects, infant mortality, low birth weight, and lack of prenatal care. Toll-
free 1-888-MODIMES (663-4637); **www.modimes.com**

SPINAL CORD INJURY

SPINAL CORD INJURY (SCI) involves damage to the nerves within the bony
protection of the spinal canal. The most common cause of cord injury
is trauma, although damage can occur from various diseases acquired
at birth or later in life, from tumors, electric shock, poisoning or loss of
oxygen related to surgical or underwater mishaps. The spinal cord does
not have to be severed in order for a loss of function to occur. In fact, in
most people with SCI, the spinal cord is bruised and intact.

Since the spinal cord coordinates body movement and sensation, an
injured cord loses the ability to send and receive messages from the brain
to the body's systems that control sensory, motor, and autonomic function
below the level of injury; this often results in paralysis.

Spinal cord injury is an age-old problem, but it wasn't until the
1940s that the prognosis for long-term survival was very optimistic. Prior
to World War II, people routinely died of infections to the urinary tract,
lungs, or skin; the advent of antibiotic drugs changed SCI from a death
sentence to a manageable condition. Nowadays, people with spinal cord
injury approach the full life span of nondisabled individuals.

Spinal cord trauma is more than a single event. The initial blunt
force damages or kills spinal nerve cells. But in the hours and days after
injury a cascade of secondary events, including loss of oxygen and the

release of toxic chemicals at the site of injury, further damage the cord. Since 1990, acute treatment for SCI trauma often included use of the steroid drug methylprednisolone, thought to limit the second wave of destruction. The drug is no longer recommended by neurosurgeons.

Acute care may involve surgery if the spinal cord appears to be compressed by bone, a herniated disk, or a blood clot. Traditionally, surgeons waited for several days to decompress the spinal cord, believing that operating immediately could worsen the outcome. More recently, many surgeons advocate immediate early surgery.

Generally speaking, after the swelling of the spinal cord begins to go down, most people show some functional improvement after an injury. With many injuries, especially incomplete injuries (some motor or sensory function preserved below the lesion level), a person may recover function eighteen months or more after the injury. In some cases, people with SCI regain some function years after the injury.

Nerve cells (neurons) of the peripheral nervous system (PNS), which carry signals to the limbs, torso, and other parts of the body, are able to repair themselves after injury. However, nerves in the brain and spinal cord, within the central nervous system (CNS), are not able to regenerate (see below for discussion of research to address this lack of self-repair in the spinal cord).

The spinal cord includes nerve cells (neurons) and long nerve fibers (axons) that are covered by myelin, a type of insulating substance. Loss of myelin, which can occur with cord trauma and is the hallmark of such diseases as multiple sclerosis, prevents effective transmission of nerve signals. The nerve cells themselves, with their tree-like branches called dendrites, receive signals from other nerve cells. As with the brain, the spinal cord is enclosed in three membranes (or meninges): the pia mater, the innermost layer; the arachnoid, the middle layer; and the dura mater, the leather-like outer layer ("dura mater," Latin for tough mother).

Several types of cells carry out spinal cord functions. Large motor neurons, or efferents, have long axons that control skeletal muscles in the neck, torso, and limbs. Sensory neurons called dorsal root ganglion cells, or afferents, carry information from the body into the spinal cord and on to the brain. Spinal interneurons, which lie completely within the spinal cord, help integrate sensory information and generate coordinated signals that control muscles.

Glia, or supporting cells, far outnumber neurons in the brain and spinal cord and perform many essential functions. One type of glial cell, the oligodendrocyte, creates the myelin sheaths that insulate axons and improve the speed and reliability of nerve signal transmission. Astrocytes, large star-shaped glial cells, regulate the composition of the biochemical fluids that surround nerve cells. Smaller cells called microglia become activated in response to injury and help clean up waste products. All of these glial cells produce substances that support neuron survival and influence axon growth. However, these cells may also impede recovery following injury; some glial cells become reactive and thereby contribute to formation of growth-blocking scar tissue after injury.

Nerve cells of the brain and spinal cord respond to trauma and damage differently than most other cells of the body, including those in the peripheral nervous system. The brain and spinal cord are confined within bony cavities that protect them, but this also renders them vulnerable to compression damage caused by swelling or forceful injury. Cells of the central nervous system have a very high rate of metabolism and rely upon blood glucose for energy—these cells require a full blood supply for healthy functioning; therefore, CNS cells are particularly vulnerable to reductions in blood flow (ischemia).

Other unique features of the CNS are the blood-brain barrier and the blood-spinal cord barrier. These barriers, formed by cells lining the blood vessels in the CNS, protect nerve cells by restricting entry of potentially harmful substances and cells of the immune system. Trauma may compromise these barriers, perhaps contributing to further damage in the brain and spinal cord. The blood spinal-cord barrier also prevents entry of some potentially therapeutic drugs.

Complete vs. incomplete injury. Those with an incomplete injury have some spared sensory or motor function below the level of injury—the spinal cord was not totally damaged or disrupted. In a complete injury, nerve damage obstructs all signals coming from the brain to the body below the injury.

While there's almost always hope of recovering some function after a spinal cord injury, it is generally true that people with incomplete injuries have a better chance of getting more return. The sooner muscles start working again, the better the chances are of additional recovery. When muscles come back later, after the first several weeks, they are more likely to be in the arms than in the legs. As long as there is some improvement and additional muscles recover function, the chances are better that more improvement is possible. The longer there is no improvement, the lower the odds it will start to happen on its own. The spinal cord is organized into segments along its length, noted by their position along the thirty-three vertebrae of the backbone. Nerves from each segment are responsible for motor and sensory functions for specific regions of the body (if you map this, it's called a dermatome, right). In general, the higher in the spinal column an injury occurs, the more function a person will lose. The segments in the neck, or cervical region, referred to as C1 through C8, control signals to the neck, arms, hands, and, in some cases, the diaphragm. Injuries to this area result in tetraplegia, or as it is more commonly called, quadriplegia.

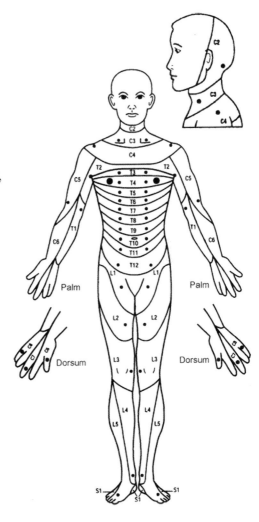

Injury above the C3 level may require a ventilator for the person to breathe. Injury above the C4 level usually means loss of movement and sensation in all four limbs, although often shoulder and neck movement is available to facilitate sip-and-puff devices for mobility, environmental control, and communication. C5 injuries often spare the control of shoulder and biceps, but there is not much control at the wrist or hand. Those at C5 can usually feed themselves and independently handle many activities of daily living. C6 injuries generally allow wrist control, enough to be able to drive adaptive vehicles and handle personal hygiene, but those affected at this level often lack fine hand function. Individuals with C7 and T1 injuries can straighten their arms and can typically handle most self-care activities, though they still may have dexterity problems with hands and fingers.

Nerves in the thoracic, or upper back region (T1 through T12) relay signals to the torso and some parts of the arms. Injuries from T1 to T8 usually affect control of the upper torso, limiting trunk movement as the result of a lack of abdominal muscle control. Lower thoracic injuries (T9 to T12) allow good trunk control and good abdominal muscle control. Those injured in the lumbar, or mid-back region just below the ribs (L1 through L5), are able to control signals to the hips and legs. A person with an L4 injury can often extend the knees. The sacral segments (S1 through S5) lie just below the lumbar segments in the mid-back and control signals to the groin, toes, and some parts of the legs.

Besides a loss of sensation or motor function, injury to the spinal cord leads to other changes, including loss of bowel, bladder, and sexual function, low blood pressure, autonomic dysreflexia (for injuries above T6), deep vein thrombosis, spasticity, and chronic pain. Other secondary issues related to injury include pressure ulcers, respiratory complications, urinary tract infections, pain, obesity, and depression. See pages 125-165 for more on these conditions; they are mainly preventable with good healthcare, diet, and physical activity.

Research on aging with disability indicates that respiratory illnesses, diabetes, and thyroid disease occur more often in people with SCI than in the rest of the population. For example, people with SCI are more prone to lower respiratory infections, resulting in lost productivity, increased healthcare costs, and increased risk of early death. These problems are common not only in those with high cervical injuries, who have loss of respiratory muscle function, but also in those with paraplegia.

Spinal cord injuries are most commonly caused by motor vehicle accidents, followed by sports-related injuries (more common in children and teenagers), falls and acts of violence. More work-related injuries (mainly construction work) occur with adults. People who sustain a spinal cord injury are mostly in their teens or twenties, although as the population in general ages, the percentage of older persons with paralysis is increasing. About four out of five people with spinal cord injuries are male. More than half of spinal cord injuries occur in the cervical area, a third occur in the thoracic area, and the remainder occur mostly in the lumbar region.

Paralysis Prevalence: Big Number

The numbers are out and they are shockingly large: there are 5.6 million Americans dealing with paralysis, roughly 1 in 50. A study from the Reeve Foundation estimates that 1.275 million Americans are living with paralysis resulting from spinal cord injuries — five times the previous commonly used estimate of 250,000. Stroke, which paralyzes 1.6 million Americans, was found to be the leading cause of paralysis; spinal cord injury was the second-leading cause, at 23 percent of cases.

The figures were gathered from a meticulously designed population-based telephone survey of about 33,000 households, It was developed by researchers at the University of New Mexico with input from top experts from around the country, including the Centers for Disease Control and Prevention as well as 14 leading universities and medical centers.

These findings have major implications for the treatment of spinal cord and paralysis-related diseases—not only for those living with these conditions, but also for their families, caregivers, healthcare providers, and employers. As the number of people living with paralysis and spinal cord injuries increases, so do the costs associated with treating them. Each year, paralysis and spinal cord injuries cost the healthcare system billions of dollars. Spinal cord injuries alone cost roughly $40.5 billion annually—a 317 percent increase from costs estimated in 1998 ($9.7 billion). People living with paralysis and spinal cord injuries are also often unable to afford health insurance that adequately covers the complex secondary or chronic conditions that are commonly linked with these conditions.

SPINAL CORD INJURY RESEARCH

THERE ARE NO DEFINITIVE TREATMENTS YET for spinal cord injury. However, ongoing research to test new therapies is progressing rapidly. Drugs to limit injury progression, decompression surgery, nerve cell transplantation and nerve regeneration, as well as nerve rejuvenation therapies, are being examined as potential ways to minimize the effects of spinal cord injury. The biology of the injured spinal cord is enormously complex but clinical trials are underway with more coming; hope for restoring function after paralysis continues to rise, and for good reason. Still, paralysis from disease, stroke or trauma is considered one of the toughest of medical problems. In fact, just over a generation ago, any damage to the brain and spinal cord that severely limited motor and/or sensory function was thought to be untreatable. In recent years, though, the word "cure" in this context has not only entered the vocabulary of the science community but also that of clinicians. Restorative neuroscience is bubbling with energy and expectation. To be sure, scientific progress is a slow but steady march. One day in the not-too-distant future there will be a host of some procedures or treatments to mitigate the effects of paralysis. But it is not reasonable to expect a one-size-fits-all "magic bullet" for restoring function. It is almost a certainty that these coming treatments will involve combinations of therapies, given at various time points in the injury process, including a significant rehab component. Here is a snapshot of work being done in several research areas.

Nerve protection: As in the case of brain trauma or stroke, the initial damage to spinal cord cells is followed by a series of biochemical events that often knock out other nerve cells in the area of the injury. This secondary process can be modified, thus saving many cells from damage. The steroid drug methylprednisolone (MP) was FDA-approved in 1990 as

Motivated mouse: epidural stimulation plus treadmill training equals function.

GREGOIRE COURTINE LAB

a treatment for acute SCI; it is still the only approved acute treatment. MP is believed to reduce inflammation if people get the drug within eight hours of injury. The medical community is not entirely sold on the effectiveness of MP; many neurosurgeons won't recommend it and suggest the steroid dosage actually causes more damage. Meanwhile, research is underway in many labs around the world to find a better acute treatment. Several drugs look promising, including Riluzole (protects nerves from further damage from excess glutamate), Cethrin (reduces inhibitors to growth), a molecule called anti-Nogo (tested in Europe, promotes spinal cord cell growth by blocking inhibition), and a magnesium chloride compound in polyethylene glycol (PEG) called AC105 (in animal studies, AC105 was neuroprotective and improved motor function in SCI and cognitive function

Ramón y Cajal

in TBI when initiated within four hours of injury). Cooling of the spinal cord is another possible acute therapy; hypothermia appears to reduce cell loss. Protocols for cooling (how cold, how long) have not been fully determined. Stem cells have also been considered as an acute therapy: The biotech firm Geron began (then abandoned) human safety trials using human embryonic stem cells to treat acute spinal cord injuries (see more on this trial below).

Well more than one hundred years ago, Spanish scientist Santiago Ramón y Cajal noted that the ends of axons broken by trauma become swollen into what he called "dystrophic endballs" and are no longer capable of regeneration. This remained a central issue in recovery of function—there seems to be some sort of barrier or scar that traps the nerve tips in place. Recent studies in several labs have revealed that these dystrophic growth cones can get unstuck using a molecule that breaks down the sugar chains forming the scar (chondroitinase, nicknamed chase). There has been much work published about the potential for chase; it has helped restore function in paralyzed animals. There have been no human trials yet; effective delivery of chondroitinase to the injury site has not been fully worked out.

Bridging: The idea of a bridge is conceptually easy—transplanted cells or perhaps a type of miniature scaffold, fill the damaged area of the cord (often a scar-lined cyst), and thus allow nerves of the spinal cord to cross through otherwise inhospitable terrain. In 1981, Canadian scientist Albert Aguayo showed that spinal cord axons could grow long distances using a bridge made of peripheral nerve, proving without doubt that axons will grow if they have the right environment. A variety of techniques has evolved through experiments to create a growth-enhancing environment, including the use of stem cells, nerve cells called olfactory ensheathing glia (OEG) that come from the upper nose, and Schwann cells (support cells of peripheral nerves that have been shown to help spinal cord and brain cells).

Another type of bridge, or perhaps more like a bypass, stitches a piece of peripheral nerve above and below the area of spinal cord lesion. This type of surgery is not used clinically in the United States. In experiments, however, a nerve bypass restored some diaphragm function and breathing in animals with high cervical injuries, and some bladder control in animals with lower injuries. The research team is hopeful this can one day benefit people.

Cell replacement: While it may be tantalizing to think broken or lost spinal cord nerve cells can be replaced by new ones, this has not been done; cell replacement is not yet a source of spare parts. Stem cells from one's own body or from other sources (including embryonic cell lines), OEG cells, fetal tissue, and umbilical cord blood cells have been used experimentally to restore function after paralysis; results have been encouraging but not because the new cells take on the identity of the lost or damaged ones. Replacements seem to offer support and help nurture surviving cells.

For discussion of what a stem cell is, see sidebar page 106. Be mindful that stem cell therapy is considered a drug by the FDA; the only approved use in the United States is bone marrow transplantation.

The first-ever embryonic stem cell trial (halted midstream in 2011 by its sponsor, Geron, citing financial priorities) hoped to use transplanted stem cells to rejuvenate existing cells in the area of an acute spinal cord injury, thereby restoring the myelin wrapping necessary for signal transmission. Five people were enrolled in the Phase I trial, looking mainly at safety; there were no adverse effects reported, but no functional gains either. The Geron cells may get a reprise; two former Geron executives acquired the rights to the cell line and formed a new company, BioTime, intending to run more trials. See **www.biotimeinc.com**

In an ongoing clinical trial in Switzerland, a California biotech, StemCells, Inc., is testing human stem cells from a fetal source in people injured three months to a year. These cells, too, are believed to restore myelin. The first trial is showing the cells are safe; early data shows some return of sensory function, too. The science behind the StemCells, Inc. trial comes from the labs of husband-and-wife team Brian Cummings and Aileen Anderson at the University of California, Irvine. Anderson is a member of the Reeve International Research Consortium on Spinal Cord Injury (see **www.ChristopherReeve.org**, click on "research"). StemCells, Inc. has begun preclinical animal studies of the company's cells as a potential treatment for long-term cervical spinal cord injury. **www.stemcellsinc.com**

A third SCI stem cell clinical trial, underway from a company called Neuralstem, is testing human neural cells in a chronic SCI model, one-to two-years post-injury. The transplanted cells are derived from stem cells native to the brain and spinal cord. The company found a way to produce them in large quantity for direct injection to the spinal cord; the same cell line has been in clinical trials for several years for ALS.

In preclinical studies using Neuralstem's human cells in animals, researchers suggest the replacement cells integrate with spinal nerves and form new relay circuits—the animals showed significantly improved function. Why do the cells seem to grow and form connections so well? This preliminary success with animals might have to do with the delivery system, using a fibrin matrix as a scaffold, plus the addition of a cocktail of growth factors. The first human trials, however, won't test the combination of matrix or factors. See **www.neuralstem.com**

Clinical trials in several countries have tested the safety and efficacy of OEG cells transplanted into the lesion area of the spinal cord; results have been promising. Meanwhile, the Miami Project has begun a clinical trial for transplanted Schwann cells, support cells of peripheral nerves that have been shown to encourage the regrowth of axons after spinal cord injury. Combining Schwann cells with other growth molecules may ultimately be more useful than transplants of Schwann cells alone. For example, a team at the Miami Project found that Schwann cells alone activated nerves to grow into a bridge but they stopped short of crossing the gap in the injured spinal cord. By adding OEG cells to the Schwann cells, the axons crossed the bridge and entered the spinal cord on the other side of the lesion. See **www.themiamiproject.org**

Regeneration: This is perhaps the toughest of the treatment possibilities. To restore a major degree of sensation and motor control after spinal cord injury, long axons must grow again and connect over long distances—as much as two feet—to precise targets. These axons cannot regenerate unless their path is cleared of poisons, enriched with vitamins, and paved with an attractive roadbed. By blocking inhibitory factors (proteins that stop axon growth in its tracks), adding nutrients, and supplying a matrix to grow on, researchers have indeed grown spinal nerves over long distances. One group of scientists at several labs used a molecular switch to turn on nerve cell growth after trauma. PTEN is a tumor suppressor gene that was discovered by cancer researchers fifteen years ago. This gene regulates cell proliferation and it turns out

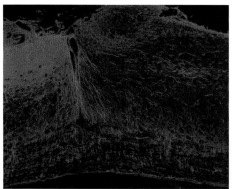

ZHIGANG HE LAB

to be a molecular switch for axon growth. When scientists deleted PTEN in a complete spinal cord injury model, cortical spinal axons—the ones needed for major movement function—regenerated at unprecedented rates. PTEN is complicated; you can't just get rid of it because it is the brake needed to stop certain kinds of cellular overgrowth (cancer). But there are ways to release it. Much work

Nerve fibers (axons), labeled red, cross the lesion site of an injured spinal cord, coaxed by genetic manipulation to release growth potential.

remains to make this relevant to human spinal cord injuries but many more labs have joined in, exploring the PTEN gene and many others related to regrowth of nerve cells.

Rehabilitation: Almost any treatment to restore function after paralysis will require a physical component to rebuild muscle, build bone, and reactivate patterns of movement. Some form of rehab will be needed after function comes back. Moreover, it appears that activity itself affects recovery: In 2002, seven years after his supposedly complete C2 injury, Christopher Reeve showed that he had regained limited function and sensation. His doctor credited his use of functional electrical stimulation, which may have kick-started the repair process, and a program of passive electrical stimulation, aqua therapy, and passive standing.

To a limited extent, Reeve also used treadmill training, a type of physical therapy that forces the legs to move in a pattern of walking as the body is suspended in a harness above a moving treadmill. The theory is that the spinal cord can interpret incoming sensory signals; the cord itself is smart. It can carry out movement commands without brain input. Locomotion is managed by a system called a central pattern generator (CPG), which activates the pattern of stepping. Stepping during treadmill training sends sensory information to the CPG, reminding the spinal cord how to step. Scientists describe the reactivation due to stepping as plasticity—the nervous system is not "hard wired" and appears to have the ability to adapt itself to new stimulation. Researchers are learning much more about the CPG and how to activate it. (See the Rob Summers story, page 104-105.) Rehabilitation techniques have evolved to the point that exercise and physical activity are an essential component of recovery. For the person with a spinal cord injury, it's best to stay active and always strive for the maximum outcome. For more on activity-based recovery, and to learn about the Reeve Foundation NeuroRecovery Network, see page 100.

SOURCES

American Association of Neurological Surgeons, Craig Hospital, Christopher & Dana Reeve Foundation, The National Institute of Neurological Disorders and Stroke.

ঌ **Below are links to spinal cord injury resources.**

Christopher & Dana Reeve Foundation funds research to develop treatments for paralysis caused by spinal cord injury or other nervous system disorders. The Foundation also works to improve the quality of life for people living with disabilities through its grants program, Paralysis Resource Center (**www.paralysis.org**), and advocacy efforts. For an overview of the Foundation's research and advocacy, details on the Quality of Life Grants Program, or to connect with an Information Specialist, visit **www.ChristopherReeve.org** or write c/o 636 Morris Turnpike, Suite 3A Short Hills, NJ 07078; toll-free 1-800-225-0292.

Reeve Foundation Peer & Family Support Program is a national peer-to-peer mentoring program providing emotional support as well as local and national information and resources to people living with paralysis, and their families and caregivers. **www.paralysis.org/peer**

Apparelyzed website provides peer support for those affected by spinal cord injuries. **www.apparelyzed.com**

CareCure Community offers discussion forums on SCI and neuroscience research, caregiving, travel, sex and relationships, sports, equipment, legislation and more. Home of the Spinal Nurses (in the Care section) and of MobileWomen. A lively, helpful, hopeful community. **http://sci.rutgers.edu**

Craig Hospital supports a dedicated nurse to answer non-emergency calls from people with SCI, Monday-Friday. Toll-free 1-800-247-0257 or 303-789-8508. Educational materials are available online. **www.craighospital.org**

Darrell Gwynn Foundation provides support for people with paralysis, donating dozens of high-tech, customized wheelchairs at no cost to deserving individuals. 954-792-7223; **http://darrellgwynnfoundation.org**

Facing Disability While spinal cord injury affects the entire family, there are few resources for families. This website provides information and peer support for people with injuries and their families. Sharing life experiences—by way of over 1000 videos—with others who have been down same road helps people find their own strength and support. **www.FacingDisability.com**

elearnSCI.org is a free online education resource for spinal cord injury prevention and comprehensive clinical practice and rehabilitation. An initiative of the physician-based International Spinal Cord Society. Visit online **www.elearnsci.org; www.iscos.org.uk**

International Spinal Cord Society, with a membership of over 1,000 clinicians and scientists from 87 countries, promotes education, research and clinical excellence; produces the journal *Spinal Cord.* **www.iscos.org.uk**

National Spinal Cord Injury Association (NSCIA), a division of United Spinal, offers a toll-free help-line, peer support, information resources. Toll-free 1-800-962-9629. **www.spinalcord.org**

Paralyzed Veterans of America (PVA) works toward quality healthcare, rehabilitation and civil rights for veterans and all citizens with spinal cord injuries and diseases. PVA offers numerous publications, fact sheets and supports the Consortium for Spinal Cord Medicine, which produces authoritative clinical guidelines for SCI. PVA supports research by way of its Spinal Cord Research Foundation. The organization sponsors the magazines *PN/Paraplegia News* and *Sports 'N Spokes.* Toll-free 1-800-424-8200. **www.pva.org**

Ralph's Riders Foundation is a peer network in Southern California area founded by Mayra Fornos in honor of her late husband, Ralph, an acivist lawyer and quadriplegic. **www.ralphsriders.org**

SCI Information Network offers information about spinal cord injury, including new injuries, and is home to National Spinal Cord Injury Statistical Center (NSCISC). **www.uab.edu/medicine/sci** or **www.nscisc.uab.edu**

Spinal Injury 101 is a video series from the Shepherd Center, with backing from the Reeve Foundation and the National Spinal Cord Injury Association. Tutorial videos on SCI, acute management, secondary conditions and more. **www.spinalinjury101.org**

SPINALpedia is an Internet social mentoring network and video archive "that allows the spinal cord injury community to motivate each other with the knowledge and triumphs gained from our individual experiences." **www.spinalpedia.com**

United Spinal Association (USA) provides expertise, connections and access to resources. 718-803-3782; **www.unitedspinal.org**

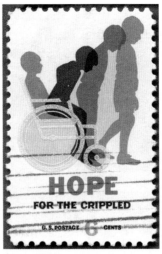

Circa 1969

The Alliance for Regenerative Medicine (ARM) promotes legislative, regulatory reimbursement, investment, technical, and other initiatives to accelerate the development of safe and effective regenerative medicine technologies. ARM also works to increase public understanding of the field. **http://alliancerm.org**

Canadian Spinal Research Organization is dedicated to physical improvement for persons with spinal cord injury or related neurological deficits, through targeted medical research. 905-508-4000; **www.csro.com**

CatWalk Spinal Cord Injury Trust was founded by New Zealander Catriona Williams, injured in a 2002 riding accident. The trust is dedicated to raising funds to support cure science. **www.catwalk.org.nz**

CenterWatch provides a list of approved clinical trials being conducted internationally. 617-856-5900; **www.centerwatch.com**

ClinicalTrials lists all federally supported clinical trials in the U.S., sorted by disease or condition, location, treatment or sponsor. Developed by the National Library of Medicine. **www.clinicaltrials.gov**

Craig H. Neilsen Foundation was formed to improve the quality of life for those living with spinal cord injury and to support scientific exploration for therapies and treatments. The foundation is the largest non-profit funding source for SCI research in the U.S. Neilsen, a casino executive, lived 21 years with paralysis before his death in 2006. **http://chnfoundation.org**

Dana Foundation provides reliable, accessible information on the brain and spinal cord, including research. The Foundation offers numerous books and publications and sponsors Brain Awareness Week every March. Deep resources. **www.dana.org**

International Campaign for Cures of Spinal Cord Injury Paralysis is a group of organizations around the world that together fund about $25 million a year in SCI research. Members include: CatWalk Spinal Cord Injury Trust, Christopher & Dana Reeve Foundation, Craig H. Neilsen Foundation, French Institute for Spinal Cord Research, International Foundation for Research in Paraplegia, Japan Spinal Cord Foundation, Miami Project to Cure Paralysis, Paralyzed Veterans of America, Rick Hansen Foundation, Spinal Cure Australia, Neil Sachse Foundation, Spinal Research, Wings for Life. **www.campaignforcure.org**

International Research Consortium on Spinal Cord Injury is a Reeve Foundation-funded collaboration of prominent neuroscience laboratories in the U.S. and Europe working toward treatments for spinal cord injury. **www.ChristopherReeve.org/research**

International Society for Stem Cell Research is a source for reliable information about stem cell research and clinical advances. **www.isscr.org**

Japan Spinal Cord Foundation takes aim "at the realization of a society where spinal cord injured persons can establish a life with independence and self-esteem regardless of the severity of their disabilities." **www.jscf.org**

Miami Project to Cure Paralysis is a research center at the University of Miami dedicated to finding treatments and, ultimately, cures for paralysis. Toll-free 1-800-STAND-UP; **www.miamiproject.miami.edu**

Mike Utley Foundation provides financial support of research, rehabilitation and education programs on spinal cord injury. Toll-free 1-800-294-4683; **www.mikeutley.org**

National Institute of Neurological Disorders and Stroke is the primary federal funding source for all research related to the brain and spinal cord and provides authoritative research overviews for all diseases and conditions related to paralysis. **www.ninds.nih.gov**

Neil Sachse Foundation was founded in Australia to support SCI research. Sachse had a sporting injury leading to quadriplegia. **www.nsf.org.au**

PubMed, a service of the National Library of Medicine, provides access to over 12 million citations in the medical literature back to the mid-1960s. Includes links to many sites providing full text articles and other related resources. Search using key word, researcher name, or journal title. **www.pubmed.gov**

Reeve-Irvine Research Center was formed by philanthropist Joan Irvine Smith in honor of Christopher Reeve to study injuries and diseases of the spinal cord that result in paralysis. Contact c/o University of California at Irvine; **www.reeve.uci.edu**

Rick Hansen Foundation was created in Canada in 1988 to support spinal cord injury research, as well as wheelchair sport, injury prevention and rehabilitation programs. 604-295-8149; toll-free 1-800-213-2131; **www.rickhansen.com**

Roman Reed Foundation is dedicated to finding cures for neurological disorders. Named for California advocate Roman Reed, injured in a college football game. **http://romanreedfoundation.com**

Sam Schmidt Paralyis Foundation helps individuals with spinal cord injuries and other illnesses by funding research, medical treatment, rehabilitation and technology advances. Named for Schmidt, a quadriplegic former race car driver. 317-236-9999; **www.samschmidt.org**

SCORE is dedicated to finding a cure for paralysis; also helps with out-of-pocket costs for home modifications, vehicle adaptations, etc., for young people who injured in sporting events. 323-655-8298; **www.scorefund.org**

Society for Neuroscience is an organization of about 40,000 basic scientists and clinicians who study the brain and nervous system, including trauma and disease, as well as brain development, sensation and perception, learning and memory, sleep, stress, aging and psychiatric disorders. 202-962-4000; **http://apu.sfn.org**

Spinal Cord Injury Project at Rutgers University works to move therapies from laboratory to clinical trial. Home of the CareCure community. 732-445-2061; see online **http://sci.rutgers.edu**

Spinal Cord Injury Research Program, U.S. Department of Defense, was established by Congress in 2009 with a $35 million appropriation to support research into regenerating or repairing damaged spinal cords and improving rehabilitation therapies. Congressionally Directed Medical Research Programs: 301-619-7071; **http://cdmrp.army.mil/scirp**

Spinal Cord Research Foundation of the Paralyzed Veterans of America (PVA) funds research to treat spinal cord dysfunction and to enhance the health of people who are paralyzed. Toll-free 1-800-424-8200; Click on "Research and Education." **www.pva.org**,

Spinal Cord Society (SCS) is a research advocacy organization that raises money to cure spinal cord injuries. 218-739-5252; **www.scsus.org**

Spinal Cure Australia (formerly Australasian Spinal Research Trust) was established in 1994 to fund scientific research to find cures for paralysis. On the Internet see **www.spinalcure.org.au**

Spinal Research (formerly International Spinal Research Trust) is a United Kingdom charity funding research to end the permanence of paralysis. Founded in 1980 by Stewart Yesner, a young lawyer paralyzed in a car accident in Zambia in 1974. **www.spinal-research.org**

StemCellAction is a grassroots group of people with chronic medical conditions and their families and friends who believe in the potential of stem cell research. Offshoot of the Genetics Policy Institute. See online **www.stemcellaction.org**; or **www.genpol.org**

Travis Roy Foundation, named for the injured Boston University hockey player, helps people with spinal cord injuries and funds cure research. The foundation has awarded grants for wheelchairs, van purchases, home modifications, and other adaptive gear. 617-619-8257; **www.travisroyfoundation.org**

United To Fight Paralysis (U2FP) advocates as "cure warriors" for SCI research. Sponsors the annual Working to Walk research science meeting. **http://u2fp.org**

Veterans Affairs Rehabilitation Research and Development Service supports the study of pain, bowel and bladder function, FES, nerve plasticity, prosthetics, and more. Publishes the *Journal of Rehabilitation R&D*, hosts the International Symposium on Neural Regeneration. **www.rehab.research.va.gov**

Wings for Life, based in Austria, finances research projects worldwide aimed at healing the injured spinal cord; projects are picked by an international group of reviewers to ensure the best possible investment of donations; **www.wingsforlife.com/en-us**

Yale Center for Neuroscience and Regeneration Research works to develop new treatments, and ultimately a cure, for spinal cord injury and related disorders. Supported by the Paralyzed Veterans of America and United Spinal Association and the Department of Veterans Affairs. 203-937-3802; **http://medicine.yale.edu/cnrr**

Spinal Cord Model Systems

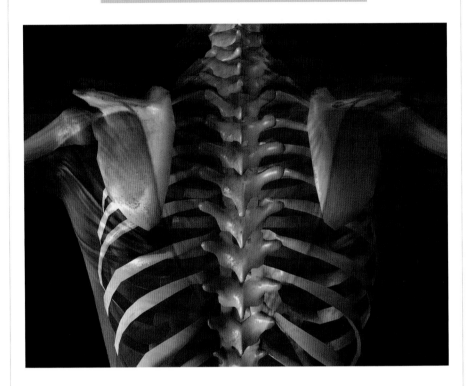

The Spinal Cord Injury Model Systems (SCIMS) Centers Program was established by the federal government in 1970; the goal of the program has been to improve care and outcomes for individuals with spinal cord injury, based on research showing the superiority of comprehensive versus fragmented care. The SCIMS Centers provide a multidisciplinary care from emergency services through rehabilitation and re-entry into community life. The centers also conduct research, provide education and disseminate information to improve the health and quality-of-life for individuals living with spinal cord injury.

There are currently 14 SCI Model Systems centers and 3 Form II centers sponsored by the National Institute on Disability and Rehabilitation Research, Office of Special Education and Rehabilitative Services, U.S. Department of Education.

UAB Model Spinal Cord Injury Care System, University of Alabama
at Birmingham, Birmingham, AL; 205-934-3283.

Southern California Spinal Cord Injury Model System, Rancho Los
Amigos National Rehabilitation Center, Downey, CA; 562-401-8111.

Rocky Mountain Regional Spinal Injury System, Craig Hospital, Englewood, CO;
303-789-8306.

South Florida Spinal Cord Injury Model System, University
of Miami, Miami, FL; 305-243-9516.

Georgia Regional Spinal Cord Injury Care System, Shepherd
Center, Inc., Atlanta, GA; 404-350-7591.

Midwest Regional Spinal Cord Injury Care System, Rehabilitation
Institute of Chicago, Chicago, IL; 312-238-6207.

Kentucky Regional Model Spinal Cord Injury System, Frazier
Rehabilitation, Louisville, KY; 502-582-7443.

New England Regional Spinal Cord Injury Center Network, Boston
University Medical Center, Boston, MA, and Gaylord Hospital, Wallingford,
CT, Hospital for Special Care, New Britain, CT; 617-638-7380.

Spaulding-Harvard Spinal Cord Injury System, Spaulding
Rehabilitation, Boston, MA; 617-573-2862.

**University of Michigan Model Spinal Cord Injury Care
System**, Ann Arbor, MI; 734-763-0971.

Northern New Jersey Spinal Cord Injury System, Kessler Foundation
Research Center, West Orange, NJ; 973-243-6973.

Regional Spinal Cord Injury Center of the Delaware Valley, Thomas
Jefferson University, Philadelphia, PA; 215-955-6579.

**University of Pittsburgh Model Center on Spinal Cord
Injury**, Pittsburgh, PA; 412-232-7949.

Northwest Regional Spinal Cord Injury System, University
of Washington, Seattle WA; 800-366-5643.

Form II Centers (previously funded Model Systems that continue to collect follow-up
data. New participants are not enrolled).

Santa Clara Valley Medical Center, San Jose, CA; 408-885-2383.

Mount Sinai School of Medicine, New York, NY; 212-659-9369.

The Institute for Rehabilitation and Research (TIRR);
Memorial Hermann, Houston, TX; 713-797-5972.

Living a Fearless Life

By Christopher Reeve

I live a fearless life on a daily basis. I'm reminded of that every time I come into New York, because I'm put in the back of a van, strapped down by four straps, and driven around by a bunch of guys who just happen to be firefighters from Yonkers. These guys are used to driving fire trucks—at great speed–so when I get into the van, I have to give it up. As a self-confessed control freak from way back in my early childhood, being able to sit in the back, assume that we're going to safely reach our destination, and actually doze off has been big for me.

This one hour van trip is a good metaphor for the journey I'd like to talk about. For so many of us, the source of our fear is the loss of control. But the more we try to control what happens to us, the greater our fear that we're no longer empowered, that there's no safety net, and that dangerous, unexpected things may happen. Ironically, the act of trying to control what happens is what actually robs us of great experiences and diminishes us.

The lesson I had to learn when I had my injury was pretty drastic because my life before that as an actor had been one of self-sufficiency, perseverance, and discipline. I had been extremely self-sufficient from the time I finished high school, all the way through college and graduate school, and as I made my way to Off-Broadway, Broadway, television and film. I had done well and was used to being in charge.

My accident was a strange and very close call. If I had landed differently, even by a millimeter in one direction, I wouldn't have been injured; if I had landed a millimeter the other way, I wouldn't be here today. I had, at best, a 40 percent chance of surviving my surgery, during which my head was actually reattached to my neck. Also during the surgery I nearly died as a result of a drug reaction. I was told I would never again move below my shoulders, that I would absolutely have no further recovery, and that my life expectancy at 42 years of age was, at best, six to seven more years.

I dealt with it with my wife Dana at my side, thank God. We just decided not to buy into the fear that people tried to instill in us. This decision was the most important of all. How many people are walking around today three years after they were told that they only had six months to live? How many of us are doing things now that we were told that we could never do? It happens all the time.

One of the keys to going ahead and conquering fear is to ignore your moods. Ignore it when you feel like you really don't want to do whatever it is today. Ignore it

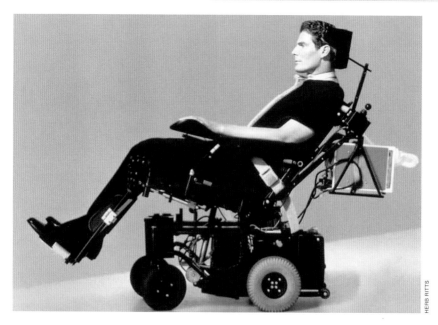

HERB RITTS

when you feel like you can't be bothered. Often you start the day feeling bad–feeling like you don't want to do something or you are treading water and getting nowhere or you can't keep going—and the day turns out to be one of the best you're ever going to have. You have to leave yourself open to possibility. By staying in the moment regardless of how you actually feel, you leave yourself open for surprises, both on a big scale and on a little scale.

I am proud of what I have achieved, but my path hasn't been without problems and difficulties. About a year ago, I was the second patient in the world to have diaphragm pacing implanted into my body. It's like a cardiac pacemaker, but it stimulates the diaphragm to create normal breathing and replace the ventilator. I felt that it was safe and that there was a good chance it would work. It didn't. It failed.

For over a year now, I've had infections and all kinds of signs of rejection by my body, and the site of implantation is still not closed. That's why I am still on this ventilator, why I can't go into the swimming pool anymore, and why I haven't moved beyond my initial level of recovery, where I plateaued. And yet I'm telling you this because it is important to know that living a fearless life means that you might go through an experience that doesn't actually work out for you. The way to stay positive, to avoid being bitter or feeling like a failure, is to look at the fact it might help somebody else. For example, this failure of the diaphragm pacing has led to modifications in how doctors perform the procedure, and the set of patients who followed me have all gotten off the ventilator.

In 1996 I was one of the first to experiment with something called "treadmill walking therapy," where I was held up by a harness and put on a treadmill, just like in a gym. This kind of therapy works because the spine has energy and memory, and so the central pattern generator in the lumbar area remembers how to walk. It doesn't take much brain power to walk. After 60 days of treadmill therapy, a lot of paraplegic patients have been able to walk again. So far in the United States alone, more than 500 people have made it out of their wheelchairs that way.

I, however, had an accident when I was put on a treadmill one day because the doctors wanted to shoot a video of how it works. They cranked up the treadmill to three and a half miles an hour. I got up on it, and I took some beautiful steps. They

Reeve addressing the Democratic National Convention, 1996

got the shot. It was perfect, and the actor in me was happy. But then I broke my leg. My femur, the big bone in my thigh, snapped right in half. I still have a 12-inch metal plate with 15 screws in there holding it together. What happened? It turned out that I had osteoporosis and my bone density wasn't strong enough to take the pace of the treadmill. So for me, there is no more treadmill at the moment. But for others, there is a new protocol, a new standard. Now they know that before they put anybody on a treadmill, they must do a bone density scan to make sure the patient doesn't have osteoporosis. Something good came out of that.

You might wonder why I went in so early on some of these experiments. I'd been pushing neuroscientists to be fearless, to not get hung up in the laboratory doing experiments forever. So, I felt that if I was pushing scientists to be fearless on the biological level, I had to do the most I could on the rehab level.

> The lesson I had to learn when I had my injury was pretty drastic . . . my life before that as an actor had been one of self-sufficiency, perseverance, and discipline.

There are also going to be times in life when living fearlessly is very simple. One of the first things that happened after surviving my surgery was that I lost my finesse. My social skills went down the drain. I realized that social skills are, to a large extent, mini-lies. Now when someone asks me a question, I have learned to tell the truth because, really, what the hell do I have to lose?

There are lots of ways of being fearless. I highly recommend it. To a large extent, the key to fearlessness is the "no matter what." Keep that in mind. It's truly amazing what we can do by allowing the spirit and mind to flourish. Our capabilities go way beyond our understanding. Trust in that and go forward. Get past the clutter, the noise inside you that says, "I can't, I can't, I'm not good enough, I don't feel like it, I'm sick, I don't want to." That is just like static on a radio. Just clear the channel, find good reception, and you'll be amazed by what you can do.

This essay was adapted from Reeve's closing speech at a Living a Fearless Life conference in New York City in the spring of 2004, hosted by The Omega Institute, www.eomega.org

Consortium for Spinal Cord Medicine

C are for people with spinal cord injuries has become more evidence-based. Since 1995, a group of 22 health professional and consumer organizations (including the Reeve Foundation), has made this its mission. The Consortium for Spinal Cord Medicine, funded and administered by Paralyzed Veterans of America, is centered around clinical practice guidelines: these are recommendations to healthcare providers based on current medical literature and research findings that expert methodologists have graded for scientific strength and validity.

Using this research along with professional and consumer input, the Consortium Steering Committee updates these guidelines and develops new ones, promoting a research agenda that encourages scientific rigor and outcome evaluation.

The Consortium's clinical practice guidelines for healthcare professionals and companion consumer guides help people living with paralysis put this information to use in their daily lives. These easy-to-understand publications provide guidance and address questions on clinical subjects ranging from pressure ulcers to bowel care to expected outcomes one year out from injury.

Printed and downloadable versions of the clinical practice guidelines and consumer guides are available. Some consumer guides are available in Spanish.

Clinical Practice Guidelines for Healthcare Professionals
- Sexuality and Reproductive Health in Adults with Spinal Cord Injury
- Early Acute Management in Adults with Spinal Cord Injury
- Bladder Management For Adults with Spinal Cord Injury
- Preservation of Upper Limb Function Following Spinal Cord Injury
- Respiratory Management Following Spinal Cord Injury
- Prevention of Thromboembolism in Spinal Cord Injury
- Acute Management of Autonomic Dysreflexia
- Pressure Ulcer Prevention and Treatment Following Spinal Cord Injury
- Outcomes Following Traumatic Spinal Cord Injury
- Depression Following Spinal Cord Injury
- Neurogenic Bowel Management in Adults with Spinal Cord Injury

Consumer Guidelines
- Bladder Management Following Spinal Cord Injury: What You Should Know

- Respiratory Management Following Spinal Cord Injury: What You Should Know
- Preservation of Upper Limb Function Following Spinal Cord Injury: What You Should Know
- Autonomic Dysreflexia: What You Should Know
- Pressure Ulcers: What You Should Know
- Expected Outcomes: What You Should Know
- Depression: What You Should Know
- Neurogenic Bowel: What You Should Know

Spanish Consumer Guides

- Ulceras por Decubito: Lo Que Usted Debe Saber (Pressure Ulcers)
- Intestino Neurologico: Lo Que Usted Debe Saber (Neurogenic Bowel)
- Reflejo Disfuncional Autonomo: Lo Que Usted Debe Saber (Autonomic Dysreflexia)

Guidelines Being Developed

- Nutrition, metabolic disorder and obesity
- Psychological adjustment and coping

Guidelines are downloadable at www.PVA.org; click on "publications"

Clinical Trials

D rugs and treatments are developed—or as the research community says it, "translated" —from laboratory experiments. Clinical research is usually conducted via a series of trials that begin with a few people and become progressively larger as safety, efficacy, and dosage are better understood.

Because full-scale clinical trials are expensive and time consuming, usually only the most promising of treatments emerging from research labs are selected in the translation process. A National Institute of Neurological Disorders and Stroke panel noted that future trials on treating paralysis should be based on minimum risk with significant benefit in a relevant animal model that has been independently replicated by other labs. Questions remain as to what minimal level of clinical improvement would warrant various levels of risk and expectation.

Once laboratory and animal studies show promise, a Phase I clinical trial is initiated, used to test the safety of a therapy for a particular disease or condition.

A Phase II clinical trial usually involves more subjects at several different centers and is used to test safety and efficacy on a broader scale, such as to test different dosing for medications or to perfect techniques for surgery.

A Phase III clinical trial involves many centers and sometimes hundreds of subjects. The trial usually involves two patient groups comparing different treatments, or, if there is only one treatment to test, patients who do not receive the test therapy get a placebo (dummy drug) instead.

Many Phase III trials are double-blinded (neither the subjects nor the doctors treating them know which treatment a subject receives) and randomized (placing subjects into one of the treatment groups in a way that can't be predicted by the patients or investigators). Success in Phase III leads to approval by the FDA for clinical use. A Phase IV might be carried out after approval to detect possible rare undesirable side effects that previous phase did not detect.

Informed consent: The government has strict safeguards to protect people who participate in clinical trials. Every clinical trial in the United States must be approved and monitored by an Institutional Review Board (IRB), an independent committee of physicians, statisticians, community advocates, and others who assess risk and ensure that the trial is ethical and that the rights of study participants are protected. The IRB makes sure participants know as much as possible.

Informed consent is a process that stresses the need for participants to understand the key facts about a clinical trial before deciding whether or not to join. These facts include why the research is being done, who the researchers are, what the researchers want to accomplish, what will be done during the trial and for how long, what risks and what benefits can be expected, and what the possible side effects are. Informed consent continues as long as you are in the study. Before joining a trial, participants must meet the study's eligibility guidelines, such as age, type of disease, medical history, and current medical condition. People may leave a trial at any time. For information about all clinical trials taking place in the United States, see *http://clinicaltrials.gov* (search by condition or diagnosis). Be very cautious before joining a trial outside the jurisdiction of the FDA or seeking an unproven or experimental treatment. Legitimate clinical trials never charge patients to participate. See also *www.closerlookatstemcells.org*

NACTN: Clinical Trials Network

S pinal cord injury research has evolved to a new era, one where clinical trials are being held, or planned, for several promising therapies. This era of translational research—moving from laboratory science to clinical application—requires new infrastructure to manage the process, coordination of preclinical data, clinical assessment, treatment and outcome measures, and, at some point, commercialization and reimbursement.

To help select and move promising therapies from the lab to the clinic, the Christopher & Dana Reeve Foundation formed the North American Clinical Trials Network, a group of ten clinical research centers plus data management and pharmacology centers.

> There can be no progress without partnerships, without collaborations, without alliance-building.

Created in 2004, NACTN is a consortium of university hospital neurosurgical and neurorehabilitation teams. NACTN's lead investigator, neurosurgeon Robert G. Grossman (Methodist Hospital, Houston), explains that given the complexity of SCI and the high cost of mounting trials, "There can be no progress without partnerships, without collaborations, without alliance-building. Spinal cord injury is too difficult and too expensive to go-it-alone and there is no room for failure due to ill-conceived planning or lack of cutting-edge spinal cord expertise."

The network is currently evaluating the drug Riluzole, a neuroprotective that is given soon after injury. NACTN successfully concluded a Phase I safety and pharmacokinetics trial and completed data analysis in preparation for a Phase II-III trial to study dosage and timing, and efficacy.

Running trials is not NACTN's only concern. The organization has created an important database to quantify the natural history of human SCI, building a

multicenter registry to document all SCI cases, including age, gender, nature of injury, and mechanism of injury. This gives NACTN a statistical baseline upon which to compare any potential therapy. The registry will help with outcome prediction, by stratifying SCI cases more carefully. So far more than 500 detailed cases are in the registry. NACTN and a European registry are pursuing several research questions via a data sharing agreement. NACTN is also studying better

Dr. Robert Grossman

ways to measure return of function. A device called GRASSP (Graded Redefined Assessment of Strength Sensibility and Prehension) has been developed to capture information after cervical SCI at any point during recovery (acute, subacute, chronic). Current measures are not sensitive enough to pick up subtle changes in the hand and upper limb. This more sensitive measure will enable researchers to better understand the benefits of new treatments. *www.christopherreeve.org/nactn*

NeuroRecovery Network

The NeuroRecovery Network (NRN) is a cooperative group of innovative rehabilitation centers that develop and deploy therapies to promote functional recovery and improve the health and quality of life for people living with paralysis.

The basis of NRN therapy is Locomotor Training (LT), in which the body of the paralyzed patient is suspended in a harness over a treadmill, while specially trained therapists move his or her legs to simulate walking. As the patient regains function, improvements in sitting, standing, reaching, grasping or walking occur. LT derives from recent advances in scientific understanding about neural plasticity (the ability of the neurons in the nervous system to develop new connections and "learn" new functions) and the role the spinal cord plays in controlling stepping and standing. LT "awakens" dormant neural pathways by repetitively stimulating the muscles and nerves in the lower body – allowing patients whose lower bodies may seem disconnected from input from the brain to regain motor abilities and achieve rehabilitation goals.

Participants in the NRN become part of a network-wide database that is collecting comprehensive medical information about the progress of each patient. While most of the data collected on treadmill locomotion has featured people with incomplete cervical and thoracic injuries, the program is now open to those with complete injuries.

NRN centers report that all participants experience beneficial changes as a result of the therapy. A significant number who were unable to walk when they entered the program are now able to walk. For others, there are significant improvements in trunk control, endurance, speed of walking and balance, which translate into better ability to perform activities of daily living and reduced dependence on caregivers;

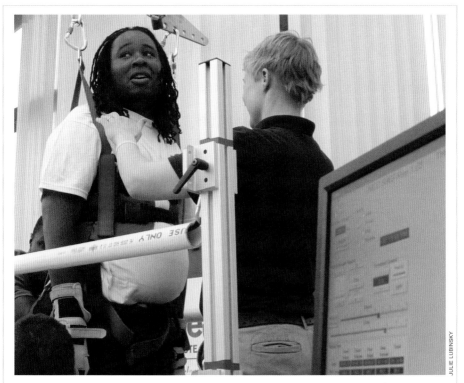

JULIE LUBINSKY

Eric LeGrand, injured playing football for Rutgers in 2010, doing Locomotor Training

there are measurable improvements in cardiovascular, pulmonary, and bladder function, and increased bone density. In general, NRN participants show improved overall physical well-being and quality of life.

During training, each session lasts about an hour and a half. Patients start out five days a week. As they progress through the phases of recovery, the number of days per week declines. The average NRN participant receives the therapy for three to four months, with about 60 sessions. Each patient is re-evaluated every 20 sessions.

"Our results support the concept that human spinal cord circuitry can respond to task-specific sensory cues, which can result in recovery in walking," said Susan J. Harkema, Ph.D., Director of the NRN, University of Louisville professor of neurosurgery and rehabilitation, and research director of the University of Kentucky's Spinal Cord Research Center. "The existence of the NRN and standardization of locomotor training protocols are crucial to determining the outcomes of these and future studies. By standardizing protocols across all NRN centers, we have an improved ability to understand the capacity for recovery in a chronic spinal cord injury population."

NRN Centers

Eight NRN Centers:

- Craig Hospital, Englewood, CO
- Frazier Rehab Institute, Louisville, KY
- The Institute for Rehabilitation & Research, Houston, TX
- Kessler Institute for Rehabilitation, West Orange, NJ
- Magee Rehabilitation Hospital, Philadelphia, PA
- Shepherd Center, Atlanta, GA
- Ohio State University Medical Center, Columbus, OH
- Toronto Rehabilitation Insitute, Toronto, ON

NRN Community Fitness Centers:

There are also several NRN Community Fitness and Wellness facilities that work with individuals with walking difficulties related to any cause (not just SCI); these fitness facilities host activity-based exercise programs designed specifically for individuals with physical disabilities. The community centers are operated more like fitness facilities.

- Courage Center, Minneapolis, MN
- Frazier Rehab Community Fitness and Wellness, Louisville, KY
- NextSteps Chicago, Willow Springs, IL
- NextStep Fitness, Lawndale, CA
- Neuroworx, South Jordan, UT

For more information or to apply to participate in NRN studies or programs: *http://www.christopherreeve.org/nrn*

Community-Based Recovery

Janne Kouri has an ironman work ethic and a relentless routine. Kouri's not just training, though. He's recovering. Before: total paralysis. Now: walking with a walker. Kouri puts himself through the paces at a facility he and his family created, NextStep Fitness near Los Angeles. The gym is a community-based facility in the Reeve Foundation's NeuroRecovery Network (NRN), the activity-based program that to maximizes health and function after paralysis.

Kouri, born in Sweden and raised in New York, broke his neck in 2006 diving into the Pacific and hitting a sandbar. He and his then-fiancée Susan Moffat checked out his rehab options—all over California, and beyond. They weren't hearing the word recovery. Said Kouri, "I wanted a proactive, progressive place, not one where you just learn how to live your life in a wheelchair." They heard about Frazier Rehab in Louisville, the lead center in the NRN, ground zero for locomotor training. The head of Frazier's rehab research, Susan Harkema, Ph.D., urged Kouri to come to there. "She was the only one who gave us hope," he said. "She said 'we'll push him, get him up on the treadmill.'"

"After about four months of five days a week training, I was able to wiggle my big toe," he said. "But the more immediate results were better muscle tone, cardiovascular health and improved blood pressure." There's also a mental part: "Simply put, it felt great to stand up and 'walk' again."

Janne Kouri

SAM MADDOX

When it was time to move back to California, Kouri could move his arms again and maneuver a wheelchair but he wanted to continue the aggressive therapy. He and Susan soon discovered that there were no locomotor training sites on the West Coast. If they wanted it they'd have to build it. With encouragement from Harkema and the NRN, Kouri opened NextStep as a nonprofit, the first NRN facility that's not in an academic or medical setting. "We want to bring the idea of lifetime wellness into many communities," said Kouri. "People should not have to move their families to get needed exercise."

Rob Summers

Unprecedented NeuroRecovery

This was a remarkable study, funded in part by the Reeve Foundation: Rob Summers, a young man who aspired to a career as a major league baseball pitcher, was spinal cord injured by a hit-and-run driver. He has a complete C7-T1 spinal cord injury, and no muscle control below mid-chest. In 2011, five years after his injury, an epidural stimulator was surgically placed over his lumbar spinal cord; when turned on, Summers was able to rise up from his chair, fully bear his weight, and stand unassisted. This is not the same as functional electrical stimulation (FES) which activates muscles directly. The epidural stimulation did not directly affect his leg muscles; it activated circuits of the spinal cord not controlled by the brain; he was able to animate his lower extremities because the stimulation made the spinal cord more sensitive to sensory cues. The lumbar cord, on its own, is thought to be "smart."

After seven months of locomotor training (at the University of Louisville, under the direction of Susan Harkema, Ph.D.), Summers could also voluntarily move his toes, ankles, knees, and hips. The research team was surprised by this, speculating that this recovery of function may have been caused by the epidural stimulation awakening residual but weak spinal nerves. Summers also had functional gains in bladder control, sexual function, and temperature regulation.

Since the first experiment, several other completely injured subjects have undergone epidural stimulation; the scientists report similar results: All regained function when the lumbar cord was stimulated.

Why this is cool: It shows that recovery of movement after complete SCI is possible, and it won't necessarily require regeneration or replacement of damaged nerve connections between brain and body. A new strategy may emerge, taking advantage of the body's powerful ability to reorganize spinal nerve circuits, based on activity. Scientists speculate on what might come next: Imagine taking this training-based recovery and then adding some yet-to-come biological or regenerative therapy—this could lead to significant functional recovery.

Susan Harkema, Ph.D., Rob Summers and Reggie Edgerton, Ph.D. Summers was able to stand on his own, benefiting from the research of Harkema and Edgerton.

Stem Cells

In 1998, scientists isolated pluripotent stem cells from early human embryos and grew them in culture. In the few years since this discovery, evidence has emerged that these stem cells can become almost any of the 350 known specialized cells of the body; this leads to the notion that stem cells can repair or replace cells or tissues that are damaged or destroyed by disease and injuries.

There is tremendous expectation for stem cell therapy; it's too soon to say just how or when stem cells will be recognized as standard treatment for disease or trauma, but research and some clinical trials are beginning to show promise. What follows is a brief primer on stem cell terminology.

Stem cell: A cell from the embryo, fetus, or adult that, under certain conditions, has the ability to reproduce itself for long periods or, in the case of adult stem cells, throughout the life of the organism. A stem cell can give rise to specialized cells that make up the tissues and organs of the body.

Pluripotent stem cell: A cell that can develop and self-replicate, from the embryonic germ layers, from which all cells of the body arise.

Induced pluripotent stem cells (iPSCs): Until recently the only known sources of human pluripotent stem cells were human embryos or certain kinds of fetal tissue; in 2006, scientists in Japan discovered a way to genetically reprogram skin cells to become very similar to embryonic stem cells. Since these cells are specific to the donor, this increases compatibility if such cells were to be used for therapies, thus forming the basis for personalized medicine. However, as with embryonic stem cells, researchers do not fully understand how iPSCs are locked in to their cell lineages. Research is moving quickly: iPSCs are being tested experimentally in numerous disease models, including SCI; moreover, iPSCs are also being used widely as tools to model disease states in a culture dish, providing a unique way to screen therapeutic agents.

Embryonic stem cell: Derived from embryos that develop from eggs that have been fertilized in vitro in a fertilization clinic and then donated for research purposes with informed consent of the donors. The current challenges: to direct differentiation of embryonic stem cells into specialized cell populations; to devise ways to control their proliferation once placed in people. Uncontrolled, these cells can form teratomas, a benign form of cancer.

Differentiation: The process by which an unspecialized cell (such as a stem cell) specializes into one of the many cells that make up the body. During differentiation, certain genes become activated and others are inactivated in an intricately regulated fashion.

Adult stem cell: An undifferentiated (unspecialized) cell that occurs in a differentiated (specialized) tissue, renews itself, and becomes specialized to maintain and repair the tissue in which it is found. Adult stem cells are capable of making identical copies of themselves for the lifetime of the organism. These cells have been identified in brain, bone marrow, peripheral blood, blood vessels, skeletal muscle, skin, teeth, heart, gut, liver, ovarian epithelium, fat and testis.

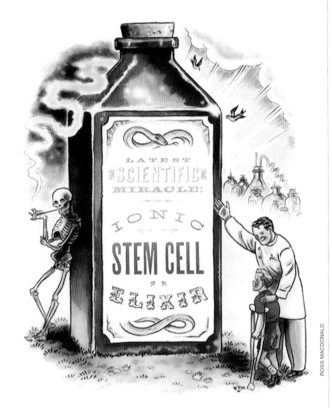

Progenitor or precursor cell: This type of cell can occur in fetal or adult tissues and is partially specialized. When a progenitor/precursor cell divides, it can form similar cells or it can form two specialized cells, neither of which is capable of replicating itself.

Somatic cell nuclear transfer (also known as therapeutic cloning): This process involves removing the nucleus of an unfertilized egg cell, replacing it with the material from the nucleus of a "somatic cell" (e.g., skin, heart, or nerve cell), and stimulating this cell to begin dividing. Stem cells can be extracted five to six days later.

Source: NIH: http://stemcells.nih.gov/info/basics; see also International Society for Stem Cell Research, www.isscr.org

Stem Cell Caution

Be hopeful. But also cautious: There is indeed a great deal of promise regarding stem cells. Between newspaper headlines and Internet testimonials, it is indeed tempting to think cures are right around the corner. But the stem cell field is still very new. Not enough is known about how stem cells work; moving from research to the clinic is long and complicated. Clouding the picture are high expectations for stem cells, fueled by lots of Internet noise. There are many clinics outside the United States and outside mainstream medicine that offer, for large fees, unproven stem cell therapies. None of these clinics can back up claims of recovery with published, credible science. Fueled by very motivated patients who seem to feel they have nothing to lose, stem cell tourism is a big business — despite warnings from reputable scientists and numerous reports of stem cell scams and fraud. Before you or someone you know considers such a treatment, be a responsible consumer; make an effort to understand the risks. Ask lots of questions. Please visit the Closer Look At Stem Cells website from the International Society for Stem Cell Research, *www.closerlookatstemcells.org/*

Some essential questions to ask a stem cell clinic:

- Is the treatment FDA-approved, and if not, why not?
- Will this affect whether I can get into another clinical trial?
- What benefits can I expect?
- How will this be measured, and how long will it take?
- What other medications or special care might I need?
- How is this stem cell procedure done?
- What is the source of the stem cells?
- How are the stem cells identified, isolated, and grown?
- Are the cells differentiated into specialized cells before therapy?
- How do I know if the cells are delivered to the right part of my body?
- If the cells are not my own, how will my immune system be prevented from reacting to the transplanted cells?
- What do the cells actually do, and is there scientific evidence that this procedure could work for my disease or condition? Where is this published?

SPINAL MUSCULAR ATROPHY

SPINAL MUSCULAR ATROPHY (SMA) refers to a group of inherited neuromuscular diseases that affect the nerve cells (motor neurons) and the control of voluntary muscles. SMA, the leading genetic cause of death in infants and toddlers, causes lower motor neurons in the base of the brain and the spinal cord to disintegrate, preventing them from delivering the necessary signals for normal muscle function.

Involuntary muscles, such as those that control bladder and bowel function, are not affected in SMA. Hearing and vision are not affected, and intelligence is normal or above average.

The three major childhood-onset forms of SMA are now usually called Type 1, Type 2, and Type 3. All three types are also known as autosomal recessive SMA—both parents must pass on the defective gene in order for their children to inherit the disease.

All forms of SMA affect the skeletal muscles of the trunk and limbs. In general, those muscles closer to the center of the body are more affected than those farther away. SMA Type 1, the most severe form, mostly affects the neurons controlling the mouth and throat muscles and therefore involves more problems with chewing and swallowing. Respiratory muscles are involved to varying degrees in all forms of the disease. In SMA Type 1, the onset of the disease is noted within the first six months of the child's life. Children with SMA Type 1 are unable to sit without support, and death usually occurs before age two.

SMA Type 2 is an intermediate form of the disease. Onset is between seven and eighteen months. Children with SMA Type 2 usually learn to sit without support, but they don't learn to stand or walk without aid. The child's survival depends in large part on the degree of respiratory and swallowing difficulties.

SMA Type 3 is a milder form of this condition. Onset occurs after the age of eighteen months and most often between the ages of five and fifteen. Weakness of the muscles of chewing and swallowing is rare, and respiratory effects are generally not as severe as in the first two forms. These children may live into adulthood. Respiratory complications, if they occur, pose the most serious threat to life.

At present, there is no known treatment that will stop or reverse SMA. Physical therapy and orthopedic devices can help preserve walking function. Braces or surgery may also help to counteract scoliosis, or curvature of the spine.

Researchers around the world have collaborated to find the causes of SMA, which in most cases result from a deficiency of a protein called SMN (survival of motor neuron). This deficiency occurs when a mutation is present in both copies of the SMN1 gene—one on each chromosome 5. Scientists hope to characterize the genes, study gene function and disease course, and find ways to prevent, treat, and, ultimately, cure these diseases.

SOURCES

Spinal Muscular Atrophy Foundation, Muscular Dystrophy Association, National Institute of Neurological Disorders and Stroke

📖 **Below are links to resources.**

Spinal Muscular Atrophy Foundation hopes to accelerate the development of a treatment or cure for SMA. Toll-free 1-877-FUND-SMA; **www.smafoundation.org**

Families of Spinal Muscular Atrophy (FSMA) raises funds to promote research into the causes and treatment of the spinal muscular atrophies; supports families affected by SMA. Toll-free 1-800-886-1762; **www.fsma.org**

Muscular Dystrophy Association (MDA) provides services and supports research for a group of hereditary muscle-destroying disorders, including spinal muscular atrophies. Toll-free 1-800-572-1717; **www.mda.org**, search under "Diseases."

SPINAL TUMORS

BRAIN AND SPINAL CORD TUMORS feature abnormal tissue growth inside the skull or the bony spinal column. Tumors are classified as benign (noncancerous) if the cells that make up the growth are similar to normal cells, grow slowly, and are confined to one location. Tumors are malignant (cancerous) when the cells are different from normal cells, grow quickly, and can spread easily to other locations.

Because the central nervous system (CNS) is housed within rigid, bony quarters (the skull and spinal column), any abnormal growth can place pressure on sensitive nerve tissues and impair function. While malignant cells elsewhere in the body can easily seed tumors inside the brain and spinal cord, malignant CNS tumors rarely spread out to other body parts.

Most spinal cord cancers are metastatic, meaning that they arise from a wide variety of primary cancers. These include lung, breast, prostate, head and neck, gynecologic, gastrointestinal, thyroid, melanoma, and renal cell carcinoma.

When new tumors begin within the brain or spinal cord, they are called primary tumors. Primary CNS tumors rarely grow from neurons— nerve cells that perform the nervous system's important functions – because once neurons are mature they no longer divide and multiply. Instead, most tumors are caused by out-of-control growth among cells that surround and support neurons. Primary CNS tumors—such as gliomas and meningiomas—are named by the types of cells comprising them, their location, or both.

The cause of most primary brain and spinal cord tumors remains a mystery. Scientists don't know exactly why and how cells in the nervous system or elsewhere in the body lose their normal identity and grow uncontrollably. Some of the possible causes under investigation include viruses, defective genes, and chemicals. Brain and spinal cord tumors are not contagious or, at this time, preventable.

Spinal cord tumors are less common than brain tumors. About 10,000 Americans develop primary or metastatic spinal cord tumors each year. Although spinal cord tumors affect people of all ages, they are most common in young and middle-aged adults.

Brain tumors affect about 40,000 Americans each year. About half of these tumors are primary and the remainder are metastatic.

Brain and spinal cord tumors cause many diverse symptoms, which generally develop slowly and worsen over time. Some of the more common symptoms of a brain tumor include headaches; seizures (a

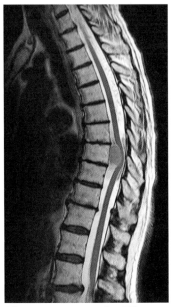

disruption of the normal flow of brain cell electricity that can lead to convulsions, loss of consciousness, or loss of bladder control); nausea and vomiting; and vision or hearing problems. Increased intracranial pressure can also decrease blood flow in the eye and trigger swelling of the optic nerve, which in turn causes blurred vision, double vision, or partial visual loss. Other symptoms of a CNS tumor may include the following: behavioral and cognitive symptoms, motor or balance problems, pain, sensory changes such as numbness, and decreased skin sensitivity to temperature.

Tumor mass compressing T6

Diagnosis: Special imaging techniques, especially computed tomography (CT) and magnetic resonance imaging (MRI), have greatly improved the diagnosis of CNS tumors. In many cases, these scans can detect the presence of a tumor even if it is less than half an inch across.

Treatment: The three most commonly used treatments are surgery, radiation, and chemotherapy. When a tumor compresses the spinal cord or its surrounding structures, corticosteroids may be given to reduce the swelling and preserve nerve function until the tumor can be removed.

Surgery to remove as much tumor as possible is usually the first step in treating an accessible tumor—as long as there is little risk of neurological damage. Fortunately, neurosurgical advances now make it possible for doctors to reach tumors that were previously considered inaccessible.

Doctors treat most malignant, inaccessible, or inoperable CNS tumors with radiation and/or chemotherapy. Radiation therapy bombards tumor cells with lethal beams of energy. Chemotherapy uses tumor-killing drugs that are given orally or injected into the bloodstream. Because not all tumors are vulnerable to the same anticancer drugs, doctors often use a combination of drugs for chemotherapy.

The overall outcome of radiation therapy is not always good. Radiation can damage spinal cord myelin, which can lead to paralysis. Researchers are looking for better ways to target radiation or enhance its effectiveness, perhaps by making tumor tissue more vulnerable. Researchers are studying brachytherapy (small radioactive pellets implanted directly into the tumor) as the optimum way to deliver radiotherapy to the tumor while sparing surrounding normal tissues.

Some cells within tumors are quite resistant to radiation. Using a gene therapy approach, scientists hope to kill these cells by inserting a "suicide" gene that could make the tumor cells sensitive to certain drugs or program the cancerous cells to self-destruct.

Blocking the formation of blood vessels (angiogenesis) is a very promising tool for the treatment of various cancers. Since brain tumors are the most angiogenic of all cancers, blocking their blood supply might prove to be especially effective.

The gamma knife is a newer tool that provides a precisely focused beam of radiation energy that delivers a single dose of radiation on target. The gamma knife does not require a surgical incision; doctors have found it can help them reach and treat some small tumors that are not accessible through surgery.

Although most primary tumors of the spinal cord are not life threatening, they can cause significant disability. Goals of rehabilitation include functional improvement in mobility, self-care, and pain management.

SOURCES

National Institute for Neurological Disorders and Stroke, American Brain Tumor Association, National Cancer Institute

꙾ **Below are links to resources:**

The American Brain Tumor Association (ABTA) supports medical research and offers information and support for people with tumors and their families. 773-577-8750, toll-free 1-800-886-2282; **www.abta.org**

National Brain Tumor Society funds research to find treatments and improve clinical care for brain and spinal cord tumors. It offers information and access to quality of life and psychosocial support. 617-924-9997; **www.tbts.org**

Musella Foundation for Brain Tumor Research is dedicated to improving the quality of life and survival times for brain tumor survivors. The Foundation has information on clinical trials, treatment outcomes. 516-295-4740, toll-free 1-888-295-4740; **www.virtualtrials.com**

Making Headway Foundation offers services and funds research for children with brain or spinal cord tumors. 914-238-8384; **http://makingheadway.org**

National Cancer Institute, part of the National Institutes of Health and the Department of Health and Human Services, with an annual research budget of about $5 billion, is the leading U.S. agency to fight cancer of all kinds. Includes resources and information on brain and spinal cord cancers; **http://cancer.gov**

Spinal Cord Tumor Association, Inc. supports tumor survivors and their families; **www.spinalcordtumor.org**

STROKE

A STROKE OCCURS WHEN THE BLOOD supply to the brain is suddenly blocked or when a blood vessel in the brain bursts. Deprived of oxygen, nerve cells in the affected area of the brain can't function and die within minutes. A person with loss of blood flow to the heart is said to be having a heart attack; similarly, a person with loss of blood flow to the brain or sudden bleeding in the brain can be said to be having a "brain attack."

Although stroke is a disease of the brain, it can affect the entire body, including cognitive and memory deficits, speech problems, emotional difficulties, daily living problems, and pain. Paralysis is a common outcome of stroke, often on one side of the body (hemiplegia). The paralysis or weakness may affect only the face, an arm or a leg, or it may affect one entire side of the body and face.

A person who suffers a stroke in the left hemisphere of the brain will show right-sided paralysis, or paresis. Likewise, a person with a stroke in the right hemisphere will show deficits on the left side of the body.

There are two main types of stroke. Ischemic strokes occur as a result of an obstruction (clot) within a blood vessel supplying blood to the brain; ischemic strokes account for about 87 percent of all cases. Hemorrhagic strokes result from a weakened blood vessel that ruptures and bleeds into the surrounding brain.

Stroke is the nation's fourth leading cause of death and is a leading cause of serious, long-term disability in the United States. About 4,500,000 stroke survivors are alive today.

Risk factors: The most important risks for stroke are hypertension, heart disease, diabetes, and cigarette smoking. Others include heavy alcohol consumption, high blood cholesterol levels, illicit drug use, and genetic or congenital conditions, particularly vascular abnormalities. An increase in the red blood cell count is another risk factor for stroke— excess red blood cells thicken the blood and make clots more likely. Eighty percent of strokes are preventable.

Symptoms: The symptoms of a stroke include sudden numbness or weakness, especially on one side of the body; confusion or trouble speaking or understanding speech; vision impairment in one or both eyes;

sudden difficulties walking; dizziness or loss of balance or coordination; severe headache with no known cause.

Treatment: Ischemic stroke is treated by removing the obstruction and restoring blood flow to the brain. In hemorrhagic stroke, doctors attempt to prevent the rupture and bleeding of aneurysms and arteriovenous malformations.

When blood flow to the brain is interrupted, some brain cells die immediately, while others remain at risk. The damaged cells can often be saved by early intervention with a clot-dissolving drug called tissue plasminogen activator (t-PA) if administered within three hours of the onset of the stroke. Unfortunately, only 3 to 5 percent of those who suffer a stroke reach the hospital in time to receive treatment.

The appropriate response to a brain attack is emergency action—every minute lost, from the onset of symptoms to the time of emergency room contact, cuts into the limited window of opportunity for intervention. Meanwhile, other neuroprotective drugs are being developed to prevent the wave of damage after the initial attack.

Early recovery: The brain often compensates for the damage caused by stroke. Some of the brain cells that do not die may resume functioning. Sometimes, one region of the brain takes over for a region damaged by the stroke. Stroke survivors sometimes experience remarkable and unanticipated recoveries that can't be explained.

5 SUDDEN WARNING SIGNS OF STROKE

WEAKNESS

VISION PROBLEMS

DIZZINESS

TROUBLE SPEAKING

HEADACHE

CALL 9-1-1

IF YOU SEE ANY OF THESE SIGNS

SOMEONE'S LIFE COULD BE IN YOUR HANDS

General recovery guidelines show that 10 percent of stroke survivors recover almost completely; 25 percent recover with minor impairments; 40 percent experience moderate to severe impairments requiring special care; 10 percent require care in a nursing home or other long-term care facility; 15 percent die shortly after the stroke.

Rehabilitation: This doesn't reverse the effects of a stroke but rehab builds strength, capability, and confidence so a person can continue daily activities despite the effects of stroke. Such activities may include the following: self-care skills such as feeding, grooming, bathing, and dressing; mobility skills such as transferring, walking, or moving a wheelchair; communication skills; cognitive skills such as memory or problem-solving; social skills for interacting with other people.

Rehabilitation starts in the hospital, and as soon as possible. For those who are stable, rehab may begin within two days after the stroke has occurred and continue as necessary after release from the hospital. Rehabilitation options may include the rehab unit of a hospital, a subacute care unit, a specialty rehab hospital, home therapy, outpatient care, or long-term care in a nursing facility.

Stroke may cause problems with thinking, awareness, attention, learning, judgment, and memory. A stroke survivor may be unaware of his or her surroundings. Language problems are common, usually the result of damage to the left lobes of the brain. Also, stroke survivors may experience pain, uncomfortable numbness, or strange sensations, due to many factors including damage to the sensory regions of the brain, stiff joints, or a disabled limb.

Many people who have had strokes are affected by spasticity, which causes stiff, tight muscles. Muscle tightness prevents people from doing everyday things such as holding a spoon or tieing a shoe. A combination of medication and physical therapy can loosen the muscles. Some stroke survivors may be candidates for intrathecal baclofen, which places a pump into the abdominal wall to deliver small doses of liquid baclofen into the fluid surrounding the spinal cord. This relaxes the muscles without the mind-numbing side effects often associated with the drug.

A stroke can also lead to emotional problems. Stroke patients may have difficulty controlling their emotions or may express inappropriate emotions in certain situations. One common disability that occurs with many stroke patients is depression. A depressed person may refuse or neglect to take medications, may not be motivated to perform exercises that will improve mobility, or may be irritable. Depression can create a vicious cycle – it deprives the stroke survivor of social contacts, which could in turn help dispel depression. Family can help by stimulating interest in other people or by encouraging leisure activities. Chronic depression can be treated with counseling, group therapy, or antidepressant medications.

Stroke survivors often find that once-simple tasks around the house become extremely difficult or impossible. Many adaptive devices and techniques are available to help people retain their independence and function safely and easily. The home usually can be modified so the stroke survivor can manage personal needs. See page 280 for more on home modification and adaptive equipment.

There are numerous research projects related to preventing and treating stroke. When a stroke occurs, some brain cells die immediately; others remain at risk for hours and even days due to an ongoing sequence of destruction. Some damaged cells can be saved by early intervention with drugs. The search for so-called neuroprotective drugs, ongoing for many years, has been difficult and frustrating, as one drug after another that showed great promise in animal studies and early human trials was found ineffective in large-scale clinical studies.

Meanwhile, the only approved clot-busting treatment, t-PA, is underutilized. New delivery methods and refinements of t-PA are being developed, including intra-arterial t-PA, which is infused into a main artery in the neck or even smaller arteries in the brain for faster, safer delivery.

Here are some of the research leads for treating stroke:

- An enzyme (DSPA) found in saliva from vampire bats may help dissolve blood clots in the brains of stroke survivors. This enzyme may be much more potent than existing anticoagulant drugs and may cause fewer bleeding problems because it only targets the clot itself.
- Erythropoietin, a hormone produced by the kidney, appears to protect some neurons from executing genetically programmed "cell suicide" missions.

- A protein called fibronectin may protect against serious brain damage from stroke.
- Trials have taken place to see if taking amphetamines for several weeks after a stroke will help kick-start the process of self-repair in the brain. Results have been inconclusive but more research is needed.
- For many years, doctors have relied on warfarin, a drug with potentially dangerous side effects (it is also used as rat poison), to reduce the risk of stroke in people at risk for clotting in the heart.
- Cell transplantation has shown some early-trial success in humans who have had a stroke. To be sure, there is great excitement for stem cells as a stroke treatment.
- A study called Pilot Investigation of Stem Cells in Stroke (PISCES) from a British company called ReNeuron is recruiting participants to test the safety of a manufactured neural stem cell line delivered by injection into the damaged brains of male patients 60 years of age and older who have remained moderately to severely disabled six months to five years following an ischemic stroke. See **www.reneuron.com**
- Researchers have reported that transplanted adult stem cells (from bone marrow) restored function in laboratory animals with stroke. Human trials have begun.
- Human umbilical cord blood cells have been effective in animal models; trials are underway to test these cells in children with strokes. For information on clinical trials see **www.clinicaltrials.gov**
- Research advances have led to new therapies and new hope for people who are at risk or who have had a stroke. For example, the Heart Outcomes Prevention Evaluation (HOPE) study found a 33 percent reduction in stroke incidence in diabetics who were given the hypertension drug ramipril. Treatment with statins (cholesterol lowering drugs) decreases the risk of stroke as well as heart attacks in people with known coronary heart disease.

Clinical trials have tested the safety and effectiveness of a protein called E-selectin, administered by way of a nasal spray, to prevent the formation of blood clots that could cause stroke.

The National Institute of Neurological Disorders and Stroke (NINDS) has initiated a program called Specialized Programs of Translational Research in Acute Stroke (SPOTRIAS). This is a national network of centers that perform early phase clinical projects, share data, and promote new approaches to therapy for acute stroke. The network currently includes eight stroke research centers. The goal is to reduce the disability and mortality of stroke survivors by promoting rapid diagnosis and effective interventions. See **www.spotrias.org**

In the area of stroke rehabilitation, an approach called constraint-induced movement-based therapy (CIT) has improved recovery in people who have lost some function in a single limb. The therapy entails immobilizing a patient's good limb to force use of the weakened limb. CIT is thought to promote a remodeling of nerve pathways, or plasticity.

SOURCES

American Stroke Association, National Stroke Association, National Institute of Neurological Disorders and Stroke

⅋ **Below are links to resources:**

American Stroke Association (ASA), affiliated with the National Heart Association, covers the full spectrum, including medical, rehabilitation, recovery, caregiving, prevention, and research. ASA features the Stroke Family Support Network, which provides information and support to stroke families at any stage of recovery. Toll-free 1-888-478-7653; **www.strokeassociation.org**

National Stroke Association (NSA) offers information and support, including publications. Toll-free 1-800-787-6537; **www.stroke.org**

TRANSVERSE MYELITIS

TRANSVERSE MYELITIS (TM) is a neurological disorder caused by inflammation of the spinal cord. Attacks of inflammation can damage or destroy myelin, the fatty insulating substance that covers nerve cell fibers. This causes scars that interrupt communication between the nerves in the spinal cord and the rest of the body.

Symptoms of TM include a loss of spinal cord function over several hours to several weeks. What usually begins as a sudden onset of lower back pain, muscle weakness, or abnormal sensations in the toes and feet can rapidly progress to more severe symptoms, including paralysis. Demyelination (loss of nerve fiber conductivity) usually occurs at the thoracic level, causing problems with leg movement and bowel and bladder control.

Some people recover from TM with minor or no lasting problems, while others have permanent impairments that affect their ability to perform ordinary tasks of daily living.

Transverse myelitis occurs in adults and children, in men and women, and in all races. No familial predisposition is apparent. The peak number of new cases per year appears to occur in people between ten and 19 years and 30 and 39 years of age. About 1,400 new cases of transverse myelitis are diagnosed annually in the United States, and approximately 33,000 Americans have some type of disability resulting from TM.

The exact causes of transverse myelitis are not known. The inflammation that damages the spinal cord may result from viral infections, abnormal immune reactions, or insufficient blood flow through the blood vessels located in the spinal cord. Transverse myelitis may also occur as a complication of syphilis, measles, Lyme disease, and some vaccinations, including those for chickenpox and rabies. Transverse myelitis often develops following viral infections due to varicella zoster (the virus that causes chickenpox and shingles), herpes simplex, Epstein-Barr, influenza, human immunodeficiency virus (HIV), hepatitis A, or rubella. Bacterial skin infections, middle-ear infections, and bacterial pneumonia have also been linked with TM.

Some experts believe that infection causes a derangement of the immune system, which leads to an indirect autoimmune attack on the spinal cord. The immune system, which normally protects the body from foreign organisms, mistakenly attacks the body's own tissue, which causes inflammation and, in some cases, damage to the spinal cord myelin.

Treatment: As with many disorders of the spinal cord, no effective cure exists for people with transverse myelitis. The best medicine has to offer is symptom management.

Therapy generally begins when the patient first experiences symptoms. Physicians may prescribe steroids during the first few weeks of illness to decrease inflammation. The goal is to keep the body functioning, hoping for complete or partial spontaneous recovery of the nervous system. Some who don't respond to steroids may undergo plasma exchange therapy (plasmapheresis). This involves replacing plasma, thus removing antibodies that may be involved in inflammation.

People with acute symptoms, such as paralysis, are most often treated in a hospital or in a rehabilitation facility under the care of a specialized medical team. Later, if patients begin to recover limb control, physical therapy to help improve muscle strength, coordination, and range of motion begins.

Transverse myelitis usually includes the following symptoms: (1) weakness of the legs and arms, (2) pain, (3) sensory alteration, and (4) bowel and bladder dysfunction. Most patients will experience weakness of varying degrees in their legs; some also experience it in their arms.

Pain is the primary symptom of transverse myelitis in about half of all patients. The pain may be localized in the lower back or may consist of sharp sensations that shoot down the legs or arms or around the torso. Most people with transverse myelitis report heightened sensitivity to heat, cold, or touch; for some a light touch with a finger may cause significant pain (called allodynia).

The prognosis: Recovery from transverse myelitis usually begins within two to 12 weeks of the onset of symptoms and may continue for up to two years. However, if there is no improvement within the first three to six months, significant recovery is unlikely. About one-third of people affected with TM experience good or full recovery. Another one-third show fair recovery and are left with deficits such as spastic gait, sensory dysfunction, and urinary urgency or incontinence. The remaining one-third show no recovery, using wheelchairs, perhaps with marked dependence on others for basic functions of daily living.

Research: The National Institute of Neurological Disorders and Stroke (NINDS) supports research to clarify the role of the immune system in TM and other autoimmune diseases or disorders. Other work focuses on strategies to repair demyelinated spinal cords, including approaches using cell transplantation. The ultimate goals of these studies are to encourage regeneration and to restore function to patients dealing with paralysis.

SOURCES

National Institute of Neurological Disorders and Stroke (NINDS), Transverse Myelitis Association

📖 **Below are links to resources.**

Transverse Myelitis Association (TMA) features news and information for the TM community; facilitates support and networking. 614-766-1806; **www.myelitis.org**

Johns Hopkins Hospital Department of Neurology has established a specialized center in Baltimore to care for people with transverse myelitis. The center has gathered physicians and healthcare experts in a variety of disciplines, including neurology, urology, rheumatology, orthopedic surgery, neuroradiology, rehabilitation medicine, and physical and occupational therapy. Johns Hopkins Transverse Myelitis Center, 410-502-7099, toll-free 1-800-765-5447; online see **www. hopkinsneuro.org/tm**

The Cody Unser First Step Foundation raises research funds to fight paralysis and to build awareness of transverse myelitis and living actively. 505-890-0086; **www.codysfirststep.org**

2
Health Management

A secondary condition is any medical, social, emotional, mental, family, or community problem that a person with a primary disabling condition (stroke, MS, brain injury, etc.) likely experiences.

SECONDARY CONDITIONS

Autonomic Dysreflexia

Autonomic dysreflexia (AD) is a potentially life-threatening medical emergency that affects people with spinal cord injuries at the T6 level or higher. Although rare, some people with T7 and T8 injuries can develop AD. For most people, AD can be easily treated as well as prevented. The key is knowing your baseline blood pressure, triggers and symptoms.

Autonomic dysreflexia requires quick and correct action. AD can lead to stroke. Because many health professionals are not familiar with this condition, it is important for people who are at risk for AD, including the people close to them, to know all about it. It is important for at-risk people to know their baseline blood pressure values and to be able to communicate to healthcare providers how to identify potential causes as well as manage an AD emergency.

Some of the signs of AD include high blood pressure, pounding headache, flushed face, sweating above the level of injury, goose flesh below the level of injury, nasal stuffiness, nausea and a slow pulse (slower than 60 beats per minute). Symptoms vary by individual; learn yours.

What to do: If AD is suspected, the first thing to do is sit up or raise the head to 90 degrees. If you can lower your legs, do so. Next, loosen or remove anything tight. Check blood pressure every five minutes. An individual with SCI above T6 often has a normal systolic blood pressure in the 90–110 mm Hg range. A blood pressure reading of 20 mm to 40 mm Hg above baseline in adults may be a sign of autonomic dysreflexia, or 15mm above baseline in children, and 15mm to 20mm above baseline in adolescents. Most importantly, locate and remove the offending stimulus, if possible. Begin by looking for your most common causes: bladder, bowel, tight clothing, skin issues. Keep in mind as you remove the cause that your AD may get worse before it gets better.

Autonomic dysreflexia is caused by an irritant below the level of injury, usually related to bladder (irritation of the bladder wall, urinary tract infection, blocked catheter or overfilled collection bag) or bowel (distended or irritated bowel, constipation or impaction, hemorrhoids or anal infections). Other causes include skin infection or irritation, cuts, bruises, abrasions or pressure sores (decubitus ulcers), ingrown toenails, burns (including sunburn and burns from hot water) and tight or restrictive clothing.

AD can also be triggered by sexual activity, menstrual cramps, labor and delivery, ovarian cysts, abdominal conditions (gastric ulcer, colitis, peritonitis) or bone fractures.

What happens during an episode of AD? Autonomic dysreflexia indicates over-activity of the autonomic nervous system—the part of the system that controls things you don't have to think about, such as heart rate, breathing and digestion. A noxious stimulus (would be painful if one could sense it) below the injury level sends nerve impulses to the spinal cord; they travel upward until blocked at the level of injury. Since these impulses cannot reach the brain, the body doesn't respond as it would normally. A reflex is activated that increases activity of the sympathetic portion of the autonomic nervous system. This results in a narrowing of the blood vessels, which causes a rise in blood pressure. Nerve receptors in the heart and blood vessels detect this rise in blood pressure and send a message to the brain. The brain then sends a message to the heart, causing the heartbeat to slow down and the blood vessels above the level of injury to dilate. However, since the brain is not able to send messages below the level of injury, blood pressure cannot be regulated. The body is confused and can't sort out the situation.

Generally speaking, medications are used only if the offending stimulus cannot be identified and removed, or when an episode of AD persists even after the suspected cause has been removed. A potentially useful agent is nitroglycerine paste (applied topically above level of injury). Nifedipine and nitrates are commonly used, in immediate-release form. Hydralazine, mecamylamine, diazoxide, and phenoxybenzamine might also be used. If an erectile dysfunction drug (e.g. Cialis, Viagra) has been used within 24 hours, other medications should be considered as blood pressure could drop dangerously low.

For the most part, autonomic dysreflexia can be prevented. Keep catheters clean; adhere to your catheterization and bowel schedules.

SOURCES

Paralyzed Veterans of America, Miami Project to Cure Paralysis/ University of Miami School of Medicine

ℰ❧ **Below are link sto resources.**

> **Paralysis Resource Center** offers a free wallet card (adult or pediatric version, in English or Spanish) describing AD and its emergency management. Make sure your providers are informed. Call toll-free 1-800-539-7309 or search "AD card" at **www.ChristopherReeve.org**

> **Paralyzed Veterans of America**, in support of The Consortium for Spinal Cord Medicine, offers authoritative clinical practice guidelines for autonomic dysreflexia. Toll-free 1-800-424-8200; **www.pva.org**, click on Publications. A consumer guide to AD is available.

Bladder Management

Paralysis at any level usually affects bladder control. The nerves controlling these organs attach to the very base of the spinal cord (levels S2–S4) and are therefore cut off from brain input. Although it may not be possible to regain the control one had before paralysis, a wide range of techniques and tools are available to manage what is termed a neurogenic bladder.

Here's how an unaffected bladder works: Urine, the excess water and salts that are extracted from the bloodstream by the kidneys, is piped down thin tubes called ureters, which normally allow urine to flow only in one direction. The ureters connect to the bladder, which is basically a storage bag that does not like pressure. When the bag is full, pressure rises and nerves send a message via the spinal cord to the brain. When one is ready to empty the bladder, the brain sends a message back down the spinal cord to the bladder, telling the detrusor muscle (the bladder wall) to squeeze and the sphincter muscle (a valve around the top of the urethra) to relax and open. Urine then passes down the urethra to exit the body.

It is a rather elegant process of muscle coordination just to go pee.

After paralysis, however, the body's normal system of control goes haywire; messages can no longer pass between the bladder muscles and the brain. Both the detrusor and the sphincter may be overactive due to lack of brain control. An overactive detrusor can contract at small volumes against an overactive sphincter; this leads to high bladder pressures, incontinence, incomplete emptying, and reflux – along with recurrent bladder infections, stones, hydronephrosis (kidney distention), pyelonephritis (kidney inflammation), and renal failure.

The neurogenic bladder is usually affected in one of two ways:

1. Spastic (reflex) bladder: when the bladder fills with urine, an unpredictable reflex automatically triggers it to empty; this usually occurs when the injury is above the T12 level. With a spastic bladder you do not know when, or if, the bladder will empty. Physicians familiar with spinal cord injury often recommend a bladder relaxing medication (anticholinergic) for reflexive bladder; oxybutynin (Ditropan) is common, with a primary side effect of dry mouth. Tolterodine, propiverine, or transdermal oxybutinin may result in less dry mouth. Botulinum toxin A (Botox) may be an alternative to anticholinergics. It has been FDA approved for detrusor overactivity treatment in individuals with SCI and multiple sclerosis. The advantage: Botox is used focally in the bladder, thus avoiding systemic side effects, including dry mouth.

2. Flaccid (non-reflex) bladder: the reflexes of the bladder muscles are sluggish or absent; it can become over-distended, or stretched. Stretching affects the muscle tone of the bladder. A flaccid bladder may not empty completely. Treatments may include sphincter relaxing medications (alpha-adrenergic blockers) such as terazosin (Hytrin) or tamsulosin (Flomax). Botox injected into the external urinary sphincter may improve bladder emptying. Also, surgery is an option to open the sphincter. Bladder outlet surgery, or sphincterotomy, reduces pressure on the sphincter and thus allows urine to flow out of the bladder easier. An alternative to sphincterotomy is placement of a metal device called a stent through the external sphincter, thus ensuring an open passage. One drawback to both sphincterotomy and stenting is that sperm from an ejaculation ends up in the bladder (retrograde), rather than coming out the penis. This doesn't rule out having a child but complicates it; sperm can be collected from the bladder but can be damaged by urine.

Dyssynergia occurs when the sphincter muscles do not relax when the bladder contracts. The urine cannot flow through the urethra, which can result in the urine backing up into the kidneys (called reflux), which can lead to serious complications.

The most common method of bladder emptying is an intermittent catheterization program (ICP), which drains the bladder on a set schedule (every four to six hours is common). A catheter is inserted in the urethra to drain the bladder, then removed. An indwelling catheter (Foley) drains the bladder continuously. If drainage originates from a stoma (a surgically created opening) at the pubic bone area, bypassing the urethra, it's called a suprapubic catheter. Advantage: unrestricted liquid intake. Disadvantage: besides the need for a collection device, indwelling catheters are more prone to urinary tract infection. An external condom catheter, which also drains continuously, is an option for men. Condom catheters also require a collection device, e.g. legbag.

Sterile vs. Clean

The rules were changed a few years ago. No longer is it necessary to reuse a catheter over and over again, rinsing it out after 30 or 40 uses. Medicare and other payers now reimburse for single use intermittent catheters. It makes perfect sense that disposable caths might reduce the incidence of bladder infection, especially the closed "no touch" systems with a tip that remains sterile. Still, Medicare is not so compelled as to pay for sterile catheters, at least not until a person gets really sick from a bladder infection – twice – and then gets a doctor's prescription. A regular catheter is enormously cheaper (less than $200 a month versus $1500 a month or more for disposable sterile caths). Another type of premium catheter on the market features a super slippery hydrophilic coating to allow easier insertion. There is evidence these are associated with fewer UTIs and reduced urethral trauma compared to conventional polyvinyl chloride catheters. LoFric is a well-known brand; most major urological companies have a hydrophilic line now. You can get these paid for, too, once you prove your urethral openings are at risk.

Cranberries?

As for cranberries and bladder health, well, a lot of folks swear by the juice or dried fruit, a lot of people say forget about them; there are published reports in support of both sides. The National Center for Complimentary and Alternative Medicine leans toward the pro-cranberry side, and suggests that cranberries limit the ability of e-coli bacterial to stick to the wall of the bladder. The center admits that research hasn't been well conducted, or clear. Of course the berry and supplements industries lead the cheers, and a paper a few years back from Scotland noted some evidence that cranberry juice may decrease the number of symptomatic bladder infections over a 12 month period in women. More recently, a group at the Kessler Institute in New Jersey suggested that cranberry supplements have no effect in preventing urinary tract

infections. In this study, 21 people with SCI were given either cranberry tablets or dummy pills. After four weeks, they crossed over to the other group. Urinary pH between the cranberry and placebo groups was compared weekly. There was no statistically significant effect for cranberry supplements in reducing bacterial counts or UTIs. Bottom line: can't hurt you to try.

There are several surgical alternatives for bladder dysfunction. A Mitrofanoff procedure constructs a new passageway for urine using the appendix; this allows catheterization to be done through a stoma in the abdomen directly to the bladder, a great advantage for women and for people with limited hand function. Bladder augmentation is a procedure that surgically enlarges the bladder, using tissue from the intestines, to expand bladder capacity and thus reduce leaking and the need for frequent catheterization.

It is common for people with multiple sclerosis and other spinal cord diseases to have problems with bladder control. This can involve a little leaking after a sneeze or laugh, or loss of all control. For many people, appropriate clothing and padding can compensate for lack of control. Some women benefit from strengthening the pelvic diaphragm (Kegel exercises) to improve retention of urine.

Urinary tract infection: People who are paralyzed are at a high risk for urinary tract infection (UTI), which until the 1950s was the leading cause of death after paralysis. The source of infection is bacteria, a group or colony of tiny, microscopic, single-celled life forms that live in the body and are capable of causing disease. Bacteria from the skin and urethra are easily brought into the bladder with ICP, Foley and suprapubic methods of bladder management. Also, many people are not able to completely empty their bladder; bacteria are more likely to grow in urine that stays in the bladder.

Some of the symptoms of UTI are cloudy, smelly urine, fever, chills, nausea, headache, increased spasms and autonomic dysreflexia (AD). One may also feel burning while urinating, and/or discomfort in the lower pelvic area, abdomen or lower back.

Once symptomatic, the first line of treatment is antibiotics, including the fluorquinolones (e.g. ciprofloxacin), trimethorprin, sulfamethoxazole, amoxicillin, nitrofurantoin and ampicillin. The key to preventing UTI is to halt the spread of bacteria into the bladder. Meticulous hygiene and proper handling of urinary care supplies can help prevent infection. Sediment in the urine can collect in tubing and connectors. This can make it harder for your urine to drain and can make it easier for bacteria to spread. Clean skin is also an important step in preventing infection.

Drinking the proper amount of fluids can help with bladder health, by washing bacteria and other waste materials from the bladder. Cranberry juice, or cranberry extract in pill form, can be an effective preventative for bladder infections. It works by making it hard for bacteria to stick to the wall of the bladder and colonize. Another way to keep the bacteria from colonizing on the bladder wall is the use of D-mannose, a type of sugar available at health food stores. It appears to stick to the bacteria so the bacteria can't stick to anything else.

A complete medical check-up is recommended at least once a year. This should include a urologic exam, including a renal scan or ultrasound to know that the kidneys are working properly. The exam may also include a KUB (kidneys, ureters, bladder), an X-ray of the abdomen that can detect kidney or bladder stones.

Bladder cancer is another concern. Research shows a moderate increase in the risk of bladder cancer among those who have been using indwelling catheters for a long period of time. Smoking also increases the risk for developing bladder cancer.

SOURCES

National MS Society, Spinal Cord Injury Information Network, University of Washington School of Medicine

ᕒ Below are links to resources

Paralyzed Veterans of America, in support of The Consortium for Spinal Cord Medicine, offers authoritative clinical practice guidelines for bladder management. Toll-free 1–800–424–8200; **www.pva.org**, click on Publications. A consumer guide is available.

Urine Control program features details on bladder issues. Developed at Case Western Reserve Medical School, Center for Health Care Research and Policy and MetroHealth Medical Center. **www.chrp.org/empowering**

The Spinal Cord Injury Rehabilitation Evidence (SCIRE) project is a Canadian research collaboration of scientists, clinicians and consumers that reviews, evaluates, and translates research knowledge to establish best practices following SCI. **www.scireproject.com**

Bowel Management

The digestive tract in its entirety is a hollow tube beginning at the mouth and ending at the anus. The bowel, the final portion of the tract, is where the waste products of digested food are stored until they are emptied from the body in the form of stool, or feces.

After food is swallowed, it moves through the esophagus to the stomach, which is basically a storage bag, and then on to the intestines or bowels. The absorption of nutrients occurs in the small intestines, the duodenum, the jejunum and the ileum. Next is the colon, which encircles the abdomen, starting on the right with the ascending colon, passing across the top with the transverse colon, and down the "s"-shaped sigmoid colon to the rectum, which opens at the anus.

Feces move through the bowel by coordinated muscular contractions of the colon walls called peristalsis. This motion is managed by a network of nerve cells at several different levels. The myenteric plexus nerves direct local intestinal movement, seemingly without input from the brain or spinal cord. More than 100 years ago it was discovered that the intestines, even when removed from the body, have an inherent tendency to produce peristalsis. If the intestine wall is stretched, the myenteric plexus triggers the muscles above the stretch to constrict and those below to relax, propelling material down the tube.

The next level of organization comes from autonomic nerves from the brain and spinal cord to the colon, which receives messages through the vagus nerve. The highest level of control comes from the brain. Conscious perception of a full rectum permits discrimination between solid material and gas, and the decision to eliminate fecal matter when appropriate. Messages relayed via the spinal cord produce voluntary relaxation of the pelvic floor and anal sphincter muscles, allowing the defecation process to occur.

Paralysis disrupts the system. There are two main types of neurogenic bowel, depending on level of injury: an injury above the conus medullaris (at L1) results in upper motor neuron (UMN) bowel syndrome; a lower motor neuron (LMN) bowel syndrome occurs in injuries below L1.

In a UMN or hyperreflexic bowel, voluntary control of the external anal sphincter is disrupted; the sphincter remains tight, which promotes constipation and retention of stool, which cannot be ignored; it is associated with episodes of autonomic dysreflexia. UMN connections between the spinal cord and the colon remain intact, thus reflex coordination and stool propulsion remain intact. Stool evacuation in people with UMN bowel occurs by means of reflex activity caused by a stimulus introduced into the rectum, such as a suppository or digital stimulation—best triggered at socially appropriate times and places.

LMN or flaccid bowel is marked by loss of stool movement (peristalsis) and slow stool propulsion. The result is constipation and a higher risk of incontinence due to lack of a functional anal sphincter. To minimize formation of hemorrhoids, use stool softeners, minimal straining during bowel efforts, and minimal physical trauma during stimulation.

Bowel accidents happen. The best way to prevent them is to follow a schedule, to teach the bowel when to have a movement. Most people perform their bowel program at a time of day that fits with their lifestyle. The program usually begins with insertion of either a suppository or a mini-enema, followed by a waiting period of approximately 15–20 minutes to allow the stimulant to work. After the waiting period, digital stimulation is performed every 10–15 minutes until the rectum is empty. Those with a flaccid bowel frequently start their programs with digital stimulation or manual removal. Bowel programs typically require 30–60 minutes to complete. Preferably, a bowel program can be done on the commode. Two hours of sitting tolerance is usually sufficient. But those at high risk for skin breakdown need to weigh the value of bowel care in a seated position, versus a side-lying position in bed.

Constipation is a problem for many people with neuromuscular-related paralysis. Anything that changes the speed with which foods move through the large intestine interferes with the absorption of water and causes problems. There are several types of laxatives that help with constipation. Laxatives such as Metamucil supply the fiber necessary to add bulk, which holds water and makes it easier to move stool through the bowels. Stool softeners, such as Colace, also keep the water content of the stool higher, which keeps it softer and thus easier to move. Stimulants such as bisacodyl increase the muscle contractions (peristalsis) of the bowel, which moves the stool along. Frequent use of stimulants can actually aggravate constipation – the bowels become dependent on them for even normal peristalsis.

Faster than a speeding ... There are two main types of suppositories, both based on the active ingredient bisacodyl: those with a vegetable base (e.g. Dulcolax) and those with a polyethylene glycol base (e.g. Magic

Bullet). Bullets are said to be about twice as fast as the alternative.

Antegrade continence enema is an option for some people with difficult bowel problems. This technique involves surgery to create a stoma, or opening, in the abdomen; this allows introduction of liquid above the rectum, thus causing an effective flushing of fecal material from the bowel. This method may significantly decrease bowel care time and allow for the discontinuation of some bowel medications.

Here are some bowel facts for better digestive management:

- It is generally not necessary to have a bowel movement every day. Every other day is okay.
- Bowels move more readily after a meal.
- Fluid intake of two quarts daily aids in maintaining a soft stool; warm liquid will also aid bowel movement.
- A healthy diet including fiber in the form of bran cereals, vegetables and fruits helps keep the digestive process working.
- Activity and exercise promote good bowel health.

Some medications commonly used by people with paralysis can affect the bowel. For example, anticholinergic medications (for bladder care) may slow bowel motility, resulting in constipation or even bowel obstruction. Some antidepressant drugs, such as amitryptyline; narcotic pain medications; and some drugs used for the treatment of spasticity, such as dantrolene sodium, contribute to constipation.

Many people report significant improvements in quality of life after colostomy. This surgical option creates a permanent opening between the colon and the surface of the abdomen to which a stool collection bag is attached. Colostomies sometimes become necessary because of fecal soiling or pressure sores, continual stool incontinence, or excessively long bowel programs. Colostomy enables many people to manage their bowels independently, plus, colostomy takes less time than bowel programs. Studies have shown that people who get colostomies are pleased and would not reverse the procedure; while many may not have embraced the idea of a colostomy at the outset, the procedure can make a huge difference in quality of life, cutting bowel time from as much as eight hours a day to no more than 15 minutes.

SOURCES

Spinal Cord Injury Information Center/University of Alabama at Birmingham, University of Washington School of Medicine, ALS Association of America, National Multiple Sclerosis Society

ֲֶ **Below are links to resources**

Paralyzed Veterans of America, in support of The Consortium for Spinal Cord Medicine, offers (no charge) authoritative clinical practice guidelines for bowel management. Toll-free 1–800–424–8200; **www.pva.org**, click on Publications. A consumer guide is available.

The Spinal Cord Injury Rehabilitation Evidence (SCIRE) project is a Canadian research collaboration of scientists, clinicians and consumers that reviews, evaluates, and translates research knowledge to establish best practices following SCI. **www.scireproject.com**

Deep Vein Thrombosis

People with spinal cord injury (SCI) are at particular risk for deep vein thrombosis (DVT) during their acute hospital course. Deep vein thrombosis is a blood clot that forms in a vein deep in the body, most often in the lower leg or thigh. This can result in a life-threatening danger if the clot breaks loose from the leg vein and finds its way to the lung, causing a pulmonary embolism.

Doctors use anticoagulants, commonly called blood thinners, to prevent blood clots. In spinal cord injury, anticoagulants are generally given with the first 72 hours after injury to all patients. The thinners are usually given for about eight weeks. The most common type of blood thinner used in SCI is a low molecular weight heparin such as enoxoparin or dalteparin. These medications slow the time it takes for blood to clot and also prevent growth of a clot. Blood thinners do not remove existing clots; that sometimes involves surgery.

Some SCI centers use a type of blood filter called an inferior vena cava (IVC) filter in people at high risk for thromboembolism – including those with high cervical injuries or long bone fractures. The appropriateness of IVC filter use as a preventative has not been fully worked out. A recent study showed that placement of an IVC filter may actually increase risk of DVT.

The risk for DVT is highest in the acute phase of SCI but some risk for blood clot formation remains in the SCI population. Routine use of graduated compression stockings is common in people with paralysis.

SOURCE:

National Heart, Lung and Blood Institute

ઽૐ **Below are links to resources**

> **National Blood Clot Alliance** is a patient advocacy group that promotes awareness of risk, prevention and treatment of blood clots. **www.stoptheclot.org**

Vascular Disease Foundation produces educational materials and promotes public awareness about various vascular diseases. See **http://vasculardisease.org,** click on Deep Vein Thrombosis.

Paralyzed Veterans of America, in support of The Consortium for Spinal Cord Medicine, offers (no charge) authoritative clinical practice guidelines for deep vein thrombosis. Toll-free 1–800–424–8200; **www.pva.org,** click on Publications.

Depression

Depression is common among people who are paralyzed, but it's not normal – becoming discouraged, grief-stricken or sad is normal, but depression represents a condition that is a health problem unto itself. Most forms of depression, however, can be treated.

While about 10 percent of the U.S. non-disabled population is said to be moderately or severely depressed, research shows that about 20 to 30 percent of people with long-term disabilities have a depressive condition.

Depression affects a person in many ways. It involves major changes in mood, outlook, ambition, problem solving, activity level and bodily processes (sleep, energy and appetite). It affects health and wellness: People with a disability who are depressed may not look after themselves; they may not drink enough water, take care of their skin, manage their diet. It affects one's social world. Friends and families are tuned out. Depressed people can't find pleasure, success or meaning. Substance abuse may develop. Thoughts of suicide often occur when things look most hopeless. In spinal cord injury, for example, risk is highest in the first five years after the injury. Other risk factors include dependence on alcohol or drugs, lack of a spouse or close support network, acess to lethal means, or a previous suicide attempt. People who've tried to kill themselves before are likely to try again. The most important factors in preventing suicide are spotting depression early, getting the right treatments for it, and instilling problem solving skills.

Taking Care

Mental Health America offers these tips to reduce depression:

- Stay connected
- Stay psitive
- Get physically active
- Help others
- Get enough sleep
- Create joy and satisfaction
- Eat well
- Take care of your spirit
- Deal better with hard times
- Get help if needed

Many factors contribute to depression. These may include the effects of disability – pain, fatigue, changes in body image, shame, and loss of independence. Other life events, such as divorce, loss of a loved one, loss of a job or financial problems can also lead to or magnify depression.

There are effective ways for helping people cope with the stresses of paralysis. Depression is highly treatable using psychotherapy, pharmacotherapy (antidepressants), or a combination of both. Tricyclic drugs (e.g., imipramine) are often effective for depression but may have intolerable side effects. SSRIs (Selective Serotonin Reuptake Inhibitors, e.g., Prozac) have fewer side effects and are usually as effective as tricyclics. SSRIs may exacerbate spasticity in some persons.

Among the newest antidepressants, venlafaxine (e.g., Effexor) is chemically similar to tricyclics and has fewer side effects. In theory, it may also alleviate some forms of neurogenic pain, a huge contributor to depression. In fact, aggressive treatment of pain problems is crucial to the prevention of depression.

Among those with MS, some experience mood swings and/or uncontrollable laughing or crying (called emotional lability). These result from damaged areas in emotional pathways in the brain. It is important for family members and caregivers to know this and realize that people with MS may not always be able to control their emotions. Mood stabilizing medications such as amitriptyline (e.g., Elavil) and valproic acid (e.g., Depakote) are used to treat these emotional changes. It is also important to recognize that depression is very common in MS – even more so than in other equally disabling chronic illnesses.

Life is worth living, despite what health professionals are sometimes prone to judge: According to a Colorado survey, 86 percent of SCI high-level quadriplegics rated their quality of life as average or better than average, while only 17 percent of their ER doctors, nurses, and technicians thought they would have an average or better quality of life if they acquired quadriplegia.

If you are depressed, get help, including professional counseling or participation in a support group. An active lifestyle can also help to break through depression.

SOURCES

Rancho Los Amigos National Rehabilitation Center; Paralyzed Veterans of America; National Multiple Sclerosis Society

ॐ **Below are links to resources.**

Paralyzed Veterans of America, in support of The Consortium for Spinal Cord Medicine, offers clinical practice guidelines for depression as a secondary condition of paralysis. PVA, toll-free 1-800-424-8200, **www.pva.org**, click on Publications, then Medical Guidelines.

National Action Alliance for Suicide Prevention envisions a nation free from the tragic experience of suicide. **http://actionallianceforsuicideprevention.org**

Mental Health America is dedicated to addressing all aspects of mental health and mental illness, including depression. Contact MHA toll-free at 1-800-969-6642; visit **www.mentalhealthamerica.net**

Not Dead Yet opposes legalized assisted suicide and euthanasia. NDY notes that the duration of disability almost always correlates with acceptance in persons with spinal cord injury paralysis. **www.notdeadyet.org**

Anxiety and Depression Association of America (ADAA) promotes education, training, and research for anxiety, depression, and stress-related disorders Links people who need treatment with healthcare professionals. **www.adaa.org**

Fatigue

Fatigue is a very common symptom of many conditions related to paralysis. About 80 percent of people with multiple sclerosis report that fatigue significantly interferes with their ability to function. It gets worse as the day progresses; it's aggravated by heat and humidity and may be the most prominent complaint in many MSers who otherwise have few other symptoms.

Fatigue is also a prominent symptom of post-polio syndrome. People who had polio long ago, even those who made complete recoveries from their original polio, sometimes begin years later to feel a lack of energy —tiring much faster than in the past, feeling that once simple things now take a huge effort. These symptoms may be caused by the gradual wearing out of already weakened and damaged nerve cells. Some believe chronic fatigue syndrome, which affects about 500,000 people in the United States, may be related to undiagnosed post-polio syndrome. More than 60 percent of people with SCI who experience changes in function identified fatigue as a major problem.

Underlying medical problems such as anemia, thyroid deficiency, diabetes, depression, respiratory problems or heart disease may be factors in a person's fatigue. Also, medications such as muscle relaxants, pain drugs and sedatives can contribute to fatigue. Low fitness levels may result in too little energy reserves to meet the physical demands of daily life. People should consult a physician if fatigue becomes a problem.

Disrupted sleep is reported in up to 35 percent of people with MS; daytime fatigue may be caused by sleep apnea, periodic leg movements, neurogenic bladder problems, spasticity, pain, anxiety or depression. Better sleep starts with better symptom management. See your doctor about options for treating pain, depression, sleep apnea, etc. There isn't a single remedy for fatigue. Listen to your body; use your energy wisely.

SOURCES

National Multiple Sclerosis Society, Rancho Los Amigos Hospital, Paralyzed Veterans of America

Dealing with Fatigue

A few ideas for reducing fatigue:

- Better nutrition. Caffeine, alcohol, smoking and a diet high in refined carbohydrates, sugar and hydrogenated fats rob your energy. Lack of protein can also lead to fatigue.

- Rest. Take it easy on yourself. Give yourself down time as needed. Reach for the best-feeling thoughts, enjoy a laugh whenever you can, and structure relaxation time at least twice a day using yoga, meditation or prayer.

- Stay cool. People with MS are less fatigued when they avoid heat and/or use cooling devices (vests, ice packs, etc.).

- Find new ways, including the tools of occupational therapy, to simplify work tasks and implement energy saving strategies.

- Use adaptive equipment to preserve the energy you do have. There is a wonderful array of gadgets and timesavers on the market (see page 260 for more). For a person with post-polio, this could mean using a wheelchair instead of a walker. Wheelchair users might add a power assist or move up to a full-power unit.

- Cut stress. Some people benefit from stress management, relaxation training, membership in a support group or psychotherapy. Although the link between fatigue and depression is not fully understood, psychotherapy has been shown to lessen fatigue in people with MS who are depressed.

- Build stamina through exercise. Physical activity was once thought to worsen fatigue, but aerobic exercise may benefit those with mild disabilities.

- Vitamins, herbs, etc. Some people say their fatigue is improved after taking supplements such as adenosine monophosphate, coenzyme Q-10, germanium, glutathione, iron, magnesium sulfate, melatonin, NADH, selenium, l-tryptophan, vitamins B12, C and A, and zinc. Others include astragalus, borage seed oil, bromelain, comfrey, echinacea, garlic, Ginkgo biloba, ginseng, primrose oil, quercetin, St. John's wort and Shiitake mushroom extract.

- For MS, doctors often prescribe amantadine and pemoline to relieve fatigue. Since one of the side effects of both drugs is insomnia, they work best if taken in the morning and at noon.

Other Complications

Heart disease: People with spinal cord dysfunction have an increased risk of developing heart disease at an earlier age than those in the rest of the population. Cardiovascular diseases are reportedly the leading cause of death for persons who have had a spinal cord injury for more than 30 years. People with SCI are prone to certain metabolic risk factors. They are generally more insulin resistant, which affects the body's ability to transform blood sugar into energy, and can lead to heart disease, diabetes and other conditions. Contributing to the abnormalities are loss of muscle mass (atrophy), increase in body fat, and a harder time maintaining cardiovascular fitness. Prevention strategies: screening for blood sugar problems, healthy diet, no smoking, moderation with alcohol, regular physical exercise.

Orthostatic hypotension is a condition that results in a decrease in blood pressure when sitting or standing up, causing light-headedness or fainting. It occurs more commonly after spinal cord injury at T6 or above, in response to lowered blood pressure. Elastic hose and abdominal support help prevent it. It is also helpful to come to a sitting or standing position gradually.

Heterotopic ossification (HO) is the development of bone deposits in soft (non-skeletal) tissue, primarily around the hip and knee joints. It occurs in many spinal cord injured individuals and may develop within days following the injury. In most cases, HO causes no significant additional physical limitations but may limit joint motion, cause swelling or increase spasticity in the leg. Drugs are prescribed to treat HO; surgery is sometimes necessary.

Hypo/hyperthermia: Paralysis can cause the temperature of the body to fluctuate according to the temperature of the environment. Being in a hot room may increase temperature (hyperthermia); a cold room may decrease temperature (hypothermia). Temperature management is essential for some people.

Chronic Pain

Pain is a signal triggered in the nervous system to alert us to possible injury. Acute pain, the result of sudden trauma, has a purpose. This kind of pain can usually be diagnosed and treated so the discomfort is managed and confined to a given period of time. Chronic pain, though, is much more confounding. It is the kind of alarm that doesn't go away and is resistant to most medical treatments. There may be an ongoing cause of difficult to treat pain—arthritis, cancer, infection – but some people have chronic pain for weeks, months and years in the absence of any obvious pathology or evidence of body damage. A type of chronic pain called neurogenic or neuropathic pain often accompanies paralysis—it is a cruel irony for people who lack sensation to experience the agony of pain.

Pain is a complicated process that involves an intricate interplay between a number of important chemicals found naturally in the brain and spinal cord. These chemicals, called neurotransmitters, transmit nerve impulses from one cell to another.

There is a critical lack of the essential inhibitory neurotransmitter GABA (gamma-aminobutyric acid) in the injured spinal cord. This may "disinhibit" spinal neurons that are responsible for pain sensations, causing them to fire more than normal. This disinhibition is believed to be the root of spasticity, too. Recent data also suggest that there may be a shortage of the neurotransmitter norepinephrine, as well as an overabundance of the neurotransmitter glutamate. During experiments, mice with blocked glutamate receptors show a reduction in their responses to pain. Other important receptors in pain transmission are opiate-like receptors. Morphine and other opioid drugs work by locking on to these receptors, switching on pain-inhibiting pathways or circuits, and thereby blocking pain.

Following injury, the nervous system undergoes a tremendous reorganization. The dramatic changes that occur with injury and persistent pain underscore that chronic pain should be considered a disease of the nervous system, not just prolonged acute pain or a symptom of an injury. New drugs must be developed; current medications for most chronic pain conditions are relatively ineffective and are used mostly in a trial by error manner; there are few alternatives.

The problem with chronic nerve pain is not just the distraction of hurting. Pain can lead to inactivity, which may lead to anger and frustration, to isolation, depression, sleeplessness, sadness, then to more pain. It's a spin cycle of misery with no easy exit, and modern medicine doesn't offer a wide range of help. Pain control becomes a matter of pain management; the goal is to improve function and allow people to participate in day-to-day activities.

Types of pain: Musculoskeletal or mechanical pain occurs at or above the level of spinal cord lesion and may stem from overuse of remaining functional muscles after spinal cord injury or those used for unaccustomed activity. Wheelchair propulsion and transfers are responsible for most mechanical pain.

Central pain or deafferentation pain is experienced below the level of SCI and is generally characterized by burning, aching and/or tingling. Central pain doesn't always show up right away; it may take weeks or months to appear and is often associated with recovery of some spinal cord function. This type of pain is less common in complete injuries. Other irritations, such as pressure sores or fractures, may increase the burning of central pain.

Psychological pain: Increased age, depression, stress and anxiety are associated with greater post-spinal cord injury pain. This doesn't mean the sensation of pain is in your head—it's real, but pain appears to have an emotional component, too.

Treatment options for neuropathic pain:

Heat and massage therapy: sometimes these are effective for musculoskeletal pain related to spinal cord injury.

Acupuncture: this practice dates back 2,500 years to China and involves the application of needles to precise points on the body. While some research suggests this technique boosts levels of the body's natural painkillers (endorphins) in cerebrospinal fluid following treatment, acupuncture is not fully accepted in the medical community. Still, it is noninvasive and inexpensive compared to many other pain treatments. In some limited studies, this method helps relieve SCI pain.

Exercise: SCI patients who underwent a regular exercise program showed significant improvement in pain scores; this also accounted for improved depression scores. Even light to moderate walking or swimming can contribute to an overall sense of well-being by improving blood and oxygen flow to tense, weak muscles. Less stress equals less pain.

Hypnosis: has been shown to have a beneficial effect on SCI pain. Visual imagery therapy, which uses guided images to modify behavior helps some people alleviate pain by changing perceptions of discomfort.

Biofeedback: trains people to become aware of and to gain control over certain bodily functions, including muscle tension, heart rate and skin temperature. One can also learn to effect a change in his or her responses to pain, for example, by using relaxation techniques. With feedback and reinforcement one can consciously self-modify out-of-balance brain rhythms, which can improve body processes and brain physiology. There are many claims made for treating chronic pain with biofeedback, especially using brain wave information (EEG).

Transcranial electrical stimulation (TCES): treatment applies electrodes to an individual's scalp, allowing electrical current to be applied and presumably stimulate the underlying cerebrum. Studies indicate this newer treatment may be useful in reducing SCI-related chronic pain.

Transcutaneous electrical nerve stimulation (TENS): is used for pain and has been shown to help with chronic musculoskeletal pain. In general, TENS has not been as effective for pain below injury level.

Transcranial magnetic stimulation (TMS) applies electromagnetic pulses to the brain; it has helped with post-stroke pain and in limited studies has reduced post-SCI pain over long-term use.

Spinal cord stimulation: electrodes are surgically inserted within the epidural space of the spinal cord. The patient triggers a pulse of electricity to the spinal cord using a small box-like receiver. This is most commonly used for lower back pain but some people with MS or paralysis can benefit.

Deep brain stimulation: is considered an extreme treatment and involves surgical stimulation of the brain, usually the thalamus. It is used

Current medications for most chronic pain conditions are relatively ineffective and the options for treatment are limited. More research is needed.

for a limited number of conditions, including central pain syndrome, cancer pain, phantom limb pain and other types of neuropathic pain.

Magnets: are usually dismissed as pseudoscience, but proponents offer the theory that magnetic fields may effect changes in cells or body chemistry, thus producing pain relief.

Drugs: options for chronic pain include a ladder of drugs, starting with over the counter nonsteroidal anti-inflammatories such as aspirin, all the way to tightly controlled opiates such as morphine. Aspirin and ibuprofen may help with muscle and joint pain but are of minimal use for neuropathic pain. This includes COX-2 inhibitors ("superaspirins") such as celecoxib (Celebrex).

At the top of the ladder are opioids, drugs derived from the poppy plant that are among the oldest drugs known to humankind. They include codeine and the king of opiates, morphine, named for Morpheus, the god of dreams. While morphine is still the go-to therapy at the top of the treatment ladder, it is not usually a good long-term solution. It depresses breathing, causes constipation and fogs the brain. And people develop tolerance and addiction for it. Moreover, it isn't effective against many types of neuropathic pain. Scientists hope to develop a morphine-like drug that will have the pain-deadening qualities of morphine but without the drug's debilitating side effects.

There is a middle ground of medications that work for some types of chronic pain. Anticonvulsants were developed to treat seizure disorders, but are also sometimes prescribed for pain. Carbamazepine (Tegretol) is used to treat a number of painful conditions, including trigeminal neuralgia. Gabapentin (sold as Neurontin) is commonly prescribed "off label" (unapproved by the FDA) for neuropathic pain. (Pfizer, the company that owns Neurontin, pled guilty in 2004 to felonies and agreed to millions of dollars in fines for aggressive marketing of the drug for unapproved uses.)

Meanwhile, Pfizer received FDA approval in 2012 of a newer anticonvulsant to target pain, this time specific to SCI. Approval of pregabalin, marketed as Lyrica, was based on two randomized, double-blind, placebo-controlled Phase 3 trials, which enrolled 357 patients. Lyrica reduced neuropathic pain associated with SCI from baseline compared to placebo; patients receiving Lyrica showed a 30 percent to 50 percent reduction in pain compared to those getting placebo. Lyrica won't work for everyone. And it comes with a wide range of possible side-effects, including anxiety, restlessness, trouble sleeping, panic attacks, anger, irritability, agitation, aggression, and a risk for suicidal behavior.

For some, tri-cyclic antidepressant drugs can be helpful for the treatment of pain. Amitriptyline (sold as Elavil and other brands) is effective in the treatment of post-SCI pain – at least there is some evidence it works in depressed individuals.

In addition, the class of anti-anxiety drugs called benzodiazepines (Xanax, Valium) act as muscle relaxants and are sometimes used to deal with pain. Another muscle relaxant, baclofen, applied by an implanted pump (intrathecally), improves chronic post-SCI pain, but may only work when it is related to muscle spasms.

Botulinum toxin injections (Botox) which is used to treat focal spasticity, can also have an effect on pain.

Nerve blocks: employ the use of drugs, chemical agents or surgical techniques to interrupt the transmission of pain messages between specific areas of the body and the brain. Types of surgical nerve blocks include neurectomy; spinal dorsal, cranial, and trigeminal rhizotomy; and sympathetic blockade.

Physical therapy and rehabilitation: are often utilized to increase function, control pain and speed a person toward recovery.

Surgeries: for pain include rhizotomy, in which a nerve close to the spinal cord is cut, and cordotomy, where bundles of nerves within the spinal cord are severed. Cordotomy is generally used only for the pain of terminal cancer that does not respond to other therapies. The dorsal root entry zone operation, or DREZ, destroys spinal neurons corresponding to the patient's pain. This surgery can be done with electrodes that selectively damage neurons in a targeted area of the brain.

Marijuana: is illegal by federal law, but its proponents place pot alongside other pain remedies. In fact, for many years, it was sold in cigarette form by the U.S. government for just that purpose. Numerous states have partially decriminalized marijuana for medical reasons but that does not exempt users from federal prohibition laws, nor does it allow doctors to prescribe marijuana. There is medical evidence, however, to support further study; marijuana appears to bind to receptors found in many brain regions that process pain information.

Research in neuroscience will lead to a better understanding of the basic mechanisms of pain, and to more and better treatments in the years to come. Blocking or interrupting pain signals, especially when there is no apparent injury or trauma to tissue, is a key goal in the development of new medications.

SOURCES

National Institute of Neurological Disorders and Stroke (NINDS), National Multiple Sclerosis Society, Dana Foundation

☙ **Below are links to resources.**

American Chronic Pain Association (ACPA) offers peer support and education for individuals with chronic pain. Toll-free 1-800-533-3231; **www.theacpa.org**

The Spinal Cord Injury Rehabilitation Evidence (SCIRE) project is a Canadian research collaboration of scientists, clinicians and consumers that reviews, evaluates, and translates research knowledge and establishes best rehabilitation practices following SCI. There is a lengthy section on pain. **www.scireproject.com**

Respiratory Health

As we breathe, air is brought into the lungs and into close contact with tiny blood vessels that absorb oxygen and transport it to all parts of the body. At the same time, the blood releases carbon dioxide, which is carried out of the lungs with exhaled air.

Lungs themselves are not affected by paralysis, but the muscles of the chest, abdomen and diaphragm can be. As the various breathing muscles contract, they allow the lungs to expand, which changes the pressure inside the chest so that air rushes into the lungs. This is the process of inhaling—which requires muscle strength. As those muscles relax, the air flows back out of the lungs.

If paralysis occurs in C3 or higher, the phrenic nerve is no longer stimulated and therefore the diaphragm does not function. This means mechanical assistance – usually a ventilator – will be required to facilitate breathing. When the injury is between C3 to C5 (the diaphragm is functional), respiratory insufficiency still occurs: The intercostals and other chest wall muscles do not provide the integrated expansion of the upper chest wall as the diaphragm descends during inspiration.

People with paralysis at the mid-thoracic level and higher may have trouble taking a deep breath and exhaling forcefully. Because they may not have use of abdominal or intercostal muscles, these people also lose the ability to force a strong cough. This can lead to lung congestion and respiratory infections.

Clearing Secretions: Mucous secretions are like glue, causing the sides of airways to stick together and not inflate properly. This is called atelectasis, or a collapse of part of the lung. Many people with paralysis are at risk for this. Some people have a harder time knocking down colds or respiratory infections; they have what feels like a constant chest cold. Pneumonia is a serious risk if secretions become the breeding ground for various bacteria. Symptoms of pneumonia include shortness of breath, pale skin, fever and an increase in congestion.

Ventilator users with tracheostomies have secretions suctioned from their lungs on a regular basis; this may be anywhere from every half hour to only once a day.

Mucolytics: Nebulized sodium bicarbonate is frequently used to make tenacious secretions easier to eliminate. Nebulized acetylcysteine is also effective for loosening secretions, although it may trigger reflex bronchospasm.

It is important to be aggressive with pulmonary infections: Pneumonia is one of the leading causes of death for all persons with spinal cord injury, regardless of the level of injury or the amount of time since the injury.

Cough: An important technique for clearing secretions is the assisted cough: An assistant firmly pushes against the outside of the stomach and upward, substituting for the abdominal muscle action that usually makes for a strong cough. This is a much gentler push than the Heimlich maneuver; it's also important to coordinate pushes with natural breathing rhythms. Another technique is percussion: this is basically a light drumming on the ribcage to help loosen up congestion in the lungs.

Postural drainage uses gravity to drain secretions from the bottoms of the lungs up higher into the chest where one can either cough them up and out or get them up high enough to swallow them. This usually works when the head is lower than the feet for 15–20 minutes.

Glossopharyngeal breathing can be used to help obtain a deeper breath, by "gulping" a rapid series of mouthfuls of air and forcing the air into the lungs, and then exhaling the accumulated air. It can be used to help with coughing.

There are several machines on the market that may help people on ventilators cough. The Vest (Hill-Rom; **www.thevest.com**), consists of an inflatable vest connected by air hoses to an air pulse generator, which can rapidly inflate and deflate the vest, thus applying gentle pressure to the chest wall to loosen and thin mucus and move it to the central airways to be cleared by coughing or suctioning.

The CoughAssist (Philips Respironics; **www.coughassist.com**) is designed to boost cough function by mechanically simulating the cough maneuver. This device blows in an inspiratory pressure breath followed rapidly by an expiratory flow. This generates enough peak air flow to clear secretions. Both the Vest and the CoughAssist have been approved by Medicare for reimbursement if determined to be a medical necessity.

Researchers at the Cleveland FES Center have devised an electrical stimulation protocol to initiate a forceful cough in tetraplegic patients, on demand. The system is under evaluation and not yet clinically available. See **http://fescenter.org**

Ventilators: There are two basic types of mechanical ventilators. Negative pressure ventilators, such as the iron lung, create a vacuum around the outside of the chest, causing the chest to expand and suck air into the lungs. Positive pressure ventilators, which have been available since the 1940s, work on the opposite principle, by blowing air directly into the lungs. Ventilators are invasive – an air passage is made in the throat area, fitted with a device most people call a "trach."

Noninvasive breathing: Some people, including high-level tetraplegics, have had success using a noninvasive breathing system. Positive pressure air is supplied to a mouthpiece from the same type of ventilator used with a trach. The user takes puffs of air as needed. A primary advantage reported for noninvasive ventilation is that because there is no open trach, there may be less chance of bacterial entry and therefore fewer respiratory infections. Also, some patients on non-invasive systems attest to a better, more independent quality of life because they don't have a trach in their neck and they don't have to suction the trachea as frequently. Clearly, noninvasive ventilation is not for everyone. Candidates must have good swallowing function; they also need a full support network of pulmonary specialists. There are not many clinicians with expertise in the method, thus its availability is limited.

Another breathing technique involves implantation of an electronic device in the chest to stimulate the phrenic nerve and send a regular signal to the diaphragm, causing it to contract and fill the lungs with air. Phrenic nerve pacers have been available for many years. Two companies offer diaphragm stimulation systems. The Avery pacemaker has been in use since before the FDA approved medical devices, going back to the mid-1960s. The Avery has been implanted in over 2,000 patients, with about 600 in use now, some continuously for almost 40 years. The procedure involves surgery through the body or neck to locate the phrenic nerve on both sides of the body. The nerves are exposed and sutured to electrodes. A small radio receiver is also implanted in the chest cavity;

this is activated by an external antenna taped to the body. For details see **www.averylabs.com**

The Synapse system, pioneered in Cleveland, was used in an early clinical trial by Christopher Reeve in 2003. The Cleveland system, FDA approved for implant in people with spinal cord injury in 2008, is more simply installed, using an outpatient laparoscopic technique. Two electrodes are placed on each side of diaphragm muscle, with wires attached through the skin to a battery powered stimulator. Synapse also has FDA approval to implant the devices in people with ALS. For more see **www.synapsebiomedical.com**

For those with a progressive neuromuscular disability, such as ALS, morning headaches are often the first sign that breathing needs help. Since breathing is shallower during sleep, any drop in volume can lead to trouble – including retention of carbon dioxide, which causes headache.

Others may wake up repeatedly during the night as the shallow breathing causes a sudden jolt. Broken sleep causes daytime sleepiness, lethargy, anxiety, irritability, confusion and physical problems such as poor appetite, nausea, increased heart rate and fatigue. BiPAP (Bi-level Positive Airway Pressure), a type of noninvasive ventilation, is often called for. BiPAP is not a life-support machine—it cannot completely take over breathing. Using a removable mask over the nose, the system delivers

Off the Vent

Lazlo Nagy became a C4 tetraplegic on a vent after he crashed his motorcycle a few years ago. Eventually, he wound up in a nursing home with around-the-clock care, and remained quite unsettled. "I used to cry myself to sleep every night because of the anxiety. I was constantly worried, would my battery go dead, would the machine go all night?" After Nagy heard about Christopher Reeve's experience in a diaphragm pacing clinical trial, he too got a diaphragm pacing implant. "The change in my life has been truly remarkable," says Nagy. "The nursing facility was billing Medicaid $16,000 a month. After getting the [pacing] surgery, it went to $3000—a savings of $13,000 a month. Eventually I returned to work, I got married, I feel confident I can go out in the world by myself, without an attendant. It's given me a lot more freedom. I feel safe. I don't worry that I'm going to suddenly die."

a pressurized breath of air into the lungs, then drops the pressure to allow an exhale. The most common use is for people with sleep apnea, characterized by snoring and lack of oxygen during sleep. Sleep apnea is linked to high blood pressure, stroke and cardiovascular disease, memory problems, weight gain, impotency and headaches.

For reasons that are not completely clear, sleep apnea is significantly more common to people with spinal cord injuries, especially tetraplegics, among whom an estimated 25-40 percent have the condition. Obesity, common in the SCI population, is a risk factor for sleep apnea. Many people with SCI can't change sleep positions and may remain on their backs, which often leads to breathing obstruction. Respiratory muscle weakness is very likely involved. It may also be that certain medications (baclofen, for example, is known to slow down breathing) affect sleep patterns. People with higher cervical injuries who rely upon neck and upper chest muscles to help with breathing may be susceptible to sleep

Preventing Respiratory Issues

- Maintain proper posture and mobility. Sit up every day and turn regularly in bed to prevent the buildup of congestion.
- Cough regularly. Have someone perform manual assist coughs, or perform self-assist coughs; use a machine to help.
- Wear an abdominal binder to assist intercostal and abdominal muscles.
- Follow a healthy diet and manage your weight — problems are more likely to occur if you are too heavy or too light.
- Drink plenty of water. Water helps keep congestion from becoming thick and difficult to cough up.
- Do not smoke or be around smokers: Smoking not only causes cancer, but also decreases oxygen in the blood, increases congestion in the chest and windpipe, reduces the ability to clear secretions from lungs, destroys lung tissue, and increases the risk for respiratory infections.
- Exercise. Every person living with paralysis can benefit from some type of exercise. For those with a high level of paralysis, it may be helpful to do breathing exercises.
- Get vaccinations for both influenza and pneumonia.

apnea because these muscles are inactive during deep sleep.

For people with neuromuscular disease, BiPAP can improve the quality of life while delaying the need for invasive ventilation, or diaphragm pacing, by months or years. Some people use BiPAP as an intermediary step before going on a ventilator.

Tracheostomy care: There are many potential complications related to tracheostomy tubes, including the inability to speak or swallow normally. Certain tracheostomy tubes are designed to direct air upward during exhalation and thus permit speech during regular, periodic intervals. Another tracheostomy-associated complication is infection. The tube is a foreign body in the neck, and thus has the potential of introducing organisms that would ordinarily be stopped by natural defense mechanisms in the nose and mouth. Cleaning and dressing of the tracheostomy site daily is an important preventive measure.

Weaning (removing ventilator support): In general, those with complete neurologic injuries at C2 and above have no diaphragmatic function and require a ventilator. Those with complete injuries at C3 or C4 may have diaphragmatic function and usually have the potential for weaning. People with complete injuries at C5 and below have intact diaphragmatic function and may at first require a ventilator; they are usually able to wean. Weaning is important because it reduces the risk of some health issues related to tracheostomy, and also because weaned individuals generally require much less paid assisted care.

Exercise: respiratory muscles are both metabolically and structurally plastic and they respond to exercise training. Respiratory muscle training can improve respiratory muscle performance but may also dramatically reduce respiratory infections. There are a number of commercially available hand-held devices for inspiratory muscle training.

SOURCES

Craig Hospital, University of Miami School of Medicine, University of Washington School of Medicine/Department of Rehabilitation Medicine, ALS Association of America

&❧ **Below are links to resources.**

International Ventilator Users Network (IVUN), a resource for people who use ventilators, pulmonologists, pediatricians, respiratory therapists, and ventilator manufacturers and vendors to discuss home ventilation. Features a newsletter, articles from healthcare professionals and venturesome vent users. **www.ventusers.org**

The Center for Noninvasive Mechanical Ventilation Alternatives and Pulmonary Rehabilitation. The New Jersey–based center, under the direction of Dr. John Bach, says it has removed dozens of tracheostomy tubes from vent users and taught many to breathe without ventilators. **www.theuniversityhospital.com/ventilation**

Paralyzed Veterans of America, in support of The Consortium for Spinal Cord Medicine, offers authoritative clinical practice guidelines for respiratory management. Toll-free 1–800–424–8200; **www.pva.org**, click on Publications. A consumer guide is available.

The Spinal Cord Injury Rehabilitation Evidence (SCIRE) project is a Canadian research collaboration of scientists, clinicians and consumers that reviews, evaluates, and translates research knowledge and establishes best rehabilitation practices following SCI. There is a section on respiration. **www.scireproject.com**

Skin Care

People with paralysis are at high risk of developing skin problems. Limited mobility coupled with impaired sensation can lead to pressure sores or ulcers, which can be a devastating complication.

The skin, the largest organ system in the body, is tough and pliable. It protects the underlying cells against air, water, foreign substances and bacteria. It is sensitive to injury and has remarkable self-repair capabilities. But skin just can't take prolonged pressure. A pressure ulcer involves damage to the skin and underlying tissue. Pressure ulcers, also called bed sores, decubiti or decubitus ulcers, range in severity from mild (minor skin reddening) to severe (deep craters that can infect all the way to muscle and bone). Unrelieved pressure on the skin squeezes tiny blood vessels, which supply the skin with nutrients and oxygen. When skin is starved of blood for too long, tissue dies and a pressure ulcer forms.

Sliding around in a bed or chair can cause blood vessels to stretch or bend, leading to pressure ulcers. An abrasion can occur when a person's skin is pulled across a surface instead of lifted. A bump or fall may cause damage to the skin that may not show up right away. Other causes of pressure sores are braces or hard objects that put pressure on your skin. Also, people with limited sensation are prone to skin injuries from burns.

Skin damage from pressure usually begins on the body where the bones are close to the skin surface, such as the hip. These bony prominences apply pressure on the skin from within. If there is a hard surface on the outside, too, the skin is pinched off from circulation. Because the rate of circulation is reduced by paralysis to begin with, less oxygen is available to the skin, lowering the skin's resistance. The body tries to compensate by sending more blood to the area. This may result in swelling, adding still more pressure to the blood vessels.

A skin sore begins as a red area on the skin. This reddened area may feel hard and/or hot. For those with darker skin, the area may appear shiny. At this stage, the progression is reversible. The skin will return to its normal color if the pressure is removed.

If the pressure is not removed, a blister or scab may form—this means that the tissue underneath is dying. Remove all pressure over the area immediately.

In the next stage, a hole (ulcer) forms in the dead tissue. Frequently, this dead tissue is small on the skin surface, but damaged tissue may extend deep to the bone.

A skin sore can mean several weeks or even months of hospitalization or bed rest in order for the sore to heal. Complex pressure sores may require surgery or skin grafting. All of this can cost thousands of dollars and mean valuable time away from work, school or family.

Stages of a Pressure Sore

Stage One: Skin is not broken but is red; color does not fade 30 minutes after pressure is removed. What to do: stay off the sore, keep clean and dry. Explore causes: check out mattress, seat cushion, transfer procedures and turning techniques.

Stage Two: The top layer of skin, the epidermis, is broken. The sore is shallow but open; drainage may be present. What to do: Follow steps in Stage One but cleanse wound with water or saline solution and dry carefully. Apply either a transparent dressing (e.g. Tegraderm) or a hydrocolloid dressing (e.g. DuoDERM). If there are signs of trouble see your healthcare provider.

Signs of Trouble: The sore is getting bigger; the sore starts to smell bad or the drainage becomes greenish in color. Fever is a bad sign.

Stage Three: Skin has broken down further, into the second layer of skin, through the dermis into the subcutaneous fat tissue. You must see a care provider at this point; this is getting serious and may need special cleaning or debriding agents. Don't wait.

Stage Four: The skin has broken down all the way to the bone. A lot of dead tissue is present and there is also a lot of drainage. This can be life threatening. You may be looking at surgery.

Healing: This occurs when the sore gets smaller, when pinkish skin forms along the edges of the sore. Bleeding might occur but take this as a good sign: circulation is back and that helps healing. Be patient. Skin repair isn't always speedy.

When is it safe to put pressure on the affected area again? Only when the sore is completely healed—when the top layer of skin is unbroken and normal looking. The first time pressure is applied, start with 15-minute intervals. Build up gradually over periods of a few days to allow skin pressure tolerance to build. If redness occurs, keep pressure off the area.

Skin wound treatment by any means is complicated by hard-to-treat infections, spasticity, additional pressure and even the psychological makeup of the person (pressure sores have been linked to low self-esteem and impulsive behavior). It is an oversimplification to say pressure sores are always preventable but that's almost true; with vigilant care and good overall hygiene, skin integrity can be maintained.

A wide variety of pressure-relieving support surfaces, including special beds, mattresses, mattress overlays or seat cushions are available to support your body in bed or in a chair. Work with your therapists to know what is available. See page 268 for more on the various types of seating options. Search **www.abledata.com** for specific seating and sleep surface products. Here's an example of a product to help people who can't turn at night and who may not have an attendant to do it for them: Freedom Bed is an automatic lateral rotation system that quietly turns through a 60-degree range of rotation; **www.pro-bed.com**

Christopher Reeve's Passing

The death of Christopher Reeve in 2004 was attributed to heart failure due to sepsis (also known as septicemia), an infection that spreads from a specific location (such as a skin sore or bladder infection) to the blood and other organs. What exactly happened to Reeve isn't known. Clearly, his death was related to pressure sores; to be sure, Reeve had been battling more than one skin sore and had even experienced life-threatening sepsis just weeks before he died. But according to people who were with him on his last day, Reeve did not appear to have symptoms that would red-flag recurrent sepsis (he did not exhibit fever, chills, fatigue, malaise, anxiety, confusion).

The cause of death was not directly related to Reeve's pressure sores. According to Dana Reeve, the more likely cause of death was a reaction to an antibiotic Reeve was given for a developing infection (he had a history of drug sensitivity). Reeve's body immediately went into shock (anaphylactic) but not septic.

Reeve chose to live his life fully and well, and as much as possible on his own terms. That is his most lasting legacy.

Remember that the first line of defense is to be responsible for your own skin care. Look at it: Check your skin daily, using a mirror for hard-to-see areas. Skin stays healthy with good diet, good hygiene and regular pressure relief. Keep the skin clean and dry. Skin that is moist from sweat or bodily discharges is more likely to break down. Drink plenty of fluids. A healing wound or sore can lose more than a quart of water each day. Drinking 8 to 12 cups of water a day might not be too much. Note: Beer and wine do not count; alcohol actually causes you to lose water or become dehydrated. Watch your weight, too. Being too thin causes you to lose the padding between your bones and your skin and makes it possible for even small amounts of pressure to break down the skin. Getting too heavy is risky, too. More weight may mean more padding, but it also means more pressure on skin folds. Don't smoke. Research has shown that heavy smokers are more prone to skin sores.

SOURCES

Paralyzed Veterans of America, Craig Hospital, National Library of Medicine, University of Washington School of Medicine/Rehabilitation

≈ Below are links to resources.

Paralyzed Veterans of America, in support of The Consortium for Spinal Cord Medicine, offers authoritative clinical practice guidelines for skin care. PVA, toll-free 1-800-424-8200, **www.pva.org**, click on Publications, then Medical Guidelines.

Craig Hospital, with funding from the National Institute on Disability and Rehabilitation Research, has developed educational materials to help people with spinal cord injuries maintain their health. **www.craighospital.org**, click on "Spinal Cord Injury," then "Health and Wellness."

Spasticity

Spasticity is a side effect of paralysis that varies from mild muscle stiffness to severe, uncontrollable leg movements. Generally, doctors now call conditions of extreme muscle tension spastic hypertonia (SH). It may occur in association with spinal cord injury, multiple sclerosis, cerebral palsy, or brain trauma. Symptoms may include increased muscle tone, rapid muscle contractions, exaggerated deep tendon reflexes, muscle spasms, scissoring (involuntary crossing of the legs) and fixed joints.

When an individual is first injured, muscles are weak and flexible because of what's called spinal shock: The body's reflexes are absent below the level of injury; this condition usually lasts for a few weeks or several months. Once the spinal shock is over, reflex activity returns.

Spasticity is usually caused by damage to the portion of the brain or spinal cord that controls voluntary movement. Since the normal flow of nerve messages to below the level of injury is interrupted, those messages may not reach the reflex control center of the brain. The spinal cord then attempts to moderate the body's response. Because the spinal cord is not as efficient as the brain, the signals that are sent back to the site of the sensation are often over-exaggerated in an overactive muscle response or spastic hypertonia: an uncontrollable "jerking" movement, stiffening or

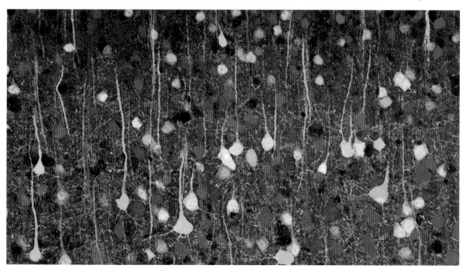

Neurons are labeled with different colors in the cerebral cortex of a "Brainbow" mouse, imaged on a laser-scanning confocal microscope at the Lichtman Lab, Harvard University.

straightening of muscles, shock-like contractions of a muscle or group of muscles, and abnormal tone in the muscles.

Most individuals with SCI have some spasms. Persons with cervical injuries and those with incomplete injuries are more likely than those with paraplegia and/or complete injuries to experience SH. The most common muscles that spasm are those that bend the elbow (flexor) or extend the leg (extensor). These reflexes usually occur as a result of an automatic response to painful sensations.

While spasticity can interfere with rehabilitation or daily living activities, it is not always a bad thing. Some people use their spasms for function, to empty their bladders, to transfer or to dress. Others use SH to keep their muscles toned and improve circulation. It may also help maintain bone strength. In a large Swedish study of people with SCI, 68 percent had spasticity but less than half of those said that their spasticity was a significant problem that reduced activities of daily living or caused pain.

Changing spasticity: A change in a person's spasticity is something to pay attention to. For example, increased tone could be the result of a cyst or cavity forming in the spinal cord (post-traumatic syringomyelia). Untreated, cysts can lead to further loss of function. Problems outside your nervous system, such as bladder infections or skin sores, can increase spasticity.

Treatment for spasticity usually includes medications such as baclofen, diazepam or zanaflex. Some people with severe spasms utilize refillable baclofen pumps, which are small, surgically implanted reservoirs that apply the drug directly to the area of spinal cord dysfunction. This allows for a higher concentration of drug without the usual mind-dulling side effects of a high oral dosage.

Physical therapy, including muscle stretching, range of motion exercises, and other physical therapy regimens, can help prevent joint contractures (shrinkage or shortening of a muscle) and reduce the severity of symptoms. Proper posture and positioning are important for people in wheelchairs and those at bed rest to reduce spasms. Orthotics, such as ankle-foot braces, are sometimes used to limit spasticity. Application of cold (cryotherapy) to an affected area can also calm muscle activity.

For many years doctors have used phenol nerve blocks to deaden nerves that cause spasticity. Lately, a better but more expensive nerve block, botulinum toxin (Botox), has become a popular treatment for spasms. An application of Botox lasts about three to six months; the body builds antibodies to the drug, reducing its effectiveness over time.

Sometimes, surgery is recommended for tendon release or to sever the nerve-muscle pathway in children with cerebral palsy. Selective dorsal rhizotomy may be considered if spasms interfere with sitting, bathing or general caretaking.

Spasticity comes with the territory for many people who are paralyzed. Treatment strategy should be based on one's function: Is the spasticity keeping you from certain activities? Are there safety risks, such as losing control while driving your power chair or car? Are spasticity drugs worse than the symptoms, affecting concentration or energy? Check with your physician to discuss your options.

SOURCES

The National Institute of Neurological Disorders and Stroke, National Multiple Sclerosis Society, United Cerebral Palsy Association, The National Spinal Cord Injury Statistical Center, Craig Hospital

๛ **Below are links to resources.**

Medtronic manufactures implantable pumps for delivery (intrathecally) of drugs such as baclofen to control spasticity. **www.medtronic.com**

National Multiple Sclerosis Society offers information and resources on spasticity. Toll-free 1-800-344-4867 or search "spasticity" at **www.nationalmssociety.org**

Craig Hospital, with funding from the National Institute on Disability and Rehabilitation Research, has developed educational materials to help people with spinal cord injuries maintain their health. **www.craighospital.org**, click on "Spinal Cord Injury," then "Health and Wellness."

Syringomyelia | Tethered Cord

Syringomyelia and tethered spinal cord can occur from months to many decades after spinal cord injury. In post-traumatic syringomyelia (sear-IN-go-my-EE-lia) a cyst or fluid-filled cavity forms within the cord. This cavity can expand over time, extending two or more spinal segments from the level of SCI. The clinical symptoms for syringomyelia and tethered spinal cord are the same and can include progressive deterioration of the spinal cord, progressive loss of sensation or strength, accompanied by sweating, spasticity, pain and autonomic dysreflexia (AD) -- new levels of disability long after a person has had a successful rehabilitation.

Tethered spinal cord is a condition where scar tissue forms and holds the spinal cord itself to the dura, the soft tissue membrane that surrounds it. This scarring prevents the normal flow of spinal fluid around the spinal cord and impedes the normal motion of the spinal cord within the membrane. Tethering causes cyst formation; it can occur without evidence of syringomyelia, but post-traumatic cystic formation does not occur without some degree of cord tethering.

Magnetic resonance imaging (MRI) detects cysts in the spinal cord, unless rods, plates or bullet fragments are present.

Tethered cord and syringomyelia are treated surgically. Untethering involves a delicate surgery to release the scar tissue around the spinal cord to restore spinal fluid flow and the motion of the spinal cord. In addition, a small graft may be placed at the tethering site to fortify the dural space and decrease the risk of re-scarring. If a cyst is present, a shunt may be placed inside the cavity to drain fluid from the cyst. Surgery usually leads to improved strength and reduced pain; it does not always bring back lost sensory function.

Syringomyelia also occurs in people who have a congenital abnormality of the brain called a Chiari malformation. During development of the fetus, the lower part of the cerebellum protrudes from the base of the head into the cervical portion of the spinal canal. Symptoms usually include vomiting, muscle weakness in the head and face, difficulty swallowing, and varying degrees of mental impairment. Paralysis of the arms and legs may also occur. Adults and adolescents with

Chiari malformation who previously showed no symptoms may show signs of progressive impairment, such as involuntary, rapid, downward eye movements. Other symptoms may include dizziness, headache, double vision, deafness, an impaired ability to coordinate movement, and episodes of acute pain in and around the eyes.

Syringomyelia can also be associated with spina bifida, spinal cord tumors, arachnoiditis, and idiopathic (cause unknown) syringomyelia. MRI has significantly increased the number of diagnoses in the beginning stages of syringomyelia. Signs of the disorder tend to develop slowly, although sudden onset may occur with coughing or straining.

Surgery results in stabilization or modest improvement in symptoms for most people although delay in treatment may result in irreversible spinal cord injury. Recurrence of syringomyelia after surgery may make additional operations necessary; these operations may not be completely successful over the long term. Up to one half of those treated for syringomyelia have symptoms return within five years.

SOURCES

National Institute of Neurological Disorders and Stroke, American Syringomyelia & Chiari Alliance Project

❧ **Below is a link to resources.**

American Syringomyelia & Chiari Alliance Project
offers news on syringomyelia, tethered cord and Chiari malformation, sponsors research. Toll-free 1-800-ASAP; **www.asap.org**

HEALTHY LIVING

Coping & Adjustment

Individuals who are new to paralysis, whether from a sudden accident or the progression of a disease, will most likely experience grief. Families, too, enter this strange, new why-me world with its hallmarks of mourning, helplessness, second-guessing and regret. While everyone deals with loss and change in their own way, there are aspects of the adjustment process that many people share.

At first, many react to paralysis as if nothing really happened, refusing to accept that changes in their body and in their ability to move are not going to get better or heal in ways they always have. Some may see the injury as an annoyance similar to getting the flu that will pass with time. Psychologists call this denial. Elisabeth Kübler-Ross, who has famously outlined the stages of grieving, notes that denial has a beneficial function as a "buffer" after unexpected shocking news.

Some people find refuge in the denial stage for a long time, using it as an excuse to do nothing, or to do too much to overcome limitations and act "normal." Most, however, will begin to gain knowledge about their condition and have some perspective on what has happened. As denial fades, hope emerges. Thus begins the process of adjustment.

When denial can no longer be maintained, it is often replaced with other dark feelings—anger, rage, envy and resentment. These can be seen as defense mechanisms that allow a person time to mobilize other defenses. Guilt may be part of the mix, too, especially in people whose poor judgment or self-destructive behavior may have contributed to their disability. Self-loathing may also appear when one's notion of "normal" is turned upside down.

Many people within the universe of disability – including those who experience paralysis first hand as well as family members—can become extremely frustrated. They may see themselves as victims whose lives are ruined because they can never live the happy life they always knew they would; they see no way out. These people may react with hostility to others. This, of course, adds stress to caregivers and loved ones. There's nothing wrong with anger—unless you hold on to it and let it smolder. The best advice, easier said than done, is to let anger run its course, and let it go. How? Some find relief in religion, others by quieting the mind using meditation.

Fear is another common feeling: Where is all this chaos leading? Will it get worse? Will my spouse stay with me? Will I ever love or work or be taken seriously again? For many people, the greatest fear is losing control over their lives. These thoughts are common for individuals who are newly paralyzed; many persons continue to hold on to them, even the irrational ones, long after their injury.

Extreme sadness is natural after paralysis – there has, of course, been great loss. Sadness passes. It's important not to confuse the blues we all experience when something bad happens with depression. Depression is a medical condition that can lead to inactivity, difficulty concentrating, a significant change in appetite or sleep time, and feelings of dejection, hopelessness or worthlessness. A depressed person may have thoughts about suicide. Suicide is greater for people with spinal cord injuries compared to the nondisabled population. It is the leading cause of death for people with SCI younger than 55.

To be sure, paralysis ignites many emotions and feelings, most of them negative. A person's reactions to all this baggage may result in behavior that is bad for health and happiness. For example, a person who feels worthless may not take proper care of his or her bladder or skin or nutrition. Also, people with a history of alcohol and/or substance abuse may return to old patterns of self-destruction. Others may start drinking or taking drugs to quiet their anxieties. Unhealthy behavior leads to unhealthy results. Neglect of personal care (which has been called "existential suicide") risks a wide range of health problems such as respiratory complications, urinary tract infection, and pressure sores.

In time, one processes the toxic feelings. Another phase of adjustment begins. Generally, at some point following paralysis, people may begin to admit that they have a serious condition, though they may hold on to the belief that the situation is not a long-term problem.

As the process continues, it is important for people to contact others who share similar experiences. There are peer support groups for every sort of condition related to paralysis in most communities, including the

Reeve Foundation Peer and Family Support Program. The Internet is a great tool for connecting with paralysis survivors who have been down the same path and can testify that there is still a future ahead full of life and rewarding experience.

Given time, a person will eventually come to terms with their loss and reach the final stage of the grieving process: acceptance. Most people come to accept a realistic view of their condition, find meaning in life, and begin to make plans for the life ahead of them.

Adjustment may ultimately depend on motivation. Early on, people may be motivated to work hard at therapy to gain strength and function, still believing, perhaps, that paralysis can be beaten by sheer will power. Many people with spinal cord injuries continue to hope that they will walk again. While treatments for paralysis are coming, the best approach is to move forward and live a full life now. Hope for restoring function is fine and not unrealistic, but if it means waiting on the sidelines until medical research delivers the cure, it's an aspect of denial.

People who adjust well to life after paralysis are motivated by personal goals – getting through college, getting a good job, raising a family. People who set these kinds of goals report greater life satisfaction,

Anger Management

You can't eliminate anger, and it wouldn't be a good idea even if you could. Life will always deliver your share of frustration, pain, loss, and the unpredictable actions of others. You can't change that; but you can change the way you let such events affect you, especially if anger is an issue.

Simple relaxation techniques, such as deep breathing and pleasing imagery, can help calm down angry feelings. Try this:

• breathe deeply, from your diaphragm; breathing from your chest won't relax you. Picture your breath coming up from your stomach.

• slowly repeat a calm word or phrase such as "relax," or "take it easy." Repeat it to yourself while breathing deeply.

• use imagery; visualize a relaxing experience, from your memory or your imagination. Practice these techniques daily and remind yourself that the world is "not out to get you."

Source: American Psychological Association; www.apa.org

and they feel less shameful about their condition. How do you get motivated? It may help to think about what you always wanted out of your life before. Most people have the same personality, the same sense of style and humor as they did before being paralyzed; there is no reason not to strive for the same things.

Of course getting things done after losing function to paralysis is a challenge. It may mean learning lots of new ways to solve problems. It may be necessary to ask others for help, even when doing everything on your own becomes a stubborn way to assert your independence. Asking for help is okay – it's one of the ways to get what you need and get things done.

Adjustment to paralysis is a process; changing one's thoughts, feelings, and behavior doesn't happen overnight. It takes time to know what is true, what is realistic, what is rational. It takes time to rebuild one's identity, to find a new balance in relationships, to discover that what is important is what is happening now. Negative emotions are self-limiting, but they can be transformed. Keep your options open as best you can. Don't ignore the support and problem-solving experiences of others in similar circumstances. Figure out what's next and how to get there.

SOURCES

University of Alabama at Birmingham Research and Training Center on Secondary Conditions of Spinal Cord Injury/UAB Spain Rehabilitation Center; National Multiple Sclerosis Society; Quebec Paraplegic Association; Paralyzed Veterans of America; American Stroke Association

❧ **Below is a link to resources.**

Reeve Foundation Peer & Family Support Program
(PFSP) provides emotional support, guidance and the sharing of real-world experiences from mentor/peers who are living well after paralysis. Call toll-free 1-800-539-7309 or see **www.paralysis.org/peer**

Live the LIfe You Have

I t is possible to find peace in the wake of suffering." That is one of clinical psychologist Daniel Gottlieb's main messages. Another one is that "there is no relationship between disability and happiness." A third, one he often uses in various iterations, is this: "Don't spend so much of your energy pursuing the life you want or avoiding the life you fear. Have the faith to live the life you have—and live it fully, with great love and gratitude."

Daniel Gottlieb, Ph.D.

Gottlieb's personal narrative—the inspiration and wisdom of the archetypal wounded healer who's spent half his life as a quadriplegic – shapes those messages. Dr. Dan, as he goes by, is well known in the Philadelphia area, where he makes his home and where he hosts a weekly program on public radio, "Voices in the Family." He began his psychology practice in 1969; he and his wife had two daughters. In 1979 he survived a nasty automobile accident which left him paralyzed from the chest down. He describes years of despair, compounded by more and more pain and loss. He says he was filled with self-loathing, insecurity, shame and depression; he came to hate his body, which he described as a "terrorist."

"Most of what I was engaged in," says Gottlieb, "was self-pity and feeling victimized." His parents and sister died; his marriage broke up and his ex-wife later died of cancer. His grandson was born with a learning disability. His own health has taken many unpredictable spirals over the years.

Along the way, Gottlieb discovered a powerful resilience. Tapping into his reserves of compassion, he has armed himself to ride out the storms. "Don't fight with the life you have," he says. "Yes, there's a great deal of suffering out there. And there are ways to diminish suffering. But we all have a certain narrative in our head how to fix this, how it will happen. It's either when we walk again, or when our bladder starts working, or when we lose the pounds, or when our spouse changes, or when the insurance company comes through – we get a picture in our head of the circumstances we need to make ourselves happy. Live the life you have instead of waiting for the life you want or longing for the life you had."

> Live the life you have instead of waiting for the life you want or longing for the life you had.

Gottlieb often encounters people with disabilities who have hope for a certain outcome. "They live their lives waiting for tomorrow telling themselves 'that's when I will be happy.' To me, hope is all about believing that tomorrow can bring joy regardless of today's circumstances."

Gottlieb blogs regularly about dealing with disability and convenes a live forum at *Christopherreeve.org* called "Healing the Mind and Heart." The open, communal discussions allow Gottlieb to help people process anger and soothe grieving.

Peer and Family Support Program

A new injury or diagnosis can be overwhelming and scary—for the entire family. One of the surest ways to process the confusion and to begin to see a full and active life ahead is to connect with someone who has already navigated the same currents. The Reeve Foundation's Peer and Family Support Program (PFSP) makes sure someone will be there to help. In communities across the United States, the PFSP provides emotional encouragement, as well as local and national resources, to people living with paralysis, and to their families and caregivers. Mentors empower people living with paralysis, including our service members, to achieve a healthy and full life.

The PFSP provides one-on-one support to anyone, new to paralysis or not, who would like to talk to a mentor—someone who shares and understands the circumstances and who can offer advice, connections and friendship, and maybe provide the spark to get a person moving forward again. There are some things, personal and confidential, that can't be comfortably discussed except with another person in a similar circumstance. That's what the PFSP is about; there are issues related to medical care and adaptive equipment, or very personal issues, that an experienced hand is well suited to help with.

Here's an example of how it works. Steve Kenny, from Jacksonville, Fla., has been living with a C5/C6 spinal cord injury from a 1993 diving accident. He is the Southeast Regional Coordinator of the PFSP and has been mentoring individuals with recent spinal cord injuries as a volunteer locally at Brooks Rehabilitation. Since becoming a certified mentor for the PFSP, Kenny and other Reeve/Brooks mentors have helped dozens of individuals. Kenny helped one newly injured man from falling into despair.

"I met with an individual with a high-level spinal cord injury while he was still in intensive care at a trauma center in Jacksonville," says Kenny. "He had requested a DNR [do not resuscitate]. His mother, of course, was overwhelmed. I spoke with the young man and his mom and showed them how I live a full and happy life. The next day the DNR was removed and they decided to proceed with treatment." Encouraged by Kenny's ongoing mentorship, the man progressed to outpatient therapy and joined

a specialized day-gym program that allowed him to continue independent physical activity and strengthening.

If you are you living with paralysis, or perhaps you are the parent, spouse, family member or friend of an individual living with paralysis, you might benefit from someone who has experienced what you are experiencing. The Reeve Foundation peer mentors are adept at sharing their personal knowledge and training to help you. And there is never a charge for their services.

Peer Mentors empower people living with paralysis, including service members, families, friends and caregivers, to achieve health and wellness and to avoid the common secondary health conditions that accompany paralysis.

The PFSP is always interested in adding new mentors. If you are a person living with paralysis, someone who is upbeat and thriving, and can demonstrate life skills that might empower others to reach for their goals, why not become a mentor and share your experience? The goal of the PFSP is to match clients with certified mentors who are of similar age, gender, level of paralysis, ethnicity, etc., whenever possible. Veterans are encouraged to join the mentoring effort, as are family, friends and caregivers.

If you would like to speak with a mentor, or to be one, contact the PFSP, toll-free 1-800-539-7309; email *peer@ChristopherReeve.org* or visit **www.ChristopherReeve.org/peer**

Alternative Medicine

There are many alternative medicine approaches that may have benefits for those with spinal cord injury or disease. Although these approaches to wellness and healing fall outside of mainstream traditions, they may offer a bridge between eastern and western medicine. Don't think of these alternatives as an either/or substitute for your regular care but rather as a compliment.

Laurance Johnston, Ph.D., former head of research for the Paralyzed Veterans of America, has compiled information on alternative therapies for SCI. His book, *Alternative Medicine and Spinal Cord Injury: Beyond the Banks of the Mainstream*, details numerous treatments that you won't hear about in most rehab centers. His take on this is open-minded: "to expand the healing spectrum available to individuals with physical disability, especially SCI and multiple sclerosis, and allow these individuals to make informed decisions about their own healthcare."

Johnston points out that doctors might warn people from using alternatives, but mainstream medicine is hardly safe: more than 100,000 people die from adverse drug reactions in hospitals; two million people enter hospitals and get infections there they didn't have before; medical mistakes kill as many as 100,000 people annually. "These statistics are

Aging: Not for the Weak

Prior to World War II, life expectancy for people with spinal cord injury was about 18 months. Now, life expectancy more closely resembles that of the general population. Alas, people with paralysis can now expect many of the same health problems as their nondisabled contemporaries. But unlike the general population, where heart disease, cancer, or stroke are the leading killers, SCI survivors are more likely to succumb from diseases of the respiratory system, infections, other heart disease, benign or malignant tumors, or hypertensive and ischemic heart disease. This is from SCI Model Systems data.

People with SCI are five times more likely to die from pneumonia than the general population. Studies have found that spinal cord injury survivors are twice as likely to die if they have a heart attack or stroke; coronary artery disease is a contributing factor in nearly one in four of all SCI deaths. Higher rates of diabetes and obesity, lower levels of physical activity, and changes in body composition add to the risk.

especially relevant to people with spinal cord dysfunction, who are often prone to overmedication, life-threatening infections, and more hospitalization," Johnston says.

Worried that alt-med therapies are not validated by rigorous clinical studies? Indeed, they are not backed by high-grade evidence. But according to Johnston, only 10-20 percent of what physicians practice has been scientifically proven. "Most conventional, as well as alternative, medicine is based on a history of use and experience," says Johnston. Here are a few highlights of medical alternatives:

Acupuncture: there are claims that it improve sensation, bowel and bladder function, may improve muscle spasms, vision, sleep, sexual functioning, and bladder control in people with MS.

Qigong: may reduce central cord pain.

Ayurveda: India's ancient holistic medicine attempts to keep one healthy and disease free. Certain spices are recommended for clearing toxins after any sort of injury, including turmeric, black pepper, ginger, coriander, fennel, and licorice.

Herbal Remedies: Many herbs specifically support and nourish the nervous system. Fresh extract of skullcap (of the mint family) may reduce nerve inflammation; a tincture of milky oats (i.e., immature oat seeds) may rebuild the neuronal myelin sheath; an external liniment of Cow Parsnip, (a common weed of the parsley family) is a traditional Southwestern Hispanic remedy for treating injured nerves and stimulating regeneration.

Aromatherapy: Essential oils are used to prevent respiratory infections, promote mucus clearing, fight depression, and promote sleep. They're cheap and have no side effects.

Magnets: There are claims they enhance circulation, promote wound healing, and reduce carpal tunnel syndrome.

Edgar Cayce: America's most famous medical intuitive believed the main cause of multiple sclerosis was the lack of gold; his therapy involved administering gold vibrational energy through two electrotherapy devices, the wet cell battery and radial appliance. Cayce's recommendations for SCI also emphasized the use of gold vibrational energy.

See **www.healingtherapies.info** and National Center for Complementary and Alternative Medicine, **http://nccam.nih.gov**

Mindfulness, Meditation, Prayer

Mindfulness is the practice of letting go of the noise in our head. Instead of doing and reacting and trying to fix everything, being mindful is about sitting still, being aware of what is happening in this present moment—not with words and thinking, but by listening fully with a mind free of judgments and opinions and all the rest of the baggage that become a major source of stress. Observe thoughts and emotions but let them pass without judgment.

Mindfulness meditation is not hard, there is no right or wrong way to do it, but it may take practice to quiet the mind for an extended period of time. Your mind will wander. That's ok, just pay attention to the thoughts and let them go by.

Start by setting aside 10 to 20 minutes a day at first. No special gear needed. No cost. All you'll need is a quiet space. Most people meditate with closed eyes, but you can focus on an object, a candle, for example. Concentrating on the flame might make it easier to clear the noise.

The main idea is to focusing your attention; this is what helps free your mind from the many distractions that cause stress and worry. Focus attention on such things as  a specific object, an image, a mantra. One way to start is to focus on breathing. Concentrate on the inhale and the exhale, slow and relaxed. Always bring the wandering mind back to the breath.

As your meditation skills increase, consciously visualize the release of tension, beginning at the head, eyelids, shoulders, fingers, and moving slowly down to the toes. Breathe relaxation into all the muscles and all parts of the body.

Prayer is the best known and most widely practiced example of meditation. Some people use religious mantras to focus, relax and quiet the mind.

The clinical effects of meditation are becoming more clear. Mindfulness is taught at many medical centers to help people cope with a broad range of physical and psychological symptoms, including reducing anxiety, pain, and depression, enhancing mood and self-esteem, and decreasing stress. Some people use meditation to enhance creativity or improve performance.

For information see National Center for Complementary and Alternative Medicine. *http://nccam.nih.gov/health/meditation/overview.htm*

Fitness and Exercise

If not now, when? It's never too late to get a fitness program going. Exercise is good for mind and body, and almost anyone can do it, regardless of functional capabilities. Some people exercise to buff up. Others do it to get stronger, to build endurance and stamina, to help keep joints loose and flexible, to reduce stress, to get more restful sleep, or just because it makes them feel better.

No doubt about it, exercise is good for you. It prevents secondary conditions such as heart disease, diabetes, pressure sores, carpal tunnel syndrome, obstructive pulmonary disease, hypertension, urinary tract infections and respiratory disease. Research shows that people with multiple sclerosis who joined an aerobic exercise program had better cardiovascular fitness, better bladder and bowel function, less fatigue and depression, a more positive attitude and increased participation in social activities.

In 2002, seven years after his injury, Christopher Reeve demonstrated to the world that he had recovered modest movement and sensation. Reeve's recovery defied medical expectations but had a dramatic effect on his daily life. He believed his improved function was the result of vigorous physical activity. He began exercising the year he was injured. Five years later, when he first noticed that he could voluntarily move an index finger, Reeve began an intense exercise program under the supervision of Dr. John McDonald, then at Washington University in St. Louis, who suggested that these activities may have awakened dormant nerve pathways, thus leading to recovery.

Reeve included daily electrical stimulation to build mass in his arms, quadriceps, hamstrings and other muscle groups. He rode a functional electrical stimulation (FES) bicycle, did spontaneous breathing training and also participated in aquatherapy. In 1998 and 1999, Reeve underwent treadmill (locomotor) training to encourage functional stepping. See below for more on FES bicycle ergometry; see pages 100-101 for more on locomotor training.

Not everyone can or should expect to get function back by exercising. But here's another great reason to get fit: Exercise helps us stay smart, and it keeps the brain healthy. Neuroscience research supports the notion that exercise enhances brain cell proliferation, fights degenerative disease and improves memory. A number of human studies have shown that exercise increases alertness and helps people think more clearly.

Whatever motivates you to exercise is a good reason. Weight loss is a start. There is an epidemic of obesity in the United States. Unfortunately, people with disabilities are even more prone to carrying excess weight due to a combination of altered metabolism and decreased muscle mass, along with a generally lower activity level.

There are compelling reasons to shed the extra pounds. Research shows that people who use wheelchairs are at risk for shoulder pain, joint deterioration and even painful rotator cuff tears, due to the amount of stress they place on their arms. The more weight to push, the more stress on the shoulder. Plus, extra pounds adds risk to the skin. As people gain weight, the skin traps moisture, greatly increasing the risk of pressure sores. Inactivity can also result in loss of trunk control, shortening or weakness of muscles, decreased bone density and inefficient breathing.

But people with paralysis may not be hearing the message. According to the President's Council on Physical Fitness and Sports, people with disabilities are less likely to engage in regular moderate physical activity than people without disabilities. It's the same as in the general population. It's often the "work" part of working out that keeps people from getting a fitness program going.

Physical activity, however, need not be strenuous to achieve health benefits. You don't have to be an athlete. Significant health benefits can be obtained with a moderate amount of physical activity, preferably daily. Adequate activity can be obtained in longer sessions of less intense activities (such as 30–40 minutes of wheeling oneself in a wheelchair) or in shorter sessions of more strenuous activities (such as 20 minutes of wheelchair basketball).

Additional health benefits can be gained through greater degrees of physical activity. People who can maintain a regular routine of physical activity that is of longer duration or of greater intensity are likely to derive greater benefit. Previously sedentary people who begin physical activity programs should start with short intervals of physical activity (5–10 minutes) and gradually build up to the desired level of activity.

CHRISTOPHER VOELKER

Fitness is medicine. Laquita Conway and son Aaron Baker: Says the former full-time power chair user, "Who knows what's possible?" To encourage his continuing recovery Aaron and his mom teamed with trainer Taylor Isaacs; the trio later opened an L.A. area specialty gym, CORE; www.corecenters.info

For paralyzed people unable to perform voluntary exercise, functional electrical stimulation (FES) has been shown to build muscle mass, improve circulation and metabolism, and favorably alter muscle fiber composition. According to a team at the Miami Project to Cure Paralysis, FES cycling reverses cardiac muscle atrophy in quadriplegics. FES works, but it's not available widely and it's not for everyone. See below for more. And ask your doctor about it.

Set realistic fitness goals but stick with a program. Stop exercising if you feel any pain, discomfort, nausea, dizziness, lightheadedness, chest pain, irregular heartbeat, shortness of breath or clammy hands. Always stay hydrated. People with paralysis should consult a physician before beginning a new program of physical activity. Over training or inappropriate activity can be counterproductive. For example, in people with multiple sclerosis, exercise can lead to a condition called cardiovascular dysautonomia, which lowers heart rate and decreases blood pressure. Also, because exercise tends to warm up the body, sensitivity to heat (especially in people with MS) can induce fatigue, loss of balance and visual changes; use cooling aids as needed (cool vests, ice packs). **www.steelevest.com** or **www.coolsport.net**

SOURCES

National Center on Health, Physical Activity and Disability, President's Council on Physical Fitness and Sports, National MS Society, Craig Hospital, Paralyzed Veterans of America

ॐ **Below are links to resources.**

> **National Center on Health, Physical Activity and Disability (NCHPAD)** features resources on fitness, exercise and recreation. A good place to start when you decide to get fit. Toll-free 1-800-900-3086; **www.nchpad.org**
> **The Cleveland FES Center** promotes techniques to restore function for persons with paralysis. Home of the FES Information Center. 216-231-3257; **http://fescenter.org**

FES Bikes

Functional electrical stimulation (FES) is an assistive device that provides low-level electrical current to muscles in a paralyzed body. Electrodes may be applied to the skin as needed or they may be implanted under the skin. FES can power the legs in order to power a stationary bike (or ergometer as they are called). An FES system was FDA approved and commercialized for tetraplegics to initiate a grip using a shoulder shrug (very effective, patients loved having use of their hands, but the company did not survive). FES has been used to facilitate standing, breathing, coughing, and urinating.

FES biking, the most commercially developed form, has been shown since the 1980s to be a very good means of working out a paralyzed body. FES builds muscle mass, is good for the heart and lungs, may help with bone strength and immune function. Some people have used FES systems to help them walk, with braces. FES or any physical activity improves overall health and well being. Might FES activity affect recovery, too?

John McDonald, MD, Ph.D., who runs the International Center for Spinal Cord Injury at the Kennedy Krieger Institute in Baltimore, believes it does. "Maximizing spontaneous recovery of function is something that is possible in the majority of those paralyzed, including the most severe," he claims.

McDonald clearly likes the concept; he helped start a company, Restorative Therapies, Inc. (**www.restorative-therapies.com**). The RT bike, the RT300 (also available with arm FES) competes with the original FES bike, the Ergys (**www.musclepower.com**). The primary difference is that the RT is smaller and is ridden without transferring from a wheelchair. Both cost north of $15,000; some insurance carriers will pay for FES. So far, Medicare has not reimbursed for FES bikes.

RT300 from Restorative Therapies, Inc.

Jen French: NeuroTech

Neurotechnology is not just about electrical stimulation. It is a whole category of medical devices and therapies that interact with the human nervous system. They can be used in various ways; to provide meaningful function, to treat a specific condition or to supplement therapy. Devices can be applied externally such as to the surface of the skin or implanted with a surgical procedure. For paralysis, options can range in the following:

- breathing, cough or respiratory systems
- hand, arm and shoulder systems
- bladder or bowel control
- spasticity or pain management
- pressure sore prevention and wound healing
- standing and ambulation systems
- exercise and rehabilitation systems

Jen French and JP Creignou, silver medalists, sailing, 2012 Paralympics.

Whether you are looking to extend the rehabilitation process or combat the common secondary conditions, neurotechnology may be an option. It is important to first learn about the technologies then consult with a trained medical professional prior to initiating any program.

How do I know? I have been using neurotechnology devices since my spinal cord injury in 1998 from a snowboarding accident. I used surface electrical stimulation to help rehabilitate my upper extremities and FES cycling for exercise early in my rehabilitation process. Later, I was implanted with experimental electrodes in my lower extremities from the Cleveland FES Center. The system allows me to fight off common secondary conditions such as muscle atrophy and pressure sores.

I also use it for daily function. In my wheelchair, I use it for trunk control and to aid in propelling my manual wheelchair. It also gives me the freedom to stand out of my wheelchair; to reach high items, make difficult transfers, join a standing ovation and walk down the aisle at our wedding. Take the time to learn more about neurotechnologies and how they may be right for you. *www.neurotechnetwork.org*   **—Jen French**

Nutrition

It goes without saying, or at least it should, that good health depends on good nutrition. Food affects how we look and feel, and how our bodies work. Eating right provides energy, boosts our immune system, keeps us at the proper body weight, and keeps all body systems in harmony. Eating wrong can cause weight gain, diabetes, heart disease, cancer and other "ailments of civilization."

Eating well is even more essential for persons who are paralyzed. Because of changes that occur to the body after trauma or disease, it's more important than ever to understand the role nutrition plays in maintaining health.

After a spinal cord injury, most people lose some weight. The injury puts stress on the body as it uses its energy and nutrients to repair itself. Stress ramps up the metabolic rate; the body burns calories faster. Moreover, many newly injured people are not able to eat a regular diet. As muscles atrophy, the weight loss continues—for about a month. Later, the problem isn't too few pounds, it's too many. People living with SCI are more prone to inactivity, and thus don't burn calories. That's the pathway to obesity.

Compared to the general population, people with spinal cord injuries are prone to two diet-related problems: heart disease and diabetes. For reasons that are not fully understood, blood chemistry becomes impaired: Insulin tolerance is too high. (The body produces more and more of the hormone insulin to transport energy to the body tissues. This is one of the pathways to diabetes.) Meanwhile, "bad" cholesterol and triglycerides are too high, and "good" cholesterol is too low.

There are no clear guidelines for people living with SCI to manage their metabolic profile. The advice is what doctors say to everyone: moderate your lifestyle; don't eat so much; get some exercise; don't smoke; don't get heavy.

For some it isn't just the food, it's the way the food is presented. People with amyotrophic lateral sclerosis and other conditions who have problems swallowing must regulate the consistency and texture of foods. Food should be softer and cut into smaller pieces that can slide down

There are no clear guidelines for people living with SCI to manage their metabolic profile. The advice is what doctors say to everyone: moderate your lifestyle; don't eat so much; get some exercise; don't smoke; don't get heavy.

the throat with minimum chewing. If food or drinks are too runny, some of the liquid can run into the airway to the lungs and cause coughing. If food is too dry, such as toast, it tends to irritate the throat and causes coughing. This problem can often be solved by adding butter, jam, etc. Foods that may be easier to manage include custards, sherbet, puddings, plain yogurt, canned fruit, applesauce, crustless toast with butter, dark chicken, salmon, thick soups, scrambled eggs, and mashed potatoes. Avoid extra-spicy or acidic foods, soft bread, cookies, crackers, dry cereal, graham crackers, peanut butter, lettuce, celery, rice, and fruits and vegetables with skin or seeds (peas, corn, apples, berries).

Bowel management is directly related to diet. Since the messages from the brain that control the muscular movements of the bowel are out of order, it's difficult for food to move through the intestinal system. A high fiber diet – 25-35 grams of fiber every day – and plenty of fluids is recommended. True, that's a lot of fiber. Where does it come from? Vegetables, fruits, nuts, popcorn. Some people take supplements, such as Metamucil. What to avoid: high-fat foods. They don't easily move through the system.

For some people with paralysis due to disease, diet and nutrition become almost a religious issue, though certainly not without some confusion, and controversy. There are many adherents, for example, of special diets for people with multiple sclerosis. The National Multiple Sclerosis Society recommends the standard food pyramid, with a low-fat, high-carbohydrate program with a variety of grains, fruits and vegetables. The Swank MS diet, originated by an Oregon doctor almost 50 years ago, prescribes a strict no-fat, no-dairy routine. Roy Swank has claimed to reduce the frequency and severity of recurrences in his MS patients by cutting out animal fat – this being the one essential first step for anyone with MS, he says.

Roger MacDougall, an Oscar-nominated Hollywood writer in the 1950s, had a severe case of MS – his legs were paralyzed, he was almost blind, he had no voice. Using a high-protein, low-carbohydrate diet that has become known as the "Paleolithic diet," he says he got completely better. "I have not been cured. I am simply experiencing a remission – but a remission which I firmly believe to be self-induced." MacDougall's premise is that until the advent of agriculture, 10,000 years ago, we were all hunter-gatherers and ate meats and nuts and berries from natural sources; we have not evolved to deal with the processed food products of modern agriculture and thus we can become allergic to certain types of foods – wheat and other glutens, refined sugar and high-fat meat. He suggests that these allergies can lead to autoimmune disease, such as MS, arthritis, etc. MacDougall's answer: Eat like a caveman. Or at least eat more sporadically. The latest diet trend: Eat what you want for five days, fast for two. There might well be something to that: scientists know that rats, mice, and worms that eat very little live longer than those that eat normal diets. The same may be true for humans – people who carefully regulate their calories and eating patterns may stay healthier and extend their life span. It is always best to consult with your healthcare team before beginning any diet or fast.

SOURCES

Spinal Cord Injury Information Network; Rehabilitation Research and Training Center on Aging and Spinal Cord Injury, Rancho Los Amigos; National ALS Association

ð **Below are links to resources.**

Nutrition.gov is a resource on diet and food, including ways these relate to disease, activity, etc. **www.nutrition.gov**

National Institutes of Health: Office of Dietary Supplements offers reliable information on nutritional supplements. **www.ods.od.nih.gov**

Dietary Concerns Related to Paralysis

Pressure ulcers: An active pressure ulcer requires a diet high in protein, vitamins, and minerals.

Kidney or bladder stones: Some individuals with spinal cord dysfunction may be prone to stones. Certain beverages are more likely to create calcium crystals in the urine (beer, coffee, cocoa, cola drinks). Dairy products (milk, cheese, yogurt, ice cream) can also lead to trouble. The best way to avoid kidney or bladder stones is to drink a lot of water.

Urinary tract infection: Carbonated beverages (soda), orange juice and grapefruit juice may cause the urine to become alkaline, a breeding ground for bacteria that can cause UTI.

Weight control: Obesity is on the rise across the United States and people with disabilities are part of the picture. Extra weight decreases mobility, endurance and balance. It can make transfers difficult and increases the risk of pressure sores. There are dangers to being underweight, too; it increases the risk for infections and pressure sores, resulting in less energy and more fatigue.

General guidelines: Most nutritionists stick pretty close to the standard food pyramid (most calories from complex carbohydrates — breads and starches – with plenty of dairy and avoidance of refined sugars and fat). This foundation of American eating habits has been challenged in recent years by many popular high-protein diets.

Going against prevailing dogma, there is research suggesting that carbohydrates are also a problem in obesity, diabetes and heart disease. Nonetheless, the usual rehab nutrition program typically recommends a carbohydrate intake representing 50-60 percent of total calories, with protein being 20 percent of total calories.

Protein: People with mobility limitations generally need more protein in their diets to help prevent tissue or muscle breakdown. At least two 4-ounce servings of a high-protein food should be consumed every day; eat even more than that if there is an active pressure sore.

Fiber: To promote normal bowel functioning and prevent constipation and diarrhea, nutritionists recommend whole grain breads and cereals, fresh fruits and vegetables, raw nuts and seed mixes with dried fruits and peanut butter.

Fluids: A lot of water is necessary to prevent dehydration and to keep your kidneys and bladder flushed.

Minerals and vitamins: Fruits and vegetables are good sources of vitamin A and the family of B vitamins. There is some evidence that taking extra vitamin C and a zinc supplement helps keep the skin healthy.

Antioxidant vitamins: These round up free radicals that can damage the body's cells, and may stimulate the immune system. Many people with chronic neurological disease take supplements, including vitamins A (beta-carotene), C and E. Fruits and vegetables are good sources. Grape seed extract, co-enzyme Q 10 and pycnogenol are other sources.

Vitamin D: good idea to take a supplement if you don't get out in the sun much. There is data showing a link between vitamin D and multiple sclerosis: the farther away from the equator a person lives, the higher the risk of MS.

SEXUAL HEALTH

For Men

Paralysis affects a man's sexuality both physically and psychologically. Men wonder, "Can I still do it?" Men worry that sexual pleasure is a thing of the past. They worry that they can no longer father children, that mates will find them unattractive, that partners will pack up and leave. It is true that, after disease or injury, men often face changes in their relationships and sexual activity. Emotional changes occur, of course, and these too can affect a person's sexuality.

Erections are the number one issue after paralysis. Normally, men have two types of erections. Psychogenic erections result from sexual thoughts or seeing or hearing something stimulating. The brain sends these arousing messages through the nerves of the spinal cord that exit at the T10–L2 levels, then relays them to the penis, resulting in tumescence. The ability to have a psychogenic erection depends on the level and extent of paralysis. Generally, men with an incomplete injury at a low level are more likely to have psychogenic erections than men with high-level, incomplete injuries. Men with complete injuries are less likely to experience psychogenic erections.

A reflex erection occurs when there is direct physical contact to the penis or other erotic areas such as the ears, nipples or neck. A reflex erection is involuntary and can occur without sexual or stimulating thoughts. The nerves that control a man's ability to have a reflex erection are located in the sacral segments (S2–S4) of the spinal cord. Most paralyzed men are able to have a reflex erection with physical stimulation unless the S2–S4 pathway is damaged.

Spasticity is known to interfere with sexual activity in some people with SCI. During genital stimulation, spasticity is more likely to be increased and autonomic dysreflexia may occur, thus requiring temporary cessation of sexual activity. In addition, ejaculation has been reported to decrease spasticity for up to 24 hours.

Indeed, ejaculation is the number two issue. Researchers report that ejaculation occurs in up to 70 percent of men with incomplete lower-level injuries and in as many as 17 percent of men with complete lower-level injuries. Ejaculation occurs in about 30 percent of men with incomplete upper-level injuries and almost never in men with complete upper-level injuries.

While many men who are paralyzed can still "get it up," the erection may not be hard enough or last long enough for sexual activity. This condition is called erectile dysfunction (ED). Numerous treatments and products (pills, pellets, shots and implants) are available for treating ED but paralyzed men may have special concerns or problems with their use. It is important to see your doctor or urologist for accurate information on the various treatments as they relate to specific conditions.

Research and reported experience of men with paralysis show that Viagra, Cialis and Levitra significantly improve the quality of erections and the satisfaction of sex life in most men with ED who have injuries between T6 and L5. Men who have low or high blood pressure or vascular disease should not take these drugs. Some medications cannot be taken with ED drugs—review this with the prescribing physician

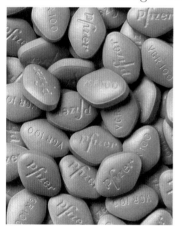

especially if you are likely to experience autonomic dysreflexia.

Penile injection therapy is an option that involves injecting a drug (papavarine or alprostadil) or a combination of drugs into the side of the penis. This produces an erection that can last for an hour or two and is firm enough for sexual intercourse in about 80 percent of men, regardless of age or the cause of ED. If not used correctly, these drugs can result in a prolonged erection, called priapism, which, untreated, can damage the penile tissue. Other risks from the injection are bruising, scarring or infection. An injection erection is a more difficult option for those with limited hand function.

Another option is called medicated urethral system erection (MUSE), wherein a medicated pellet (alprostadil, the same drug used in penile injection therapy) is placed into the urethra for absorption into the surrounding tissue. Intraurethral medications are not generally considered to be effective in men with SCI and are seldom prescribed.

Beyond drug options, vacuum pumps produce an erection. The penis is placed in a cylinder and the air is pumped out, causing blood to be drawn into the erectile tissues. Tumescence is maintained by placing an elastic constriction ring around the base of the penis. It's important to remove the ring after intercourse to avoid the risk of skin abrasion or breakdown. A battery-operated vacuum model is an available option. Premature loss of rigidity and lack of spontaneity are unwanted side effects. See **http://postvac.com**

A penile prosthesis, often the last treatment option for ED because it is permanent and requires surgery, involves inserting an implant directly into the erectile tissues. There are various types of implants available, including semi-rigid or malleable rods and inflatable devices. Generally, the penis may not be as firm as a natural erection. There are risks of mechanical breakdown, and the danger that the implant could cause infection or push out through the skin. Research showed that 67 percent of females interviewed were satisfied with results of implant treatment for their partner's ED.

Orgasm: A study of 45 men with SCI and 6 able-bodied controls demonstrated that 79 percent of the men with incomplete lesions and 28 percent of those with complete injuries achieved orgasm in the laboratory setting. Predictors of orgasm were completeness of injury and prior history of orgasm post-injury.

Paralyzed men with ED should have a thorough physical exam by a urologist familiar with their condition before using any medications or assistive devices. Men with spinal cord injuries above the T6 level must be watchful for signs of autonomic dysreflexia (AD). Signs include flushing in the face, headaches, nasal congestion and/or changes in vision. See page 125 for more on AD.

Fertility is the third biggest issue: Men with paralysis usually experience a change in their ability to biologically father a child, due to the inability to ejaculate. Some men experience retrograde ejaculation: Semen travels in reverse, back into the bladder. The number of sperm a man produces does not usually drop in the months or years after paralysis. However, the motility (movement) of the sperm is considerably lower than for non-paralyzed men. There are options, though, for improving the ability to father children.

Penile vibratory stimulation (PVS) is an inexpensive and fairly reliable way to produce an ejaculation at home. Vibrostimulation is most successful in men with SCI above T10. A variety of vibrators/massagers are available for this purpose. Some are specifically designed with the output power and frequency required to induce ejaculation while minimizing skin problems. See **www.reflexonic.com**

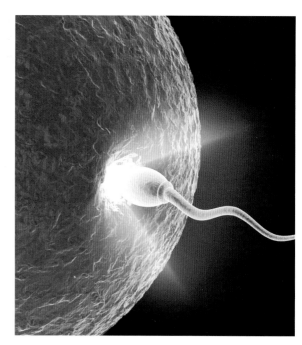

Rectal probe electroejaculation (RPE) is an option (albeit in a clinic with several technicians around) if the vibratory method is not successful. RPE, borrowing from animal husbandry, places an electrical probe in the rectum; a controlled electrical stimulation produces an ejaculation. Electroejaculation is generally a safe and effective way to obtain a sperm sample, although using a vibratory stimulus generally produces samples with better sperm motility than from electrostimulation.

The sperm from men with SCI are healthy but usually not strong swimmers, and often not hardy enough to penetrate the egg. Because of their reduced motility, the sperm need a little high-tech help. Men with SCI stand a good chance of becoming biological fathers when they have access to specialized clinics and care. The recent development of intracytoplasmic sperm injection (ICSI), which involves the direct injection of a single mature sperm into an oocyte (egg), can often solve the problem of conception.

If sperm cannot be retrieved using PVS or RPE, minor surgery can be performed to remove sperm from the testicle.

There are lots of success stories but high-tech, assisted fertility is not a slam-dunk. It can be emotionally draining and also quite expensive. Get the facts and treatment options from a fertility specialist experienced in issues of paralysis. Some couples grappling with infertility have successfully utilized donor sperm (from a sperm bank) to impregnate the woman. Couples may also want to explore the very rewarding options available to adopt children.

Sex after stroke: Heart disease, stroke or surgery doesn't mean that a satisfying sex life must end. After the first phase of recovery is over, people find that the same forms of lovemaking they enjoyed before are still rewarding. It is myth that resuming sex often causes a heart attack, stroke or sudden death. Still, fears about performance can greatly reduce sexual interest. After recovery, stroke survivors may feel depressed. This is normal, and in 85 percent of the cases it goes away within three months.

To be sure, a man can continue or initiate a romantic and intimate relationship with a partner after a paralyzing disease or injury. Good communication with his partner is essential. It is important for both partners to understand the physical changes that have occurred, but it is equally important to talk about each other's feelings. The couple can then explore and experiment with different ways to be romantic and intimate.

For people with limited arm and hand function, it is often necessary to ask caregivers to provide physical assistance prior to sexual activity. Help might be needed with undressing, preparation, and positioning.

Many couples consider oral-genital intercourse. Whatever seems satisfying and pleasurable is acceptable as long as both partners agree.

Here's something in the adaptive equipment realm for men with paralysis: IntimateRider is a swing chair that offers a natural gliding motion to improve what the company calls "sexual mobility." The IntimateRider was designed by a C6-C7 tetraplegic to improve his sex life after spinal cord injury. The chair moves with very little pushing effort, allowing the pelvis to thrust during sex. **www.intimaterider.com**

While it's been said that the largest sex organ is the brain, it's not always easy to make major adjustments in one's sexual persona. Professional counseling can help in working through feelings of fear or anxiety over establishing or continuing a healthy relationship after paralysis. A counselor can also work with couples on healthy ways to communicate their needs and feelings.

Safe sex: The risk of sexually transmitted disease (STD) is the same both before and after paralysis. STDs include diseases such as gonorrhea, syphilis, herpes and the HIV virus; these can cause other medical problems, such as infertility, urinary tract infections, pelvic inflammatory disease, vaginal discharge, genital warts and AIDS. The safest, most effective way to prevent sexually transmitted diseases is to use a condom with a spermicidal gel.

SOURCES

The American Urological Association, University of Miami School of Medicine, Cleveland Clinic

❧ **Below are links to resources.**

Paralyzed Veterans of America, in support of The Consortium for Spinal Cord Medicine, offers authoritative clinical practice guidelines for sexuality and reproductive health. PVA, toll-free 1-800-424-8200, **www.pva.org**, click on Publications, then Medical Guidelines.

The Spinal Cord Injury Rehabilitation Evidence (SCIRE) project is a Canadian research collaboration (scientists, clinicians and consumers) that reviews, evaluates, and translates research knowledge to establish best rehabilitation practices following SCI. Includes section on sexuality. **www.scireproject.com**

For Women

Paralysis itself doesn't affect a woman's libido or her need to express herself sexually, nor does it affect her ability to conceive a child. Generally speaking, sexuality in the paralyzed female is less affected than in the male; it is physically easier for the woman to adapt her sexual role, even though it may be more passive than that of a non-disabled woman. The main difference in sexual functioning between women with disabilities and those without can be accounted for by the difficulties women with disabilities have in finding a romantic partner. Their level of sexual desire may be the same, but the level of activity is generally less because fewer women with disabilities have partners.

There are no physiological changes after paralysis that prevent women from engaging in sexual activity. Positioning can be an issue but can usually be accommodated. Autonomic dysreflexia can be anticipated and controlled. Many women experience a loss of vaginal muscle control and many are unable to produce vaginal lubrication. Both problems are likely the result of the interruption in normal nerve signals from the brain to the genital area. There is no remedy for muscle loss. Lubrication, of course, can be augmented.

Typically, lubrication occurs as a psychogenic (mental) and reflex (physical) response to something sexually stimulating or arousing. It has been suggested that lubrication in women is the physiological equivalent of the erection in the male, and is probably innervated in the same way. Women can substitute water-based (never oil-based, such as Vaseline) lubricants such as K-Y Jelly.

Low sex drive is common among women with paralysis; indeed, it is reported among all women. Meanwhile, Viagra was clinically tested by a group of women with spinal cord injuries; almost all reported that the drug stimulated arousal. In some, it enhanced lubrication and sensation during intercourse.

In some conditions of paralysis, such as multiple sclerosis, cognitive problems can undermine sexuality. People with short-term memory or concentration loss may drift off during sexual activities in a way that can be disheartening to the partner. It requires love and patience, with lots of communication, to bring this out in the open and to seek the needed psychological or medical treatment.

Women who are paralyzed often fear bowel and bladder accidents during times of intimacy. There are a number of ways to reduce the chance of accidents. The first is to limit fluid intake if a sexual encounter is planned. Women who use intermittent catheterization should empty the bladder before beginning sexual activity. Women who use a suprapubic or Foley catheter find that taping the catheter tube to the thigh or abdomen keeps it out of the way. The Foley can be left in during sexual intercourse because, unknown to many men and even women, the urethra (urinary opening) is separate from the vagina.

The best way to avoid a bowel accident is to establish a consistent bowel program. Women may also want to avoid eating right before engaging in sexual activity. With good communication, an occasional bladder or bowel accident won't destroy a rewarding sex life.

Orgasm: Sexual success is often measured, wrongly, by whether or not partners achieve orgasm. A woman with paralysis, like men with similar levels of function, can achieve what is described as a normal orgasm if there is some residual pelvic innervation. Dr. Marca Sipski of the University of Alabama/Birmingham School of Medicine thinks paralyzed women retain an orgasm reflex that requires no brain input. The ability to achieve orgasm seems unrelated to the degree of neurological impairment in women with lesions down to T5 level; her research indicates the potential is still there, but women may give up trying to have orgasms because they lack the ability to feel touch in the genital area.

A small body of research suggests that women with SCI can achieve orgasm using a clitoral vacuum suction device (Eros device), FDA approved to treat female orgasmic dysfunction. The device increases blood flow, thus creating clitoral engorgement; this in turn may increase vaginal lubrication and heighten orgasm response.

Some paralyzed men and women, with practice and focused thought, are able to experience a "phantom orgasm," through reassignment of sexual response; this involves mentally intensifying an existing sensation from one portion of their body and reassigning the sensation to the genitals.

Women with paraplegia or tetraplegia who are of childbearing age usually regain their menstrual cycle; nearly 50 percent do not miss a single period following injury. Pregnancy is possible and generally not a health risk. While most paralyzed women can have normal vaginal deliveries, certain complications of pregnancy are possible, including increased urinary tract infections, pressure sores and spasticity. Autonomic dysreflexia (AD) is a serious risk during labor for those with injuries above T6 (see page 125). Also, loss of sensation in the pelvic area can prevent the woman from knowing that labor has begun.

Another potential risk of pregnancy is the development of thromboembolism, in which blood vessels become blocked by clots. With high thoracic or cervical lesions, respiratory function may be impaired with the increased burden of pregnancy or the work of labor, requiring ventilator support.

Women with disabilities often do not receive adequate healthcare services. For example, routine pelvic exams are not done due to lack of awareness of the need, problems getting onto the exam table, or not being able to find a doctor with knowledge about their disability. Providers might wrongly assume that women with disabilities are not having sex, especially if their disability is severe, and therefore may neglect to screen these women for sexually transmitted diseases (STDs) or even perform a full pelvic exam. Unfortunately, some healthcare providers even suggest to women with disabilities that they abstain from sex and not bear children, even if they can conceive children.

Breast health: Women with disabilities must be aware that they are among the one in eight women who will get breast cancer. Screening is essential. Women with limited use of their arms and hands may need to perform exams using alternate positions or with the help of an attendant or family member. In the clinic, getting a wheelchair in the door is the easy part; services or programs provided to patients with disabilities must be equal to those provided for persons without disabilities.

Birth control: since paralysis does not usually affect fertility in the female, contraception is important. There are also some special considerations. Oral contraceptives are linked to inflammation and clots in blood vessels, and the risk of these is greater with SCI. Intrauterine devices cannot always be felt in the paralyzed woman and may cause undetected complications. Use of diaphragms and spermicides can be difficult for those with impaired hand dexterity.

Sexuality does not disappear after paralysis. Explore sexuality with an open heart and an open mind.

SOURCES

The Center for Research on Women with Disabilities, Spain Rehabilitation Center, Paralyzed Veterans of America

&❧ **Below are links to resources.**

The Center for Research on Women with Disabilities (CROWD) focuses on issues related to health (including reproduction and sexuality), aging, civil rights, abuse and independent living. CROWD hopes to expand the life choices of women with disabilities to fully participate in community life: believe in oneself, honor the body, defy the myths, demand answers. 713-798-5782 or toll-free 1-800-44-CROWD; **www.bcm.edu/crowd**

National Resource Center for Parents with Disabilities, from Through the Looking Glass, a resource on childbirth and parenting, adaptive equipment for childcare, networking and support. Toll-free 1-800-644-2666; **www.lookingglass.org**

MobileWomen is an Internet magazine for women with disabilities. The site, supported in part by the Reeve Foundation, features articles, resources and a place to share experiences and solutions. **www.mobilewomen.org**

3
Acute Care & Rehab

The best way to deal with the confusion and helplessness of a spinal cord injury is to be armed with reliable information. Start here.

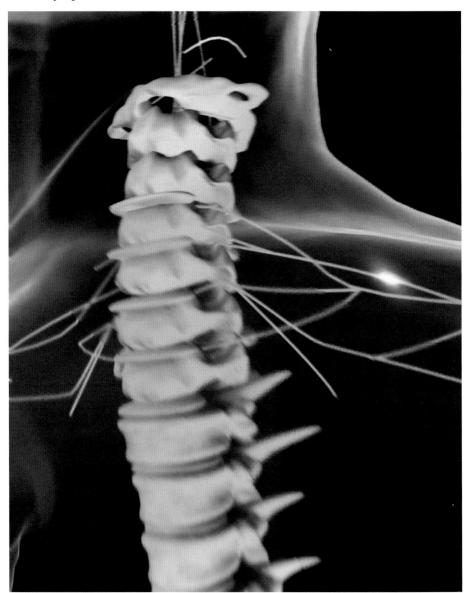

Learning that a family member or friend has had a spinal cord injury is devastating and overwhelming news. The best way to combat your feelings of helplessness and confusion is to arm yourself with information on what a spinal cord injury is, and what it means in terms of short-term planning and long-range goals. This section of the book helps those who are beginning to locate spinal cord injury information for a loved one or friend who has been recently injured.

ACUTE CARE AND ON TO REHAB

NAVIGATING THE WORLD OF NEUROTRAUMA can certainly be confusing. The Information Specialists at the Paralysis Resource Center specialize in answering questions about new injuries. You can speak to a member of the IS team at 1-800-539-7309, or make an appointment for a call-back. If you have not done so already, please visit the PRC website at **www. paralysis.org** for a wealth of information for the newly injured as well as for those living with SCI for years. You will find numerous links to other organizations as well as information specific to advances in SCI research. You don't have to go this alone: Join the online Paralysis Community to connect with and gain support from others whose circumstances are similar to yours. Paralysis Community: **www.ChristopherReeve.org** click on Community Forums.

The following section concerns issues common to acute SCI. Since each injury is different as to its level and severity, the information is provided in general terms.

Acute Management

The first few hours are critical after a spinal cord injury, as life-saving interventions and efforts to limit the severity of the injury take precedence. Fewer people are coming away from accidents with complete paralysis. A generation ago, the number of spinal cord injured people considered neurologically incomplete was 38 percent; it's now well over half, an improvement attributed to more careful management of medical emergencies at the scene. Ideally, a spinally injured person should be transported to a Level I trauma center for multidisciplinary expertise. If cervical spine injury is suspected, the head and neck are immediately stabilized. The spine should never be allowed to bend. Since SCI rarely occurs without other complications, acute management must address possible brain injury (especially for upper cervical injuries), fractures, lacerations, contusions, etc.

Beginning in 1990, most people with SCI in the United States were given large doses of the steroid drug methylprednisolone; it was thought to preserve spinal cord tissue vulnerable to the "cascade" of biochemical responses secondary to the initial trauma. According to the most recent clinical practice guidelines for SCI, however, there is not enough evidence to support administration of any neuroprotective drug or therapy for SCI, including methylprednisolone, and including the use of hypothermia (cooling) of the spinal cord. Cooling has been tested in clinical trials and appears promising, but protocols for temperature, duration, etc. have not been determined. Other acute SCI therapies are under investigation, including Riluzole (see North American Clinical Trials Network, page 99).

Once a person reaches the acute hospital, several basic life-support procedures may occur. Respiratory issues must immediately be

addressed. Tracheostomy or endotracheal intubation is often done even before location of injury is established. Bladder management is begun, typically with an indwelling catheter. Commony, SCI patients undergo MRI.

Early surgery (within hours of injury) to decompress or align the spinal canal is often done. Evidence from animal studies supports this as a means to

What is a Spinal Cord Injury?

What is a spinal cord injury? Spinal cord injuries commonly lead to paralysis; they involve damage to the nerves within the bony protection of the spinal canal. The most common cause of spinal cord dysfunction is trauma (including motor vehicle accidents, falls, shallow diving, acts of violence, and sports injuries). Damage can also occur from various diseases acquired at birth or later in life, from tumors, electric shock, and loss of oxygen related to surgical or underwater mishaps. The spinal cord does not have to be severed in order for a loss of function to occur. The spinal cord can be bruised, stretched, or crushed. Since the spinal cord coordinates body movement and sensation, an injured spinal cord loses the ability to send and receive messages from the brain to the body's system that controls sensory, motor, and autonomic function.

improve neurologic recovery but the timing of this intervention is subject to debate; some surgeons wait several days to allow swelling to subside before decompressing the cord.

For cervical fractures, the spine is often stabilized by a bone fusion, using grafts from the fibula (calf bone), tibia (shin bone) or iliac crest (hip). To stabilize spinal bones, a spinal fusion might be done, using metal plates, screws, wires and/or rods and sometimes small pieces of bone from other areas of the body.

A spinal cord injured patient will typically encounter several external devices, including braces, traction pulleys, skull tongs, turning frames, molded plastic jackets, collars and corsets. Bracing devices are often used early on; they allow vertebral bones to heal but allow patients to be up and around, protecting them from the effects of bed rest. A halo-brace is a stainless steel hoop placed around the patient's head and secured to the skull by four stainless steel pins. It can be applied in the emergency room. The brace is secured to upright pieces extending up from a pelvic girdle.

Classifying the Injury: Once physicians determine the level and extent of the injury the patient will also undergo a thorough neurological examination. This looks for signs of sensation, muscle tone and reflexes of all limbs and the trunk. The classification of injury may differ from what is seen on the x-rays or scans because it is based on function, reflected by

Outcomes That Often Occur

By level of injury, here are summaries of outcome expectations (remember, these are averages, not hard, cold facts): the level of injury and function may change.

Level C1-3: total paralysis of the trunk, all extremities. These folks are most likely to be ventilator dependent and typically need 24-hour attendant care with total assistance with bowel, bladder, bed mobility, transfers, eating, dressing, grooming, bathing and transportation. These high quads can power an electric wheelchair and can be independent communicators with the right equipment; they need to be able to explain everything an assistant needs to know about their care.

Level C4: Total paralysis but some respiratory reserve possible, may be able to breathe without a ventilator, otherwise, similar profile as the C1-3 group: total assistance needed for all tasks except power wheelchair use. Some neck and shoulder movement.

Level C5: Possible shoulder flexion, elbow flexion, weak hands and wrists. Low respiratory endurance; may need help clearing secretions. These people can eat independently if meals are set up for them but still need some assistance for grooming, bed transfers, dressing. Personal care assistance needed daily. Some people with a C5 injury can drive a vehicle with the right specialized equipment and training.

Level C6: Total paralysis of trunk and legs but more independent. Some help may be needed for bowel, uneven transfers, bathing. No wrist flexion or hand movement but can push a manual chair and do weight shifts. Personal care needed but on a limited basis – getting up in the morning, grooming, going to bed. Driving is very doable.

Level C7/8: Paralysis of trunk and legs but with greater arm and hand dexterity, including elbow, wrist and thumb extension. Still some limits to respiratory endurance and reduced vital capacity. Mostly independent for bladder and bowel self-care, eating, grooming, etc. Personal care attendant may be needed on limited basis.

Level T1-9: Lower trunk paralysis but full arm and hand function. Some compromised vital capacity but independent for almost all functional self-care activities. Minimal assistance needed for daily living, work and homemaking.

Level T10-L1: Paralysis of legs but good trunk stability, intact respiratory system. Independent in functional activities. Minimal help needed in the home.

Level L2-S5: Partial paralysis of legs, hips, knees, ankles and feet, good trunk support. Independent for all functions of wheelchair life. No assistance in the home.

Get a copy of *Expected Outcomes, What You Should Know*, (choose the one for your level of injury). Free download from *www.pva.org*, see publications section.

what is called the ASIA scale. This is a tool that assigns the spinal cord injury patient into a category: ASIA A (no motor control, no sensation); B (no motor, some sensation); C (some motor function), D (motor incomplete with more function below lesion area); or E (normal). During an ASIA classification the physician, looking at a variety of determinants such as muscle movement and range of motion, notes whether or not the person can feel light touch or sharp and dull sensations.

The location and severity of the spinal cord injury determines what parts of the body are affected. The doctor will also determine if the injury is complete or incomplete. An incomplete injury means that the ability of the spinal cord to convey messages to or from the brain is not completely lost. A complete injury is indicated by a total lack of sensory and motor function below the level of injury. But the absence of motor and sensory function below the injury site does not necessarily mean that there are no remaining intact axons or nerves crossing the injury site, just that they do not function appropriately following the injury.

Extra care must be given to protecting the skin; as many as half of new SCI patients get some degree of pressure ulcer in the first month post-injury. Pressure relief is needed at least every 30 minutes.

The first days after a SCI are also the most crucial to begin formal rehabilitation. It is essential to optimal recovery to initiate rehab interventions immediately after injury to prevent secondary complications, including thromboembolism, skin breakdown, and respiratory issues; bowel and bladder care must also be managed.

It is also important to immediately begin addressing psychosocial issues related to SCI, paying attention to family issues, depression, social supports, coping strategies and suicidal ideation. This is also the key time to discuss assistive devices and information services, insurance issues, Internet resources, etc.

Depending on other medical issues related to the injury, most people leave the acute hospital within days and enter into rehabilitation.

See "Early Acute Management in Adults with Spinal Cord Injury," a guide from the Consortium for Spinal Cord Medicine. This publication, along with nine additional Clinical Practice Guidelines, can be downloaded at no cost; go to **www.pva.org**, click on publications section.

I Have No Health Insurance

Being uninsured or underinsured does not mean there are no avenues to get health coverage. Hospitals that accept federal money must provide a certain amount of free or reduced-fee care. Check with the hospital's financial aid department to see if you qualify for reduced or charity care. To start the process, meet with a caseworker at the hospital to gather relevant paperwork and begin applying for Medicare/Medicaid and Social Security. Not everyone will qualify for Medicaid, a state administered program established to provide healthcare to low-income individuals and families. Applications and rules vary from state to state, so contact your local Medicaid office directly or work with the hospital caseworker. Be aware of any deadlines or required documentation. Contact relevant benefit offices to set up any appointments or interviews needed to expedite the process; confirm the documentation needed. Be sure to keep accurate and thorough records of everyone you are in contact with. If you are doubtful of your eligibility, it is best to apply and have a caseworker or lawyer review your application. Caseworkers or social workers are sometimes assigned by your hospital (though you may have to ask for one). They are there to assist you in managing your family member's care.

Medicaid is an assistance program. Medical bills are paid from federal, state and local tax funds. It serves low-income people under the age of 65. Patients usually pay no costs for covered medical expenses, although a small co-payment may be required. For more, call the Centers for Medicare and Medicaid Services (CMS), 1-877-267-2323.

Medicare is an insurance program. Medical bills are paid from trust funds which those covered have paid into. It mainly serves people 65 and over, whatever their income, and serves younger disabled people after they have received disability benefits from Social Security for 24 months. Patients pay part of costs through deductibles for hospital and other costs. Small monthly premiums are required for non-hospital coverage. Medicare is a federal program. For more information on Medicare call 1-800-MEDICARE.

Children: If the patient is under 18 year of age, look into your state's health insurance program for children (SCHIP). SCHIPs provide low-cost insurance coverage to families and children. Eligibility is determined by each state and is income- and disability-based. Each state's SCHIP program may have a different name. It is important to note that your child may qualify for SCHIP coverage even if denied Medicaid. Children may also be eligible for some disability benefits from Supplemental Security Income.

To help you navigate the Medicaid/Medicare process or SCHIP program: Center for Medicare and Medicaid Service: *www.cms.hhs.gov* or *www.medicaid.gov*

CHOOSING A REHABILITATION SETTING

How can you predict the quality of care you or a loved one will receive when entering a rehabilitation program? How do you know what facility to choose? Is there really a choice? Does rehab really matter?

Most people have no experience with rehab or the effects of paralysis, so assessing the quality of a rehab program can be stressful and complex. The final choice may come down to which program is covered by insurance or by which one is closest to the support systems of one's family and community, but it is possible to make an informed decision. Rehabilitation centers are not all the same; they can be compared.

At the top of the list of qualifying factors is experience in rehabilitation for your specific needs. Medical rehab is increasingly specialized; the more patients a facility regularly treats with needs similar

to yours, the higher the expertise of the staff. How do you know what a facility is best at? Ask the facility how many beds are dedicated to your rehab situation. For example, if 85 percent of a unit's beds are dedicated to stroke survivors, this may not be the ideal place for a young person with a spinal cord injury. Get a sense of the facility's reputation and standing. Ask around; connect to others by way of support groups (e.g., Reeve Paralysis Community, CareCure Community, American Stroke Association, National Multiple Sclerosis Society; turn to page 411 for a list of online communities).

High-quality programs are often located in facilities devoted exclusively to providing rehabilitation services or in hospitals with designated units.

Here are a few questions to consider in choosing a facility:

- Is the place accredited, that is, does it meet the professional standards of care for your specific needs? Generally speaking, a facility with accredited expertise is preferable to a general rehabilitation program.

Money for Rehab

H ow can I locate funding for rehabilitation and equipment? Depending upon the cause and the nature of the injury, you should seek out various insurance policies that may cover medical emergencies (homeowners, auto, and worker's compensation) in addition to your health insurance. If you still need assistance, there are some non-profit organizations that do provide grants for individuals. However, funding levels and guidelines do vary from organization to organization. Please call the Reeve Foundation at 1-800-539-7309 for more information on organizations that provide grants to individuals as well as those that provide wheelchairs and other equipment. Fundraising is another option to consider. An organization called HelpHopeLive assists individuals with raising funds from their communities and social networks for uninsured expenses related to catastrophic injury. Donors receive tax deductions. HelpHopeLive: Toll-free 1-800-642-8399; *www.helphopelive.org*

For example, recognition by the Commission on Accreditation of Rehabilitation Facilities (CARF) for spinal cord injury indicates that the facility meets a minimum standard level of care, has a wide range of specialized services and is well connected in the local community. CARF also accredits programs in assisted living, mental health and substance abuse, brain injury, and pediatric rehab.

- For those with a spinal cord or brain injury, there are groups of specialized hospitals called Model Systems Centers. These are well-established facilities that have qualified for special federal grants to demonstrate and share medical expertise (see pages 45 and 90).

- Does the place offer a wide variety of specialized personnel who offer therapies with a coordinated team approach? Rehab teams should include doctors and nurses, plus social workers, occupational and physical therapists, recreational therapists, rehabilitation nurses, rehabilitation psychologists, speech pathologists, vocational counselors, nutritionists, respiratory experts, sexuality counselors, rehab engineering experts, case managers, etc.

- Does the facility offer connections to peer support and contact with others with a similar disability? Peer support is often the most reliable and encouraging source of information as people make their way in the new world of rehab and recovery.

You might also ask these types of questions: What have been the results for people like me who have used your services? How will services be individualized? How much can my family participate in the program? Are you close to public transportation? Are there bilingual staff or sign language interpreters? The ultimate measure of good rehab is the breadth and quality of the professional staff on hand. The professions you can expect to find represented on a rehabilitation team are as follows:

Physiatrist

A physiatrist (pronounced fizz-ee-AT-trist, or more commonly, fizz-EYE-a-trist) is a doctor with a specialty in physical medicine and rehabilitation. Physiatrists treat a wide range of problems from sore shoulders to acute and chronic pain and musculoskeletal disorders. Physiatrists coordinate the long-term rehabilitation process for people with paralysis, including those with spinal cord injuries, cancer, stroke or other neurological disorders, brain injuries, amputations and multiple sclerosis. A physiatrist must complete four years of graduate medical education and four years of postdoctoral residency training. Residency includes one year spent developing fundamental clinical skills and three years of training in the full scope of the specialty.

Rehab Nurse

Rehab nurses begin to work with individuals and their families soon after the onset of injury or illness. They have special training in rehabilitation and understand the full range of medical complications related to bladder and bowel, nutrition, pain, skin integrity and more, including vocational, educational, environmental and spiritual needs. Rehab nurses provide comfort, therapy and education and promote wellness and independence. The goal of rehabilitation nursing is to assist individuals with disabilities and chronic illness in the restoration and maintenance of optimal health. Nurses are the hands-on people who carry out the directives of the medical team.

Occupational Therapist

Occupational therapists (OTs) are skilled professionals who have studied the social, emotional and physiological effects of illness and injury. An OT helps individuals learn—or relearn—the day-to-day activities they need for maximum independence. OTs offer treatment programs to help with bathing, dressing, preparing a meal, house cleaning, engaging in arts and crafts or gardening. They recommend and train people in the use of adaptive equipment to replace lost function. OTs also evaluate home and job environments and recommend adaptations. The occupational therapist guides family members and caregivers in safe and effective methods of home care; he or she will also facilitate contact with the community outside of the hospital.

Physical Therapist

Physical therapists (PTs) treat people with motor and/or sensory impairments, helping to increase strength and endurance, improve coordination, reduce spasticity and pain, maintain muscles, protect skin from pressure sores, and gain greater control of bladder and bowel function. PTs also treat joints and help expand their range of motion.

Staying in Touch

Staying in touch with loved ones and friends while also managing a healthcare challenge can be difficult. But staying connected is a crucial component to getting and staying well—for both patients and caregivers. One very good way to stay connected with family, friends and colleagues before, during and after hospitalization and rehabilitation is by way of a private, personalized website such as Caring Bridge, Lotsa Helping Hands or CarePages. These free websites allow you to post entries on the condition and care of your loved one in the care of a hospital or rehabilitation center. You can also receive messages of encouragement to help sustain you during this difficult transition in your life. *www.caringbridge.org*, *www.lotsahelpinghands. com*, or *www.carepages.com*

PTs use a variety of equipment including weights, pools and bikes (including the functional electrical stimulation types). When pain is an issue, physical therapy is often the first line of defense; therapists use a variety of methods including electrical stimulation and exercise to improve muscle tone and reduce contractures, spasticity and pain.

PTs will also demonstrate techniques for using assistive devices such as wheelchairs, canes or braces. Physical therapy is not a passive activity that is "done" to you; a PT program requires active participation from both practitioner and patient—it's hard work to restore body function lost to injury or disease. Once a maintenance program has been developed by a physical therapist, it is the client's responsibility to follow it at home.

Recreation Therapist

Recreation therapists help people discover the wide range of options for active living in their community. It has been well established that exercise, fitness and relaxation reduce stress and contribute to improved cardiovascular and respiratory functioning, increased strength, endurance and coordination. Activity clearly reduces secondary medical complications related to paralysis. Skin sores and urinary tract infections, for example, are significantly reduced in wheelchair athletes, as compared to non-athletes. Rec therapists push physical activity for social as well as medical reasons. Active involvement in recreation leads to improved life satisfaction, better social relationships and lower levels of depression.

Vocational Counselor

Vocational counselors perform many of the same functions that career counselors do—they assess a client's job skills and help with a smooth reentry into the workforce or school. Then they work with various government agencies to obtain equipment, training and placement. Vocational therapists also educate disabled individuals about their rights and protections under the Americans with Disabilities Act, which requires employers to make "reasonable accommodations" for disabled employees. Vocational therapists may mediate between employers and employees to negotiate reasonable accommodation.

Speech-Language Pathologist

Speech-language pathologists help people with aphasia or other communication problems relearn language or develop alternative means of communication. They also help people improve their ability to swallow. Sometimes, changing body position and posture while eating can bring about improvement. The texture of foods can be modified to make swallowing easier. Speech-language pathologists help people with paralysis develop strategies for language disabilities, including the use of symbol boards or sign language. They also share their knowledge of computer technology and other types of equipment to enhance communication.

Neurologist

A neurologist is a doctor who specializes in the diagnosis and treatment of disorders of the nervous system (brain, spinal cord, nerves and muscles). A neurologist makes an initial evaluation, diagnoses the injury and consults on one's immediate care.

Rehabilitation Psychologist

A psychologist helps people deal with life-changing injury or disease, offering tools to cope with the effects of disability. A psychologist offers support for families as well. Therapy might be offered individually or in a group to speed the adjustment to changes in physical, cognitive and emotional functioning. The psychology team also offers marital and family therapy and sexual or family planning counseling. Biofeedback and relaxation techniques may be included.

Case Manager

A case manager oversees many aspects of rehab, including preparing a discharge plan and working with insurance companies to communicate the rehab team's goals. A case manager may arrange for purchases of special equipment and/or home modifications.

Social Worker

A rehab social worker connects many aspects of the recovery process, delving into a patient's personality, lifestyle, emotional behavior, past relationships, education, work history, special interests and financial background in order to help the rehab team create an optimal rehabilitation program within the hospital and back home in the community.

SOURCES

American Occupational Therapy Association, American Physical Therapy Association, American Academy of Physical Medicine and Rehabilitation, Commission on Accreditation of Rehabilitation Facilities, Association of Rehabilitation Nurses, American Therapeutic Recreation Association

ॐ Below are links to resources

The American Academy of Neurology (AAN) is a medical specialty society established to advance the art and science of neurology and to promote the best possible care for patients with neurological disorders. Toll-free 1-800-879-1960; **www.aan.com**

The American Academy of Physical Medicine and Rehabilitation is the national medical society for physicians who are specialists in the field of physical medicine and rehabilitation (physiatrists). The website includes a physician directory. 847-737-6000; **www.aapmr.org**

The American Congress of Rehabilitation Medicine serves people with disabling conditions by promoting rehabilitation research and the transfer of technology. 703-435-5335; **www.acrm.org**

The American Occupational Therapy Association (AOTA) is a professional society that advances the field of occupational therapy through standard setting, advocacy, education and research. 301-652-2682; **www.aota.org**

American Physical Therapy Association is the main membership organization for the PT profession, furthering the prevention, diagnosis and treatment of movement dysfunction. Toll-free 1-800-999-2782; **www.apta.org**

American Speech-Language-Hearing Association (ASHA) is the professional association for audiologists, speech-language pathologists, and speech, language and hearing scientists. Toll-free 1-800-638-8255; **www.asha.org**

The American Therapeutic Recreation Association (ATRA) represents the interests of recreational therapists and promotes recreation as a means of improving health and well-being. 601-450-ATRA; **www.atra-online.com**

Christopher Reeve and his rehab entourage, getting therapy in the pool.

Association of Rehabilitation Nurses promotes and accredits rehab nurses and sets forth the philosophy of care of the nursing professional. Toll-free 1-800-229-7530; **www.rehabnurse.org**

Commission on Accreditation of Rehabilitation Facilities (CARF) is an independent, nonprofit accrediting body that establishes rigorous standards to assure the quality, value and outcome of rehab services. 520–325–1044; toll-free 1-888-281-6531; **www.carf.org**

National Center for Medical Rehabilitation Research (NCMRR), a component of the National Institute of Child Health and Human Development (NICHD), supports research on enhancing the functioning of people with disabilities in daily life. **www.nichd.nih.gov**, click NCMRR.

The National Institute on Disability and Rehabilitation Research (NIDRR) supports research aimed at improving the lives of individuals with disabilities from birth through adulthood. NIDRR: 202-245-7640; **www.ed.gov/osers/nidrr**

Spinal Cord Injury Model Systems and Traumatic Brain Injury Model Systems are federally funded medical and/or rehabilitation centers across the United States. These centers research best practices for SCI and TBI. For a list see **www.msktc.org**

4
Active Living

Challenge the world, explore the boundaries, escape the ordinary, take risks. Most of all—have fun, stay fit, with friends and family.

JOHN JEFFERSON

Christiaan Bailey drops in.

R ecreation. What relief to get away from our day-to-day routines, to recreate mind and body with fun activities, sports and games with friends and family, or in solitude. Paralysis is a ready excuse to stay indoors and inactive. But the benefits of escaping the ordinary, of being challenged, of exploring the boundaries of limitation, and sharing this with people you like to be with is all very fulfilling and meaningful.

THE PHYSICAL BENEFITS of active living promote health and wellness, reduce stress and help us think more creatively. The social and psychological reasons add balance to life with disability. We need to do things that focus on activity and not limits. Recreation and adventure enable people to explore themselves, to take risks, to get the blood going, to gain a fresh perspective.

We're here to discuss fun, though, not therapy. Many recreational activities, sports and competitions are inclusive and accessible. Here's the real bottom line: No matter your level of function or your physical limitations, if you want to try something—anything—there's almost always a way to do it. Jump out of an airplane ... hooked up to a ventilator? Been done. Climb the rock face of El Capitan in Yosemite, with just arm power? Done. Bag an elk with a large caliber rifle, by a high quad sitting in a wheelchair? Sure, if that fits your notion of recreation. Surf the waves off Malibu, with no hand or leg power? Of course. Bungee jumping, swimming the English Channel, riding the rapids in the Grand Canyon, skiing the black diamonds in Vail, sailing or flying solo around the world—all have been done by people living with paralysis.

The point isn't to raise the recreation bar to the level of the extreme achiever. Recreation doesn't have to be measured or scored, or even noticed by anyone but the participants. There is recreation for everyone. Find your own rec groove. Below is a list of some popular individual activities that for the most part can be shared with family and friends (see also team sports listed on page 236). Some require adaptive gear, such as cycles, skis and clubs. Some require a bit of fitness going in. All require a spirit of fun and a readiness to recreate.

RECREATION SPORTS

Billiards

This is a great game for wheelchair users. The rules and regulations are basically the same as in the stand-up game; individuals with upper body limitations must stay seated (one bun on the chair at all times) during play and are allowed to use adaptive devices for shooting control. Modified pool cues or a roller attachment at the end of a cue stick allow players with limited hand use to enjoy the sport and be competitive with the best players.

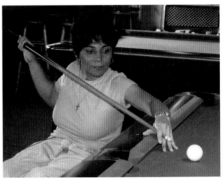

Rozanna Quintana

Some wheelchair players compete quite well against nondisabled players. Contact the National Wheelchair Pool Players Association, 703-817-1215; **www.nwpainc.org**

Bowling

Wheelchair bowling, like basketball, emerged as part of social and physical rehab programs for disabled World War II vets. The sport is easy to learn and does not require enormous strength. It is played just as the stand-up version, with the exception of special push tools and ball-drop ramps for bowlers with limited arm mobility. Special snap handle balls are available for those who can't get a good grip on the ball. Can you do well against nondisabled bowlers? Ask George Holscher, a para from Virginia Beach, or Shawn Beam from Fort Worth. They both rolled perfect 300s in 2012. To find out about leagues and adaptive gear, contact the American Wheelchair Bowling Association: 713-849-9052; **www.awba.org**

Camping

Some people's idea of roughing it is being far enough from home that WiFi will no longer work. While "rough" is a relative term, there is more to camping than getting out of the city service area. It's a way to be close to nature, to simplify, to cut the electronic umbilical cords and

Chair Bowler's Perfect Game

I know I said I can't feel my knees, but let me tell you, they were weak." So says George Holscher as he rolled the last ball in the 10th frame for the first 300 of his bowling career.

For George and his team, it was just another Monday night of bowling league, November 26, 2012, at Indian River Lanes in Virginia Beach, VA. Little did he know how special this night was going to be for him and all those who watched as the 12th ball rolled down the lanes and George rolled into wheelchair bowling history. He became only the second person in the American Wheelchair Bowling Association's 50+ year history to throw a perfect game. Shawn Beam of Fort Worth, TX was the first, in May of 2012.

George Holscher

"When you're on a streak like that, the whole house gets quiet," Holscher says. "Everyone else stops bowling. It gets tense." With a deep breath to steady his nerves, he let the last throw leave his fingers. "The 60 feet to the pins seemed like 60 miles. Everyone just went crazy. It was amazing."

conveniences we take for granted. Getting away might mean car or motorhome camping within a designated site. It might mean getting off the beaten path and deep into the woods. Wheeling into the wilderness isn't easy for people who are paralyzed, but it's not impossible with a bit of preparation and determination.

Where to go? State and national parks are a good place to start. As mandated by the Americans with Disabilities Act, these parks have accessible accommodations, bathrooms and level ground—usually. Progress toward accessibility continues but you can find many camp areas that are already inclusive. Be prepared and be creative. To get started, check with your state's outdoor recreation or state parks agency. You may need to make reservations.

What to bring? There may be no way to avoid the necessities of mobility, medications and hygiene. But go lightly—you don't need the handheld satellite TV or the Swiss Army microwave. Remember, the idea is to escape the mundane and the routine.

Resources: U.S. National Parks are visited by more than 275 million visitors every year. Includes 43,162 miles of shoreline. **www.nps.gov**. Residents of the United States with disabilities can obtain a free Access Pass, a lifetime entrance pass to over 2,000 national parks, monuments, historic sites, recreation areas and wildlife refuges. The Pass also provides a 50 percent discount on fees for camping, swimming, parking, boat launching and tours. **http://store.usgs.gov/pass/access.html**

Flying

By its very nature flight is restrictive—by gravity, of course, and by licensing agencies and cost, but not necessarily by paralysis. If a person has normal health and has either quick reflexes or a suitable alternative control, most likely he or she can fly. Flying does not require great strength although good headwork is a must. Hundreds of paraplegics, quadriplegics and amputees have successfully flown over the years, even as commercial pilots, having proven their abilities to the FAA and other licensing authorities throughout the world.

A good information resource is the International Wheelchair Aviators, which began in 1972 as a monthly "fly to lunch" group of four paraplegic aviators from Southern California. IWA has information and resources on adaptive flying. IWA: 817-229-4634; for more see **www.wheelchairaviators.org**. Freedom's Wings International, a New Jersey organization, has a fleet of adapted motorless sailplanes. Gliders are towed into the sky by a regular airplane and then released for a quiet ride back to the airport. When conditions permit, sailplane pilots ride the natural thermal currents to stay aloft for hours. People with disabilities can come along either as passengers or by joining the flight training program. FWI: toll-free 1-800-382-1197; **www.freedomswings.org**

Gardening

Digging in the dirt, planting seeds and growing flowers or food is pleasurable and rewarding. Gardening provides exercise and mental stimulation. Many people claim it's also therapeutic—there's an organization called the American Horticultural Therapy Association (see **http://ahta.org**) that promotes physical and mental health through gardens and plants. Gardening can relieve tension. With its clear cause-and-effect nature, it can foster a sense of expectation, of accomplishment, self-reliance and responsibility. Moreover, with some adaptations (raised beds and special tools, for example), gardening can be barrier-free and fully inclusive. The Paralysis Resource Center library carries several books on accessible gardening. Go to **www.paralysis.org,** click on library, search for gardening; books available free by way of interlibrary loan.

Golf

Such a simple game. Maddeningly simple. Simply maddening. Hit the ball down the grassy fairway, get it on the green, and sink it in the hole. Easier to say than do, but that's part of the fun of it. The game is quite adaptable to the seated player. Custom clubs and special carts, some with single-passenger swivel seats and tires that won't damage the greens, open the game to players who have limited leg function.

Golf is growing in popularity among disabled players, not only because of equipment innovation but also because of the changes in law. The Americans with Disabilities Act requires all public accommodations, including golf courses, to provide goods and services to people with disabilities on an equal basis with the rest of the general public. Public entities, such as states and local governments, must make golf courses and other facilities accessible to people with disabilities and all new golf course facilities must be accessible. The ADA also requires

SAM MADDOX

Tim Gilmer tees off.

removal of architectural barriers in existing facilities when "readily achievable," or when it can be done without much difficulty or expense for that facility. Before you show up at a golf club expecting an equal basis experience, check ahead. You may need to work with the management and perhaps enlist the help of organizations such as the United States Golf Association, 908-234-2300; **www.usga.org**; or American Disabled Golfers Association, 772-335-3820; **www.americandisabledgolfersassociation.com**

Hand Cycling

Hand cycling really took off once the technology came of age with sophisticated three-wheel, multi-geared cycles. Hand cranking has become quite popular across the country and abroad, and for good reason. It's fun, fast and family oriented. It's great for fitness, too. A rider can move the three-wheelers along at a steady 20 mph pace, enough to keep up with nondisabled bike riders. Many riders have hand-powered over the thin air of Colorado's highest mountain passes, or even around the world. Hand cycling has emerged as an elite competitive sport, too; it's included in the Paralympics. The handcycle is used in triathlons for the cycling portion of the competition and in cycling events like century rides. There are several variations on the hand-power theme: Some cycles clamp on to a standard manual wheelchair, with a chair-driven front wheel to more or less pull the chair along. Clamp-ons are best for cruising around the

neighborhood. Serious road travel or competition requires a trike: they are lighter and deliver more power to the drive wheel, have greater stability at speed, and offer much less wind resistance. The big wheelchair companies Invacare and Sunrise Medical offer handcycle lines. For information about bikes see **www.freedomryder.com**, **www.varnahandcycles.com** or

Sarah Cantor handcycling in San Diego

CHRISTOPHER VOELKER

Ron Scanlon is a master of Kung Fu San Soo, an ancient fighting art. He teaches others, including people in wheelchairs, to be prepared. When Ron was nine, he was in an auto accident that injured his spinal cord. However, he did not let this stop him from achieving his dreams. "We all suffer from traumas, maybe its a disability, maybe its a divorce maybe its losing a family member but at some point when you get through the grief you have to wake up and say 'time to get on with my life!'"

www.bike-on.com. The United States Hand Cycling Federation (USHF) is the official governing body for recreational and competitive hand cycling in America. USHF, 720-239-1360; **www.ushf.org**

Hunting

Very few limits to this sport. If you can exhale a puff, you can fire a gun. Here are some connections to hook up with others who like to shoot.

- Disabled Hunting Magazine: **http://dhuntmag.com**
- Outdoors Without Limits breaks down barriers and removes stereotypes. 803-480-0167; **www.outdoorswithoutlimits.net**
- United Foundation For Disabled Archers sponsors free bowhunts for members with disabilities. **www.uffdaclub.com**
- Be Adaptive: manufactures sip'n puff triggers, gun mounts, etc. **www.beadaptive.com**

Pinball

The game of pinball has always been out of reach to many players. The machines are usually too high for wheelchair users, and for those with less than normal hand function, there just isn't any way to activate the flippers. But a New Jersey company has made pinball accessible. Ron Kochel and Gene Gulich created a game that a disabled player and nondisabled player can share on equal terms. Using the U Can Do controls, players can become wizards whether they use one hand or two, or one foot or two. Players can use fists, elbows, head switches or even a sip and puff method, moving the steel ball around the game by blowing or sucking air out of a straw. Every independent living center and accessible recreation program should have one. Toll-free 866-822-6362; **www.ucandocentral.com**

Racing

Wheelchair racing can take place anywhere there is running, on the track or on the road. The racing wheelchair has three wheels, one small one up front and two larger wheels that the person sits between; it looks like a mini dragster. Almost all running road races from 5K to marathon length have wheelchair divisions. The Summer Paralympics features a

wheelchair marathon, and numerous track races. Click on Paralympics at
www.teamusa.org

Riding

Horseback riding is an exhilarating recreation that's doable for many
people who are paralyzed, using padding or specially made saddles and a
mounting ramp. While riding can be done simply because it's pleasurable,
for some people the activity is therapeutic. The rhythmic motion and
warmth of a horse can be helpful; riding can facilitate cognitive as well as
sensory and motor development. Moreover, it can help foster a sense of
responsibility and self-confidence while reducing spasticity and improving
strength, and stimulating good posture, balance and flexibility for more
functional independence off the horse. The Equestrian event Dressage,

where horse and rider perform a series of predetermined movements, has been included in the Paralympics since 1996. There are many riding programs across the United States that cater to disabled riders. The best source of information is the Professional Association of Therapeutic Horsemanship International, toll free 1-800-369-7433; **www.pathintl.org**

Sailing

Sailing can be a peaceful and relaxing way to explore and enjoy the world of water. The sport also offers great adventure and challenges to instincts we forgot (or never knew we had). It's a lot of fun if you're along for the ride, but it is especially so if you're the skipper, reading the wind, setting the course and piloting the boat. Sailboats can accommodate people with varying degrees of paralysis. There are boats that are quite accessible for

the wheelchair sailor (a transfer box helps with the hardest part—getting aboard). In fact, there are boats that can be single-handed by people with no hand function whatsoever. A sip 'n puff control has been adapted to a fleet of boats called Martin 16s. These were originally designed to be quad friendly, with inspiration from Sam Sullivan, a high-quad sailor from British Columbia (former mayor of Vancouver). These boats are affordable, comfortable, safe and accessible to anyone. For more visit **www.martin16.com**

Another accessible boat called an Access Dinghy, which can also be controlled using a joystick, is available for rent at many sailing centers. Sailors are seated low in the boat for added stability. A servo-assist joystick can operate the electric winches and can be controlled by hand, foot, chin or any moving body part. The Access Dinghy brings full inclusion to the marina, **www.accessdinghy.org**

For some, the most fulfilling way to enjoy sailing is to see who's got the fastest boat. Sailing is something of an aquatic equalizer—nondisabled sailors have no particular advantage when it comes to boat handling and navigation skill. There are also many disabled-only races, including the Paralympic Games. For information on racing: The United States Sailing Association, 401-683-0800; **http://home.ussailing.org**

There are numerous sailing programs across the country that offer boats and instruction for people with disabilities. Check your local marinas; many programs are listed on the USSA Website.

Scuba

Scuba diving opens a fantastic new world to the gravity-bound. And for those with limitations of mobility, underwater sports offer an exhilarating "aquatic equality" unsurpassed on land. With training and some assistance getting in and out of equipment, even high-quads can enjoy scuba diving, and perhaps the clear, 85-degree water of the beautiful reefs of the Caribbean. There are dive programs all over the United States that specialize in getting disabled divers trained and certified. There are special tour companies that target the wheelchair diver, and there are even resorts in such exotic places as Bonaire in the Caribbean that offer fully "walk 'n roll" accessible dive vacation packages.

Join Team Reeve

Run or push a marathon, or maybe half of one. Complete a triathlon, bike a trail, swim the tides, host a bake sale, plan a party, or organize any kind of event that interests you—all to benefit Team Reeve and the Reeve Foundation. Turn your passions into a mission to help others. Team Reeve is a charity participant in several major marathons, including the Virgin London Marathon, Bank of America Chicago Marathon, Marine Corps Marathon and the ING New York City Marathon. Team Reeve runners get coaching and personalized training advice, fundraising assistance and most of all, tremendous satisfaction both for themselves, and for helping the Foundation. See *www.ChristopherReeve.org/TeamReeve*

CHRISTOPHER VOELKER

Cody Unser was diagnosed with transverse myelitis when she was 12; two years later, after having already started the Cody Unser First Step Foundation, she learned to scuba dive. Says Cody, "You're free in the water, you're not dependent on your wheelchair to move you around. With scuba diving, I realized that life does go on and I didn't have to get swallowed up in what was happening to me." These days Cody spreads the word on the benefits of diving, with Operation Deep Down, and Cody's Great Scuba Adventure programs that will offer expense-paid trips to wounded military veterans to get certified in scuba diving.

Many divers have been trained by instructors certified by the Handicapped Scuba Association (HSA), a California nonprofit that's been running scuba and underwater education programs for nearly thirty years. HSA bases diving proficiency on one's ability to assist another diver in the water. Level A divers are certified to dive with one other person; a Level B diver must dive with two other nondisabled divers. Level C divers require two dive buddies and one must be trained in diver rescue. Says HSA founder Jim Gatacre, "Virtually everyone I've ever trained will tell you that their lives have been changed by the diving. Just about anybody can do it; if a person has fair respiratory function, even if he or she can't move at all, there are ways to teach diving so anyone can have a wonderful diving experience." HSA International, 949-498-4540; see **www.hsascuba.com**. Site includes a list of dive instructors across the United States. The Cody Unser First Step Foundation also supports a robust scuba program. See **http://cody.sks.com/scuba.htm**

Skiing (Alpine)

This is a sport that's been well adapted for people with disabilities, thanks to technology. Depending on one's level of function, there are three ways a person can get from the top of the mountain down the snowy trails to the bottom. At the highest end of the tech scale is the mono-ski, best for those with good upper body strength and trunk balance. The

Hall of fame mono-ski racer Sarah Will, in 2002

skier sits in a molded shell mounted to a frame above a single ski with a shock absorber linking the frame to the ski. Two outriggers are used for balance and turning. Mono-skiing closely resembles stand-up skiing—the skier can become highly skilled, carving turns in tight formation and taking on the deep and the steep. Ski all day without anyone's help: The mono-ski self-loads onto the chairlift.

The bi-ski, a bucket seating system similar to the mono ski, sits atop two heavily shaped skis and can be balanced with attached or hand-held outriggers. Bi-skis are used by individuals who have more significant

WALLY MARSH

Candace Cable

physical limitations and are tethered or skied from behind by an instructor. A definite thrill ride!

The sit-ski, akin to a toboggan, works for people with even more significant limitations. Those with some hand function can steer the sit-ski with short ski poles and by leaning. The sit-ski is tethered to an instructor.

There are many disabled ski programs across the United States. Among the largest is the National Sports Center for the Disabled, which runs recreation programs year-round, at Winter Park in Colorado. NSCD, 303-316-1518; **www.nscd.org.** Another big Colorado program is the Breckenridge Outdoor Education Center: **www.boec.org.** See the National Ability Center, Park City, UT, 435-649-3991; **www.discovernac.org**. A full-scale California program can be found at Alpine Meadows, in the Tahoe region: **www.dsusafw.org**. The Adaptive Sports Foundation at Windham Mountain runs a large program on the East Coast: **www.windhammountain.com**

Skiing has a very active competitive and Paralympic side, too. Contact **www.paralympic.org/AlpineSkiing**

CHRISTOPHER VOELKER

Patrick Ivison was 14 months old when a car backed over him and injured his spinal cord. He's currently a film student at the University of Southern California and an advocate for active living. He's an avid surfer and inveterate optimist: "It is important to get back out there and live life to the fullest, with or without an injury."

Jesse's Life, Rolling On

In 1996, Jesse Billauer, on the verge of becoming a professional surfer, sustained a spinal cord injury after being tossed from his board in Malibu. When he was in the hospital with a broken neck, Jesse got a call from someone named Christopher. He says he didn't know anyone named Christopher but he took it. Turns out it was Christopher Reeve, who had joined the quad club the previous year. "He told me to keep my positive outlook." That he did. Jesse was a quadriplegic but his love of the ocean drew him back to the waves. With the help of friends and professional surfer Rob Machado, Jesse began surfing again; he teamed up with "They Will Surf Again" (TWSA), a foundation that worked to introduce adaptive surfing to the paralysis community.

Meanwhile, Jesse and his family created the Life Rolls On Foundation (LRO) to fund

spinal cord injury research and educate the public. In 2004, TWSA merged with LRO; with a handful of surfers and volunteers, LRO's first TWSA event was produced in Newport Beach, CA. The program has grown to include surf events from coast to coast, offering at no cost to participants who were dealing with paralysis a chance to ride the surf.

TWSA added adaptive skate and snowboarding programs as LRO shifted its focus from cure to active living and quality of life programs.

In 2010, Life Rolls On became a subsidiary of the Reeve Foundation and serves as its West Coast headquarters. Jesse is National Outreach Director; that means he'll continue to raise awareness, raise money and put on events, such as LRO's annual Night by the Ocean dinner. He's glad to help out with peer-to-peer counseling. "When I was first hurt the most important part of my rehab was the people who came in to see me. These are people who've been through it instead of doctors and nurses who are walking around. I learned about the real world and how it is to deal with it in a wheelchair. I've done the same for others. I go in there, be myself, talk about their hopes and dreams. I tell them to live their lives. Tomorrow is not guaranteed, bad things happen to good people, but never let anyone tell you your dreams can't come true." See *www.liferollson.org*

CHRISTOPHER VOELKER

Skiing (Cross Country)

This manner of sit skiing imitates the experience of hiking in the wilderness and is a great aerobic and strength workout. Cross country sit skis have molded or canvas seats mounted on frames that are simple and light weight, creating more independence. The frames are attached to two cross country skis for snow skiing or a mountain-board for summer trails. The skier propels along the course using cross country ski poles that have straps to support any limited hand function. There are no chair lifts to ride, no tickets to buy, and this sport will really work your muscles, including some you didn't know you had.

Surfing

Well, dude, it's bitchin, that's why. Jesse Billauer, a quad after a surfing accident, started Life Rolls On (LRO, a subsidiary of the Reeve Foundation) to raise awareness about quality of life and spinal cord injury. Jesse, of course, got back on his board, riding huge waves on his stomach, with help from some stand-up surfers to get in and out. To share the joy, he started They Will Surf Again, a program that gets people in wheelchairs

Pro surfer Christiaan Bailey rides the surf

out riding the waves, on surfboards, at beaches across the United States. LRO also features They Will Skate Again, showing how wheelchair users can have fun at the skatepark. LRO: **www.liferollson.org**

Tennis

Wheelchair tennis is played with the same rules as stand-up tennis, except the wheelchair player is allowed two bounces of the ball. Decent wheelchair players can actively compete against stand-up players, making this one of the best activities to share with friends and family. In wheelchair tennis, the player must master the game as well as the wheelchair. Learning mobility on the court is exciting and challenging, and it helps build strength and cardiovascular fitness. The competitive side of tennis is robust and international in scope. Tennis is also a Summer Paralympic sport. International Tennis Federation, click on "wheelchair" at **www.itftennis.com**

Tennis (Table)

Not your daddy's ping pong game. This is a fast and fun indoor/outdoor option. For information on competitive action (this is a Summer Paralympic sport), contact USA Table Tennis, **www.teamusa.org**

Triathlon

The sport of triathlon is expanding for people with disabilities. Triathlon distances include the shorter course (half mile swim, 12 mile bike, 3.1 mile run), or the longer Ironman course (2.4 mile swim, 112 mile bike, 26.2 mile run). The adaptive division completes the same courses. The 2016 Summer Paralympics will debut the triathlon event with the Olympic distance of swimming, biking and running. Sit-down athletes use a handcycle for the bike and a racing wheelchair for the run portions of the Triathlon. **www.usatriathlon.org**

Video games

The modern video game has better graphics, better games, better interactivity than ever before. No problem for anyone with decent hand function to join the action. But can a high quad play? If you can sip and puff, the answer is yes. A company called KY Enterprises has been in the accessible gaming business for twenty years and makes a joystick controller for Playstation games. It takes a bit of practice to become skillful with six switch modes on the sip-and-puff unit, which doubles as a joystick, and two buttons operated by the lip. But if a gamer is motivated, this popular activity is wide open. There are some PS2 games that are not compatible (those that require analog-only control, which is the mushroom thumb control on a regular control unit. See the box of the video game; it will indicate if analog is required). Most driving games, sports games and other popular titles don't require analog. 406-586-2376; **www.quadcontrol.com**

A company called Broadened Horizons, founded by Mark Felling, a C5 quad, develops products targeting people with upper extremity limitations; a number of video game controllers are available for all game platforms, as well as gear for personal independence, communications, transportation, education, employment, and recreation; online see **www.broadenedhorizons.com**. The Able Gamers Foundation advocates for accessible gaming. **www.ablegamers.com**

Water Skiing

Water skiing is a terrific heat-beating summer sport that's been adapted so that skiers of almost all abilities can participate with family and friends. If skiers get good at it and have the urge to compete, there are various water ski meets around the United States. The sit skis are varied in width of 10 to 15 inches, depending on the skier's ability; some skis have outriggers or short ski tips attached to either side of the sit ski for balance. The towropes have a modified handle so individuals with hand disabilities can hook up to a boat and thrill to the speed and wake-crashing fun of water skiing. Skis are available commercially; many have been added to recreation programs in many communities across the country.

Water ski tournaments for skiers with mobility limitations include slalom, tricks and jumping events. Competition is organized by the Water Skiers with Disabilities Association (WSDA), a division of USA Water Ski, the national governing body for the sport in the United States. WSDA promotes the recreational aspects of the sport with clinics, teaching materials, equipment development and by way of a network of water ski resources. Contact WSDA, 863-324-4341; **http://usawaterski.org**

Weightlifting

Granted, many don't hear the calling for this strenuous, get-pumped recreation, but it is not hard to adapt lifting weights to people with lost function due to paralysis. The activity has clear benefits for fitness but lifting has also emerged as a very competitive activity at the international level. Online, check out powerlifting under the Paralympics section at **www.teamusa.org**

Wheelchair bodybuilding

This sport has come a long way with numerous competitions across the U.S., and internationally, even sporting a professional division. Want to oil up, pump and pose? Try this site: **www.wheelchair-bodybuilding.com**; see also the sit-down division of the International Federation of Body Builders, **http://ifbbwcbb.com**

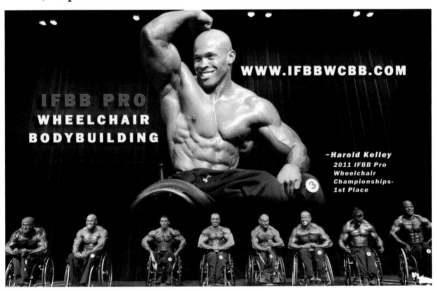

TEAM SPORTS

Basketball

Basketball is probably the most well-developed sport for wheelchair users in the United States, for good reason. The game has been played for almost seventy years, originated by World War II vets in rehab on the East and West coasts. There are teams and divisions all over the country for men, women and juniors. Some colleges suit up wheelchair hoops teams. The game is fast and fun, and quite entertaining to watch. Contact the National Wheelchair Basketball Association, telephone 719-266-4082; **www.nwba.org**

Quad Rugby

Quad Rugby, or murderball, is a combination of soccer, keep-away and demolition derby that emerged from the cold northern winters of Winnipeg, Manitoba, to become an international sport. Rugby fans say it's the fastest growing wheelchair sport in the world. There are dozens of competitive teams in the United States; each team utilizes four players, mostly quads (players must have all four limbs affected

by disability). A player has fifteen seconds to advance the ball into the opponent's half-court. The player with the ball must pass or dribble every ten seconds or a turnover is awarded. The idea is to cross the end line on the court and score a point. The other guys do what they can to stop you. It's not a game for polite recreation. U.S. Quad Rugby Association, 512-791-2644; **www.quadrugby.com**

Sled hockey

Sled hockey is played by people who use their arms to propel themselves by digging picks on the ends of two short hockey sticks into the ice. Players are seated on sleds, which are affixed to two hockey skate blades under the seat. The sleds are about three inches off the ice and are anywhere from two to four feet long, depending on the size of the player. There are few differences between this and the stand-up game. The puck is the same, as are the pads. Protection is needed, as there is a lot of checking. International competition is fierce, including the Paralympic Games. USA Hockey, 719-576-USAH (8724); **www.usahockey.com**

Softball

It's not easy to field full teams of wheelchairs for a Saturday afternoon pick-up game. The best chance for action occurs at an annual tournament sponsored by the National Wheelchair Softball Association, where thirty or so teams show up to compete. The game is much the same as slow-pitch softball, using a sixteen-inch slow-pitch ball, with base paths shortened to fifty feet. There is no adaptive equipment. For more, contact NWSA, **www.wheelchairsoftball.org**

Volleyball

Volleyball has been adapted to include seated persons with many types of disability. The net is about three feet high and the court is smaller than a standard volleyball setup. Bump, set, spike—the major differences between the standing game and the sitting game are that players can block the serve and that one bun must be in contact with the floor when a player makes contact with the ball. USA Volleyball, 719-228-6800; **www.usavolleyball.org**

৵ **Below are recreation resources.**

Achilles International, with chapters in more than sixty-five locations in the United States and abroad, encourages disabled people to participate in long-distance running. ATC provides support, training and technical expertise to runners with all kinds of disabilities. Achilles has programs for children and war veterans. Achilles Track Club, 212-354-0300; **www.achillesinternational.org**

BlazeSports America, an outgrowth of the 1996 Paralympic Games held in Atlanta, empowers children and adults with physical disabilities through sport, health enhancement, and the promotion of universal human rights. The program is named after the Atlanta Paralympics mascot, Blaze. 404-270-2000; **www.blazesports.org**

Challenged Athletes Foundation steps in where rehabilitation and health insurance end by funding sports wheelchairs, handcycles, mono-skis and sports prosthetics, as well as expenses for training and competition. Based in San Diego. 858-866-0959; **www.challengedathletes.org**

Disabled Sports USA, formed in 1967 by a group of disabled veterans, offers nationwide sports programs to anyone with a physical disability. Activities include winter skiing, water sports, summer and winter competitions, fitness and special sports events. Participants include those with visual impairments, amputations, spinal cord injury, dwarfism, multiple sclerosis, head injury, cerebral palsy and other neuromuscular and orthopedic conditions. 301-217-0960; **www.dsusa.org**

National Center on Health, Physical Activity and Disability (NCHPAD) offers multimedia information on accessible fitness, recreation and sports programs, stress management, nutrition, equipment vendors, etc. NCHPAD, toll-free 1-800-900-8086; **www.nchpad.org**

Paralympics: United States Olympic Committee manages the U.S. Paralympic team. With minor exceptions, services provided to disabled athletes are comparable to those provided to nondisabled Olympic athletes. The USOC is dedicated to the integration and advancement of elite disabled athletes into open competition whenever possible. The Paralympics are open to elite athletes who meet the rigid qualifying standards of their sport. Athletes are categorized by a combination of functional and medical determinations. The Paralympic Games have been contested since 1960 and now feature competition in twenty sports. The Paralympic Winter Games showcase five sports. For more, contact U.S. Paralympics, 719-632-5551; **www.usparalympics.org**. Also see International Paralympic Committee, **www.paralympic.org**

Sports 'N Spokes is a magazine about sports and recreation for people with paralysis, published by the Paralyzed Veterans of America; SNS offers details on wheelchair athletics and competition, recreation, exercise, training, nutrition, event schedules and other topics of interest to the active wheeler. Toll-free 1-888-888-2201; 602-224-0500; **www.sportsnspokes.com**

Turning P.O.I.N.T. teaches people with mobility impairments the skills necessary to fully enjoy the outdoors. The organization sponsors opportunities for paralyzed people of all shapes, sizes and ages to camp, fish, sail, scuba dive, hunt, water ski or take pictures from a pontoon boat in the scenic swamps of East Texas. Based on the notion that it's okay to get together with other people with disabilities without feeling embarrassed. 972-524-4231; **www.turningpointnation.org**

Wheelchair and Ambulatory Sports, USA was founded in 1956 as the National Wheelchair Athletic Association to provide mobility-limited athletes the chance for recreational and competitive sports. WASUSA offers national sports programs and linkage to the Paralympics through a widespread regional structure. WASUSA, 732-266-2634; **www.wsusa.org**

World T.E.A.M. Sports brings individuals with and without disabilities together in unique athletic events (mountain climbing, white water rafting, biking, rides around the world, rides through Vietnam, etc.). The program promotes diversity and increased awareness, acceptance and integration of those with disabilities. 855-987-8326, **www.worldteamsports.org**

ART AND CREATIVITY

THE ARTS ENRICH OUR LIVES IN COUNTLESS WAYS, whether we create art or appreciate its beauty, truth or abstraction. The worlds of creative endeavor and artistic expression are inclusive; there are no limitations on imagination. There are only a few restrictions on accessing the tools of art; musical instruments, paintbrushes, pencils or video cameras are fairly adaptable. Because art is infinite and unconditional, people with disabilities are free to express themselves without physical, social, or attitudinal barriers. The arts are not recreation, per se, but they can be uplifting, refreshing and socially involving.

The arts provide unlimited possibilities for personal, academic, and professional success. By engaging in the arts, people with disabilities are able to greatly contribute to their communities, help extinguish old stereotypes regarding disability, and create a culture truly representative of all people. The arts help forge a collective identity. People with disabilities share common experiences through the expression of their struggles and histories—in art, dance, music and other performing arts, including motion pictures and television.

👪 **Below are links to resources:**

Arts and Healing Network is an Internet resource regarding the connection between art and healing. Stinson Beach, CA. **www.artheals.org**

Association of Foot and Mouth Painting Artists is a fifty-year-old international organization that offers significant financial support to painters accepted in the group. American affiliate is Mouth and Foot Painting Artists Inc., Atlanta. 770-986-7764; **www.mfpausa.com**

AXIS Dance Company has become an internationally known resource for physically integrated dance and is one of several companies setting a standard for professionalism in this emerging field. AXIS Dance Company, Oakland, CA, 510-625-0110; **www.axisdance.org**

Ballroom Dancing: This graceful, dramatic style is catching on with wheelchair dancers. Among U.S. programs are Philadelphia-based American Dance Wheels, see **www.americandancewheels.com** and San Diego's Wheelchair Dancers Organization, **www.wheelchairdancers.org**

Coalition for Disabled Musicians introduces disabled musicians to each other, offers an accessible rehearsal and recording studio, helps with adaptive techniques for pain, endurance, etc. Bay Shore, NY. 631-586- 0366; or see **www.disabled-musicians.org**

Creative Growth Art Center offers art programs, independent living training, and vocational links for adults who are physically, mentally and emotionally disabled. Oakland, CA. 510-836-2340; **www.creativegrowth.org**

Full Radius Dance explores the human experience in a world of diversity in attitude, action and outcome. Atlanta, GA. 404-724-9663; **www.fullradiusdance.org**

Inclusion in the Arts promotes and advocates for full inclusion of artists of color and performers with disabilities at all levels of production in theatre, film, television, and related media. **http://inclusioninthearts.org**

Media Access Office promotes the employment and accurate portrayal of persons with disabilities in all areas of the media and entertainment industry, ensuring that people with disabilities are part of the cultural diversity. **http://mediaaccessawards.com**

National Arts and Disability Center (NADC) is an information, technical assistance and referral center dedicated to full inclusion of children and adults with disabilities into the visual, performing, media, and literary arts. NADC, Tarjan Center for Developmental Disabilities; UCLA. 310-825-5054; **www.semel.ucla.edu/nadc**

National Institute of Art and Disabilities (NIAD) is a visual arts center that serves adults with developmental and physical disabilities. **www.niadart.org**

ReelAbilities Disabilities Film Festival presents award-winning films by and about people with disabilities in multiple locations. 646-505-5738; **www.reelabilities.org**

Stunts-Ability trains disabled persons for stunts, acting and effects for the entertainment industry. Stunts-Ability, see **www.stuntsability.com**

That Uppity Theatre Company produces the Disability Project, an ensemble of conversation, writing, sound, movement and theatrical exercises to empower individuals, honor their stories, enhance awareness about disability. St. Louis, MO; 314-534-1454; **www.uppityco.com**

VSA (formerly Very Special Arts) offers numerous opportunities for creative writing, dance, drama, music and the visual arts for people with disabilities. There are affiliates in almost all states and in dozens of countries. VSA is affiliated with the Kennedy Center for the Performing Arts in Washington, D.C. Toll-free 1-800-444-1324; **www.vsarts.org/education/vsa**

CHRISTOPHER VOELKER

Ruben Rios was 18 when he was shot in the neck at close range. He was 24-hour dependent on a ventilator. Ruben was a painter and a member of the prestigious Association of Foot and Mouth Painting Artists. "I create art mostly the same way I did when I started, a kind of pointillism. I use fine point felt tip pens and I "stipple" or dot my way through the piece. First, I draw an outline with pencil and then I'll color in the sketch, dropping in different colors and layers. It takes anywhere from 20 to 60 hours to complete a piece from beginning to end with this method. My art has been the biggest thing in my life that has kept me goal oriented and not just stagnant. Now I have something to achieve. And if it weren't for the opportunity I was given to pursue a career as an artist, I don't think I'd be where I am today. I wouldn't have the same quality of life."

Ruben passed away on February 10, 2014. He was an ambassador for the Reeve Foundation and Paralysis Resource Center (PRC) since 2007.

5
Travel

It's a big planet. You should see it. Here's how to get ready to explore, to relax, to savor exotic cultures.

Bags packed, ready to go.

ASHLEY OLSON

> Twenty years from now you will be more disappointed by the things you didn't do than by the ones you did. So throw off the bowlines. Sail away from the safe harbor. Catch the tradewinds in your sails. Explore. Dream. Discover. — Mark Twain

Whether you're a tourist or a traveler, or even if you don't know the difference, there is great appeal in getting away from home to experience the world—on a road trip to the state next door or off to some far-flung place across land and sea. For our purposes, it's the trip that counts, not the purpose, or the destination, or the scenery. Travel is a process; sometimes it's familiar and comfortable, sometimes random or even unsettling. Unless you have an unusually high threshold for the unpredictable, the best travel plan is to have a plan. That does not necessarily mean a packaged trip with a cookie-cutter itinerary. But planning is especially important for people who use adaptive gear or need to get around with reduced mobility. No plan is bulletproof, of course, especially when it comes to transportation, lodging, scheduling, weather, and all the unforeseen tribulations that remind you that travel is an art, not a science. We'll break the planning into three steps: getting ready, getting there, and being there.

GETTING READY

FOR THOSE WHO HAVEN'T DONE A LOT OF TRAVEL with wheelchairs, walkers, and all the paraphernalia of paralysis, it's a good idea to enlist the help of someone with a lot of personal experience or perhaps a travel agent who specializes in the disability travel market. Travel professionals know how to get you where you want to go and pretty much what to expect once you get there, matching your level of adventure with your need for creature comfort. In many cases, it's best to make your maiden voyage to a destination that is familiar with people with disabilities. This would include, among many other places, San Diego, Las Vegas, Disney World in Orlando, New York, and Washington, D.C.

Your agent may also recommend a cruise—this is a very relaxing way to see exotic ports of call in an accessible, well-fed, and friendly environment including, in many cases, cabins with roll-in showers. As a whole, the cruise business does a good job anticipating the needs of travelers with disabilities, especially on the most modern sailing vessels.

Your expert friend or travel agent should know a few basic tricks (see a list of tips from veteran wheelchair travelers, including those who use mechanical ventilation, page 252). It's not an absolute requirement, but let the airline know you're coming by wheelchair. Advance notice may not be such a big deal if you're hopping a one-hour shuttle from

Lavatory Issues

How about bathroom issues on a long airplane ride for someone who uses a wheelchair? Bob Vogel, a paraplegic who has been pushing nearly thirty years and half a million air miles has this to say:

First, unless you're in a big, wide body aircraft, an accessible onboard lavatory in not a given; according to the Air Carrier Access Act, "Aircraft with more than one aisle must have at least one accessible lavatory (with door locks, call buttons, grab bars, and lever faucets) available, which will have sufficient room to allow a passenger using an onboard wheelchair to enter, maneuver, and use the facilities with the same degree of privacy as other passengers." I've used an aisle chair to get to "inaccessible" bathrooms—the transfer was "expert only," to say the least, but doable.

Most regional flights are not on two-aisle planes; some have an aisle chair, some don't, so it's a good idea to limit fluid intake before the flight. Use the restroom and catheterize immediately before boarding. Avoiding dehydration is a balancing act— the dry air in an airplane cabin can add to dehydration. I do drink water on the flight to stay hydrated—just not a lot. If you are worried about a long flight, consider using an indwelling catheter and leg bag. Alas, some folks wear pads or Depends—just in case. So here's hoping you get bumped to First Class, with plenty of free drinks on a plane with an aisle chair and accessible bathroom. Safe travels!

Los Angeles to San Francisco, but if your flight is long and involves plane changes, always let them know. If the plane has fewer than sixty seats, powerchair users may also be required to give a two-day notice. Air carriers may require up to forty-eight hours advance notice if you plan to use oxygen or the plane's power supply to operate a respirator. A note on oxygen: Most U.S. airlines can accommodate passengers requiring oxygen, although the FAA requires a physician's statement. Also, regulations prohibit the use of passenger-provided oxygen equipment during flight. Airlines will charge extra for their oxygen, and it's not cheap, so check with the carrier.

Book a direct flight whenever possible. Changing planes is a nuisance and can be unnerving, especially if your connection is tight—you have to make absolutely sure your wheelchair and other gear make the connecting flight. Airlines may try to seat you in one of their one-size-fits-all wheelchairs at the gate. In the name of comfort and safety, insist that your personal equipment be brought forth. On the subject of missing baggage, here is another pro tip: Keep your meds, catheter supplies, etc. in your carry-on bag. Never pack them in your checked luggage.

The airline industry in the United States must by law accommodate passengers with disabilities. The compliance record for all airlines is not spotless, although it has been much improved in recent years. But here's another rule of thumb experience has taught the veteran traveler with a disability: Despite federal regulations and many years of ADA sensitivity, don't assume that anyone who wears the airline's uniform knows what to

Passengers with Service Animals

Dogs are fine onboard. Ask about the airline's policy on advance seat assignments for people with disabilities. Airlines are not permitted to automatically require documentation for service animals other than for emotional support animals, but you may want to carry documentation from your physician or other licensed professional confirming your need for the service animal. Passengers with unusual service animals also may want to carry documentation confirming that their animal has been trained to perform a function or task for them.

ASHLEY OLSON

Mendocino, California trail.

do with you or your gear. It may not be necessary to pack a copy of the
Air Carrier Access Act (get a summary online at **www.faa.gov**), but you
may have to tap into the deep reserves of your patience.

Agents should know to get their mobility-restricted clients assigned
to a bulkhead seat on the airplane; it is much easier to transfer in and
out. Your travel pro should also know about general accessibility of your
destination, public transportation, rental cars with hand controls, and
other details once you arrive. Book your van well ahead of time. An agent
is going to be most helpful in arranging lodging on the other end. Just
because a hotel's brochure has the little wheelchair symbol that says it
has accessible rooms doesn't mean you can get in the bathroom. In many
cases, the agent has been there ahead of you with a tape measure and
knows what to expect, including accessibility of shops, restaurants, and
the hotel pool. There are agencies listed at the end of this chapter.

Do you need to bring an attendant? No, unless you are on a stretcher
or the air carrier cites a safety issue, which you should get in writing. As
the rule reads, an attendant may be required for "a person with a mobility
impairment so severe that the person is unable to assist in his or her own
evacuation of the aircraft."

How about bringing your service dog? No problem. Any public
or private accommodation, including restaurants, hotels, stores, taxis,

and airlines, must allow people with disabilities to bring their service animals with them wherever customers are normally allowed. You and your dog can't be denied any seat, either, unless the animal obstructs an aisle or other areas that would impede an emergency evacuation. When booking your ticket, tell your travel or ticket agent that a service dog is coming along. Bring the dog's health certificates with proof of vaccinations.

You hope your chair or scooter will survive the ride in the cargo hold. Usually there's no problem, especially for manual chairs. If you use a power wheelchair there are more reasons for concern for the well-being of your equipment. Airlines prefer that you use gel or dry-cell batteries as opposed to the more common liquid (spillable, corrosive lead acid) ones. Also, the spillable battery's regular vent caps may be replaced with spill-proof vent caps. Be sure the handlers replace the regular vent caps before reconnecting the battery so dangerous pressure does not build up in the battery during later use.

Some powerchair or scooter users remove their joystick controls and carry them on board. These devices are sensitive to abuse and difficult to repair away from home. Not leaving anything to chance, a Maryland company makes protective molded containers for folding manual wheelchairs and for power wheelchairs and scooters. **www.haseltine.com**

Sedona, Arizona.

ASHLEY OLSON

Pro Para Tips

Here are a few tips for wheelchair travelers from well-seasoned Ashley Olson, proprietress of *www.wheelchairtraveling.com*

- Tools: Bring a portable set of Allen wrenches—very handy for brake and caster adjustment.
- Tires: Check the air in your tires before leaving; consider packing a portable pump. Solid rubber wheels are an option.
- Immunity: Boost your immune system; I swear by On Guard Essential Oil, a blend of wild orange, clove bud, cinnamon, eucalyptus, and rosemary. Hand sanitizer is helpful, too.
- Compression socks: Good for circulation and for preventing leg swelling; helps the body stay warm in colder weather.
- Packing: A backpack is an essential carry-on luggage item but is also a crucial daypack throughout the trip to hold water, clothing, souvenirs, etc.
- Medical supplies: Bring extra supplies because you never know— flights get delayed, cars break down, bad weather brews.
- Flying: Check-in at the desk instead of a kiosk to arrange for boarding and on-flight wheelchairs; gate-check your wheelchair; remove everything that can fall off the wheelchair—side-guards, seat cushion, etc.
- Gloves: These are a good idea to protect your hands along the sometimes bumpy, dirty road.
- Reservations: When booking anything— a plane flight, train ride, hotel, restaurant, etc.—notify the other party that you are in a wheelchair.
- Food: Let your system adjust to new foods and spices. Don't shock your system—it could lead to indigestion and an irregular bowel.
- Public restrooms: Sometimes finding an accessible public restroom can be challenging; try looking for shopping centers, chain coffee shops, hotel lobbies, train/subway stations, airports, government buildings, banks, and fast food restaurants.
- Attitude: Be open to the new things that come your way, whether cuisine or access features, but also when situations don't go according to plan. Roll with it and you'll be guaranteed to have a more pleasant and eye-opening experience.

Bodega Bay, Northern California.

GETTING THERE

IT'S IMPORTANT TO GET TO THE AIRPORT EARLY to check in. As you are transferred to one of those skinny aisle chairs to get you to your seat (first to board, last to deplane), your chair will be tagged so the destination ground crew knows to bring it to the gate when the plane arrives. A lot of wheelchair users keep their seat cushion with them and use it on the plane. Bigger planes (more than thirty seats) must have movable armrests, so you can slide in easily.

Once onboard, the travel experience is pretty much like that of everyone else, except for using the lavatories. Newer, two-aisle planes have accessible lavatories, as long as you can maneuver yourself in the little onboard chair or have an attendant standing by. The cabin crew is not required to help you once you reach the lavatory. According to federal rules, the accessible lavatory "shall afford privacy to persons using the onboard wheelchair equivalent to that afforded ambulatory users." Still, it's a rather conspicuous and indiscrete hassle to use the toilet on a plane. It's common for people with dysfunctional bladders to restrict fluid intake before boarding the plane and to use airport facilities right before going aboard.

Pro Quad Tips

Here are a few tips for wheelchair travelers from well-traveled Mark Willits, a lawyer with C2-C3 quadriplegia who uses a respirator, and who is president of the California support organization Ralph's Riders, *www.ralphsriders.org*

- This is true: Hope for the best, plan for the worst.
- Always carry on the equipment you need to survive 24 hours at your destination, for me that's an ambu-bag, suction machine, extra batteries and charger for the ventilator, medications, etc. Airlines cannot limit the amount of medical equipment that a passenger carries on to the airplane.
- Always remember to do regular weight shifts.
- Locate ground transportation at your destination. Rental vans with a ramp or wheelchair lift and wheelchair tie-downs can be found in most major cities. (Three national rental companies are listed at the end of this chapter.)
- If you plan to use public transportation, taxis, hotel shuttles, etc., know your options before you get there. The subways of New York or Paris are great but not always available—that's completely the opposite in Washington, D.C. or Los Angeles.
- Transfers from a wheelchair to an aisle chair and then to the airplane seat are crucial; understand how this works and prepare for it. You will have to speak up and explain how to keep this process safe.
- Plan for a broken chair. It probably won't happen but ahead of arrival, always locate the closest wheelchair repair shop. You can often find this by contacting the manufacturer of your chair.
- Make sure all electrical equipment is compatible with the voltage in foreign countries. Bring a transformer or adapter if necessary.
- Chair: Remove and carry onboard everything that you can: headrest, armrest, foot rest, cushion, cords, and backpacks. Instruct airline employees on how to properly handle the wheelchair; the more explicit and simple you explain everything, the better.
- You are not required to remove the batteries or disconnect them from the wheelchair if the batteries are gel cell or dry cell batteries.
- Stay positive. Even with perfect planning, problems will occur. Be polite and courteous to the airline employees. They are always more helpful that way.

Hotline

The U.S. Department of Transportation (DOT) has established a toll-free hotline to assist travelers with disabilities. The hotline provides general information to consumers about the rights of air travelers with disabilities, responds to requests for printed consumer information, and assists air travelers with time-sensitive disability-related issues. Call 1-800-778-4838 (voice) or 1-800-455-9880 (TTY) to obtain assistance.

Air travel is an overwhelmingly positive experience for most passengers with disabilities. But if you are treated as cargo by insensitive personnel, or if your own cargo is mangled, always be prepared to assert your rights. Anyone who feels an airline has violated any provision of the access rules may report the incident to the Aviation Consumer Protection Division, C-75, Department of Transportation, 1200 New Jersey Ave., SE, Washington, DC 20590. **www.dot.gov/airconsumer**. You can be sure that complaints are taken seriously.

Mark Willits, the one in the chair, in Hawaii for a helicopter tour.

BEING THERE

PUBLIC TRANSPORTATION MAY WORK OUT FINE. Some cities are better set up with fixed route systems than others but most transit systems are sensitive to travelers using wheelchairs, so do a bit of research to obtain

Revised ADA Rules for Lodging

Ever get there and find the room you booked as accessible wasn't even close? The good news is that this is not supposed to happen anymore. ADA regulations regarding hotels, motels, and inns were revised in 2012. By law, individuals with disabilities must be able to make reservations for accessible guest rooms during the same hours and in the same manner as others. Places of lodging must identify and describe accessible features of the facility and guest rooms in enough detail to reasonably permit those with disabilities to assess independently whether a given facility or guest room meets his or her accessibility needs.

Customer service staff should know accessible routes to and through the facility; details about the configuration of accessible guest rooms and bathrooms; availability of accessibility equipment or features such as bath benches or visual alarm and alert devices; and the accessibility of common spaces such as meeting rooms, lounges, restaurants, swimming pools, or fitness centers.

When a reservation is made for an accessible guest room, the specific accessible guest room reserved must be held for the reserving customer and the room must be removed from the reservation system.

Madonna Inn, San Luis Obispo, CA.

Places of lodging that rely on third parties (i.e., travel agents, including online travel reservation services) must provide accessible rooms to at least some of the third parties and must provide information about the accessible features of the facility and the guest rooms.

Newly built lodging facilities now must comply with the 2010 ADA Standards, which include recreational spaces, such as swimming pools and spas, exercise equipment, golf courses, boating facilities, and play areas. For more, call toll-free 1-800-949-4232; *http://adata.org*

Going outside the United States?

- Learn some of the local language and keep a list of keywords so others can help you.
- Contact your insurance company; make sure you know what is covered while you're abroad.
- Make sure you research foods and their ingredients for the countries on your itinerary.
- For your power or other electrical equipment: Know what transformers, voltage converters, or plug adapters you will need.

maps and schedules ahead of time. A rental car affords flexibility and independence. Most of the major car rental companies can supply hand controls, but it's best to give them a few days notice. Several accessible van rental companies are found in major cities. These offer daily and weekly rates on a variety of accessible, full-size cars and minivans. Check ahead with the companies, listed at the end of the chapter, to make sure their rigs are configured to meet your specific needs.

Once you check in and make sure the accommodations are what you expected at the hotel or aboard the cruise ship, go do what travelers do: eat, shop, relax, go to a museum, or just watch humanity pass by. You're on holiday time now.

So, what are you waiting for? There is nothing so invigorating as travel. It renews the spirit, recharges the imagination. Travel can be a challenge no matter your level of function. But the hassles and even the horror stories supply the contrast to make the good parts all the more special. When you're ready to hit the road or the high seas, be well informed. Know what you're getting in to and to some degree, what you can expect once you get there.

You might have heard that the most important piece of luggage is a joyful heart. Or that the heaviest baggage is the empty purse. Italian writer Cesare Pavese said it well: "If you wish to travel far and fast, travel light. Take off all your envies, jealousies, unforgiveness, selfishness and fears." The best advice is to take all advice with a grain of salt, to be prepared as best you can, and be open to the adventure. Bon voyage!

✌ Below is a List of Travel Resources

AbilityTrip is a centralized information resource for the community of disabled travelers and their companions, including logistics, accommodations, activities, restaurants, and emergency services. **http://abilitytrip.com**

ABLE to Travel provides knowledgeable travel agents experienced with the issues a traveler using a wheelchair or who has limited mobility may encounter during a trip. Toll-free 1-888-211-3635; **www.abletotravel.org**

Able Travel Accessible Adventures makes adventure travel—whether for holiday, work, or study—easier for people with disabilities, seniors, and those with temporary limited mobility. **www.able-travel.com**

Access-Able Travel is an online resource for travelers with disabilities. **www.access-able.com**

Accessible Journeys, based in Pennsylvania, has nearly three decades of experience making vacations across the

Yosemite National Park.

ASHLEY OLSON

world accessible and comfortable. 610-521-0339, toll-free 1-800-846-4537; **www.disabilitytravel.com**

Amtrak has many trains and stations that accommodate travelers with disabilities. For information on reservations, accessible coaches and sleeping accommodations, boarding, use of oxygen, service animals, etc., see **www.amtrak.com/accessible-travel-services**

Emerging Horizons is a publication about accessible travel. It contains access information, resources, news, and travel tips. Editor Candy Harrington has also written several books, including *Barrier-Free Travel, Inns and B&Bs for Wheelers and Slow Walkers*, and recently, *22 Accessible Road Trips* (**http://22accessibleroadtrips.com**); Candy's point is, you don't have to go far away to get far away. For more visit **http://emerginghorizons.com**

Flying Wheels Travel, founded in 1970, has arranged group tours and independent travel for thousands of clients with disabilities. **www.flyingwheelstravel.com**

Greyhound buses offer an alternative to trains and planes. Greyhound Customers with Disabilities Travel Assistance Line, toll-free 1-800-752-4841; click on "Customers with Disabilities at **www.greyhound.com**

Mobility International USA (MIUSA) is a clearinghouse to empower people with disabilities to achieve human rights through international exchange and international development. 541-343-1284; **www.miusa.org**

Rolling Rains, from travel promoter Scott Rains, provides resources on inclusive tourism, promoting a global disability community that both enjoys and asserts the right to full inclusion. **www.rollingrains.com**

ScootAround offers scooter and wheelchair rentals in dozens of North American destinations. Toll-free 1-888-441-7575; **www.scootaround.com**

The Society for Accessible Travel & Hospitality (SATH) is a clearinghouse for accessible tourism information; dedicated to a barrier-free environment across the travel industry. 212-447-7284; **www.sath.org**

Travability is a travel agency in Australia that offers itinerary planning, flight and hotel bookings, attractions, cruising holidays, private yacht charters, escorted group tours, and can hire cars or vans with or without hand controls. **http://travability.travel**

TSA Cares is a dedicated resource for passengers with disabilities regarding questions about Transportation Security Agency screening policies, procedures, and what to expect at security checkpoints. Toll-free 1-855-787-2227.

Wheelchairtraveling.com is an international online community of wheelchair travelers sharing experiences and tips on everything from hotels to transportation to activities and attractions. Whether you are looking for something exotic or close by, let the community help you find what is out there. **http://wheelchairtraveling.com**

NATIONAL ACCESSIBLE VEHICLE RENTALS

- **Accessible Vans of America.** Toll-free 1-866-2241750; *www.accessiblevans.com*
- **Wheelchair Getaways.** Toll-free 1-800-642-2042; *www.wheelchairgetaways.com*
- **Wheelers Accessible Van Rentals.** Toll-free 1-800-456-1371; *www.wheelersvanrentals.com*

Gimp On the Go

Adam Lloyd took a passion for wanderlust and transformed it into his life platform. Lloyd, from Bethesda, Maryland, was injured during a high school swim practice in 1983 and is a C4 quad. He has never been one for sitting on the sidelines. The powerchair, of course, adds another challenge. "The amount of research, planning, and coordination that goes into every trip makes it a chore. That's really why I started Gimp on the Go. Each of us was reinventing the wheel."

Cruising is one of Lloyd's recommended escapes: "The opportunity to see the world without having to make a plethora of travel arrangements or constantly worrying about finding accessible lodging and activities makes for a wonderfully convenient, stress-free trip," he says.

Favorite destination? Las Vegas. "It's incredibly accessible and loads of fun." Any transformative experiences? "Germany was my first trip outside the Americas, and traveling through Bavaria . . . the topography, architecture, history, food, people—I felt like I was in a Grimm's fairytale. In Costa Rica, after almost twenty

Adam Lloyd gets around.

years in a chair, I was almost moved to tears at being able to trek through a genuine rainforest! It was such a unique experience, and one I never would have dared to dream could be a reality for me after my accident." See *www.gimponthego.com*

6 Tools & Technology

With the right gear, gadgets, and equipment, people living with paralysis can open the doors of opportunity, self-sufficiency, employment, or recreation.

The RoughRider Wheelchair, targeted for use in areas of rugged terrain and poor infrastructure. Ralf Hotchkiss, who began redesigning wheelchairs after he became disabled in a motorcycle accident in college, co-founded Whirlwind Wheelchair International in order to design sturdy wheelchairs that could be easily built and repaired in developing countries from locally available materials. The RoughRider frame is made from thin-walled steel tubing, available almost anywhere. The back wheels are bicycle tires. The chairs are now made in Mexico, Turkey, South Africa, Vietnam, and Indonesia; see www.whirlwindwheelchair.org

W elcome to the wonderful world of assistive technology, all the tools, the gear and gadgets that can profoundly affect the lives of people who have lost function due to paralysis. Innovation and product design offer much more than convenience, of course. There are many people thriving in their communities who would have been locked away in institutions a generation or two ago in the past.

Indeed, technology opens the doors of opportunity. The computer, for example, is a truly essential and empowering tool; it offers human contact and access to the community. It is a pipeline for information and a gateway to the marketplace. It can offer recreation and fun, and it can lead to gainful employment. With a variety of switches and software options, almost anyone can access the power of the PC – even people who cannot move a muscle.

There are dozens of accessories and gadgets not listed here, such as reachers, grabbers and all the special devices to make things easier in the kitchen, bath and bedroom. Check out one of the big home healthcare catalogs, including Sportaid (**www.sportaid.com**), Patterson Medical (**www.pattersonmedical.com**), HDIS Healthcare (**www.hdis.com**) or Allegro Medical (**www.allegromedical.com**).

Still, we've taken a fairly broad view of what might be considered a tool, from microchips to velcro. We have included computers and a variety of hands-free options for using the PC or smartphone. We have also featured personal mobility (wheelchairs, scooters and seating systems); environmental control systems (central switch boxes to run electrical functions); home modification (the design elements that make the home or workplace accommodating); automobiles and the hand controls to operate them; orthoses and bracing devices to improve function, and in some cases, ambulation; and clothing tailored for people who spend all day sitting. While most of us don't think of a dog or a monkey as a tool, we have included service animals in this section for the high utility they offer as assistive pets.

WHEELCHAIRS

THE COMMON SAYING HAS IT ALL WRONG: People are not "confined" to their wheelchairs – they are in fact liberated by their wheels. A person with paralysis can get around as quickly in a wheelchair as anyone else can walking. A wheelchair offers people access to work and shopping or any other travel outside the home. For those who are interested, a wheelchair accommodates participation in races, basketball, tennis and other sports.

In some ways a wheelchair is like a bicycle: There are many designs and styles to choose from including imports, lightweights, racing models, etc. The chair is also like a pair of shoes – there are distinct styles for special purposes, such as tennis or rugged trail use. If the fit isn't just right the user can't get comfortable and therefore can't achieve maximum function.

Selecting the right chair, especially for a first-time wheelchair user, can be confusing. It's always a good idea to work with an occupational therapist (OT) who has experience with various kinds of wheelchairs. Many people choose their first chair because it was the one the insurance company was willing to pay for. The second one, though, is often selected because of styling, performance or other features. Here are some basics on wheelchairs:

Manual Chairs

People with upper body strength typically use a manual chair – it is propelled, of course, by pushing the arms forward as the hands grab the wheel rims. A little over a generation ago the standard chair was a chrome-plated behemoth that weighed about 50 pounds. Today's standard chair comes in every color you can think of and is much less than half that weight. The modern chair is designed for far superior performance – they ride truer and are much easier to push than the clunkers of yesteryear. The lightweights, whether with a rigid frame or a folding frame, are also easier to lift in and out of cars. Generally speaking, a rigid frame (one that does not fold up) transfers more of the rider's energy into the forward motion than does a folding unit. The primary advantage of a folding chair, however, is portability; some folding units can even fit in the overhead bin of an airplane.

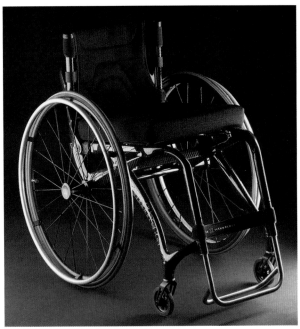

PANTHERA

In recent years, chair makers have added suspension systems as an option, which smooth the ride considerably. The trade-off in ride quality is with weight (shocks add a few pounds) and price (higher). Aftermarket products (e.g. Frog Legs, **http://froglegsinc.com**) are also available to add suspension to the front forks; these are very popular and have been approved for reimbursement by Medicare. Another key innovation is the use of super-light titanium in wheelchair frames. Light is better for the shoulders. Ti leads the pack in the U.S. (**www.tilite.com**). Panthera, from Sweden, offers a super lightweight chair, weighs under 10 lbs. with wheels (**www.panthera.se**).

There are also lots of options for wheels and tires, including innovations for performance, off-road traction and high style. A company called Spinergy branched out from the bicycle business to add a high performance line of wheelchair rims. They are light and stay true. The company recently brought out an innovative push rim – the outer part of the rim that one pushes to propel the chair. The soft rubber FlexRim bridges between the rim and the tire, allowing for an easier, low impact push that protects hands and arms from impact. **www.spinergy.com**

Propulsion alternatives: you don't have to push a rim on the wheel to make the chair go. There are a couple of lever-driven chairs on the market, both touting that shoulders don't get damaged the way they can with standard rim pushing. The Pivot Dual Lever Drive replaces

WIJIT

the quick-release rear wheels of any manual wheelchair; the Pivot comes with five levels of effort (**http://riomobility.com**). The Wijit Wheelchair Lever Driving and Braking System lets the user push half as much as they usually do with a conventional wheelchair. Says the company, citing medical literature to back it up, "The Wijit will protect you from repetitive stress injuries to your shoulders, elbows and wrists caused by wheelchair use, and protects your hands from friction burns." **http://wijit.com**

Power

A person who can't push may require a wheelchair or scooter powered by an electric motor and batteries and controlled by a joystick. Power chairs come in several basic styles. The traditional style looks like a beefed-up standard issue wheelchair, along with all the extra bulk of the batteries, motor and control systems. There are also platform-model power chairs with a more ordinary-looking seat or captain's chair fixed atop a power base. Scooters come in three- and four-wheel configurations and are most often used by people who don't require them full-time.

Twenty years or so ago, the power chair market was limited to just a few brands and models. Innovation has expanded the choices toward lighter, more powerful and much faster chairs. Most power chairs have rear-

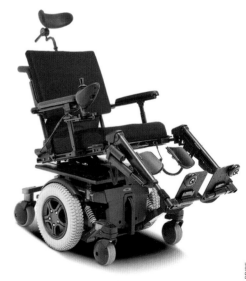

PRIDE

wheel drive, but mid-wheel and front-wheel drives have grabbed a share of the market. These are easier to turn and are quite nimble in tight spaces. There are models that are rugged and off-road ready; there are models that fold for travel; there are power chairs that can be customized for the most complex needs of people with paralysis. The right choice for each user is based on much more than style. Getting a power chair fitted and configured to one's needs requires expert help, from an OT or reputable durable medical supplier. How do you find the right supplier? Ask around, ask an OT, read the very active gear discussion boards online at **www.wheelchairjunkie.com** or **http://sci.rutgers.edu**

The IBOT was one cool wheelchair; it could stand on it's hind wheels and could even climb stairs. Despite the marketing savvy of Johnson & Johnson, they couldn't get it paid for by insurance. You still see them in use but not many were sold. The stand-up-on-two wheels Segway, which costs about $20,000 less than an IBOT did, comes from the same inventor using the same gyro technology; the Segway has now been adapted as a wheelchair. A company called Segsolutions makes a seating conversion kit for the off-the-shelf Segway; people who ride it love it. **www.segsolutions4freedom.com**

To be sure, reimbursement is a key issue for all durable medical equipment purchases, especially for high-ticket items such as power chairs (which can cost more than a fully loaded Honda). The power-mobility industry has been the target of federal investigations into Medicare fraud. According to a 2011 government report, 80 percent of Medicare claims for power wheelchairs did not meet coverage requirements and should not have been paid by Medicare. So, in an attempt to curtail fraud, Medicare has changed some of its reimbursement rules, including in some cases, prior authorization. That, along with a choice-limiting system of competitive bidding, has been met with much resistance in the disability community. To keep abreast of evolving federal reimbursement policies, see the ITEM Coalition (Independence Through Enhancement of Medicare and Medicaid; **http://itemcoalition.org**), a consumer-led coalition of national organizations, including the Reeve Foundation, whose goal is to improve access to assistive devices, technologies and related services for individuals with disabilities.

Need a new chair? You'll need to work with your funding sources, your OT and seating specialists, and your rehab supplier to get the best chair for your needs, and to defend your choice in the event of a reimbursement denial.

For more on power chairs options, the Reeve Foundation website, **www.christopherreeve.org**, presents a 32-segment Power Wheelchair Comparison video series (search for power wheelchair) with detailed test drives and consumer-friendly information on eight power chairs from the seven leading manufacturers—produced by power chair user Jenni Gold.

Batteries

Battery life is a crucial issue for power chair users. Failure to manage this power source can lead to sticky or annoying situations, especially if you're far from home. Power chair batteries must be of the 24-volt "deep-cycle" variety, discharged over long periods, as opposed to a battery in a car (12-volt) used for short bursts of power. Deep-cycle units come in several sizes: e.g., Group-22, Group-24 and Group-27. The larger the group number, the larger the battery and the more power it stores.

There are three types of batteries. Lead-acid or "wet" batteries create electrical energy when lead and sulfuric acid interact. Wet means just that: These battery cells need to be periodically filled with distilled water, maybe once a month. The main advantage of a wet-cell battery is the lower cost. The main disadvantage is that they may require special handling, especially when you fly. Gel batteries don't have liquid to spill or top off. They are more expensive than wet battery versions, but they have a longer life cycle and are much preferred for airline travel. Absorbent glass mat (AGM) batteries, like gel units, don't require maintenance and are fine for flying. They are very rugged, hold a charge better and last twice as long as standard lead-acid batteries. They are also the most expensive.

Wheelchair batteries are sometimes the same as those used in the boating industry. If you pay for your own batteries out-of-pocket, you might save money by purchasing marine deep-cycle batteries. Be sure and check with your chair manufacturer's specifications.

Power assist

A sort of hybridization has occurred. The standard lightweight manual can be tricked-up with a small, powerful motor, affixed to the wheel units or attached to the base of the chair. When the assist is turned on, a forward push on the handrim gives the chair a strong boost. The e.motion fits many types of chairs (**www.frankmobility.com**). The Xtender is available on some Quickie models (**www.sunrisemedical.com**) in two versions, one that increases the force applied to the handrims by a factor of 1.5 and one that boosts you by a factor of 3. These assist hubs add quite a bit of weight to the chair (from 38 to almost 50 pounds) and quite a bit of expense ($5,000 to $8,000), but the advantages are terrific, especially for lower-level quads and anyone with achy shoulders who won't have to struggle up steep hills. A rider's range will increase dramatically using the assist, saving personal energy and wear and tear on the rotator cuffs. What's more, the chair doesn't look like a beefed-up power unit: It looks more or less "normal."

SmartDrive is a newer power assist option for manual chairs. This is a portable drive wheel (11 pounds) that pretty easily hooks on to the base of the chair; a battery fits under the seat. The manufacturer, Max Mobility, notes that the unit is better on dry surfaces; traction is provided

by the weight of the drive unit and the grip of the drive wheel. Price is comparable to the rim-based power assist units; see **http://max-mobility.com**

Another option, this one without batteries or motors, is MagicWheels, two-gear wheelchair wheels that have a lower gear for hills when you need it, with a click of the hub, at about a third the cost of power assist units. Visit **www.magicwheels.com**

SmartDrive: portable, easy to hook up.

If users emphasize the potential increased health benefits of power assist devices (saving the shoulders), many insurance companies will cover them, including Medicare.

Kids' Chairs

Children's bodies are growing and changing, which means their chairs must be adjusted or replaced more often than adult chairs. Since chairs are not cheap and insurance providers often place limitations

SUNRISE QUICKIE ZIPPIE

on replacement, most manufacturers offer adjustable chairs to accommodate a growing child. Wheelchair companies also offer chairs for kids that don't look as "medical" as the older styles. The updated looks offer more streamlined designs, cooler upholstery and different frame colors. Colours (**www.colourswheelchair.com**) offers the Little Dipper, or the Chump, little chairs with a little attitude. Likewise, the Sunrise Quickie Zippie (**www.sunrisemedical.com**) and the Invacare Orbit (**www.invacare.com**) are made for younger wheelers who want to ride with a bit of style.

Seating and Positioning

People with paralysis are at high risk for pressure sores and therefore usually require special cushions and seating systems to give the skin some relief. There are several basic kinds of cushion material, each with benefits for certain types of users: air, foam or liquid (e.g., gel), a variety that is more dynamic, with moving parts. There is no single product that will do the job for all. The right cushion can provide comfort, correct positioning and prevent pressure sores, but it need not meet all those criteria for every user. An ambulatory person who only uses a wheelchair to go shopping doesn't have the same needs as a high-level quad who spends eighteen hours per day in a power chair, so it's important to fully understand your requirements and select the appropriate cushion, weighing the pros and cons of the different styles.

Work with your seating specialist to determine which is the right one to fit your body, lifestyle and budget.

Foam is the least expensive material for a cushion. It's also lightweight and doesn't leak or lose air. It does wear out, though, losing its compression over time. Air flotation cushions, such as the popular ROHO model (**www.rohoinc.com**), provide support using a rubber bladder of evenly distributed air. These work well but can leak; they also require air adjustments when you change altitude. Another type of air cushion, the Vicair Vector, employs many small, permanently sealed air cells; the cushion can be adjusted by unzipping the liner and removing or adding air cells (**www.vicair.com**). The BBD air cushion (aka the "bye bye") has been around since the late Ken McRight brought them to market in 1951. The single-chamber models are still widely used for inexpensive pressure relief. **www.randscot.com**

Gel cushions, such as the Jay (**www.sunrisemedical.com**), are filled with slow-flowing gel. They are popular and effective for skin protection, but are also somewhat heavy.

Aquila is an example of a dynamic cushion; it features an oscillating pump that alternates pressure. The theory is that seating can continue for longer periods of time if pressure is alternated with no pressure. This adds weight to the chair and, because the pump runs on batteries, is not as carefree as a static cushion (**www.aquilacorp.com**). Another dynamic pressure-changing cushion is the Ease (**http://easecushion.com**). Some users might benefit from a custom cushion, made to fit their body. The Aspen line uses a thin contoured plastic shell generated from client mold. **www.ridedesigns.com**

For a list of available cushions and seating systems see AbleData (**www.abledata.com**) or USA TechGuide (**www.usatechguide.org**), which includes reviews of many wheelchair-related products. It's best to work with a seating and positioning expert to pick the right product.

Tilt or Recline

Some people use special wheelchairs to distribute pressure and thus reduce the risk of skin sores. These chairs also increase comfort and

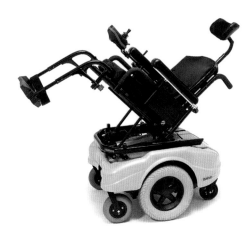

sitting tolerance. One type of chair, called "tilt in space," changes a person's orientation while maintaining fixed hip, knee and ankle angles. In effect, the whole seat tilts. The other chair option is a recline system, which basically changes the seat-to-back angle, flattening out the back of the chair and, in some cases, raising the legs to form a flat surface.

A tilt system redistributes pressure from the buttocks and posterior thighs to the posterior trunk and head. The system maintains posture and prevents sheering (the friction on tissues from dragging across a surface). A drawback: If a user sits at a workstation, for example, the tilt requires that he or she move back from the table to avoid hitting it with the knees or footrests.

Recline systems open the seat-to-back angle and, in combination with elevating leg rests, open the knee angle. There are some advantages to a recline system for eating, making transfers or assisting with bowel or bladder programs, as all are easier when lying down. Generally speaking, the recline system offers more pressure relief than tilt, but with a higher risk of sheer. Elevating the legs may be beneficial to people with edema. Both tilt and recline must be fitted and prescribed by seating and positioning experts.

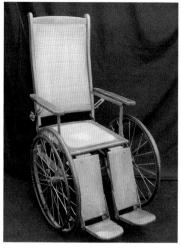

Old school: recline yes; tilt no.

Standing

Standing chairs act as normal manual chairs but also help the rider rise to a standing position. There are many advantages to being tall at home, in school and in the workplace. Some manual chairs come with a power assist to activate the rising mechanism. Some power chairs also enable the rider to rise to a standing position, with the advantage of eye-to-eye contact with others. The drawback: They are not cheap and are heavy for an everyday chair. Standing has physical benefits, too. It helps to prevent pressure sores, improves circulation and range of motion and, for some, reduces spasms and contractions. A few years ago the Hines VA reported that people who stand for 30 minutes or more per day "had significantly improved quality of life, fewer bed sores, fewer bladder infections, improved bowel regularity, and improved ability to straighten their legs." See Lifestand (**www.lifestandusa.com**), Levo (**www.levousa.com**, now Permobil) or Redman (**www.redmanpowerchair.com**).

Ready Stalls Standing Frames

Standing frames are also available (they don't retract to a seat). EasyStand offers several models, including a pediatiric unit (www. easystand.com). Some, such as the Stand Aid (**www.stand-aid.com**), are motorized. Other standing frames are more rudimentary—basically a static frame that supports a paralyzed person in the standing position. **www.stand-rite.com** or **www.ReadyStalls.com**

There are other specialty chairs available, including ultra lightweight three-wheelers for road racing; chairs with extra camber for tennis and basketball (they don't tip over); heavy duty four-wheelers for off-road use; chairs with big puffy tires for the beach, and even chairs with tractor treads for those who cannot resist negotiating the roughest of terrain.

SOURCES

AbleData, USA TechGuide

❧ **Below are links to wheelchair and seating resources.**

WheelchairJunkie is a resourceful and opinionated website operated by self-described "power chair gonzo" Mark E. Smith. Says he: "WheelchairJunkie.com is about mobility, not manufacturers, so the voices expressed here represent only users." **www.wheelchairjunkie.com**

Mark Smith

USA TechGuide is an Internet guide to wheelchairs and assistive technology, including numerous reviews of mobility gear. Sponsored by United Spinal Association. **www.usatechguide.org**

Wheelchair and scooter companies include:
- Invacare, **www.invacare.com**
- Sunrise Medical/Quickie, **www.sunrisemedical.com**
- Permobil, **www.permobil.com**
- Colours, **www.colourswheelchair.com**
- TiSport, **www.tilite.com**
- Pride Mobility (Jazzy brand), **www.pridemobility.com**
- Redman Power Chair, **www.redmanpowerchair.com**

Spinlife is one of several online dealers of durable medical equipment. **www.spinlife.com**; other online dealers include Preferred Health Choice, **www.phc-online.com** and Sportaid, **www.sportaid.com**

Wheelchair accessories: Here is a source for backpacks, trays, cup holders, canopies, umbrellas and other cool stuff for your chair. Diestco, **www.diestco.com**

Environmental Control

Paralysis often restricts control over one's living space. An environmental control unit (ECU) can help people regain power over their environment and maximize functional ability and independence at home, school, work and leisure.

Generally, an ECU is a remote control unit designed to operate a variety of switches and appliances – such as opening a door, turning on the television, dialing a telephone, adjusting the lights, etc. The ECU can operate with an array of switches, by voice command, by computer or by sip and puff. The unit can also be operated by motion detection switches; for example, one can control the environment with as little movement as an eye blink.

&♥ **Below are resources on ECUs and other tools.**

X-10 technology is a nifty and inexpensive remote switching system that uses existing wiring in the home or workplace, or with a smart phone; toll-free 1-800-675-3044; **www.x10wti.com**

Quartet Technology Incorporated (QTI) offers high-end ECU units that operate by voice, switches or computer mouse; 978-957-4328; **www.qtiusa.com**

Home Automated Living (HAL) makes software that turns the home computer into an ECU controllable from anywhere. HAL, Inc., toll-free 1-855-442-5435; **www.automatedliving.com**

Able-Phone makes adaptive telephones designed for persons with little or no arm and hand function. 530-846-7466; **www.ablephone.com**

The Association of Assistive Technology Act Programs supports implementation of the AT Act and promotes full access to AT devices and services: It's a good idea to try out various ECU or computer operating systems before purchase. One way to shop for adaptive technology is to check in with your state's federal Tech Act office. For a list of resources see **www.ataporg.org**

Rehabtool.com features a comprehensive collection of links to the largest AT catalogs, databases and vendor directories in North America. **www.rehabtool.com**

United Spinal Association features an AT site with product listings and reviews. **www.usatechguide.org**

Closing the Gap is a national publication offering great resources in print and online on assistive equipment and adaptive gear. **http://closingthegap.com**

Assistivetech.net is an online resource providing up-to-date information on assistive technologies, adaptive environments and community resources. **www.assistivetech.net**

Save Those Wrists and Shoulders

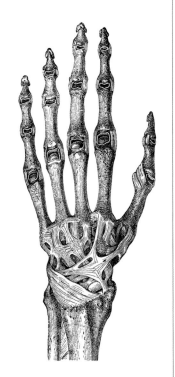

This is right out of the medical literature but it's no secret: the arms were not designed to be the legs, too. As people live 40-50 or more years with paralysis, overuse of the upper limbs is inevitable. "…pain and injury are highly prevalent in people with spinal cord injury and the consequences are significant." So it says in the clinical guidelines from The Consortium for Spinal Cord Medicine, *Preservation of Upper Limb Function Following Spinal Cord Injury* (download a free copy from PVA at *www.pva.org)*. The guidelines recommend a series of things wheelchair users should do to minimize wrist and shoulder pain.

- Minimize the frequency of repetitive upper limb tasks. This includes decreasing the frequency of the stroke during wheelchair propulsion, decreasing the number of transfers needed each day, decreasing the frequency of other repetitive tasks.

- Minimize the force required for upper limb tasks. This can be achieved by maintaining an ideal weight, improving wheelchair propulsion techniques, using optimal biomechanics during weight bearing, and minimizing exposure to high loads as part of daily activities.
- For the wrist: avoid extremes of motion, particularly maximum extension when weight bearing during transfers.
- For the shoulders: avoid tasks that require the arm to be above shoulder height.
- Wheelchair: the guidelines strongly recommend that users should be provided with a high-strength, fully customizable manual wheelchair made of the lightest possible material. Lighter wheelchairs require less force to propel. Titanium chairs, for example, are super light but also dampen vibration, protecting the spine and shoulder from the damaging effects of vibration.
- Rear axel: Adjust the rear axle as far forward as possible without compromising the stability of the user. This requires less muscle effort, fewer strokes to go the same speed, and decreases rolling resistance, therefore increasing propulsion efficiency. Of course moving the axel forward makes a chair more tippy. The panel recommends an incremental change in axel position so the user can get used to the stability. As a general rule, the seat height and rear axle should be adjusted so that when the hand is placed at the top dead-center position on the pushrim, the angle between the upper arm and forearm is between 100 and 120 degrees.
- Stroke: use long, smooth pushes that limit impact on the pushrim. After the push, it is recommended that the hand drop below the pushrim in a semi-circular pattern for better biomechanical form.
- Transfers: keep them level if at all possible. The guidelines strongly recommend using a transfer device (sliding board, etc.) if there is any arm pain or upper limb weakness.
- Power mobility: yes, power will save the joints but there may be a stigma about it—maybe the idea of a motorized wheelchair brings on thoughts of dependency, loss of access. Consider one of the newer power-assist devices that power up a manual chair or supplement the force applied to the pushrim (see page 267).

Hands-Free Computing

Hands-free technology is available for tetraplegics and people with upper-body restrictions to fully and independently operate a computer and almost all software. It's also possible to navigate the World Wide Web by using only voice, eyes, head or breath. Soon the world of computing will be accessed using no touch at all, just brain waves.

🐾 **Here is a rundown on hands-free cursor control alternatives.**

The HeadMouse Extreme translates the movements of a user's head into movements of a computer mouse using a wireless optical sensor that tracks a tiny target placed on the user's forehead or glasses. Full computer control facilitated by an onscreen keyboard. Prentke Romich, **www.prentrom.com**

TrackerPro is a computer input device that takes the place of a mouse for people with little or no hand movement; it works just like a mouse (no additional software required). Prentke Romich, **www.prentrom.com**

HeadMouse model is also available from Origin Instruments Corporation, **www.orin.com**

Cyberlink allows hands-free control of cursors, video games and external devices. Users wear a headband with sensors to detect electrical signals from facial muscle, eye movement and brain wave activity. **www.broadenedhorizons.com/braincontrol.htm**

NaturalPoint SmartNAV is a hands free ergonomic mouse. Increase productivity by moving your head to control the computer. **www.naturalpoint.com/smartnav**

Quad-Joy is a hands-free system that uses a joystick-operated mouse, controlled by the lips, or sip and puff. **www.quadjoy.com**

Dragon Systems: This voice activation software is widely used at home and in the office to translate voice to text; it's easy and reliable. **www.nuance.com/dragon**

RJ Cooper & Associates offers dozens of assistive technology solutions, including custom adaptations for the iPad. Call 1-800-RJCooper; **http://rjcooper.com**

Hands Free: Three Ways to Go

No question about it, my computer is my most valuable possession. It's an incredible tool for communication, for learning, for fun, for shopping, for running one's home environment, and best of all, for making a living. There are lots of ways to operate the computer without using hands. I use a mouth stick, which I make myself. I can type fairly quickly with it. *—Pete Denman, C4*

If you have access to a computer, you're able to communicate with the outside world. They won't even know you have a disability unless you tell them. I use Morse code and a sip-n-puff. I tried a lot of ways to do this and this seems to work the best. Once you memorize the codes, it's just automatic. *—Jim Lubin, C2*

I do a lot of work on the computer. I spend hours and hours every day on the computer. I use a voice-activated system called Dragon: Naturally Speaking, which works very well for me. For me to move the mouse, which I use pretty extensively, it works through the wheelchair system. The mouse is infrared, and it sends a signal from my wheelchair to the computer. I have a little remote control that sits on the roof of my mouth, and I hit little buttons with my tongue. *—Brooke Ellison, C2*

Christopher Reeve and Brooke Ellison, on the set of The Brooke Ellison Story, directed by Reeve, 2004

A Man and His Gear

PHOTOS: SAM MADDOX

Mark is a heavy computer user. He works his rig two ways: with a Jouse joystick he can operate with his mouth (www.jouse.com); this input is synced with an onscreen keyboard (www.imgpresents.com). He can also write, send and receive email or surf the web by voice activation (Dragon NaturallySpeaking software, www.nuance.com).

Mark Willits recently celebrated what he called his 50-50 day: half his life walking, half as a vent-dependent C3 tetraplegic. He had a big party at his house outside Los Angeles, with lots of family and friends to share the day; he gives this support system credit for his success. Mark broke his neck as a teenager, on his family's farm in Iowa; he went on to college, first in Iowa and then in Arizona. He then went to law school at UCLA. "In May 2008, I graduated from the UCLA School of Law," says Mark, "while my girlfriend graduated from Pepperdine University one week later. At our joint graduation party, she got down on one knee and proposed to me. We were married in November 2008 at our home."

Mark is a practicing attorney; he is president of the L.A. area peer network Ralph's Riders. He and his wife Sheila travel extensively (see page 252 for his tips for vent trekking). Says Mark, "Your limitations can only limit you if you let them."

Here is a glimpse of the gear Mark uses to work and stay connected.

Exercise is a major part of Mark's lifestyle. To get a workout he straps into a functional electrical stimulation device from Restorative Therapies (www.restorative-therapies.com). He can work his lower extremities, or arms and legs simultaneously.

Left: Mark uses an Invacare power chair with tilt, and relies on a Pulmonetics LTV 1100 ventilator (see www.carefusion.com). Below: he hooks either phone or iPad to a flexible mount from Loc-Line Modular Hose (see www.modularhose.com). He activates the capacitive touch screens with mouthsticks from iFaraday (www.ifaraday.com).

Home Modification

The world isn't flat or paved, of course, and for the most part no one was thinking about people using wheelchairs or walkers when they designed all our streets and buildings. But things are changing as people with disabilities — joined by the largest ever U.S. generation heading toward its senior years – have pushed to open up access to all people, including those with paralysis or mobility problems.

The concept of universal design goes beyond ramps, retrofits and curb cuts. It isn't just about accessibility. It is a way of looking at the designed world knowing that thoughtful plans from the get-go will accommodate any user across his or her lifespan – whether it's getting in the office, the ballpark, or on the Internet.

The late Ron Mace, creator of the term "universal design," and founder of the Center for Universal Design at North Carolina State University, put it this way: "Universal design is the design of products and environments to be usable by all people, to the greatest extent possible, without the need for adaptation or specialized design." What he means is that design should work for all of us, across our lifespans, transparently.

There are laws on the books making schools, transportation, housing, public accommodations and sidewalks fully accessible in every city. For most people, day-in and day-out access has more to do with getting in and out of the house, working in the kitchen, using the bathroom.

Home modification can be as simple as a doorknob that's easy to work, a grab bar in the right place or a ramp to get in through the back door. It may involve widening a door or installing a special sink or elevator. It gets as fancy or as complicated as any architect can make it. There are solutions that don't cost much and there are serious money pits.

Home access and ease-of-use modifications are for the most part still viewed as an exception: Builders will not include them unless consumers ask for them, and consumers won't ask for them unless they have a significant need. So be informed, know what's out there. What follows are resources to help you assess your needs, weigh your many product options and locate contractors and vendors to make your home or work environment accessible.

ε♦ **Below are links to resources.**

Center for Universal Design evaluates, develops and promotes universal design in housing, public and commercial facilities, and related products. Toll-free 1-800-647-6777; **www.design.ncsu.edu/cud**

National Resource Center on Supportive Housing and Home Modification, based at the University of Southern California, promotes aging at home for frail elderly and persons aging with a disability, 213-740-1364; **www.homemods.org**

Handi Habitats is a contractor service available in many states to evaluate and install home modifications. Toll-free 1-877-467-5617; **www.handihabitats.com**

MAX-Ability specializes in products and consultation services for accessibility accommodation in the home, school, and healthcare facilities. National coverage. Toll-free 1-800-577-1555; **http://max-ability.com**

Shower Bay is a portable shower designed for wheelchair users, without requiring dangerous wet-environment transfers or expensive home renovations. Can be quickly assembled in any room of the house -- connect to a standard faucet, turn on the pump, ready to go. Toll-free 1-877-223-8999; **www.showerbay.com**

Mac's Lift Gate designs and engineers vertical lifts for everyday use. Toll-free 1-800-795-6227; **www.macslift.com**

ThyssenKrupp Access Solutions supplies mobility solutions in homes and public areas, including stairlifts, platform lifts, home elevators. **www.tkaccess.com**

AbleData is a national resource database on adaptive technology products, including every sort of device and tool for home or workplace modification. Funded by the National Institute on Disability and Rehabilitation Research; toll-free 1-800-227-0216; **www.abledata.com**

Access Board is an independent federal agency devoted

to improving accessibility for people with disabilities. The board develops and enforces accessibility requirements for the built environment, transit vehicles, telecommunications, electronic and information technology. Toll-free 1-800-872-2253; **www.access-board.gov**

Accessibility Equipment Manufacturers Association is a trade group of companies that make elevators and lifts, stairway chairlifts and similar products. Toll-free 1-800-514-1100; **www.aema.com**

The Institute for Human Centered Design (IHCD), founded in 1978 as Adaptive Environments, is an international organization committed to advancing excellence in design, balancing expertise in legally required accessibility with best practices in universal design. **http://humancentereddesign.org**

Center for Inclusive Design and Environmental Access (IDEA) is dedicated to improving the design of environments and products by making them more usable, safer and appealing to people with a wide range of abilities, throughout their life spans. **www.ap.buffalo.edu/idea**

AARP spotlights universal design for people of all ages. **www.aarp.org/families/home_design**

The Ramp Project offers an inexpensive, modular, reusable, easy to build wheelchair ramp design. The manual, "How to Build Ramps for Home Accessibility," contains step-by-step instructions and engineering drawings for ramps and stairs. **www.wheelchairramp.org**

Concrete Change works to make all homes visitable, that is, accessible to all. Minimum standards: at least one entrance with zero steps, 32-inch passages through interior doors and at least a half-bath on the main floor. **http://concretechange.org**

AdaptMy is a resource for remodeling ideas for kitchen, bath, bedroom, etc. **www.adaptmy.com**

Design Linc provides information on universal design products, technical information, other resources. **www.designlinc.com**

Cars and Driving

There's more to having a set of wheels than getting from here to there. Jumping in a car is a ticket to freedom, independence and adventure. For people new to paralysis, driving is a sure way to get back into the swing of things. But can you do it? Can a paralyzed person get behind the wheel and handle the machine and the traffic? Driving is quite possible for many people who are paralyzed, even those with very limited hand and arm function. A wide range of adaptive driving equipment and vehicle modifications are on the market today.

Driving with a disability often means relearning to drive. The rules of the road don't change, but the controls do. Depending on one's specific needs, an adapted vehicle may include hand controls for braking/accelerating, power assist devices for easy steering, touch ignition pads and gear shifts, adjustable driver's seats, automatic door openers and even joysticks for people with extremely limited hand function (see sidebar on joystick driving, page 288). For a person who has had a stroke, a spinner knob might be attached to the steering wheel for one-hand steering. A left gas pedal may be adapted if the right foot can't operate the gas.

The first step in the process is to get an evaluation from a qualified driver trainer. This will determine your basic driving set up, specific modifications and driving equipment to match your needs. An evaluation also includes vision screening and assessment of muscle

The MVI, made in America, designed from the ground up for the wheelchair market.

strength; flexibility and range of motion; hand-eye coordination and reaction time; judgment and decision making; and the ability to handle adaptive equipment. An evaluator may also take into account medications a potential driver is taking.

To find a qualified evaluator, visit your local rehabilitation center or contact the Association for Driver Rehabilitation Specialists (ADED – see page 286), which maintains a list of certified specialists throughout the country.

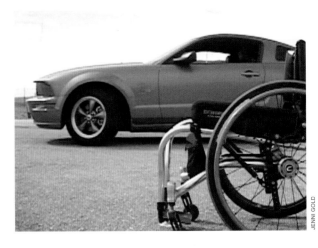

JENNI GOLD

As for getting a new driver's license, most states require a valid learner's permit or driver's license to receive an on-the-road evaluation. You cannot be denied the opportunity to apply for a permit or license because you have a disability, but you may receive a restricted license, based on adaptive devices you may require.

Once you get the green light from the evaluation and your state's motor vehicle department, it's time to think about the kinds of vehicles that suit your abilities and needs. Choosing the right car may lead you to more practical wheels than you might have chosen before paralysis (two-seater sports cars may fit the image you have of yourself but are pretty low on the practical scale; minivans, those dreaded mom-wagons you swore to avoid are of much higher utility). See what other people with similar disabilities drive. Then be sure and collaborate with the evaluator and a qualified vehicle modification dealer.

People who sit in their wheelchair while driving or riding in minivans or full-size vans need either a manual tie-down or power lockdowns for safety. The manual systems usually require help getting in and out. Power units allow for more independence – you just roll into place and the chair automatically locks down. Because there is no way a person can operate a van from a scooter, users must be able to transfer to the vehicle seat to drive; electronic seats are available to help with the transfer.

The following can help with vehicle selection and perhaps adaptation of a car you already own:

- Does the necessary adaptive equipment require a van, or will a smaller passenger car do? In other words, will you be driving from a wheelchair or can you transfer to the car seat? If you can transfer in to drive a car, your choices are much wider.
- Will you fit in a minivan? A person may sit taller in the chair and may not clear the ceiling.
- Can the vehicle accommodate the hand controls or other needed driving equipment?
- Will there be enough space to accommodate other passengers once the vehicle is modified?
- Is there adequate parking space at home and at work for the vehicle and for loading/unloading a wheelchair or walker? Be aware that full-size vans might not fit in your garage or public garages or even in certain parking spaces.
- If a third party is paying for the vehicle, adaptive devices, or modifications, are there limitations or restrictions on what is covered? Get a written statement on what a funding agency will pay before making your purchase.
- If you are adapting a used van or family vehicle, make sure the technician has lots of experience. All lifts are not created equally; some just won't fit. Also, some lifts are built for wheelchair users; scooter users may not be able to use them.

The cost of modifying a vehicle varies greatly. A new vehicle modified with adaptive equipment can cost anywhere from $20,000 to $80,000. Be a savvy shopper; investigate public and private financial assistance. Contact your state's department of vocational rehabilitation or another agency that provides vocational services and, if appropriate, the Department of Veterans Affairs. Also, consider the following:

- Some nonprofit groups that advocate for individuals with disabilities have grant programs that help with adaptive devices.
- If you have private health insurance or workers' compensation, you may be covered for adaptive devices and vehicle modification. Check with your insurance carrier.

- Several auto manufacturers, including Toyota, Chrysler, Ford, and General Motors, have rebate or reimbursement plans for vehicles that will be modified (see facing page).
- Some states waive the sales tax for adaptive devices if you have a doctor's prescription for their use. You may also be eligible for medical expense-related savings on your federal income tax return; consult a tax specialist.

Find a qualified dealer to modify your vehicle. Ask questions, check credentials and references. Do they work with evaluators? Will they examine your vehicle before you purchase it? Do they require a prescription from a physician or other driver evaluation specialist? Do they provide training on how to use the equipment? Do they provide service? What is the cost? How long will it take to do the work? What is the warranty? Have fun. Be safe.

SOURCES

U.S. Department of Transportation, Association for Driver Rehabilitation Specialists

❧ **Below are links to resources.**

The Association for Driver Rehabilitation Specialists (ADED) certifies driver trainers who are experts in adaptive driving and vehicles. The organization offers several fact sheets for drivers with various types of disabilities. Call toll-free 1-866-672-9466; **www.driver-ed.org**

National Mobility Equipment Dealers Association (NMEDA) is a trade group of companies that sell adaptive driving equipment. Call toll-free 1-866-948-8341; **www.nmeda.org**

National Highway Traffic and Transportation Safety Administration offers advice on driver training, vehicle selection and vehicle modification; Search under "adaptive." at **www.nhtsa.gov**

Disabled Dealer is a publication featuring used vehicles (and all sorts of other rehab and medical gear). Regional editions feature numerous pre-owned adapted vans and cars. **www.disableddealer.com**

Cars and driving: the Reeve Foundation presents a multi-segment Accessible Driving video series, with two segments on Hot Rides – custom adaptations and hot rods, California style; produced by power-chair-user Jenni Gold. Search under "driving" at **www.ChristopherReeve.org**

Vehicle Discounts

Ford Mobility Motoring offers up to $1,000 of assistance toward the cost of adaptive equipment on a new Ford, Lincoln or Mercury vehicle. Ford Mobility Motoring Customer Care Center; 1-800-952-2248.

GM Mobility Program with OnStar offers up to $1,000 reimbursement ($1,200 on Chevy Express/GMC Savana vans) plus two extra years of the OnStar safety and security service on an eligible new GM vehicle (except Cadillac); 1-800-323-9935.

Toyota Mobility Program provides cash reimbursement of up to $1,000 toward aftermarket adaptive equipment or conversion installed on any eligible purchased or leased new Toyota; 1-800-331-4331.

The Chrysler Automobility Program provides up to $1,000 in financial assistance toward the installation of adaptive equipment on new Chrysler, Jeep and Dodge vehicles; 1-800-255-9877.

Hyundai Mobility Program offers $1,000 toward the cost of adaptive equipment. See dealer for more; 1-800-633-5151.

Lexus Mobility Program provides Lexus retail vehicle buyers with a cash reimbursement of up to $1,000 to help offset expenses incurred for adaptive mobility equipment; 1-800-255-3987.

Volvo Mobility Program reimburses up to $1,000 toward the cost of adaptive equipment added to a new Volvo. Mobility by Volvo Center; 1-800-803-5222.

Joystick Motoring

The joystick has enabled a fleet of quads who'd otherwise be riding shotgun to hit the freedom freeway.

Joystick car systems have been around long enough to establish their safety, reliability and performance. You may face a choice between a mechanical/hydraulic system (like an airplane) or electronic system (like a PlayStation). It may come down to your comfort level with electronics and any worries about a total power shutdown at 70 mph.

SAM MADDOX

A California company called dSi custom fits its Scott mechanical system to each driver. The firm says mechanical is more reliable and more refined than electronic. They like to use big Ford vans and stay in touch with drivers (including some with spinal cord injury up to C4/C5) who've logged more than 300,000 miles on the system.

EMC offers an electronic solution called Aevit 2.0. A main advantage is that Aevit does not require modification of original equipment brakes, steering and airbag assemblies. This means you can resell the vehicle without the mods. Also, an Aevit system can be operated by a non-disabled driver. The Scott system, by contrast, is joystick only.

If you're thinking about going joystick, you can't get one without a referral from a driving instructor (see ADED, page 286). Also, the importance of training cannot be overstated. Oh, you may need to line up a trunkload of money, too. A joystick system will run you $40,000 to $65,000, plus the cost of the van. Third parties, including private insurance, voc rehab and the VA, have paid for lots of these, so investigate your options.

For details, ask each manufacturer for user references and if at all possible, check out each system yourself. Contact EMC, 207-512-8009; *www.emc-digi.com*; dSi-Scott, 818-782-6793; *http://drivingsystems.com*

Clothing

For a person with limited mobility or who may be sitting a great deal of the time, dressing can be a challenge. Off-the-rack clothing presents problems: seams may be placed in areas that could cause skin breakdowns; trousers may not be long enough or may bunch up in the lap; jackets bunch up; buttons and fasteners might not be handy. There are, however, options.

Several companies market to people with paralysis:

AbleApparel offers outerwear and accessories for children and adults. **www.ableapparel.com**

Adaptive Clothing: tops, pants, sleepwear, shoes, custom. Toll-free 1-800-572-2224; **www.adaptiveclothing.com**

Adaptations by Adrian designs capes, pants, sweatshirts, jackets. **www.adaptationsbyadrian.com**

Easy Access Clothing has pants, jeans, outerwear. Call toll-free 1-800-775-5536; **www.easyaccessclothing.com**

Professional Fit Clothing features alterations, as well as a line of capes and clothing protectors. 1-800-422-2348; **www.professionalfit.com**

Specially For You: offers a line of gowns, dresses, pants. **www.speciallyforyou.net**

USA Jeans offers a line of jeans friendly to the seated body. Toll-free 800-935-5170. **www.wheelchairjeans.com**

Rolli Moden: men's and women's fashion and accessories. **www.rollimoden.de/epages/RolliModen.sf**

Endless Ability makes a cool line of jeans for men. **www.endlessability.com**

Able Tailor offers jeans and denim. **http://abletailor.com**

SAM MADDOX

Warren helps Mike.

Service Animals

You may not think of an animal as an assistive device or tool, but it's easy to see that dogs, and even less conventional animals such as monkeys, can make a real difference in people's lives. Service animals increase their owner's independence and enhance their quality of life. A dog can help to turn on a light switch, pull a wheelchair, pick up dropped keys or open a cupboard door. Dogs are great companions in general, and from what people who own service animals report, they are great icebreakers when meeting the public. Most service dogs are mild-mannered golden retrievers or Labrador retrievers, although some dogs without pedigree are rescued from shelters and trained to be service dogs.

There are numerous organizations across the United States and abroad that train service dogs or provide training for people to use their own dogs.

❧ Here are several sources of information:

Assistance Dogs International maintains a list of assistance dog centers across the U.S. and abroad. Visit **www.assistancedogsinternational.org**

Canine Companions for Independence is a nationwide program that provides assistance dogs at no cost to the person with a disability. Toll-free 1-800-572-BARK; **www.caninecompanions.org**

PAWS with a Cause offers service dogs. Toll-free 1-800-253-PAWS; **www.pawswithacause.org**

National Education for Assistance Dogs Services provides service dogs for people who are deaf or who use wheelchairs. 978-422-9064; **www.neads.org**

Service Monkeys

Helping Hands provides capuchin monkeys at no cost to people with disabilities. These animals (small organ-grinder-type monkeys) can fetch things, turn on switches, and help with grooming. Candidates must be at least one

Webster helps Allison.

year post-injury, must spend most of their time at home and must be able to control a power chair. Kid-free homes only. Program offers foster placement to train the animals. Helping Hands Monkey Helpers for the Disabled, **www.monkeyhelpers.org**

Walking Systems and Braces

Orthoses and braces are tools common in rehabilitation, though somewhat less so than in years past. This is due in part to cost cutting, limited clinical expertise and reduced patient time in rehab. There is also a general feeling among many users that orthoses are cumbersome and appear too bionic or "disabled" looking. An orthosis might be used for positioning a hand, arm or leg, or to magnify or enhance function. The orthosis could be as simple as a splint or as complex as a functional electrical stimulation (FES) brace for ambulation in paraplegics.

Here are several options for orthoses:

Wrist-Hand Orthosis (WHO) transfers force from an active wrist to paralyzed fingers; this offers prehension (grasping) function for those with cervical injuries (usually between C4 and C7). The WHO, also called a tenodesis splint, has been modified and simplified over the years, sometimes with the addition of batteries for power.

There are several types of orthoses for lower limb function:

Ankle-Foot Orthosis (AFO) is commonly used in people who've had strokes, multiple sclerosis and incomplete spinal cord injury to assist the ankle and allow the foot to clear the ground during the swing phase of walking. There are many varieties of AFO; most have a molded heel cup that extends behind the calf.

Knee-Ankle-Foot Orthosis (KAFO) allows a paralyzed person (usually L3 and above) to stabilize the knee and ankle. While it's very hard work; people using KAFOs, even those with no hip flexion, can ambulate by swinging their legs through steps while supported by forearm crutches. There are many varieties of KAFO, including plastic and metal braces.

Reciprocating Gait Orthosis (RGO), which originated in Canada for children with spina bifida, consists of a pair of KAFOs with solid ankles, locking knee joints, and leg and thigh straps. Each leg of the brace is attached to a pelvic unit with a hip joint; this permits hip flexion and extension. A steel cable assembly joins the two hip joints to limit step length. By rotating the torso, the user shifts the weight to the forward leg; this permits the opposite leg to move forward. This kind of walking is stable and balanced, but slow and requires great energy. Clinicians have added FES to the RGO to assist walking. For more: The Center for Orthotics Design, 1-800-346-4746; **www.centerfororthoticsdesign.com**

Parastep is a "neuroprosthesis," a device that affects both the structure of the body (as a brace) and the nervous system (a substitute for damaged nerves). It is a portable FES system that facilitates reciprocal walking by stimulating leg muscles on cue. The movement is a bit robotic, but independent and functional for short periods. Most people with spinal cord injuries between T4 and T12 can use Parastep, which requires a physical therapy regimen of 32 training sessions. The device is covered by Medicare for qualified users. Sigmedics, 937-439-9131; **www.sigmedics.com.**

Exoskeletons: several exoskeleton walking devices are coming to market for people with paralysis. These are battery powered bionic legs, with small motors on the joints.

The Hybrid Assistive Limb, or HAL, developed by Japanese robot maker Cyberdyne, is moving through the medical device approval processes; **www.cyberdyne.jp/english.** ReWalk comes from Israel and Europe and is being tested in several U.S. centers. **http://rewalk.com**.

The Ekso comes from California-based Ekso Bionics; a commercial version has been made available to hospitals and rehabilitation centers, the everyday model is not yet on the market. Ekso started as a project with the military. The company hopes to offer a tool akin to an amputee's prosthetic leg: a device for walking, for rehab or daily living. For more, see **www.eksobionics.com.**

The companies suggest exoskeleton devices will do more than give users eye-to-eye contact with others. Health benefits may include better bone density, and reduced pain. There is anecdotal evidence that robotic walking helps bowel and bladder function.

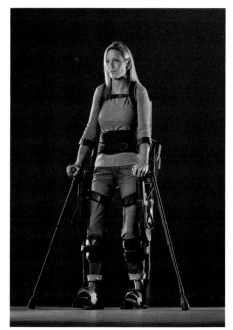

The Ekso brand exoskeleton.

7
Working the System

To get what you need and what you are entitled to, you have to know how the system works. You have to know your rights.

GEORGE H.W. BUSH PRESIDENTIAL LIBRARY

On July 26, 1990, President George Bush signed the Americans with Disabilities Act into law. With him on the South Lawn of the White House are (from left to right, sitting) Evan Kemp, Chairman of the Equal Employment Opportunity Commission, and Justin Dart, Chairman of the President's Committee on Employment of People with Disabilities; and (left to right, standing) Rev. Harold Wilke and Swift Parrino, Chairperson, National Council on Disability.

oming to grips with "the system" is a fact of life in the world of paralysis. This system is a complex and formidable weave of regulation, red tape and mostly good intentions; it directly affects people who want to exercise their rights as citizens, get an education, find jobs or get medical care.

WHAT IT REALLY COMES DOWN TO is getting what you are entitled to, getting what you paid for, getting what you deserve. Forewarned is forearmed: Federal and state policies regarding disability must be understood and sometimes challenged in order for people to succeed. Know your rights.

This chapter focuses on the policies, legalities and practicalities of surviving paralysis; it also looks at the agencies that write and enforce the rules. Underpinning much of the discussion are the basic civil rights of people with disabilities set forth by the Americans with Disabilities Act.

The healthcare benefits section looks at Medicare, Medicaid and the effect of the Affordable Care Act (aka Obamacare), in both the private and public sectors. We will look at how Part A (hospital insurance) works, and when Part B (medical insurance) comes into play. We will consider the basics of state programs, including Medicaid and Medigap, and Children's Health Insurance Program (CHIP). Also, the steps for filing an appeal of a denial will be outlined.

The section on Social Security makes sense of the rather complex rules for getting and keeping benefits under the entitlement of federal law, for both Supplemental Security Income (SSI) and Social Security Disability Insurance (SSDI). We will also look at the appeals process.

If getting a job is your goal, there are programs to help. Vocational rehabilitation programs exist in all states to help people with disabilities train for or find work. Also, there are government programs that allow people to work and keep healthcare benefits: PASS (Plan for Achieving Self-Support) and Ticket to Work help people join the workforce without fear of losing health insurance.

Education benefits are the cornerstone of public policy regarding children with disabilities. Herein is a primer. Also, resources are listed for college-age people with disabilities.

Lastly, we list the best contacts to help explain disability policies and assure that the laws are enforced fairly.

BASICS OF THE ADA

THE AMERICANS WITH DISABILITIES ACT (ADA), which became law in July 1990, is the cornerstone of civil rights for people with disabilities. The law guarantees full participation in American society for all people with disabilities, just as the Civil Rights Act of 1964 guaranteed the rights of all people regardless of race, sex, national origin or religion.

The ADA covers every person with a disability, defined as a person who has a physical or mental impairment that substantially limits one or more major life activities, has a record of such an impairment, or is regarded as having such an impairment.

The law is written in several sections, or titles. Title I of the ADA prohibits private employers, state and local governments, employment agencies and labor unions from discriminating against qualified people with disabilities regarding job applications, hiring, firing, advancement, pay scale, job training, and other conditions and privileges of employment. A qualified employee or applicant with a disability is someone who,

Ed Roberts was the principal architect of the independent living movement, the Center for Independent Living, Berkeley, CA in the 1960s. He died in 1995.

LYDIA GANS

with or without reasonable accommodation, can perform the essential functions of the job in question.

Reasonable accommodation may mean making existing facilities accessible and usable by persons with disabilities. It may also include job restructuring, modifying work schedules, acquiring or modifying equipment or devices, modifying training materials or policies, and providing readers or interpreters.

An employer is required to make an accommodation to the known disability of a qualified applicant or employee unless it imposes an "undue hardship" on the operation of the business. Undue hardship would indicate significant difficulty or expense, considering an employer's size, financial resources and the nature of its operation. An employer is not required to lower quality or production standards to make an accommodation.

Employers are not allowed to ask a job applicant about the existence, nature or severity of his or her disability. Applicants may be asked about their ability to perform specific job functions. A job offer may be conditioned on the results of a medical examination, but only if the examination is job related and required for all employees entering similar jobs.

Title II of the ADA prohibits discrimination against qualified individuals with disabilities in all programs, activities and services of public entities. This applies to all state and local governments, their departments and agencies, and any other special districts of state or local governments, including public transportation.

Title III of the ADA prohibits discrimination on the basis of disability by "private entities" operating places of "public accommodation." Businesses governed by Title III include banks, restaurants, supermarkets, hotels, shopping centers, privately owned sports arenas, movie theaters, private daycare centers, schools and colleges, accountant or insurance offices, lawyer and doctor offices, museums and health clubs.

If you feel your rights under the ADA have been abused, contact the U.S. Department of Justice. For job-related discrimination, contact the U.S. Equal Employment Opportunity Commission. To protect your rights you must know what they are.

SOURCES

U.S. Equal Employment Opportunity Commission, U.S. Department of Justice, National Institute on Disability and Rehabilitation Research

ᤞ **Below are links to resources.**

Disability.gov is the federal government website for comprehensive information on disability programs and services in communities nationwide. The site links to more than 14,000 resources. Here are answers to questions about everything from Social Security benefits to employment to affordable and accessible housing. **www.disability.gov**

U.S. Department of Justice (DOJ) enforces the laws, including the ADA. Businesses, state and local governments, or others can ask questions about general or specific ADA requirements, including questions about the ADA Standards for Accessible Design. ADA specialists are available daily. Spanish language service is available. Includes full instructions for filing complaints. Toll-free 1-800-514-0301; **www.ada.gov**

U.S. Equal Employment Opportunity Commission (EEOC) enforces the laws against employment discrimination. If you believe you have been discriminated against by an employer, labor union or employment agency when applying for a job or while on the job because of race, color, sex, religion, national origin, age, or disability, you may file a charge of discrimination with the EEOC. Toll-free 1-800-669-4000; **www.eeoc.gov**

Disability and Business Technical Assistance Centers (DBTACs) provide technical assistance on the ADA. Toll-free 1-800-949-4232; **www.adata.org**

U.S. Access Board (Architectural and Transportation Barriers Compliance Board) is an independent federal agency devoted to accessibility for people with disabilities. It offers technical assistance on the ADA Accessibility Guidelines. Toll-free 1-800-872-2253; **www.access-board.gov**

World Institute on Disability promotes independence and inclusion of people with disabilities in society, and works to strengthen the disability movement through research, training, advocacy, and public education. **www.wid.org**

Disability Rights Education and Defense Fund (DREDF) is a national law and policy center for disability rights. DREDF offers advocacy, education, training and technical assistance to persons with disabilities, lawyers, service providers and policy makers about disability civil rights laws and policies. **www.dredf.org**

Disability Rights Legal Center advances the rights of people with disabilities through education, advocacy, and litigation. **www.disabilityrightslegalcenter.org**

Disability Rights Advocates is dedicated to protecting and advancing the civil rights of people with disabilities. **www.dralegal.org**

SOCIAL SECURITY AND DISABILITY

THERE ARE TWO MAIN SOCIAL SECURITY PROGRAMS that support people with disabilities: Social Security Disability Insurance (SSDI) and Supplemental Security Income (SSI).

SSDI: Social Security Disability Insurance benefits are available to workers who have "medically determinable" impairments that prevent them from staying on the job or from performing any "substantial gainful activity." SSDI is the safety net for workers who cannot be helped by adjustments and adaptations called "reasonable accommodations" set forth by the Americans with Disabilities Act (ADA).

Disability under Social Security is based on one's inability to work.

Under the rules, you are considered disabled if you cannot do the work you did before and it is concluded that you cannot adjust to other work because of your medical condition. It must be expected that your disability will last for at least one year or result in death. In addition, you must have worked long enough and recently enough under Social Security to qualify for disability benefits. This means that a person must have worked at least 5 of the 10 years immediately before the disability and paid FICA taxes during that time.

A high percentage of initial SSDI claims are denied by Social Security, but there are various levels of the appeals process. To win a claim at any level, an applicant must provide medical evidence of a disabling condition. The best source of this evidence is the applicant's doctor, not the applicant.

SSI: Supplemental Security Income is a program that provides monthly payments to people who have limited income and resources if they are 65 or older or if they have a disability. SSI benefits are not based on your work history or that of a family member. Depending on the state where you live, the benefits and services that come with SSI include food stamps and paid Medicare premiums (all states). In most states, SSI recipients can also get Medicaid coverage for hospital stays, doctor bills, prescription drugs, and other health costs.

The Appeals Process

Social Security, ever vigilant toward waste and fraud, does not always make it easy to get or keep benefits. If the agency decides that you are not eligible or are no longer eligible for benefits, or that the amount of your payments should be changed, you will receive a letter explaining the decision. If you don't agree, you can ask them to look at your case again. If you wish to appeal, you must make your request in writing within 60 days of the date you receive the letter. There are four levels of appeal.

- A reconsideration is a complete review of your claim by someone who didn't take part in the original decision. This person will look at all the evidence submitted when the original decision was made, plus any new evidence.

- If you disagree with the reconsideration, you may ask for a hearing. The hearing will be conducted by an administrative law judge who had no part in either the first decision or the reconsideration of your case. You and your representative, if you have one, may come to the hearing and explain your case. You may review anything in your file and provide new information.

- If you disagree with the hearing decision, you may ask for a review by the Social Security's Appeals Council. The Appeals Council looks at all requests for review, but it may deny a request if it believes the hearing decision was correct. If the Appeals Council decides to review your case, it will either decide your case itself or return it to an administrative law judge for further review.

- If you disagree with the Appeals Council's decision or if the Appeals Council decides not to review your case, your final option is to file a lawsuit in a federal district court.

Because the rules are complicated, many applicants hire lawyers who specialize in Social Security law. The National Organization of Social Security Claimants' Representatives may be able to suggest local referrals; see **www.nosscr.org**. For any questions about SSI, SSDI or other disability benefits programs, contact the nearest Social Security office.

SOURCE

Social Security Administration

෴ Below is a link to resources.

> **Social Security Administration**: all the rules and applications are here. From the home page click on "Disability" at **www.socialsecurity.gov**

MEDICARE AND DISABILITY

YOU ARE ELIGIBLE FOR HEALTHCARE COVERAGE from Medicare if you or your spouse worked and paid taxes for at least 10 years, you are at least 65 years old, and are a citizen or permanent resident of the United States. You might also qualify if you are a younger person with a disability.

Note: Medicare is not the same as Medicaid, which is a joint federal and state program that helps with medical costs for some people with low incomes and limited resources. About 14 million individuals with disabilities were covered by Medicaid in 2011. Almost 80 percent were eligible because they received cash assistance through the SSI program. The remainder generally qualified for Medicaid by incurring large hospital, prescription drug, nursing home, or other medical or long-term care expenses. Medicaid is the only national program that pays for the complete range of services that enable many persons with disabilities to live in their own homes and communities. Most states, however, spend 70 percent or more of their Medicaid funding on nursing homes.

Medicaid is means-tested; it has extensive rules for determining an individual's income and resources. Furthermore, because it is not a uniform federal program like Medicare, Medicaid coverage and eligibility varies from state to state. In an effort to encourage more states to provide Medicaid to working individuals with disabilities, Congress permitted states to expand their Medicaid programs through a Medicaid "buy-in." This allows people with disabilities to continue to receive Medicaid services even if they return to work. Most states allow waivers for some eligibility restrictions. Check with your state's Medicaid office (see page 308).

Medigap policies are Medicare supplement insurance policies sold by private insurance companies to fill "gaps" in what is called Original Medicare Plan coverage, such as out-of-pocket costs for Medicare coinsurance and deductibles or services not covered by Medicare. These policies can reduce out-of-pocket costs if those costs exceed the monthly Medigap premiums.

Medicare Part A (hospital insurance) is available when you turn 65. You don't have to pay premiums if you are already receiving retirement benefits from Social Security or the Railroad Retirement Board and you or your spouse had Medicare-covered government employment. Most people get Part A automatically when they become 65. If you (or your spouse) did not pay Medicare taxes while you worked and you are age 65 or older, you still may be able to buy Part A.

If you are not yet 65, you can get Part A without having to pay premiums if you have received Social Security or Railroad Retirement Board disability benefits for 24 months.

Medicare Part B (medical insurance) is an option that helps pay for doctors and related services, outpatient hospital care, and some things Part A does not cover, such as physical and occupational therapy and home healthcare when it's medically necessary.

The Part B premium is $105 per month in 2013. This cost might be higher for those who did not choose Part B when they first became eligible at age 65. The cost of Part B may go up 10 percent for each 12-month period that you could have had Part B but did not sign up for it, except in special cases.

It is important to know that Medicare does not cover everything; it does not pay the total cost for most services or supplies that are covered.

Talk to your doctor to be sure you are getting the service or supply that best meets your healthcare needs.

The Original Medicare Plan usually pays 80 percent of the approved amount for certain approved pieces of medical equipment. Ask your supplier "Do you accept assignment?" This could save you money. Medicare pays for some home healthcare costs. Benefits are available if people meet four conditions: Their doctor says they need medical care in their home and makes a plan for that care; they need intermittent skilled nursing care, physical therapy, speech language services, or occupational therapy; they are homebound; and the home health agency caring for them is Medicare-approved.

Medicare does not pay for 24-hour a day care at home; it does not pay for all prescription drugs; meals delivered to the home; homemaker services such as shopping, cleaning and laundry; personal care given by home health aides such as bathing, toileting or dressing when this is the only care needed.

Find a Medicare approved home health agency by asking your doctor or hospital discharge planner, using a community referral service, or looking

GIL GARCETTI

The Reeve Foundation and Life Rolls On commemorated the 20th anniversary of the passage of the Americans with Disabilities Act by breaking the Guinness World Record for wheelchairs in a moving line, with 193 people, pictured at Dodger Stadium, July 26, 2010.

in the telephone directory under "home care" or "home healthcare." You are free to choose any agency that meets your medical needs.

If you have questions about your home healthcare benefits and you are in the Original Medicare Plan, contact Medicare (see page 308) to get the number for your Regional Home Health Intermediary. If you have questions about home healthcare and you are in a Medicare managed care plan, call your plan.

Although the Original Medicare Plan does not provide prescription drug coverage, your state may offer discounted or free medications programs. Check with your state's Department of Aging or local Area Agency on Aging. For those numbers, contact Medicare. Your state also has programs that pay some or all of the Medicare premiums for people with limited incomes. Call your state's Medical Assistance Office to learn about Medicare Savings Programs (or contact Medicare; see page 308).

You have the right to file an appeal for any unsatisfactory decision about your Medicare services. Ask your provider for any information related to the bill that might help your case. Your appeal rights are on the back of the Explanation of Medicare Benefits or Medicare Summary Notice mailed to you from the company that handles bills for Medicare.

If you are in a Medicare managed care plan, you can always appeal if your plan does not pay for, does not allow, or stops a service that you think should be covered. If you think having to wait for a decision could seriously harm your health, ask the plan for a fast decision. The plan must answer you within 72 hours. A Medicare managed care plan must tell you in writing how to appeal. After you file an appeal, the plan will review its decision. If your plan does not decide in your favor, the appeal is reviewed by an independent group that works for Medicare, not for the plan.

Medicare Part D is a program that provides assistance for prescription drugs. The drug benefit is not provided within the traditional Medicare program. Instead, beneficiaries must enroll in one of many Part D plans offered by private companies. Medicare drug benefits are available through two types of private plans: beneficiaries can join a Prescription Drug Plan (PDP) for drug coverage only or they can join a Medicare Advantage plan (MA) that covers prescription drugs (MA-PD). There are 34 PDP regions and 26 MA regions in the U.S. The drug plans

The Affordable Care Act (ACA) brings the country one step closer to ensuring that people living with disabilities have access to high quality, comprehensive and affordable care that meets their individual needs and enables them to live as independently as possible.

control drug costs through a system of tiered formularies; lower cost drugs are assigned to lower tiers and thus are easier to prescribe.

Those beneficiaries who are dual eligible, having both Medicare and Medicaid, are automatically enrolled into a Prescription Drug Plan (PDP) in their area. A dual eligible person is automatically removed from the MA plan upon enrollment in the PDP.

Dozens of Medicare prescription drug plans are available. Plans cover different drugs, or classes of drugs, at various co-pays, or choose not to cover some drugs at all. Medicare has made available an interactive online tool called the Prescription Drug Plan Finder (see **www.medicare.gov**) that compares drug availability and costs for all plans in a geographic area.

The Annual Enrollment Period for Part D only runs for several weeks a year (see **www.medicare.gov** for dates). Only during this period can people with Medicare enroll in a plan or change from one plan to another. Those who are already in a plan should decide whether it will be right for them in the following year; if they do not choose to switch, they will remain in their current plan. Plans will have different costs and benefits from year to year; beneficiaries should consider their options.

Medicare Part D will provide a full drug subsidy with lower co-payments to beneficiaries with incomes up to 135 percent of the federal poverty level (FPL). Part D will also provide a partial subsidy of premium, deductible and coinsurance to beneficiaries with incomes up to 150 percent of FPL. Unlike rules for Medicare Savings Programs, which allow for a family unit of only one or two, Part D recognizes larger family units and extends coverage.

SOURCES

Social Security Administration, Medicare

Effects of the Affordable Care Act

The Affordable Care Act (ACA) includes important changes that impact the disability community. Among others, these include:

Pre-Existing Conditions—Prior to the passage of the ACA, many people living with disabilities were often denied coverage, charged higher premiums, or had their coverage rescinded following an injury. Under the ACA, in 2014 most insurance plans won't be allowed to deny or exclude coverage to any American based on a pre-existing condition, including a disability.

Lifetime and Annual Benefit Caps—One of Christopher Reeve's greatest fears was that he would exceed the lifetime or annual cap on his insurance coverage. No population is more affected by these caps than those dealing with catastrophic injury. Under the ACA, lifetime caps on benefits are prohibited. After 2014, this will include both lifetime, as well as annual caps.

Medicaid Expansion—The Medicaid program provides health coverage to some of the country's most vulnerable populations, including people with disabilities. While the ACA mandated expansion of state Medicaid programs for all Americans under 65 with incomes up to approximately $15,000, the Supreme Court decision in 2012 made state expansion optional. For information on Medicaid eligibility in your state, please visit *www.medicaid.gov*

Health Insurance Marketplaces will be established in all states in 2014. Individuals can use the "Marketplaces" to shop for health insurance—much in the same way they currently shop online for airline tickets or hotel rooms. The Marketplaces will provide information on insurance options, including eligibility for public coverage programs, as well as tax credits and premium assistance to help make insurance more affordable.

Home and Community-Based Services—The ACA expands home and community-based services offered through state Medicaid programs, making it easier for people with disabilities to live at home, rather than being forced to receive services in an institutional setting. Among others, improvements include programs such as the "Community First Choice Option," which provides home and community-based attendant services and supports for people who are eligible for an institutional level of care.

☙ **Below are links to Medicare resources**

Medicaid is a federally supported healthcare program administered by each state. For information on Medicaid eligibility in your state, see **www.medicaid.gov**

Medicare: For information about healthcare options under the Medicare program, or to locate your state's **Health Insurance Assistance Program**, which can guide you in choosing a Medicare plan, dealing with denials or appeals, or filing a complaint, call toll-free 1-800-MEDI-CARE; **www.medicare.gov**

The Medicare Rights Center (MRC) works to insure that people with disabilities get affordable healthcare. Toll-free 1-800-333-4114; **www.medicarerights.org**

Medigap is Medicare supplemental insurance, sold by private companies, which can help pay some of the costs that Original Medicare doesn't cover, such as copayments, coinsurance and deductibles. Toll-free 1-800-MEDICARE or click on "Supplements & Other Insurance" at **www.medicare.gov**

The Center for Medicare Advocacy, Inc. provides education, advocacy and legal assistance to help elders and people with disabilities obtain healthcare. **www.medicareadvocacy.org**

Centers for Medicare & Medicaid Services provides health insurance for more than 100 million Americans through Medicare, Medicaid and State Children's Health Insurance Programs. Toll-free 1-877-267-2323; **www.cms.gov**

Insure Kids Now! is a national campaign connecting children under age 18 to free and low-cost health insurance. Toll-free 1-877-KIDS-NOW; **www.insurekidsnow.gov**

Healthcare.gov provides information on health insurance options, as well as on changes under the ACA that impact all Americans, including people living with disabilities.

GETTING WORK

IT USED TO BE THAT PEOPLE WITH DISABILITIES who received Social Security benefits were effectively penalized for taking a job. Any income above certain limits set by the government was deducted from one's benefits, thus jeopardizing the only source of health insurance available to people with long-term health conditions.

While many continue to see disincentives to working (few of the people who get Social Security and SSI disability benefits leave the rolls each year to go to work), policies have improved. Want to get a job without worry about health insurance? It can be done. Below are details on two Social Security programs designed to encourage people with disabilities to enter the job force without fear of losing benefits. One is the Ticket to Work program, the other the Plan to Achieve Self-Support (PASS).

Out-of-work Superman learns to panhandle.

The Ticket to Work

The Ticket to Work and Work Incentives Improvement Act of 1999, revised in 2007, increases choices for people with disabilities to obtain rehabilitation and vocational services while removing barriers that require a choice between healthcare coverage and earning money.

Social Security sees the Ticket as a good fit for people hoping to improve their earning potential and who are committed to preparing for a long-term career in the workforce. Ticket to Work offers improved access to employment with the help of specialized providers and a variety of free employment support services. Keep benefits while you explore employment, get vocational rehabilitation, or gain on the job experience. Cash benefits often continue throughout your transition to work and are eliminated only when you maintain a certain level of earnings.

Here's how it works: Beneficiaries of Social Security and Supplemental Security Income (SSI) receive a "Ticket" to obtain vocational rehabilitation and other employment support services from an approved provider of their choice. The Social Security Administration (SSA) contracts with providers (employment agencies, independent living centers, state vocational rehab offices, community nonprofits, churches, etc.) to become Employment Networks (ENs). These providers work with beneficiaries to provide support and employment-related assistance. Beneficiaries with a Ticket may choose any EN to design an employment plan. Both you and the EN agree to work together and develop a plan that describes your employment goal and outlines what the EN will provide to help you reach that goal. A Ticket can also be used to obtain services and supports to help you become self-employed or start a business. For self-employment, tell the EN early on in the process; some ENs might not accept the Ticket assignment from someone who has self-employment as a goal. You are free to talk with as many ENs as you want before assigning your Ticket. You can always un-assign your Ticket and take it to another EN. For help choosing an EN, call the Ticket to Work hotline toll-free, 1-866-968-7842; visit **www.ssa.gov/work** or go to **www.choosework.net**

Preparing a PASS

The PASS (Plan to Achieve Self-Support) is a work incentive plan that allows people to work and keep Social Security healthcare benefits. Under regular Supplemental Security Income rules, your SSI benefit is reduced by any other income you have. But income you set aside for a PASS does not reduce your benefit: You get a higher SSI benefit when you have a PASS.

A PASS lets you use your income or other things you own to help you reach work goals, such as going to school or getting special training. The job that you want should allow you to earn enough to reduce or eliminate your need for benefits provided under both the Social Security and Supplemental Security Income (SSI) programs.

A PASS must state a specific work goal. "Getting a degree" or "buying a car" are not acceptable goals. You have to demonstrate a reasonable chance of achieving your goal, within a reasonable time frame with beginning and ending dates, and milestones to mark progress. One's plan is submitted to Social Security, usually with the help of a counselor, stating what the work goal is, what is needed to achieve it, and what it will cost. The work goal can be anything you realistically expect to accomplish that will generate adequate income. It can be part- or full-time, at home or not, working for wages or starting a business of your own.

Circa 1960

The things you buy must be related to the goal—training, testing or tuition, a car or van, a computer or tools and supplies of your trade or business, daycare for a child while you work or attend school, other sorts of adaptive technology, etc.

To start, ask your local Social Security office for a copy of PASS form SSA-545-BK. This has most of the information needed to review your plan. Next, choose a work goal for a job you want to do. Figure out what steps you need to take to reach your goal and how long it will take you to complete each step. Find out how much money you'll need to set aside each month to pay for items or services you will need to reach your goal. Get several cost estimates for the things you need.

If you're planning to set aside income for your plan, your SSI benefit will usually increase to help pay your living expenses. Contact Social Security; the agency can estimate what your new SSI payment will be. Keep any money you save for your goal separate from any other money you have; open a separate bank account for the PASS money.

If you intend to start a business, you will also need a business plan describing what kind of business you want to start, hours of operation and location. You should also explain how you will pay for your business, how you will market your product or service, who your suppliers and customers will be, and your expected earnings.

It may be a good idea to get help writing your PASS from a vocational rehabilitation counselor, an organization that helps people with disabilities, or the people at your Social Security office. After you submit your plan, Social Security will review it and decide if there is a good chance that you can reach your goal, if the things you plan to buy are necessary and reasonably priced, and if any changes are needed. They will discuss any changes with you. If your PASS is denied, there is an appeals process. If your plan is approved, Social Security will contact you from time to time to make sure that you are following your plan and on the way to your goal. Make sure that you keep receipts for the items and services you buy for the plan.

Vocational Rehabilitation (VR)

Every state has a federally funded agency that administers vocational rehabilitation, supported employment, and independent living services. VR assists people in finding jobs through local searches and by promoting self-employment and telecommuting opportunities. VR services vary widely depending upon the state but typically include medical, psychological and vocational assessments; counseling and guidance; vocational and other types of training; interpreter and reader services; services to family members; rehabilitation technology; placement; post-employment services; and/or other goods and services necessary to achieve rehab objectives. In some cases VR pays for transportation and vehicle modification.

SOURCES

Social Security Administration, Rehabilitation Services Administration

❧ **Below are links to resources.**

Social Security Administration operates the Ticket to Work
and PASS programs; toll-free 1-800-772-1213. Visit
www.ssa.gov for details on all SSA programs. Use the
search function on the home page and type in "Ticket"
or "PASS." For the Ticket, see **www.choosework.net**

Rehabilitation Services Administration (RSA) administers grant programs and projects that serve individuals
with disabilities in the areas of vocational rehabilitation,
supported employment and independent living. 202-245-
7488; **http://rsa.ed.gov**

ADA National Network: The National Institute on Disability
and Rehabilitation Research (NIDRR) has established
10 regional centers to provide information, training and
technical assistance to employers, people with disabilities
and other entities with responsibilities under the ADA.
Toll-free 1-800-949-4232; **www.adata.org**

Office of Disability Employment Policy (ODEP) is a federal
agency that works to increase job opportunities for adults
and youth with disabilities while striving to eliminate barriers to employment. Toll-free 1-866-487-2364,
www.dol.gov/odep

Job Accommodation Network (JAN) is a free consulting
service that provides information about job accommodations, the Americans with Disabilities Act (ADA), and the
employability of people with disabilities. Toll-free 1-800-
526-7234, **http://askjan.org**

National Business & Disability Council is a resource for
employers seeking to integrate people with disabilities
into the workplace and also for companies hoping
to reach them in the consumer marketplace;.
516–465–1515; **www.nbdc.com**

National Collaborative on Workforce and Disability for Youth (NCWD/Youth) works to ensure that youth with disabilities have full access to services in order to maximize opportunities for employment and independent living; toll-free 1-877-871-0744; **www.ncwd-youth.info**

Proyecto Vision connects disabled Latinos with employment services and related resources and helps Latino organizations to better serve their disabled community members; **www.proyectovision.net**

Abilities Fund is the first financial institution devoted exclusively to advancing entrepreneurial opportunities for Americans with disabilities. **www.abilitiesfund.org**

Consortium for Citizens with Disabilities is a coalition of about 100 national disability organizations working toward the self determination, independence, empowerment and inclusion of children and adults with disabilities in all aspects of society. **www.c-c-d.org**

Council for Disability Rights (CDR) believes that people should be encouraged and accommodated to live independently and to participate fully in community life. **www.disabilityrights.org**

Disabled Businesspersons Association assists enterprising individuals with disabilities to maximize their potential in the business world, and works with vocational rehabilitation, government and business to encourage full participation in the workforce. **www.disabledbusiness.com**

Just One Break, founded in 1947 by Eleanor Roosevelt, Orin Lehman, and Bernard Baruch, is the nation's oldest not-for-profit employment placement service for people with disabilities. **www.justonebreak.com**

AgrAbility Project assists people with disabilities employed in farming and ranching. The Project features a database of assistive technology for the agricultural industries, including adaptive tractors and other modified gear. **http://fyi.uwex.edu/agrability**

Financial Planning

The suddenness of a stroke, spinal cord or brain injury can be devastating emotionally and physically but also financially. This is true also for families with children with disabilities. At first, gaining control of the financial future is difficult for people who may be preoccupied with day-to-day disability issues. While situations vary, there are some basic steps to take to reduce anxiety about paying bills and affording necessary equipment and care down the road.

Get organized: ask for help; talk to your employer about disability benefits, if any; locate important financial and legal papers; estimate as best you can your medical expenses; prioritize your bills; and keep good records. Consider all sources of funds for medical care and equipment, including your health insurance, VA benefits, auto insurance, workers comp, lawsuits, etc. Try to keep your current insurance policy in force. If you lapse in coverage for two months or more, you could be denied coverage for up to a year in your next group plan. A program called COBRA allows for continuation of coverage in some cases: if your employment ends (voluntarily or involuntarily) for reasons other than gross misconduct; or your work hours are reduced to the point you no longer qualify for your employer's healthcare plan.

It is important to understand Social Security and federal healthcare benefits (see information earlier in this chapter). It is also important to know your rights and to advocate for them.

Special Needs Trust

If you receive an inheritance or settlement, this could reduce or stop benefits you may be receiving from Medicaid, SSI, or a VA pension (benefits that are paid based on your financial need. Note: SSDI and VA compensation benefits are not based on financial need and are not affected by an inheritance or settlement.)

With planning, a person with a disability can receive an inheritance that will supplement the government assistance but not replace it. A financial tool called a special-needs trust can be established to provide funds for quality-of-life items—therapy, classes, or a computer—that are not covered elsewhere. A trust is sometimes funded with an initial cash payment with additional funds added through a structured settlement that makes guaranteed payments irrevocably into the trust; payments are exempt from federal and state income taxes. A trust can hold cash, stocks, personal property and real property. It can own and/or be the beneficiary of life insurance.

A person with a disability might also be able to use his or her own income to set up a similar type of trust, called an income cap trust, in order to meet Medicaid income limits. There are restrictions on what the trust can pay. Money paid directly to the individual from the trust reduces the SSI payment. Setting up a special-needs trust requires careful planning. Work with a lawyer who knows estate planning and the rules governing assistance programs for which you may qualify now or in the future.

❧ Below are links to resources.

COBRA: The Consolidated Omnibus Budget Reconciliation Act (COBRA) provides certain former employees, retirees, spouses, former spouses, and dependent children the right to temporary continuation of health coverage at group rates. **www.dol.gov/ebsa/cobra.html**

The National Multiple Sclerosis Society offers a free 72-page book, "Adapting: Financial Planning for a Life with Multiple Sclerosis." Go to **www.nationalmssociety.org** (search "financial planning") or call 1-800-344-4867 to be mailed a copy.

Veterans: You may qualify for medical care and services from the Department of Veterans Affairs (VA). Even if you have other healthcare coverage, apply for VA benefits. Call toll-free 1-800-827-1000; **www.va.gov/vaforms**

Tap Your Network

What do you do when there is no insurance money, no settlement, not enough coverage from Medicaid and still great need? You might turn to churches or service organizations (Kiwanis, Elks, etc.) for help. Barely half of people with spinal cord injury have insurance at the time of trauma. Even when there is insurance it is usually limited. Many turn to their own community network for help. A nonprofit called HelpHopeLive (formerly NTAF) offers a step-by-step framework to raise funds locally; because the program is approved by the IRS, all funds raised are tax-deductible to donors.

HelpHopeLive collects and manages funds in the name of persons with spinal cord trauma or any other major injury. The funds are disbursed as needed, with some restrictions. Some expenses must be paid directly to vendors, including those for home or vehicle modifications, durable medical equipment, and insurance co-pays. Some things cannot be paid from these funds, including rent, mortgage, tuition, electronics or personal items, or taxes.

HelpHopeLive has helped numerous people. "At the time of my accident, I was very fortunate to have people in my life with the means and desire to offer financial support for my recovery," says Lyena Strelkoff, a T11 paraplegic from Los Angeles. "But their generosity was limited by the fact that no deduction could be taken. My relationship with HelpHopeLive allowed my donors to make sizable contributions and receive a tax deduction for their kindness."

HelpHopeLive also helps coordinate

Cicra 1963 Greek stamp; circa 300 B.C., Apollo and labyrinth

fundraising efforts. "They gave us ideas for fundraisers, shared sample materials, created flyers, and gave us valuable feedback on our fundraising materials," says Strelkoff. HelpHopeLive, toll-free 1-800-642-8399; *www.helphopelive.org*

8 Military and Veterans

The expertise of the Reeve Foundation extends to those members of the military or veteran communities who have experienced spinal cord injury or paralysis.

> In February 2007, my husband Matt, an army staff sergeant on his second tour in Iraq, was shot in the neck by sniper fire near Ramadi. This happened exactly six weeks after our wedding day. Both of our lives changed forever.   —Tracy and Matt Keil

WELCOME LETTER FROM A MILITARY FAMILY

THE BULLET WENT THROUGH THE RIGHT SIDE OF HIS NECK, hit his vertebral artery and his left lung, and exited out his left shoulder blade. The bullet severed his spinal cord, rendering him a quadriplegic. The first thing the doctors said to me when they began to explain his injury was, "Your husband has a Christopher Reeve-type injury." This is the only way I understood what the doctor was talking about: we knew who Christopher Reeve was, in fact Matt had always been a huge fan of Superman and even got a tattoo of the Superman logo on his right arm when he first joined the army at eighteen.

When the doctor said those words to me I thought about what would happen to us, how would Matt live in a wheelchair, how would we possibly cope with the chaos and uncertainty? Matt was first transferred to Germany, then to Walter Reed Army Medical Center in Washington, D.C.; once stabilized he was sent to the Department of Veterans Affairs hospital in Tampa, one of five big polytrauma units in the VA system. Because we were a military family, we got hooked up with the system of care for wounded warriors. We became well versed about TRICARE, Warrior Transition Units, and the VA, and all sorts of layers of counseling and care; we discovered many resources and many regulations.

The VA has great expertise in spinal cord injury, but we began to wonder if there were any options for a more aggressive approach. We asked, "This is what life is going to be like?" Rehab was more like a nursing home; they told us Matt would probably be there a year, living in some sort of assisted living situation, but he really wanted to get back into the community. So my sister and I did some research. We reached out to the community of vets and other organizations, including the Christopher & Dana Reeve Foundation.

I called the Foundation and asked what we were supposed to do now: How do I learn everything I need to know and how do we learn to live with my husband in a wheelchair? I spoke to a very nice woman on the phone and she told me all about this book, the **Paralysis Resource Guide**, which was sent directly to me at the hospital. She told me to read through the guide and please call back anytime with any additional questions. She said, "You will get through this, things do get better. You can live a very happy full life as a quadriplegic—Christopher Reeve was proof of that." I was very encouraged after hearing that. And this book, the PRG, it was very relevant; to this day, years later, I still go back to the guide and find things that are useful.

Tracy and Matt, with Matthew and Faith

Meanwhile, we learned that there might be options for Matt's medical care: The Department of Defense and VA allow and pay for some injured soldiers to seek care and rehab at specialized private facilities. The military healthcare system doesn't promote the private care option but we were able to transfer Matt from the VA to Craig Hospital near Denver. This was the right move for us; we found our future.

Today, injured soldiers and their families reach out to Matt and me. They hear, "You want to connect with the Keils. You want the life they found." And it's true. We know where we are going to be. We also recognize there are many past vets who fought for our benefits. We know it's our turn. We are here to help; we are never too busy to help someone get where they need to go. We want people to know they do have options.

Our lives continue to change—for the better. We live a very full life. Matt and I were married such a short time that we had not yet tried to start a family, but we discovered after his injury that children were still possible and through in-vitro fertilization, we welcomed our twins Matthew and Faith on November 9, 2010. We have traveled extensively to talk about our experience and we encourage people to ask us questions about our life after injury. Our lives have changed so much since before Matt's injury, but even Matt always says he wouldn't change a thing even if it meant he could walk again. We found a new appreciation for life, friendship, family, and each other that most people spend a lifetime learning. To me, it seemed like fate. I can't explain why, but we both feel like this was supposed to happen and that this is how our life should be.

Take this opportunity to appreciate the life you have been given. Whether you are newly injured or have just learned about this resource guide, share your experience and knowledge with others, participate in all life has to offer. There are many options: learn about them from this book. Better yet, ask a lot of questions and connect with others who have been in your situation and who can say, "Life is what you make of it."

From our family to yours, we wish you a long, healthy fun-filled life. With respect and encouragement,

—Matt, Tracy, Matthew, and Faith Keil

MILITARY AND VETERANS PROGRAM

THE REEVE FOUNDATION'S MILITARY & VETERANS PROGRAM (MVP) extends our expertise in spinal cord injury and paralysis to include resources and community connections for service men and women and veterans living with paralysis, whether through combat-related, service-related, or non–service related events. In this chapter, the Paralysis Resource Guide lists the most essential governmental, service-related, nonprofit and community-based connections for people with a military history. There are many places the wounded warrior and his or her family can get answers. The MVP Hotline is here to help. Reach out to an Information Specialist with a focus on military and veteran resources. Set up an appointment to talk to an MVP Information Specialist at your convenience. Toll-free 1-866-962-8387; email Military@ChristopherReeve.org; **www.ChristopherReeve.org/military**

Circa 1946

Department of Defense

The DOD offers myriad resources for active and reserve component service members and veterans. These resources are much deeper and much more user-friendly now than they were a generation ago, thanks in large part to the commitment of the U.S. government to make documents and policies more widely available and more understandable. And then there is the networked world—the Internet has become the most useful tool for navigating programs, services, and benefits for military personnel and vets. Connection to these resources is much easier than it used to be; anyone with a smartphone can tap into vast amounts of information and references. Also, to help military personnel and vets get connected to programs and services, many nonprofits have come into existence, especially since the war on terror began in 2001. These charities are a vital resource. Finally, what may ultimately be most useful to military or veteran personnel facing life-changing injury or medical issues is contact

MILITARY ONESOURCE

Military OneSource is a free service from DOD to support military members and their families with centralized support for a broad range of concerns, such as money management, employment and education, parenting, relocation, deployment, and the issues of families with special needs. Military OneSource provides a wounded warrior specialty consultation service, including immediate assistance to wounded warriors and their families for healthcare, facilities, or benefits. Specialty consultants work with wounded warrior programs in each service branch (listed below) and the Department of Veterans Affairs to make sure callers are connected to the most appropriate resources. The service is dedicated to providing support—for as long as it may take—to make sure injured service members and their families achieve the highest level of functioning and quality of life. Military OneSource services are available 24 hours a day, 365 days a year. Toll-free 1-800-342-9647; *www.militaryonesource.mil/wounded-warrior.*

and sharing between other service members, families, and vets who have been through the process of transitioning to civilian life, especially if that life is affected by paralysis. For an overview of the complex military bureaucracy, news, details about military topics too numerous to list, and links to hundreds of DOD related programs, visit **www.defense.gov**

Military relief organizations help service members and their dependents with certain emergency financial needs, in the form of interest-free loans or grants. Most loans and grants are for one-time financial emergencies—rent, utilities, vehicle repair, certain medical and dental expenses, and emergency travel.

- **Army Emergency Relief**: 1-866-878-6378; **www.aerhq.org**
- **Navy-Marine Corps Relief Society**: 703-696-4904; **www.nmcrs.org**
- **Air Force Aid Society**: toll-free 1-800-769-8951; **www.afas.org**

⁂ **Below are links to more DOD resources.**

Invitational Travel Orders (ITOs) are issued when doctors determine that the presence of a family member is essential to the recovery of the patient. When you receive ITOs, you are eligible to receive money for travel, lodging, and daily food expenses. For travel questions related to casualty, wounded warriors, and family members of wounded warriors, 317-212-3562, toll-free 1-888-332-7366.

Computer/Electronic Accommodations Program (CAP) provides information, resources, and assistive technology to wounded service members and their families. **www.cap.mil/wsm**

Defense & Veterans Center for Integrative Pain Management (DVCIPM) seeks to improve the management of pain in military and civilian medicine. 301-816-4723; **www.dvcimp.org**

Quality of Life programs: Each service branch has its own programs to improve the quality of life for the military community. Staff can help you locate experts on benefits, housing, transportation, and finances.

- **U.S. Army Community Services:** www.myarmyonesource.com
- **U.S. Marine Corps Community Services**: www.usmc-mccs.org
- **U.S. Navy Installations Command**: www.cnic.navy.mil
- **U.S. Air Force Airman & Family Community Services**: www.usafservices.com
- **Army National Guard**: www.arng.army.mil
- **Army Reserve**: www.arfp.org
- **Marine Corps Reserve**: www.marforres.marines.mil
- **Navy Reserve**: www.navyreserve.com
- **Air Force Reserve**: www.afrc.af.mil

SUICIDE PREVENTION

The Department of Defense has established a Military Crisis Line. Toll-free 1-800-273-8255. Each branch of the military has a suicide prevention outreach. For a list see *www.suicideoutreach.org*.

MILITARY HELPLINES

- **Army Long Term Family Case Management:** Assists surviving family members of deceased Army soldiers with questions regarding benefits, outreach, advocacy and support; toll-free 1-866-272-5841
- **Army Reserve Fort Family** 24/7 Outreach and Support Program: Gateway to family crisis assistance for Army Reserve soldiers and families. Toll-free 1-866 345-8248
- **DCoE Outreach Center**: Information and referral to military service members, veterans, their families and others regarding psychological health and traumatic brain injury; toll-free 1-866-966-1020
- **DoD Helpline**: U.S. toll-free 1-800-796-9699; Local 202-782-3577; from Europe toll-free 00800-8666-8666
- **DoD Safe Helpline**: Sexual Assault Support; toll-free 1-877-995-5247; *www.safehelpline.org*
- **DSTRESS Line**: professional, anonymous counseling for Marines, their families and loved ones; toll-free 1-877-476-7734
- **Military OneSource**: toll-free 1-800-342-9647
- **Military Severely Injured Center**: Offers centralized support so injured service members and their families achieve the highest level of functioning and quality of life; toll-free 1-888-774-1361
- **VA National Caregiver Support Line**: resource/referral center to assist caregivers; toll-free 1-855-260-3274
- **Veterans Crisis Line**: To ensure veterans in emotional crisis have free, 24/7 access to trained counselors; toll-free 1-800-273-TALK, Veterans Press 1
- **Vet Center Combat Call Center**: Confidential VA call center for combat veterans and their families to talk about military experiences or any other issues in their readjustment to civilian life; toll-free 1-877-927-8387 (1-877-WAR-VETS)
- **Vets4Warriors**: Support line providing confidential peer support, information, and referrals for all National Guard and Reserve service members; toll-free 1-855-838-8255 (1-855-VET-TALK)
- **Wounded Soldier and Family Hotline**: For wounded soldiers and their families who have problems related to medical care; toll-free 1-800-984-8523

WOUNDED, ILL, OR INJURED PROGRAMS

COMPREHENSIVE CARE FOR A SEVERELY WOUNDED service member requires coordination across agencies and disciplines, and Wounded Warrior programs offer this linkage. Each of the individual branches of military service has its own Wounded Warrior program to address specific recovery, rehabilitation, and reintegration goals. These programs provide life-time support for the service member; eligibility does not end when the service member is discharged from a military treatment facility (MTF).

Army Wounded Warrior Program (AW2) is administered by the U.S. Army Warrior Transition Command; it offers personalized recovery services for severely wounded soldiers and families from injury, throughout recovery, and for as long as they need help. All wounded, injured, and ill soldiers are assigned to a Warrior Transition Unit (WTU) to focus on healing before returning to duty or transitioning to veteran status. The U.S. Army established WTUs at major military treatment facilities around the world to provide support to wounded soldiers who require at least six months of rehabilitative care and complex medical management. Each wounded soldier has a personalized Comprehensive Transition Plan (CTP) with goals that allow them and their families to move forward toward life post-injury. To contact a specific WTU, call the Wounded Soldier and Family Hotline, toll-free 1-800-984-8523. Those with extensive medical needs are assigned a local AW2 Advocate for long-term assistance. Information is available at **http://wtc.army.mil/aw2**.

Marine Corps Wounded Warrior Regiment (WWR) was formed to maximize recuperation for wounded, ill, and injured Marines and their family members as they return to duty or transition to civilian life. The WWR program designates Recovery Care Coordinators (RCCs) to serve as the primary point of contact to assist Marines with transition plans and goals for recovery, rehabilitation, and reintegration; they provide support until the wounded warrior is able to return to the military ranks or transition back into the civilian community. District Support Cells utilize Marine reservists to conduct personal visits and outreach to service members in need; **www.woundedwarriorregiment.org**, or contact the WWR call center, toll-free 1-877-487-6299.

Marine For Life is a Marine Corps organization that provides nationwide assistance to Marines who are returning to civilian life. About one hundred Marine For Life representatives, who are Marine Corps reservists, work in cities and towns throughout the United States. For more information, call toll-free 1-866-645-8762 or visit the Internet site, **www.marineforlife.org**

U.S. Navy and U.S. Coast Guard Safe Harbor is the lead organization for coordinating the nonmedical care of wounded, ill, and injured sailors, Coast Guardsmen, and their families. Services include pay/personnel issues, invitational travel orders, lodging and housing adaptation, child and youth programs, transportation needs, legal and guardianship issues, education and training benefits, commissary and exchange access, respite care, transition support to VA, and other continuing care support; **safeharbor.navylive.dodlive.mil**

Air Force Wounded Warrior (AFW2) program provides support for airmen who have a combat or hostile-related injury or illness

Circa 1953.

requiring long-term care. The program works closely with the Air Force Survivor Assistance Program and Airman & Family Readiness Centers to make sure airmen get face-to-face support; **www.woundedwarrior.af.mil**. Call toll-free 1-800-342-9647.

U.S. Special Operations Command (SOCOM) Care Coalition provides Special Operation Forces (SOF) warriors of all services and their families an advocacy program to enhance their quality of life. All personnel assigned to or attached to or working with SOCOM at the time of injury, whether Army, Air Force, Navy, or Marine, will be provided care under the Care Coalition. For more, visit **www.socom.mil** or call toll-free 1-877-672-3039.

Transition Assistance Advisors (for National Guard/Reservists) address post-service concerns and connections to the VA services and benefits. TAAs are assigned to the Office of the Adjutant General in each state; they primarily support uniformed service members and

REAL WARRIORS

The Real Warriors Campaign encourages help-seeking behavior among service members, veterans and military families. Launched by the Defense Centers of Excellence for Psychological Health and Traumatic Brain Injury, the campaign is part of a broader Defense Department effort to encourage warriors and families to seek appropriate care and support for psychological health concerns. The campaign features stories of real service members who reached out for psychological support or care with successful outcomes, including learning coping skills, maintaining their security clearance and continuing to succeed in their military or civilian careers. Contact DCoE Outreach Center, toll-free 1-866-966-1020; online see **www.realwarriors.net**

their families by explaining the services available through the VA and the military health system. Additionally, TAAs coordinate resources for service members and their families with the service programs provided by the VA, TRICARE, Veterans Service Organizations, and other supporting agencies. Visit **www.turbotap.org/register.tpp**

Yellow Ribbon Reintegration Program (YRRP) is a post-deployment service for National Guard and Reserve members and their families. Yellow Ribbon helps to ensure that geographical separation from the military doesn't equate to emotional or social isolation. Assistance includes help with TRICARE benefits, counseling services, VA benefits and enrollment, domestic violence and sexual assault, psychological and behavioral services, marriage and singles enrichment, and employment issues. For more see **www.jointservicessupport.org/YRRP**

milConnect is a website provided by the Defense Manpower Data Center (DMDC) that allows sponsors, spouses, and their children (eighteen years and older) to access personal information, healthcare eligibility, personnel records, and other information from a database (Defense Enrollment Eligibility Reporting System, DEERS) that contains information for each uniformed service member. DEERS registration is required for TRICARE eligibility and enrollment. The DMDC Support Office answers eligibility questions. Contact toll-free 1-800-538-9552 or visit **www.dmdc.osd.mil/milconnect**

Medical Evaluation Process

Integrated Disability Evaluation System (IDES): This process is complex. Evaluation begins after an injured or ill service member has passed through the acute phases of treatment. The service member will soon have to choose to Continue on Active Duty (COAD), Continue on Active Reserve (COAR), or separate/retire from the military. The IDES process begins when it appears that a service member's condition is permanent and may interfere with his or her ability to serve on active duty.

A service member who fails to meet medical retention standards will be referred into the IDES by the medical authority when it can be reasonably determined that further treatment will not render the service member capable of performing the duties of office, grade, rank, or rating. The IDES includes a medical evaluation board (MEB), a physical evaluation board (PEB), an appellate review process and a final disposition.

The MEB is an informal process initiated by the medical treatment facility; a PEB is a formal fitness-for-duty and disability determination that may recommend one of the following:

- Return the member to duty
- Place the member on the temporary disabled/retired list
- Separate the member from active duty
- Medically retire the member

Importantly, the PEB will determine the percentage of the service member's disability compensation. This is a change from the previous process wherein both DOD and VA prescribed a disability rating, which often did not match. The percentage of disability determines whether the service member will separate or retire (ratings below 30 percent for those with less than 20 years of active service will result in a separation).

If the service member disagrees with any of the information included in the medical board documents, he or she may submit a rebuttal. The PEB reviews all medical board documentation to determine if the service member is fit for continued military service. Members found not fit for duty have the right to demand a Formal Board; an attorney is appointed to represent the service member (or the member may hire an attorney). The Board reexamines the evidence, hears testimony, and considers any new evidence before making its recommendation.

Veterans medically separated from the U.S. military between September 11, 2001 and December 31, 2009 can have their disability ratings reviewed by the Physical Disability Board of Review (PDBR) to ensure fairness and accuracy. The PDBR, legislated by Congress and implemented by the Department of Defense, uses medical information provided by the VA and the military. Once a review is complete, the PDBR forwards a recommendation to the secretary of the respective branch of the armed services. The service branch makes the final determination on disability rating.. See **www.health.mil/pdbr**

DEPARTMENT OF VETERANS AFFAIRS

THE UNITED STATES DEPARTMENT OF VETERANS AFFAIRS (VA) is a military veteran benefit system with Cabinet-level status, headed by the Secretary of Veterans Affairs. The VA is the federal government's second largest department, after the Department of Defense. With a budget of more than $500 billion, the VA employs nearly 280,000 people at hundreds of medical facilities, clinics, and benefits offices and is responsible for administering programs of veterans' benefits for veterans, their families, and survivors. Benefits include disability compensation, pension, education, home loans, life insurance, vocational rehabilitation, survivors' benefits, medical and burial benefits.

Eligibility for VA programs varies; veterans are categorized into eight priority groups, based on factors such as service-connected disabilities, income, and assets. Veterans with a 50 percent or higher service-connected disability as determined by a VA regional office "rating board" are provided comprehensive care and medication at no charge. Veterans with lesser qualifying factors who exceed a predefined income threshold make co-payments for care for non-service-connected issues. VA dental and nursing home care benefits are more restricted. No co-payment is required for VA services for veterans with military-related medical conditions (problems that started or were aggravated due to military service). Reservists and National Guard personnel who served stateside in peacetime settings or have no service-related disabilities generally do not qualify for VA health benefits. To learn more call toll-free 1-800-827-1000 or visit the comprehensive VA website at **www.va.gov**. For more on veterans' benefits, see **benefits.va.gov/benefits**

Polytrauma care is for veterans and returning service members with injuries to more than one physical region or organ system, which results in physical, cognitive, psychological, or psychosocial impairments and functional disability. When medically stable, the most severely injured are often transferred to one of five Polytrauma Rehabilitation Centers (PRCs): McGuire VA Medical Center in Richmond, Virginia; James A. Haley VA Medical Center in Tampa, Florida; the Minneapolis VA Medical Center in Minnesota; Palo Alto Health Care System in California; and the South Texas Veterans Health Care System in San Antonio, Texas. There are also 23 Polytrauma Network Sites, allowing service members to recover closer to home; see **www.polytrauma.va.gov**

The National Resource Directory (NRD) is an information portal under the supervision of the Departments of Defense, Labor, and Veterans Affairs (VA); the NRD contains information from federal, state and local government agencies; veteran service organizations; nonprofits (including the Reeve Foundation); faith-based and community organizations; academic institutions; and professional associations. **www.nrd.gov**

The Federal Recovery Coordination Program (FRCP) is a VA initiative in coordination with the Department of Defense and the Department of Health and Human Services; it is designed to cut across bureaucratic lines and reach into the private sector as necessary to identify services needed for seriously wounded and ill service members, veterans, and their families. Injured service members or veterans are assigned a Federal Recovery Coordinator (FCR), who develops a Federal Individualized Recovery Plan with input from a multidisciplinary healthcare team. Though initially based in military and VA facilities, the FRCP involvement maintains a lifetime commitment to veterans and their families. FRCP staff are available at military treatment facilities and

VA SCI CENTERS

- Long Beach SCI Center, Long Beach, CA 90822, 562-826-5701
- Palo Alto SCI Center (also Polytrauma), Palo Alto, CA 94304; 650-493-5000
- San Diego SCI Center, San Diego, CA 92161, 858-642-3128
- Miami SCI Center, Miami, FL 33125, 305-575-3174
- Tampa SCI Center (also Polytrauma), Tampa, FL 33612, 813-972-7517
- Augusta SCI Center, Augusta, GA 30904, 706-823-2216
- Edward Hines VA SCI Center, Hines, IL 60141, 708-202-2241
- Boston SCI Center, West Roxbury, MA 02132, 857-203-5128
- Minneapolis SCI Center (also Polytrauma)
- Minneapolis, MN 55417, 612-725-2000
- Jefferson Barracks Division, St Louis, MO 63125, 314-894-6677
- VA New Jersey Healthcare System, East Orange, NJ 07018, 973-676-1000
- New Mexico VA Medical Center, Albuquerque, NM 87108, 505-256-2849
- VA Medical Center, Bronx, NY 10468, 718-584-9000
- VA Healthcare System, Castle Point, NY 12511, 845-831-2000
- Cleveland SCI Center, Cleveland, Ohio 44106, 216-791-3800
- Memphis SCI Center, Memphis, TN 38104, 901-577-7373
- VA Medical Center, Dallas, TX 75216, 214-857-1757
- Houston SCI Center (also Polytrauma), Houston, TX 77030, 713-794-7128
- South Texas Veterans Health Care System, San Antonio, TX 78229, 210-617-5257
- Hampton SCI Center, Hampton, VA 23667, 757-722-9961
- Richmond SCI Center (also Polytrauma), Richmond, VA 23249, 804-675-5282
- Seattle SCI Center, Seattle, WA 98108, 206-764-2332
- Milwaukee SCI Center, Milwaukee, WI 53295, 414-384-2000
- San Juan SCI Center, San Juan, PR 00921, 787-641-7582

installations across the country, and they work within wounded warriors programs. For more information call toll-free 1-877-732-4456; or visit **www.oefoif.va.gov/fedrecovery.asp**

My HealtheVet is a free, online personal health record designed for veterans, active-duty service members, and their dependents and caregivers. Users who have a Basic account are able to view their self-entered information. Advanced or Premium account types may allow one to refill VA prescriptions online and view parts of VA health records and/or DOD Military Service Information. My HealtheVet also offers a Caregiver Assistance Center, designed to help veterans, family members, friends, and their healthcare teams achieve the best healthcare possible through education, research, and improved patient-provider communication. **www.myhealth.va.gov/index.html**

Civilian Health and Medical Program of the Department of Veterans Affairs (CHAMPVA) is a health benefits program. To be eligible for CHAMPVA, a beneficiary cannot be eligible for TRICARE. CHAMPVA provides coverage to the spouse or widow and to the children of a veteran who died or who is permanently and totally disabled. **www.va.gov/hac/forbeneficiaries/champva/champva.asp.** Primary family caregivers of eligible post-9/11 veterans may qualify for CHAMPVA; contact the Caregiver Specialty Unit toll-free at 1-877-733-7927.

GI Bill: Veterans who have served at least ninety days of active duty service after September 10, 2001 and received an honorable discharge will qualify for the Post-9/11 GI Bill. To qualify for the full benefit, a veteran must have served at least three years of active duty after September 10, 2001. Benefits include college tuition and, in some cases, housing, books, and training and retraining programs. For more call toll-

free 1-888-GIBILL-1 (1-888-442-4551); or visit **www.gibill.va.gov**

eBenefits is a one-stop personalized Internet resource for active duty military personnel and veterans. Here, with an eBenefits account, one can apply for benefits, download a DD 214 or other important documents, and view benefits status regarding compensation, housing, adaptive housing, home loans, education, healthcare, transition assistance, vocational rehabilitation, insurance, death, etc. One site, streamlined to cover many functions; **www.ebenefits.va.gov**

National Personnel Records Center, Military Personnel Records (NPRC-MPR) is the repository of millions of military personnel, health, and medical records of discharged and deceased veterans of all services during the 20th century. Start here: 314-801-0800, toll-free 1-866-272-6272; **www.archives.gov/st-louis/military-personnel**

Forms: The federal government has made it easy to find any of its hundreds of forms, for claims, benefits, taxes, licensing, etc. For federal forms see **www.usa.gov/forms**. For VA forms: **www.va.gov/vaforms**. For Social Security forms, **www.ssa.gov/online/index.html**

Returning Service Members (OEF/OIF): combat veterans can receive cost-free medical care for any condition related to their service for five years after the date of their discharge or release; OEF/OIF combat veterans may be eligible for one-time dental if applied within 180 days of separation date. Returning service members help line: toll-free 1-877-222-8387; see **www.oefoif.va.gov**

Other VA Connections:

The National Call Center for Homeless Veterans provides assistance to homeless veterans and their families. Call 1-877-4AID-VET (1-877-424-3838) to receive free, confidential support from a trained VA staff member. **www.va.gov/homeless**

Spiritual Services: Chaplains are available to care for veterans' spiritual needs and, in some cases, those of the immediate family. Contact a VA medical center to speak with a chaplain. For the nearest VA medical center, call toll-free 1-877-222-VETS.

Vet Center program is a VA community-based program

DON'T LOSE THIS NUMBER

DD 214—the Certificate of Release or Discharge from Active Duty—is one of the most important documents you will ever receive during your military service. It is your key to participation in all VA programs as well as several state and federal programs. Keep your original in a safe, fireproof place, and have certified photocopies available for reference. In many states, the DD 214 can be registered/recorded just like a land deed or other significant document. Call the National Personnel Records Center at 314-801-0800 to request an application for replacement of your DD 214.

providing counseling to veterans for war-related social and psychological readjustment problems, family military-related readjustment services, substance-abuse screening and referral, military sexual trauma counseling and referral, bereavement counseling, and employment services. Vet Centers provide services in a nonclinical environment to avoid any stigma that vets might perceive about seeking assistance. All Vet Center services are prepaid through military service. To find a Vet Center:1-877-WAR-VETS; **www. vetcenter.va.gov**

Circa 1948, memorializing four interfaith chaplains who died at sea in 1943.

Veterans Crisis Line features counselors experienced in helping veterans of all ages and circumstances. For concerns about the safety and well-being of a veteran, call **1-800-273-8255** to receive free, confidential support with issues of aging, stress, or other effects from their military service—including pain, anxiety, depression, sleeplessness, anger, or even homelessness.

More VA links:

- **Center for Minority Veterans:** www.va.gov/centerforminorityveterans
- **VA Office of Survivor Assistance (OSA):** www.va.gov/survivors
- **Center for Women Veterans:** www.va.gov/womenvet

TRICARE

IF YOU ARE A SERVICE MEMBER IN THE ARMED SERVICES, your healthcare needs are processed by TRICARE, a family of health plans for service members and their families based upon their location and status (active duty, Reserves, National Guard). Service members on active duty, including Reservists and National Guardsmen on orders to federal active duty for more than thirty days, are most likely covered by TRICARE Prime, a comprehensive managed care program coordinated by a Primary Care Manager (PCM) at a Military Treatment Facility; a PCM could also be a doctor in the civilian community who is under contract with TRICARE. If you retire, you and your family are automatically covered under TRICARE Standard and TRICARE Extra. Neither requires enrollment fees or premiums.

When a military retiree turns sixty-five, his or her primary health insurance becomes Medicare; TRICARE Standard serves as a secondary coverage under a program called TRICARE for Life. To find a TRICARE network provider, visit **www.tricare.mil/findaprovider**. For full details, visit the TRICARE website at **www.tricare.mil**. Note: Eligibility to receive care under any TRICARE program requires registration in the Defense Enrollment Eligibility Reporting System (DEERS). Active duty and retired service members are automatically registered in DEERS, but they must make sure that eligible family members are registered. For more information call the DEERS Support Office toll-free 1-800-538-9552.

🐾 **To reach the TRICARE contractor for your region:**

* **North Region** (HealthNet Federal Services, LLC): 1-877-874-2273
* **South Region** (Humana Military Healthcare Services): 1-800-444-5445
* **West Region** (United Healthcare): 1-877-988-9378

Social Security & Medicare

Military service members can receive expedited processing of disability claims from Social Security. These benefits are different than those from the VA and require a separate application. Social Security pays disability benefits through two programs: the Social Security Disability Insurance (SSDI) program, which pays if you worked long enough and paid Social Security taxes; and the Supplemental Security Income (SSI) program, which pays benefits based on financial need. File an application for disability benefits as soon as possible. Full details at **www.socialsecurity. gov/woundedwarriors**

Medicare: Coverage begins automatically after you have received disability benefits for twenty-four months. For service members who are entitled to Medicare Part A (hospital insurance) and Part B (medical insurance), TRICARE provides Medicare "wraparound" coverage. Medicare is the primary payer for these beneficiaries, and TRICARE serves as a supplement, paying the Medicare deductible and patient cost share. For more about TRICARE, visit **www.tricare.mil**

For information about Medicare, see **www.medicare.gov**

TRICARE and the Affordable Care Act

The Patient Protection and Affordable Care Act (PPACA) signed into law in 2010 meant changes in healthcare coverage for many Americans. The legislation did not apply directly to TRICARE, which is authorized by an independent set of statutes, and remains under authority of the Defense Department and the Secretary of Defense.

TRICARE provides coverage for preexisting conditions and serious illnesses; offers an array of preventive care services with no cost shares; maintains reasonable out-of-pocket costs with no or low deductibles and co-payments; and there are no annual or lifetime caps on coverage.

One benefit addressed by the PPACA, which was previously not part of TRICARE, was coverage of young adults up to age 26. However, the National Defense Authorization Act, signed into law in January 2011, led to the speedy implementation of TRICARE Young Adult (TYA), which gives eligible uniformed service dependents under twenty-six who are unmarried, and not eligible for their own employer-sponsored healthcare coverage, the option to purchase TYA. For more information about TYA and how to purchase it, go to *www.tricare.mil/tya*.

VETERANS SERVICE ORGANIZATIONS (VSO)

American Legion is a congressionally chartered mutual-aid veterans organization founded in 1919 by veterans returning from Europe after World War I. Today the group has nearly 3 million members in more than 14,000 posts worldwide. The Legion supports the interests of veterans and service members, including veterans' benefits and the VA hospital system. 317-630-1200, toll-free 1-800-433-3318; **www.legion.org**

AMVETS (or American Veterans): In one recent year, AMVETS national service officers processed more than 24,000 claims that resulted in veterans receiving $400 million in compensation. Toll-free 1-877-726-8387; **www.amvets.org**

Disabled American Veterans (DAV) was founded in 1920 to represent disabled veterans returning from World War I. DAV provides free assistance to veterans and their families in obtaining benefits and services earned through military service. Toll-free 1-877-426-2838; **www.dav.org**

Paralyzed Veterans of America (PVA) was founded by a band of service members who came home from World War II with spinal cord injuries. A core strength of PVA is its network of National Service Officers, highly trained in VA law, benefits, and healthcare. Toll-free 1-800-424-8200; **www.pva.org**

United Spinal Association is a national disability and veterans service organization that helps vets sort through the array of benefits available through state and federal agencies. Toll-free 1-800-404-2898; **www.unitedspinal.org**

Veterans of Foreign Wars of the United States (VFW) traces its roots to 1899. VFW maintains a nationwide network to assist veterans with their VA disability claims. A VFW program called Unmet Needs assists military service members and their families who run into unexpected financial difficulties; assistance grants of up to $2,500 do not need to be repaid. 816-756-3390; **www.vfw.org**

NONGOVERNMENTAL ORGANIZATIONS

For an extensive list of NGOs, please go to the MVP web page at www.ChristopherReeve.org/military

Armed Forces Foundation provides assistance to injured service members and their families, including financial assistance in the form of bill payment and hotel assistance for families while they visit injured service members. 202-547-4713; **www.armedforcesfoundation.org**

Fallen Patriot Fund provides supplemental financial support to the spouses and children of U.S. military personnel killed or seriously injured during Operation Iraqi Freedom. 214-658-7125; **www.fallenpatriotfund.org**

Fisher House is a no-charge home-away-from-home for families of patients receiving medical care at major military and VA medical centers. **www.fisherhouse.org**

Green Beret Foundation provides financial resources, immediate-need supplies, caregiver assistance, and educational scholarships to wounded or ill Special Forces warriors and their families. **http://greenberetfoundation.org**

Gulf War Veteran Resource Pages; **www.gulfweb.org**

Homes For Our Troops provides homes to men and women who served in the military. There is no cost to veterans; 508-823-3300; **www.homesforourtroops.org**

Iraq and Afghanistan Veterans of America helps veterans and their families with mental health services, access to the VA system, healthcare for female veterans, and GI Bill educational benefits. **http://iava.org**

Korean War Veterans Association: in support of the legacy of Korean vets. **www.kwva.org**

Military Order of the Purple Heart is composed of military men and women who received the Purple Heart Medal for wounds suffered in combat. Although membership is restricted, MOPH supports all veterans and their families. Visit **www.purpleheart.org**

Military.com is the largest military and veteran membership organization—10 million members strong. Military.com's free membership connects service members, military families, and veterans to government benefits, scholarships, and discounts. **www.military.com**

National Coalition for Homeless Veterans is a network of community-based service providers and local, state, and federal agencies that provide emergency and supportive housing, food, health services, job training, legal aid, and case management support. **www.nchv.org**

Operation Homefront provides emergency financial aid and other assistance to the families of service members and wounded warriors. Assistance is paid directly to mortgage lenders, mechanics, contractors, hospitals, doctors, dentists, and other providers. Items covered include food, repairs, baby items, and transitional housing. Toll-free 1-800-722-6098; **www.operationhomefront.net**

Semper Fi Fund provides immediate financial support for injured and critically ill members of the U.S. Armed Forces and their families. **www.semperfifund.org**

VA Benefits for Non-Service Injuries

Q. My spinal cord was injured in a motor vehicle accident after I returned from active duty. Do I still get VA medical benefits?

A. Yes, you are eligible for VA healthcare based on your service, which basically means you earned an honorable discharge and have a DD 214. The VA will assign you to a Priority Group based on whether you have service-connected conditions. Depending on the Priority Group in which you're placed, you may have co-pays for inpatient care, outpatient care, and prescriptions. If you have private insurance, the insurance company may get billed as well. In your case of a non-service–connected catastrophic injury, you will be assigned to Priority Group 4, following what's called a Catastrophic Disability Evaluation conducted by a VA physician. Once deemed catastrophic, a veteran's income will determine whether he or she will be responsible for co-pays.

Sherman Gillums

There are other benefits available to veterans who are non-service–connected and have a spinal cord injury. Based on being enrolled in the VA system and having loss of use of lower extremities, a veteran is entitled to two customized wheelchairs, a grant to have a vehicle modified for wheelchair ingress/egress, and a small grant for home modifications. These don't cost the veteran anything as they are administered as an extension of VA healthcare. If the veteran has a need for bowel/bladder services, the VA can pay for this contracted care in the home through a fee basis. In many instances, the spouse is the veteran's caretaker and, once trained by VA, can perform and get paid for these contracted services.

(Thanks to Sherman Gillums, Associate Executive Director, Veterans Benefits Department, Paralyzed Veterans of America.)

The SHARE Initiative at Shepherd Center provides rehabilitation and care to Iraq and Afghanistan service members with brain or spinal cord injury, or blast injury. Visit online **www.shepherd.org/patient-care,** "care for service members."

Vietnam Veterans of America: services dedicated to Vietnam-era veterans and their families. 301-585-4000; toll free: 1-800-882-1316; **www.vva.org**

Wounded Warrior Project is a nonprofit organization that offers support for wounded service members and helps them on the road to healing – both physically and mentally. **www.woundedwarriorproject.org**

World War II U.S. Veterans; in 2012, 1.5 million WW2 vets were living in the United States. **http://ww2.vet.org**

EMPLOYMENT RESOURCES

Transition Assistance Program (TAP) meets the needs of separating service members during their period of transition into civilian life by offering job-search assistance and related services. TAP is a partnership among the Departments of Defense, VA, Transportation, and the Department of Labor's Veterans Employment and Training Service (VETS) to give employment and training information to armed forces members within 180 days of separation or retirement. See **www.turbotap.org**

Disabled Transition Assistance Program (DTAP) is a key component of transition assistance for service members released because of a disability or who believe they have a disability qualifying them for VA's Vocational Rehabilitation and Employment Program (VR&E). DTAP delivers personalized vocational rehabilitation services to eligible service members by assisting with benefits; **www.taonline.com/TapOffice**

Verification of Military Experience and Training: Service members have had numerous training and job experiences, perhaps too many to recall or to include on a job or college application. Fortunately, the military has written it all down on the DD Form 2586. It's not a resume but it will help in a job search. A VMET can be downloaded from **www.dmdc.osd.mil**

America's Heroes at Work is a U.S. Department of Labor program that focuses on the employment challenges of returning service members living with traumatic brain injury (TBI) and/or post-traumatic stress disorder (PTSD). The program equips employers with tools to help the injured. **www.americasheroesatwork.gov**

Career Center for Wounded Warriors is sponsored by military.com to help with finding employment after military service. Learn about potential employers and job fairs, get help with your resume, and search for jobs near you. **www.military.com/support**

Disability.gov is managed by the U.S. Department of Labor's Office of Disability Employment Policy (ODEP) in collaboration with twenty-one federal agency partners. A major focus is employment. **www.disability.gov**

Federal Jobs for Veterans: The U.S. government has made a commitment to recruit veterans into the civil service (State Department, Department of Transportation, Homeland Security, etc.). Having a disability is not a disadvantage when applying for employment with the federal government. Visit **www.fedshirevets.gov**

Helmets to Hardhats helps service veterans, National Guard, Reserve, retired, and transitioning active-duty military members connect to career and training opportunities in the construction industry. Toll-free 1-866-741-6210; **www.helmetstohardhats.org**

Job Opportunities for Disabled American Veterans is an Internet job board. **www.JOFDAV.com**

Jobs for Vets links transitioning veterans and the employers who want them. **www.jobsforvetsalpha.org**

Mission Continues awards volunteer service fellowships to veterans who still have the desire to serve their country, but whose disabilities prevent them from continuing to serve in the military. **http://missioncontinues.org**

USAJobs: The U.S. government posts employment openings for veterans at **www.usajobs.gov**

VA for Vets facilitates reintegration, retention, and hiring of veteran employees at the VA. **http://vaforvets.va.gov**

Veterans' Employment and Training Service (VETS) prepares veterans and separating service members for careers. **www.dol.gov/vets**

Veterans' Preference gives eligible veterans priority in appointment for federal jobs over many other applicants; **www.fedshirevets.gov/job/vetpref**

VetJobs is an Internet job service operated to place veterans with technical skills, management expertise, and leadership skills. **www.VetJobs.com**

VetSuccess: A VA-supported program helping vets prepare to join the work force. **www.vetsuccess.gov**

Vocational Rehabilitation and Employment (VR&E) Program helps veterans with service-connected disabilities find jobs and offers services so disabled vets can live as independently as possible. **www.vba.va.gov/bln/vre**

FOR LOVED ONES:
BEING AN ACTIVE MEMBER OF THE RECOVERY TEAM

YOU ARE VERY IMPORTANT to your service member's recovery. But it can take a while to fully understand your active role. These suggestions can help:

- Know who is providing care. Learn names and specialties and write this information down.
- Learn everything you can about your service member's condition. Talk with doctors, nurses, case managers, social workers and other care providers.
- Be sure to read any written medical information your team provides. Knowledge will help alleviate fear of the unknown and help you make better decisions.
- Contact your Casualty Liaison, Recovery Care Coordinators (RCC) and Advocates.
- Learn the hospital's schedule and routines. Be aware of shift changes and times when staff is less available.
- Write your questions down ahead of time. It can be easy to forget things if you don't write them down.
- Ask for explanations of procedures and medications. If you don't understand something, ask questions until you do understand.
- Remember that the diagnosis and treatment plan may change.
- Be flexible and try to stay positive.
- Learn patient and caregiver rights and responsibilities. Ask for a copy of your medical treatment facility's description of patient and caregiver rights and responsibilities.
- Pay attention to moods and feelings. The healing process involves both physical and emotional aspects. It's important to talk with care providers about any behavior changes you might notice.
- Remember that your observations are unique and valuable. You will spend more time with your service member than any other member of his or her medical team.
- You don't have to go it alone; connect to other caregivers.

Hometowns honor their returning veterans, 1945

Communicating with the Recovery Team

Sometimes it will feel as though doctors and military people are speaking another language and you're the only one who doesn't understand. You will be expected to learn new words and acronyms when your mind is full of emotion and your life is in upheaval. Sometimes you will have to make important decisions after hearing unpleasant news. It can make anyone feel overwhelmed.

In circumstances like these, it can be hard to communicate well, but you will get better results if you try. Begin now to practice effective communication in order to build relationships of trust with members of the recovery team. Here are some suggestions from other people who have been in situations similar to yours:

• Be assertive in a friendly way. Don't say, "Yes, I understand," if you don't understand. Ask for clarification, again and again if necessary. There are no dumb questions and you can't afford to be shy. You need to understand as much as possible.

• Remember that the medical team takes care of many patients, but that you take care of one. Speak up to make sure that your service member's needs are met, but try to be patient when members of the

medical team are doing their best to help many people.

- Keep in mind that all these people are on your side. You are on the same team, rooting for your service member's recovery. Try to trust and support each other.

- Recognize that when you are stressed, scared, or confused you may need to step back from your emotions to communicate effectively. If you feel rushed to make a decision but can't think clearly, ask for a few minutes to clear your head. Count to ten or step outside and take some time to calm down.

- Be friendly with the people around you. You will find that they can help you in many ways. Remembering to say "please" and "thank you," even when you feel stressed, seems like a small gesture, but in the end, civilities like these can make a big difference in how you, your service member, and the rest of the recovery team feel. From *Military OneSource, Keeping It All Together.*

Caregiver Services

The VA provides benefits and services specifically to support family caregivers, both in and out of the home. Contact the VA's Caregiver Support Line, toll-free 1-855-260-3274, or connect with a Caregiver Support Coordinator at a VA Medical Center. A Caregiver Support Coordinator is a licensed professional who can match you with services and offer resources that can help you stay smart, strong, and organized. Services may include adult day care centers, home-based primary care, skilled home care, home telehealth resources, respite care, and home hospice care. Family caregivers of veterans injured post-9/11 may be eligible for additional VA services, including a stipend, travel expenses, respite care, comprehensive training, and medical coverage through VA if you are not already covered by a plan. Call the support line listed above or visit **www.caregiver.va.gov**

Stroke caregiving: Resources and Education for Stroke Caregivers' Understanding and Empowerment (RESCUE), is an online VA resource providing stroke caregivers—applicable also to caregivers of loved ones with other sudden disabilities—with information and resources to help better care for a loved one. The website also offers information to help caregivers take care of themselves. The site features forty-five easy-to-read fact sheets about stroke and stroke caregiving (also available in Spanish). **www.rorc.research.va.gov/rescue/index.cfm**

For more on the topic of caregiving, see chapter 10, page 398.

BRAIN INJURY RESOURCES

THE VA OFFERS REHABILITATION for service members with brain injuries so they receive coordinated, comprehensive care. Specialized services are available at four traumatic brain injury (TBI) Centers (Palo Alto, CA; Tampa, FL; Minneapolis, MN; and Richmond, VA). The goal is to return the brain injury survivor to the highest quality of life and functioning and to educate family members and caregivers on the patient's long-term needs. Contact your local VA medical center for more information about TBI services available.

ॐ **Below are links to resources.**

Bob Woodruff Foundation works to support injured service members with a special emphasis on the hidden injuries of war—traumatic brain injury and combat stress. **http://remind.org**

Brain Injury Association of America (BIAA) works toward brain injury prevention, research, treatment and education and to improve quality of life for all people affected by brain injury. 703-761-0750; **www.biausa.org**

National Brain Injury Information Center: Toll-free 1-800-444-6443.

Defense Centers of Excellence for Psychological Health and Traumatic Brain Injury (DCoE) evaluates and disseminates evidence-based practices and standards for the treatment of psychological health and TBI within the Defense Department. DCoE is part of the Military Health System's continuum of care—from initial accession to deployment to discharge. DCoE's centers include:

- **Deployment Health Clinical Center** (DHCC): improves deployment-related health by providing assistance and medical advocacy to military personnel and families, including assessment of post-deployment physical symptoms, specialized care programs, education and clinical and health services research. Toll free help line: 1-866-559-1627; **www.pdhealth.mil/main.asp**

- **Defense and Veterans Brain Injury Center** ensures expert care, coordination, and individualized, evidence-based treatment to maximize function and minimize disability. DVBIC provides services to enable return to duty, work, or community. Any service member or veteran with TBI covered by TRICARE or VA benefits may be referred to DVBIC; toll-free 1-800-870-9244; DVBIC Information & Referral, 1-866-966-1020; **www.dvbic.org**

- **National Center for Telehealth & Technology** (T2): designs, builds, tests and evaluates technologies in support of psychological health and traumatic brain injury recovery. 253-968-1914; **http://t2health.org**

Portraits

BY

CHRISTOPHER VOELKER

Candace Cable

ATHLETE

Here's my motto: the deal in life is how you deal. For 35 years I have used a wheelchair due to a spinal cord injury. I could not imagine living this new life: No map, no flashlight, no way. I was filled with suffering and pain (physical and emotional), with anger, resentment, worthlessness, separation, fear and confusion. Lucky me! I had family and friends to help me emerge from the darkness by creating new images of what I could do and who I could be. So I reinvented myself. Jump to present: I retired a few years ago from 27 years as a competitive athlete. I wasn't athletically motivated before my paralysis. I never dreamt of competing in the Olympics, let alone 10 Paralympic Games, five Summer, five Winter in three sports—wheelchair racing, alpine and Nordic ski racing. I took 12 medals, nine of which are gold. I wheeled over 100 marathons with 84 wins, I have ridden my hand cycle across the USA, and also to qualify for the World Championship Ironman Triathlon. Sports helped me to blend my resurrected values of perseverance, knowledge, appreciation, integrity, collaboration, resiliency, dedication, empathy and responsibility. I was the poster girl for adapt, advance, excel. I am today more We than Me; my light has expanded with service, peace, forgiveness, compassion and faith. The possibilities are limitless to make positive contributions with service. I believe I am connected to everything and true power comes from the heart. My compass is an attitude of gratitude. When I get lost and forget who I truly am, I let my light shine, find a map and begin again.

Candace is a regular contributor to the blog "Life After Paralysis," online at www.ChristopherReeve.org

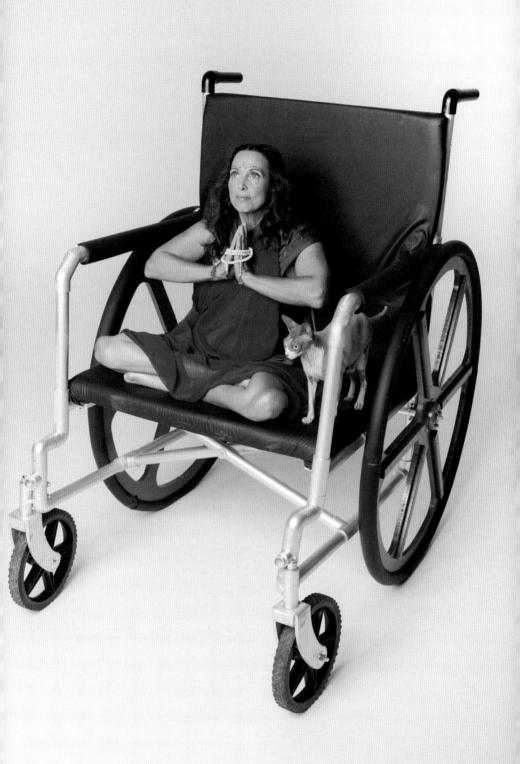

Aaron Baker

FITNESS ENTREPRENEUR

My name is Aaron Baker and I am a recovering quadriplegic, athlete, businessman, philosopher and friend. Prior to my injury I defined myself as a professional motorcycle racer. On May 26, 1999 I crashed while training, breaking cervical vertebrae 4/5/6 in my neck, instantly paralyzing my entire body. I was given a grim prognosis by multiple neurosurgeons of having only a "one in a million" chance of ever feeding myself again. The doctor's projection was instantaneously rejected by my family and me. We embraced a positive, proactive pursuit of healing, recovery and redefinition. With my mother Laquita by my side, I have pushed the bounds of possibility, setting incremental goals, building upon the flicker of a toe, the ability to brush my own teeth and tie my own shoes…My healing continues today, enabling me to walk with a cane, drive my own vehicle and pedal a bicycle (under my own power) tens of thousands of miles across the United States (twice) and ultimately to the finish line at the Para Cycling National Championships. Throughout this dynamic process of recovery, I have come to understand that I can share hope, inspiration and guidance. Through adversity comes truth, clarity and love.

Xander Mozejewski

S U R V I V O R

Every time I go to the doctor, they ask me if I'm depressed. I kinda laugh and say no and think to myself, why would I be? I lost everything I care about. Skating, snowboarding, my jobs, my girlfriend. I lost my life, so why am I not sad? Before the accident, I got to work in my dream store, I got paid to hang out with models in hot tubs and take their pictures. I learned how to tre flip, I got to skate the Berrics, I skated the marathon! I got to ride Mammoth when they were hit with 18 feet of powder, I got to drive a convertible R8. I never smoked, I fell in love, I learned how to develop and print film, I climbed the great wall of China, I touched the Hollywood sign! Even before the accident, people asked me how I was never sad, never depressed. I got to do things I never imagined, I loved life, I was living the dream. I don't care what I didn't do, or what I can't do now, because at 20 years old, I was so happy with my life, so satisfied, like soooo stoked. They thought I wasn't going to make it for two days after the accident, but I did. Then they told me what I wouldn't be able to do, but they didn't say anything about me bungee jumping, or chest pressing 300 pounds, or doing pull ups on a street light, or meeting some of the sickest people ever. It's been a year, a horrible year, but I'm still alive, still happier than everyone I know. If you're depressed or sad or bored, go and do something that will change your life, something you have always dreamed of. Who knows if you'll have the chance to do it again. "If you have the opportunity to play this game of life, you need to appreciate every moment. A lot of people don't appreciate their moment until it's passed." —Kanye West. Appreciate it all; life's dope. (*Excerpt from Facebook posting on the one year anniversary of crashing his motorcycle. Special thanks to Ekso Bionics.*)

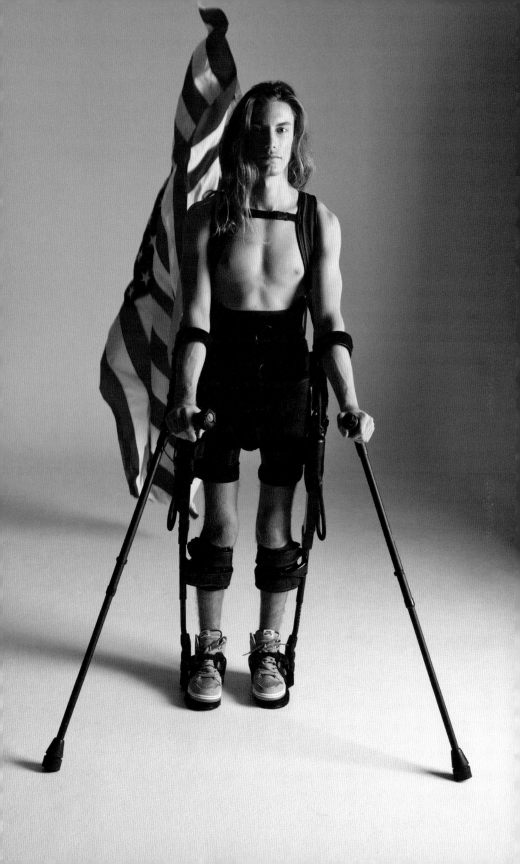

Suzy Kim

P H Y S I C I A N

Rolling into work in my titanium wheelchair with my white coat and stethoscope—that's an image I never would have imagined. While bodysurfing in my Southern California hometown, I became an incomplete C7 tetraplegic. I was 25 years prime, and living the dream in high gear: a 3rd year medical student at USC honing in on a career in sports medicine, qualifier for Boston after my first marathon, and triathlete. Life was good.

Today, living with paralysis, my mind and body have evolved to redefine familiar disciplines of fitness and health. And, guess what? Life is still good. As a board certified physician specializing in physical medicine and rehabilitation, I am one of just 500 U.S. physicians with a subspecialty certification in spinal cord injury medicine. The most valuable lessons I incorporate into my practice I gained from my experiences as a patient.

As a physiatrist, my mission is to advocate for my patient much in the way that I needed the same as a patient 15 years ago. I stress the importance of maintaining physical fitness. And I practice what I preach. I am an avid surfer (on my specially adapted surfboard), I hand-cycle, spar the punching bag, and swim five miles a week to train for triathlons. As one of six team physicians for the U.S. Paralympics team in London in 2012, my team approach to patient care incorporated working with trauma and spine surgeons, brilliant scientists and a dedicated rehabilitation team. Working with the SCI community, my mission is two-fold: live a healthy life today and prepare for future curative scientific treatments through adapted technology, exercise-based therapies and optimal medical management. Let's go people, it's time to up the ante.

Dr. Kim, who is an Ambassador for the Reeve Foundation, is Medical Director, Acute Rehabilitation Unit, Associate Clinical Professor, Department of Physical Medicine & Rehabilitation, University of California, Irvine.

Ben Lewin

F I L M M A K E R

Ben Lewin wrote and directed the 2012 film *The Sessions*, one of the most captivating films ever made about disability and the connection between two individuals. It is billed as a comedy but offers a "piercing depth of humanity," noted the *New York Times*. John Hawkes plays Bay Area poet Mark O'Brien, whose polio kept him in an iron lung; Helen Hunt plays a special kind of professional who helped O'Brien, almost 40, overcome his lack of sexual experience (Hunt was nominated for an Academy Award). Lewin, from a Australia, and himself a survivor of polio, raised money from friends and family and butted up against a Hollywood system unaccustomed to this sort of story—honest portrayal of disability with realistic but nonjudgmental (and non-erotic) sex. O'Brien died in 1999, but Lewin tracked down women who were close to him, including Cheryl Greene, a surrogate who teaches clients one-on-one how to have sex. Hunt wanted to know how they would shoot the sex scenes. Said Lewin: "I said it's just going to be part of the narrative, very mundane and ordinary; I think Helen was able to bring a lot of that real banality to it rather than anything titillating. Although there's a certain amount of shock value and it is confronting, it isn't exploitative in any way." Lewin's film is not what people expect, and that's part of the fun. "People don't want to see a depressing movie, they don't want to watch a character they're supposed to pity, and they don't want to see something that is inherently sad," said Lewin. "The combination of sex and disability is a kind of 'whoops, where are we going with this?' But in a way, that's the whole magic of the film. You're going where the Starship has not been before."

Juan Garibay & Eric Gibson

ANTI-VIOLENCE EDUCATORS

Juan Garibay and Eric Gibson both entered the spinal cord injury world by way of gun violence in the Los Angeles gang world. Eric will flat out tell you, getting shot five times at close range was a blessing of sorts—he was headed for dead, or jail, as a major gangster in the Bloods. He now dedicates himself to disarming the city and its youth. "The fact that I lived was a message to me that I needed to be doing something different," says Eric. Juan found redemption, too, and works with Eric to take a stay-out-of-gangs message to at-risk youth in the community. "Gang life is a dead end and it's been a long battle for me to make the change, but that's what keeps me going when things are hard," says Juan, who is also a life coach at the KnowBarriers program at Rancho Los Amigos Rehab Center. Both Juan and Eric received certification on drug and alcohol counseling from the University of California, Los Angeles (UCLA), and both are multicultural ambassadors for the Reeve Foundation; Juan has an even greater role within the Foundation as the West Coast regional director for the Peer and Family Support Program. Juan: "Life coaching helps clients to figure out and achieve their personal goals; the program blends the life experience of former Rancho patients, like me and Eric, who have achieved some success following our injuries. We offer a vision of success, whether it is in relationships, work, school or home. We are effective because we are living the life the new patients are facing. We validate our message by living it. Our message: set the vision for what you want in life and make it happen." *www.knowbarriers.org; www.ChristopherReeve.org/peer*

Robert David Hall

A D V O C A T E

Robert David Hall plays coroner Dr. Al Robbins on the long-running TV series *CSI: Crime Scene Investigation*. Although he lost both legs in a fiery car accident and uses a cane, his disability is not central to the role. Hall, who is a husband, father and very decent guitar player, has been active in urging Hollywood to tap into the talent pool of actors with disabilities; he also encourages the industry to produce scripts that emphasize character and not physical prowess. His own healing and recovery has been a process. "I've moved on quite a bit," he says. "Not entirely. Nobody does." But indeed Hall has learned from his disability. "Working my way through my career and my life has been challenging but interesting. The obstacles I've faced have helped to shape me and make me who I am today. Along with my parents and teachers, my experience with disability has been a great learning tool. It's helped me to begin to answer the question 'Who am I?'"

As a sort of high profile ambassador for people with disabilities (he gets invtited to the White House), Hall has visited Walter Reed Hospital many times and talked with many wounded veterans. "I don't try to preach or tell them what they ought to do," he said. "They can see I know what it's like. And all I can say is that they will get over it, working every day, if they don't give in to despair, if they have hope."

Kristina Ripatti

PATHFINDER

Kristina Ripatti was a police officer. She requested assignment to the gang unit in South Central Los Angeles. For 11 years, she loved the challenge. One night, a foot pursuit led to a chase; the man pulled a gun, shot her three times. Two bullets hit her body armor. One hit her spinal cord. Her husband Tim Pearce, a fellow officer, was first on the scene. Kristina survived as a T2 paraplegic. Kristina and Tim wondered about the promise of spinal cord injury "cure" research. "You realize pretty quickly," she said, "that there's a very fine line between hope and denial. If you stay too close to denial, that can keep you from pushing forward." For Kristina, forward meant fitness. She returned to sports and training to find herself; she competed in marathons, rode a bike across the country, worked out at the area's NeuroRecovery Network community fitness facility, NextStep. "I want to be able to live life to the fullest and to stay mentally and physically strong for the challenges I face now and the ones that will come in the future," Kristina said. She found herself in one other special way; she is mother to a boy and girl. Family, she said, reveals an essential truth: "I am still the same person, with the same core values, passions and mission."

Bill Shozan Schultz

F L U T E   M A S T E R

S ince an auto accident in 1979 I have been a level L1 paraplegic. For me, one of the hardest things was the confusion I saw in the faces of my friends and family when they were around me. It took some time for me to realize that they too were deeply affected by my accident and that it would be up to me to make them feel comfortable around me while gradually revealing to them that I was indeed still the same person that they knew prior to my injury. This was tough.

Next on the list of hard things was the change in my own attitude. I knew that I had to stop dwelling on and thinking about what I could no longer do—no more surfing, no more bicycle touring, no more comfortable sexual relations—and start to concentrate on what I could do, and to discover other things that might interest me. This process eventually led me to live in Japan studying how to play a bamboo flute called a shakuhachi. By the time I returned to Los Angeles, after 10 years in Japan, I was granted the name Shozan, had a teaching license, and was certified a shakuhachi master. I began teaching in the Ethnomusicology Department at UCLA and this eventually led to other opportunities: concert performances around the world, sound track recording for Hollywood films (*The Last Samurai* among others), and private teaching. Probably most importantly, playing shakuhachi was something I could do that did not require the use of my legs.

Lourdes Mack

L I T T L E   M I S S   W H E E L C H A I R

Lourdes Mack, 10, was crowned recently as Little Miss Wheelchair California. She wants to show the world that "having a medical condition does not limit one's dreams." Lourdes was born with spina bifida and hydrocephaly, and has had numerous surgeries. But she's been as active, or more so, than the average kid. She has been skating and surfing with Life Rolls On; she has volunteered for several local charities, including the Spina Bifida Association and Shane's Inspiration. Lourdes plays wheelchair basketball, kayaks and hand cycles with UCLA Adaptive Recreation and Rancho Los Amigos. And she's been on stage, in local musical theater and professionally—with the Joffrey Ballet in *The Nutcracker*, and in the TV series, *Private Practice*. "There may be challenges and adversity," says Lourdes, "but there is very little kids with disabilities can't do if we set our minds to it. My message to other kids with disabilities is to keep their dreams alive."

Push Girls

C H I C K S   I N   C H A I R S

They call themselves Push Girls (Angela Rockwood is in front, Mia Schaikewitz on left, Auti Angel at right, and Tiphany Adams, in back). They are four friends who live with paralysis—Angel, Tiphany and Auti from car accidents; Mia from a spinal cord blood issue. *Push Girls* became a groundbreaking TV reality series in 2012, telling stories of the girls as they navigate the brightness and darkness that is Los Angeles, trying to find love, work and affordable housing. Angela is the only tetraplegic among the group, the "Mother Earth" of the bunch. Auti was a hip hop dancer (still is, in her chair), the only one who's married and is thinking about having a baby. Mia is a graphic designer looking for Mr. Right. Tiphany is open, honest and relates well to both men and women. Says Tiphany: "The show is totally about opening people's eyes and letting them see that we live life just like they do, only we do it sitting, which is a different perspective. I call us chicks in chairs."

The Christopher & Dana Reeve Foundation partnered with Sundance Channel to promote the original docu-series, Push Girls.

R. J. Mitte

A C T O R

The hit TV series *Breaking Bad* tells the story of Walter White (played by Bryan Cranston), a high school chemistry teacher with terminal cancer; he leads a double life as a big-time methamphetamine cook to assure the financial security of his wife and family after his death. His son, Walter Jr., was written by series creator Vince Gilligan to honor a friend from his college days who had cerebral palsy (CP). RJ Mitte happened to be enrolled in acting school when the casting call came. "I have a very mild case of cerebral palsy; this affects my motor skills and the controlling of my muscles." At first Gilligan didn't think Mitte was gimpy enough; in the show, Walter Jr. is more disabled than RJ actually is. The show ends its five-year run in 2013 but Mitte hopes his impact will last (the reruns certainly will). "This kind of visibility is important in getting the public to understand and accept that people with disabilities don't have to be defined by their disability and that they can still contribute and accomplish so much." Mitte has become a spokesman for I AM PWD (Inclusion in the Arts and Media of Performers With Disabilities), an advocacy campaign around long-standing issues of people with disabilities in the entertainment industry—inclusion and accuracy of portrayal. "About 20 percent of people have disabilities, but only about 1 percent of speaking parts in television portray disability," said Mitte. "When a person with disability is featured, it's usually a stereotype—the angry or bitter person, the victim or the helpless person who becomes a hero," he said. See *www.iampwd.org*

Tara Llanes

BIKER, PHILANTHROPIST

Tara Llanes started racing BMX as a teenager, graduating a few years later to mountain bikes, pro status and gold at the X-Games. She was aggressive and fearless and had things going her way until a crash at the Jeep King of the Mountain race at Beaver Creek, CO in 2007 resulted in a spinal cord injury. After lots of rehab, and SCI-related health issues—including 3rd degree burns from falling asleep on a heating pad, which put her on her stomach for almost 10 months—she is almost ready to say the reconfigured Tara has found herself. "I've seen this for everyone who has this kind of injury," she says, "We all have to go through a whole range of emotions to get back to who we were. Some people, it may take a year. Others, ten. Some, scary to think, may never get there." And for Tara? "I'm still getting there, trying to understand who I am as a person. Everyone needs time to find themselves. The important thing is to know that you'll get there. One thing that's huge: be sure to surround yourself with positive people." Tara is married to a woman she used to race against, works in the bike industry and runs the annual Tara Llanes Classic at Tahoe's Northstar Resort, a bike event that raises money for spinal cord injury research and recovery; see *www.tarallanesclassic.org*

Cole Massey

Y O U N G   A M E R I C A N

Cole Massie is a teenager who does pretty much what every kid does, with the help of his assistance dog, a black lab named Ilia. Of course he plays video games. He's also into karate and horseback riding. He likes classical music, especially Gilbert and Sullivan and Itzhak Perlman. Says Cole: "I have cerebral palsy. Living with a disability can be kind of hard sometimes; I have to do lots of therapies and see lots of doctors. My CP mostly affects my legs and makes it hard to walk. But I'll tell you this: disabled kids CAN DO! If you have something you want to try, figure out how to do it … there's always a way."

Toby Forrest

A C T O R   &   M U S I C I A N

Toby Forrest, risk-taker for sure, made a swan dive off a rock in the Grand Canyon; the water wasn't deep enough. This happened on the same day Christopher Reeve was injured, only three years later. Toby credits Reeve's audio version of *Still Me* for getting him through rehab. "Reeve's experience—it got me through a lot of nights," Toby says. Later he received a $5,000 scholarship, funded and presented by Reeve himself, to study acting in Los Angeles. That's how he makes his living, or hopes to, anyway, on screen and TV; he also is the lead singer for Cityzen, a rocking band in Los Angeles. When he was hurt Toby remembers that he actually died. "I inhaled water and drowned. I remember thanking God for allowing me to live. I had a good life. I was ready to go. I felt love. It was the most amazing experience being bathed in blue light, I didn't have any worries, I didn't have a body. I didn't feel that life had ended but that it had just begun. I was so happy and comfortable. Meanwhile my body had floated up to the edge of the water. A guy pulled me out; of course he didn't know I had a broken neck. Picked me up like a baby. My girlfriend tried to resuscitate me, she couldn't. A doctor who was there came over; he resuscitated me. He brought me back." He thought for a moment about staying dead and cozy. "I am spiritual," says Toby. "So I have no doubt there were reasons for me coming back from the dead. Before, I was never afraid to die. Now, I'm not afraid to live." Toby's story still needs a third act. "I am hungry to do more. I love entertainment; but I'm not here to show the world people with disabilities. I'm here to show people with disabilities the world. It doesn't matter what you look like or what you can and cannot move. If you are creative, you have the right to share what you create."

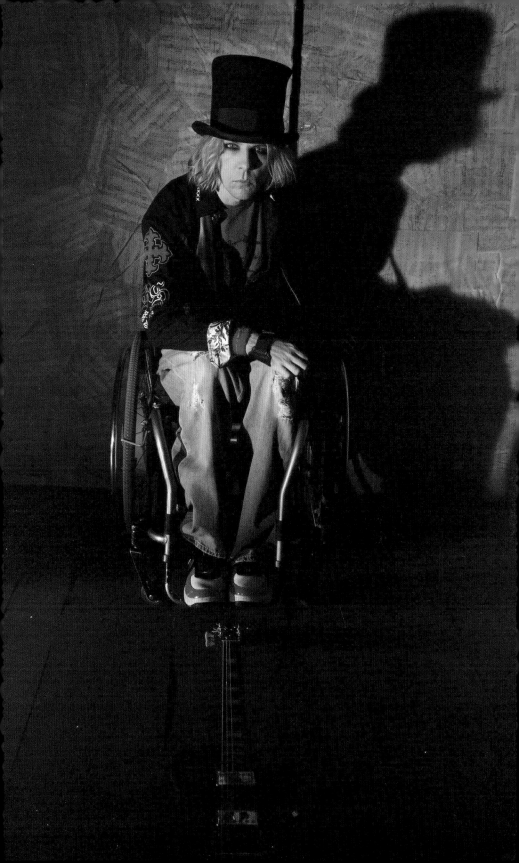

Jay Cramer & Katie Sullivan

COMIC & SPRINTER

Jay was spinal cord injured in 2006 when he fell while rock climbing. Katy was born without legs. They met at Rancho Los Amigos when Jay was in rehab. He fell for her "titanium Terminator legs" and Katy fell for his sense of humor. Jay is a writer and a stand up comic; and Katy is a TV actress and star sprinter who represented the U.S. in the London 2012 Paralympics. "I always wanted to do stand-up comedy, but never had the guts to try it until after my accident," Jay says. "I figured, how bad could it be after what I had been through?" Katy started running, she says, after Jay gave her the courage to try. She offers this advice: "When you shake up the snow globe of your life, it takes a while for the particles to settle. Remember to breathe, because 'this too shall pass.'" Says Jay, who often counsels people with new spinal cord injuries, "It doesn't matter if it's a prosthetic leg, a wheelchair or something else. Take the hand you have been dealt and be grateful for the lessons you have learned."

9
Kids' Zone

The most important tools for parents are other parents. There is no substitute for the advice and counsel of those who have been in similar circumstances.

Maile, 3, who has spina bifida and uses a wheelchair, rides the Malibu surf with Life Rolls On.

S pinal cord injury or disease in children is marked by many of the complications and secondary effects of paralysis in adults, including sensory loss, bowel and bladder loss, etc. SCI in kids is complicated by growth and developmentt. Children are skeletally immature; they have an increased risk of developing secondary skeletal conditions such as scoliosis and hip dysplasia. Their injuries may not be seen with standard x-rays so a CT scan or MRI may be needed to properly diagnose the injury. Crying may mask respiratory failure. Irritability may disguise autonomic dysreflexia, an over-activity of the autonomic nervous system that can cause an abrupt onset of extremely high blood pressure, leading to seizures, stroke and, in the most severe cases, death (see page 125 for more on this medical emergency).

A PRIMARY DIFFERENCE IN TREATING younger patients is that care becomes family centered. The parents are involved in nearly every aspect of physical care and must also nurture the child's psychological growth. It is important to foster expectations that the child will grow into an independently functioning adult.

READY FOR REHAB

WHEN A CHILD IS INJURED, a parent must first understand the injury and begin planning for the rehabilitation phase. An Information Specialist at the Reeve Foundation can provide many resources; call toll-free 1-800-539-7309. It is never too early to begin researching rehabilitation centers. Acute hospital stays are short and your child will be moving on to a rehabilitation center very soon. Make a well-informed choice based on your child's level of injury, your family's needs and your insurance guidelines. You may find that many rehabilitation centers have a minimum age requirement for admission because they are not equipped to meet the special needs of young children and their families.

Parents play a critical role in determining what is best for both child and family. Parents have a right to participate in the selection of a rehabilitation facility. Be proactive, do your research and advocate for what best meets your child's and family's needs. Remember that rehabilitation is short term—your child might be home in as few as 30 days.

A starting point in locating pediatric centers is the Commission on Accreditation of Rehabilitation Facilities (CARF). Look for a special designation of Spinal Cord Injury (SCI) as well as having the facility be an accredited rehabilitation center. There are very few programs that are specifically CARF accredited for children with spinal cord injury or disease. However, many of the major children's hospitals have rehabilitation programs and can meet your child's special needs. Additionally, many adult rehabilitation centers accept teens.

Some questions to ask a pediatric rehabilitation center:

- Do you have a specialized program for pediatric SCI patients?
- How many children with SCI does your facility admit each year?
- Do you have a specialized program for adolescents?
- How many adolescents with SCI do you admit each year?
- Do you have a program so my child can continue class work?
- Are siblings and friends allowed to visit?
- What level of involvement do you expect from parents?
- Do you provide training in care issues for the parents?
- Do you provide family housing near the hospital?
- Do you offer services to school districts that will ease my child's transition back home?
- Are there therapeutic recreation programs, as well as an opportunity to go off the hospital grounds?
- How many ventilator dependent children do you treat each year?
- What is your success rate for weaning from a ventilator?
- May I tour the facility?
- Do you have a list of former patients' families I can talk to?

Because pediatric spinal cord trauma is rare, expertise may not readily be available. Parents are advised to contact Shriners Hospitals. Shriners has taken the lead in developing clinical practice standards for children with SCI and has three comprehensive SCI rehabilitation centers designed specifically for children (Chicago, Philadelphia and Northern California). Care is often provided at no cost for children up to age 18 who have no insurance. Toll-free 1-800-237-5055; see **www.shrinershospitalsforchildren.org**

Your health insurance will play a critical role in determining where your child can go for rehabilitation. In the early days post injury, it is important to contact your insurance carrier and ask for a case manager based on your child's injury and future healthcare needs. The insurance case manager, in collaboration with the acute care hospital case manager, can assist you in selecting a rehabilitation program that meets your child's and family's needs and is covered by your insurance. If you disagree with the decision of your insurance company, you can file an appeal.

If you do not have insurance or are underinsured, it is important to apply for Medicaid as well as Social Security for your child. Each

All-access playground from Shane's Inspiration

state has financial guidelines as well as eligibility criteria that take into consideration the severity of the disability. If you do not qualify for Medicaid, the Children's Health Insurance Program (CHIP) was designed to assist families who can not afford a private health insurance policy but who make too much money to qualify for Medicaid. CHIP was created by the federal government but individual states operate their own program. Visit Medicaid and CHIP for more details; see pages 302-306.

ॐ Links to resources:

The Arc is devoted to promoting and improving supports and services for all people with intellectual and developmental disabilities; **www.thearc.org**

Parent Technical Assistance Network is a partnership of assistance centers, funded by the U.S. Department of Education for developing Parent Training and Information Centers (PTIs) and Community Parent Resource Centers (CPRCs). Toll-free 1-888-248-0822; **www.parentcenternetwork.org**

Ability Online is a social network for children and youth with disabilities or chronic illnesses to connect to each other as well as to friends, family members, caregivers and supporters. **www.abilityonline.org**

All Kids Can! is a disabilities awareness program that helps students learn acceptance, dignity and respect. Supported by CVS Caremark; **www.cvscaremarkallkidscan.com**

Council for Exceptional Children is dedicated to improving the educational success of individuals with disabilities. Toll-free 1-888-232-7733; **http://sped.org**

Camp Ronald McDonald is an accessible residential camp for kids with special needs, in Southern California. Toll-free 1-800-625-7295; **www.campronaldmcdonald.org**

Easter Seals provides services, education, outreach, and advocacy so people with disabilities can live, learn, work and play in their communities. **www.easterseals.com**

Education Resources Information Center (ERIC) is a digital library of education research and information, sponsored by the Institute of Education Sciences (IES) of the U.S. Department of Education. **www.eric.ed.gov**

Family Voices supports family-centered care for all children and youth with special healthcare needs or disabilities. Toll-free 1-888-835-5669; **www.familyvoices.org**

Island Dolphin Care, Key Largo, Fla., allows children to swim and play, and perhaps heal, with dolphins. **www.islanddolphincare.org.**

Family Center on Technology and Disability offers a range of information and services related to assistive technologies for children with disabilities. **www.fctd.info**

National Dissemination Center for Children with Disabilities is a source of information on disabilities in infants, toddlers, children, and youth. **http://nichcy.org**

Early Childhood Technical Assistance Center (ECTAC) works to ensure that children with disabilities (birth through 5 years) and their families receive and benefit from high quality, culturally appropriate and family-centered supports and services. **http://ectacenter.org**

National Organization for Rare Disorders (NORD) is a federation of voluntary health organizations dedicated to helping people with rare "orphan" diseases; **www.rarediseases.org**

Parents Helping Parents (PHP) provides lifetime guidance, supports and services to families of children with any special need and the professionals who serve them. **www.php.com**

Parent Advocacy Coalition for Educational Rights (PACER) Center works to expand opportunities and enhance the quality of life of children and young adults with disabilities and their families, based on the concept of parents helping parents. **www.pacer.org**

Sibling Support Project is dedicated to the concerns of brothers and sisters of people who have special health or developmental concerns. **www.siblingsupport.org**

Starlight Children's Foundation develops multi-media and technology projects that empower seriously ill children to deal with the medical and emotional challenges they face. **www.starlight.org**

EDUCATION

WHETHER YOUR CHILD IS A TODDLER or graduating soon from high school, it is important to be aware of available educational programs and services. There are a variety of educational programs to assist children with disabilities; most fall under the Individuals with Disabilities Education Act (IDEA), the federal law that addresses the needs of children with disabilities.

There are time frames that school systems must follow. In order to ensure that your child is ready to return to school and receive services immediately, it is important to make the referral in the early days of recovery or diagnosis. Notify your school's principal of your child's disability and to convene an Individualized Education Program (IEP) team meeting for evaluation for services. Some schools may want you to wait until your child has been discharged from the hospital. Ask if the school system will accept the hospital's assessments and recommendations—if they will, ask that communication begin between the school and hospital. Document all communication and, if necessary, put your requests in writing.

Many families feel pressure to keep their child caught up in school to continue on with classmates the following school year. While a child is in the hospital or in a rehab center, school can come directly to them. A child can be assigned a teacher and class work can be sent from school. Many rehab programs have set hours for classroom instruction.

The Individuals with Disabilities Education Act was created to ensure that all children with disabilities, regardless of the severity of their disability, have available a "free appropriate public education," including special education and related services. IDEA makes funds available for states and cities to assist in the education of infants, toddlers, preschoolers, children and youth with disabilities. As much as possible, all children with disabilities are to be educated in the regular education environment. In order to remain eligible for federal funds, states must ensure that children with disabilities receive a complete individual evaluation and assessment of their specific needs.

An Individualized Education Program will be drawn up for every

SAM MADDOX

Giant Steps therapeutic riding program, Petaluma, CA

child or youth found eligible for special education or early intervention services. An IEP is the contract between the school district and the student that lists the type and amount of services it will provide to the student.

Those receiving special education have the right to receive the related services, which may include transportation, speech pathology and audiology, psychological services, physical and occupational therapy, recreation (including therapeutic recreation), rehabilitation counseling, and medical services for diagnostic or evaluation purposes. Parents have the right to participate in all decisions related to identification, evaluation and placement of their child with a disability. Parents may appeal any decision concerning the education of their child.

Early Intervention: Birth to 3rd birthday

Services for very young children, from birth through age two, are called Early Intervention or Part C services (named for its designation in IDEA). Early intervention is an effective way to help children with disabilities and those who are experiencing developmental delays catch up or address specific developmental concerns as soon as possible in their lives.

If you believe your infant or toddler can benefit from early intervention services, you can make a referral yourself or have your hospital or doctor refer your young child. The state is responsible for implementing early intervention programs for infants and toddlers. Call your state agency (see NICHCY for contact information, below) and explain that you want to find out about early intervention services for your child. Ask for the name of the office, a contact person, and the phone number in your area where you can find out more about the program and have your child screened for a disability or delay. Even though you know that your child has paralysis, he or she will still need to be screened so that necessary services will be identified.

As with all areas of your child's health and education, keep a log of who you talked with, the date, time and any notes you may have taken.

Services for Preschoolers with Disabilities: Ages 3 through 5

Services for preschool children (ages 3 through 5) are provided free of charge through the public school system. If your child was receiving Early Intervention services and is still eligible, he or she will transition over to services for preschool, ages 3-5. Another way for very young children to become identified is through the local Child Find office; each state must have comprehensive systems to identify, locate, and evaluate children with disabilities residing in the state and who are in need of special education and related services. Your pediatrician or rehabilitation hospital may suggest that you contact the appropriate agency to have your child screened and/or evaluated to determine if he or she qualifies for services.

You don't have to wait until someone suggests that your child be screened, though. If you are concerned about your child's development, contact the local Child Find office (through your local school system) and arrange to have your child screened. These screenings are free of charge.

IDEA, Kindergarten through age 22

Before your child can receive any special education and related services (occupational therapy, physical therapy, nursing, assistive technology) he or she must be referred and evaluated. The school system has 60 days to complete the assessments—the quicker you make a referral, the faster your child can return to school. If your child qualifies for services, an Individualized Education Program will be drafted and the specific services, goals, objectives and accommodations will be outlined. For many students with disabilities, the key to success in the classroom lies in having appropriate adaptations, accommodations, and modifications made to the instruction and other classroom activities. This is particularly true for students with paralysis. Examples of related services are: physical and occupational therapy, school health services, and rehabilitation counseling. Supplementary aids and services might include an aide, a note taker, or other assistive technology.

Transition to Adulthood

If your child is 16 or older, the IEP will include transition services intended to help them move from the world of school to adulthood. As part of transition planning, the IEP team will consider post-secondary education, vocational training or employment. Often, a school's IEP team is joined by a vocational rehabilitation counselor from the state. By planning the transition process, your teen will be prepared to move onto the next phase of their life with supports in place.

Section 504 of the Rehabilitation Act of 1973 and Title II of the Americans with Disabilities Act of 1990 prohibit discrimination on the basis of disability. Practically every school district and postsecondary school in the United States is subject to one or both of these laws. Section 504 and Title II protect elementary, secondary, and postsecondary students from discrimination. Some of the requirements that apply through high school are different from those that apply beyond high school. Section 504

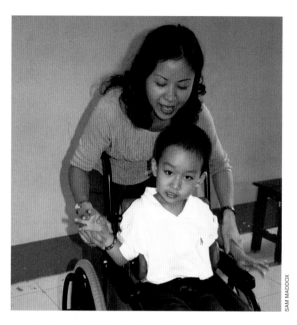

SAM MADDOX

requires a school district to provide a free, appropriate public education to each child with a disability in the district's jurisdiction. Unlike high school, however, a postsecondary school is not required to provide free services. Rather, a postsecondary school is required to provide appropriate academic adjustments as necessary to ensure that it does not discriminate on the basis of disability. If a postsecondary school provides housing to nondisabled students, it must provide comparable, convenient, and accessible housing to students with disabilities at the same cost.

If you want a postsecondary school to provide an academic adjustment, you must identify yourself as having a disability; your postsecondary school is not required to identify you as having a disability or to assess your needs. Academic adjustments may include auxiliary aids and services, as well as modifications to academic requirements as necessary to ensure equal educational opportunity. Examples of adjustments are: arranging for priority registration; reducing a course load; substituting one course for another; providing note takers, recording devices, sign language interpreters, extended time for testing, and equipping school computers with screen reading, voice recognition, or other adaptive software or hardware. A postsecondary school does not have to provide personal attendants, individually prescribed devices, readers for personal use or study, or other devices or services of a personal nature, such as tutoring and typing.

Practically every postsecondary school must have a person—frequently called the Section 504 Coordinator, ADA Coordinator, or Disability Services Coordinator—who coordinates the school's compliance with Section 504, Title II, or both laws. You may contact that person for information about how to address any concerns about discrimination. To learn more about the complaint process, call toll-free 1-800-421-3481 or see **www.ed.gov/ocr/docs/howto.html**

❧ **Below are links to resources:**

Association of University Centers on Disabilities (AUCD) is a resource for local, state, national, and international policy makers concerned about people living with developmental and other disabilities and their families. **www.aucd.org**

Career Opportunities for Students with Disabilities is a professional association of more than 600 colleges and universities and over 500 major national employers to improve the employment rate of college students and recent graduates with disabilities. **www.cosdonline.org**

Families and Advocates Partnership for Education hopes to improve educational outcomes for children with disabilities. **www.fape.org**

Federal Regional Resource Center Program supports a nationwide technical assistance network to respond to the needs of students with disabilities, especially those from underrepresented populations. **www.rrcprogram.org**

Financial aid: Resources for students with disabilities; see **www.finaid.org/otheraid/disabled.phtml**

Financial aid and scholarships for undocumented students. **www.finaid.org/otheraid/undocumented.phtml**

Going to College is about college life with a disability; aimed at high school students. **www.going-to-college.org**

HEATH is a national clearinghouse on postsecondary education for people with disabilities; develops and disseminates fact sheets, website directories, newsletters, and resource materials. **www.heath.gwu.edu**

IDEA Partnership is a collaboration of more than 50

Christiaan Bailey and Ocean Healing campers, in Mexico.

national organizations, technical assistance providers, state and local organizations and agencies working to improve educational results for children and youth with disabilities. **www.ideapartnership.org**

Kids' Chance provides scholarships for children of workers seriously injured or killed on the job. **www.kidschance.org**

National Center on Disability and Access to Education addresses issues of Internet access and technology to enhance the lives of people with disabilities and their families. **www.ncdae.org**

National Dissemination Center for Children with Disabilities (NICHCY) offers information on the full spectrum of disabilities in children, including developmental delays and rare disorders. Good source on policies regarding education, IDEA, early intervention and special education. See **http://nichcy.org**

National Dropout Prevention Center for Students with Disabilities works on dropout prevention, reentry, and school completion. **www.ndpc-sd.org**

Office of Special Education and Rehabilitative Services (OSERS), from the U.S. Dept. of Education, works to improve outcomes for people with disabilities with supports to parents and individuals, school districts and states. **www.ed.gov/about/offices/list/osers/index.html**

U.S. Dept. of Education's Tool Kit on Teaching and Assessing Students with Disabilities is focused on improving instruction, assessment, and accountability. **www.osepideasthatwork.org/toolkit/index.asp**

10 Caregiving

Caregiving duties cannot be skirted and cannot always be delegated.
But the job does not have to be performed in isolation.
Connect to others with similar situations.

Dear Caregiver,

After my husband Christopher was injured, it became obvious that paralysis is a family issue. Taking care of our families' physical, emotional, social and economic needs can be fulfilling and rewarding. But providing care to a person who is paralyzed is a job we don't always expect to get.

We mourn our loved one's loss of mobility and independence. We also mourn our own losses: We feel isolated; we have no personal time; we feel exhausted, overwhelmed. And we feel no one else understands the demands placed upon us.

A caregiver must deal with medical concerns, hygiene, transportation, financial planning, advocacy, and end-of-life issues. Being an effective caregiver means gaining some sense of control over the situation. One way this is done is through information, and by sharing experiences or solving problems with other caregivers.

Please know that you are not alone, that you are extremely valuable, and that you and your family can lead active, fulfilling lives despite the challenges of paralysis. Don't ever be embarrassed to ask our Paralysis Resource Center for assistance. Just call toll-free 1-800-539-7309.

Best Wishes,
Dana Reeve
(written in 2005, a year before her death)

THE CAREGIVER ROLE

HELPING SOMEONE YOU CARE FOR to continue living independently in the home is valuable work. Caregiving can be a satisfying experience; it demonstrates fulfillment of a commitment to a loved one. True enough, though, caregiving is not a role anyone really chooses. It seems to choose us, emerging from events and circumstances outside our expectations, beyond our control.

Family members provide the vast majority of care for people who are chronically ill or disabled. According to the Caregiver Action Network, family caregivers underpin our healthcare system in a profound way. More than 50 million people provide some level of care for a loved one, which would translate into annual wages of $375 billion—almost twice as much as is actually spent on homecare and nursing home services combined—if it weren't done for "free." As the population ages, as medical science keeps people alive longer and as healthcare policies send people home from hospitals sicker and quicker, the number of family caregivers can only grow.

Caregiving is a job that cannot be skirted and cannot always be delegated. It is frustrating. It is physically and emotionally draining. It can steal our dreams or break our hearts. It makes us sad for our loved one's loss . . . and for our own loss. While caring for loved ones can be enormously satisfying, there are days, to be sure, that offer little reward.

The job takes its toll. Caregivers suffer far more depression, stress and anxiety than the general population. Surveys show that up to 70 percent of caregivers report depression, 51 percent sleeplessness, and 41 percent back problems. Nearly three quarters of family caregivers do not go to the doctor as often as they should, and 55 percent say they skip doctor appointments; 63 percent of caregivers report having poor eating habits.

Caregivers feel isolated; they often report that their lives are not "normal" and that no one else can possibly understand what they are going through.

There is a financial impact, too. Families helping a person with a disability in daily living activities spend more than twice as much on out-of-pocket medical expenses than families without a disabled person. Frequently the caregiver must make sacrifices at work to attend to duties at home. But this is your family, your loved one. What are your choices? You can't just walk away. You learn to deal with the frustration while learning how to best get the job done. The lessons are often learned the hard way—for the most part, caregivers learn by trial and error how to manage daily routines for food preparation, hygiene, transportation and other activities at home.

Here are a few caregiving tips compiled by Paralysis Resource Center Information Specialists:

Rule number one for all caregivers is to take care of yourself. Providing care while holding down a job, running a household, or parenting can burn anyone out. A person who is exhausted or sick is more likely to make bad decisions or take out frustrations inappropriately. Stress is known to contribute to a variety of health problems. The more you keep your own well-being in balance, the more you will enhance your coping skills and stamina. By taking care of yourself, you will be better able, both physically and emotionally, to provide care for your loved one.

Connect to the caregiving community. Share and learn and benefit from the collective wisdom of the caregiver community. It is important that caregivers connect with one another to gain strength and to know that they are not alone. For many, the isolation that comes with the job is eased by attending support group meetings with others in similar situations. Support groups provide emotional support and caregiving tips, as well as information on community resources. Online support groups can be very helpful. The Reeve Foundation supports active community forums and discussions about all issues related to caregiving. See **www.spinalcordinjury-paralysis.org/discussions**

Relentless. But You Will Find Ways

Your partner gets hurt, and your life is changed because of something that happened to him. That is the hard truth. I remember saying to him, "Come back. Please come back." And he would say, "I'm trying."

A caregiver-spouse has to say at some point, "I freely choose this," in the same way as before the injury happened. And, if you don't freely choose this with your whole heart, I don't see how you can make it, because there's going to be some part of you that is always mad, that always somehow resents this other person for what they've taken away from you. Being a family caregiver is relentless. You can never, ever really

get away from it. It really helps to have a sense of humor; but, I think the most important thing isn't really how you communicate. It's the very basic choice and knowing that no one's making you do anything. If you can accept this, you'll find ways to work it out, whatever it is.

—Kate Willette

Willette chronicled her experiences as a caregiver in a book, Some Things Are Unbreakable.

Therapy or counseling may also facilitate better problem solving. Counseling can help one cope with feelings of anger, frustration, guilt, loss or competing personal, work and family demands.

Know as much as possible about your loved one's condition. Be informed about medical issues and how the disease or disability can affect a person physically, psychologically, behaviorally, etc. You are an important member of your loved one's healthcare team. Chapter 1 provides an overview of the primary causes of paralysis. The Internet is another powerful tool for learning about the medical basis of disability. Doctors and other health professionals can help you understand how a loved one's condition might change and how that change might affect the demands on the caregiver.

Take advantage of opportunities for respite care. Refresh yourself and take an occasional break from daily duties. An extended vacation may not be realistic, but it is essential for caregivers to schedule some down time. This may be a short outing, quiet time at home, a movie with a friend, etc. To get away, the caregiver may require respite care/ assistance from others. See Resources at the end of this chapter for some possible connections to help you get a break.

Be an advocate. Keep in mind you may be the only one equipped to speak out on your loved one's behalf or to ask difficult questions. Prepare your loved one's health history and take it with you to appointments. Anticipate the future as best as you can. Financial and legal planning are important considerations. Issues such as financing long-term care, protecting assets, obtaining the authority for surrogate decision making, and other matters often need attention. Make an appointment with an attorney knowledgeable in estate planning, probate, and, if possible, public benefits planning. Other areas often requiring planning include coordination between community services and involved friends and family members. Decisions about placement in a nursing home or other care options can often be facilitated by a professional familiar with brain impairments, caregiving and community resources. In some cases, it is necessary to make end-of-life decisions regarding your loved one.

Understand as best as you can how the system works for insurance,

Dana Reeve on Caregiving

After Chris was injured, we sort of operated as if it was like landing on another planet. It can look very bleak and overwhelming. There's a tremendous amount of adjustment that needs to go on mentally. And facing the new normal, facing the adjustments, the loss...you have to grieve for the loss. Because it's true - the only way for grief to be alleviated is to grieve. You need to acknowledge the loss. But at the same time, once you do that, you're opening up a whole new area where you can have tremendous hope.

Dana Reeve

Social Security and others means of public assistance. There are experts at public agencies who can help. See Chapter 7, Working the System, page 294.

Ask for help. Many caregivers are so accustomed to providing help and seeing to another person's needs that they don't know how to ask for aid themselves. Your family is your first resource. Spouses, brothers and sisters, children, and other relatives can do a lot to ease your caregiving burden. Let them know what they can and should do. Look to your place of worship for aid and counsel. Make your religious leader aware of your situation. Encourage your loved one's friends and neighbors to provide what comfort they can. If you need to hire an attendant, several good resource guides are listed below.

Know everything you can about tools and adaptive equipment. It is essential that caregivers know about the homecare products and services that might make their jobs easier. See the Tools chapter in this book, page 260, for ways to stay current and up-to-date on all that technology has to offer.

As you settle into the role of caregiver, you may find yourself making decisions for people who used to decide for you. It's sometimes a trick to balance competing needs for control. But it's important to respect the right of the person being cared for to make choices. Choice is good; by deciding things we have a sense of control over our lives. Allow your loved one as much choice as possible, from the food on the menu to their daily wardrobe to TV programming.

Gain confidence in your abilities and pride in your achievements. Easier said than done—how do you stand up for yourself, take care of yourself, and find a balance between your own needs and those of your loved ones? The Caregiver Action Network offers the following principles of empowerment caregivers are urged to live.

Choose to take charge of your life. Don't let your loved one's illness or disability always take center stage. We fall into caregiving often because of an unexpected event, but somewhere along the line you need to step back and consciously say, "I choose to take on this caregiving role." It goes a long way toward eliminating the feeling of being a victim.

Honor, value and love yourself. You're doing a very hard job and you deserve some quality time, just for yourself. Self-care isn't a luxury. It's a necessity. It is your right as a human being. Step back and recognize just how extraordinary you are. Remember, your own good health is the very best present you can give your loved one.

Seek, accept and, at times, demand help. Don't be ashamed to ask for help. When people offer assistance, accept it and suggest specific things that they can do. Caregiving, especially at its most intense levels, is definitely more than a one-person job. Asking for help is a sign of your strength and an acknowledgment of your abilities and limitations.

Stand up and be counted. Stand up for your rights as a caregiver and a citizen. Recognize that caregiving comes on top of being a parent, a child, a spouse. Honor your caregiving role and speak up for your well-deserved recognition and rights. Become your own advocate, both within your own immediate caregiving sphere and beyond.

SOURCES

Caregiver Action Network, The Family Caregiver Alliance, AARP

❧ Below are links to resources.

Caregiver Action Network educates, supports and empowers families who care for chronically ill, aged or disabled loved ones; **http://caregiveraction.org**

National Alliance for Caregiving is a coalition of national groups that supports family caregivers and the professionals who help them; **www.caregiving.org**

The Rosalynn Carter Institute for Caregiving establishes local, state and national partnerships committed to promoting caregiver health, skills and resilience; **www.rosalynncarter.org**

Well Spouse is a national organization that gives support to wives, husbands, and partners of the chronically ill and/or disabled. Addresses issues common to family caregivers: anger, guilt, fear, isolation, grief, and financial threat; **www.wellspouse.org**

Caregiving.com is an Internet community for families and healthcare professionals who care for chronically ill or disabled family members. See **www.caregiving.com**

The Family Caregiver Alliance (FCA) is the lead agency in California's system of Caregiver Resource Centers and operates the National Center on Caregiving to develop support programs for family caregivers in every state. FCA champions the caregivers' cause through education, services, research and advocacy. 415-434-3388, toll-free 1-800-445-8106; **www.caregiver.org**

AARP offers a caregiving resource center, including legal issues, long distance caregiving, end-of-life issues. Toll-free 1-877-333-5885; **www.aarp.org/home-family/caregiving**

Caregiver Media Group publishes Today's Caregiver magazine and offers topic-specific newsletters, online discussion lists, chat rooms and an online store. **www.caregiver.com**

National Respite Coalition Network and National Respite Locator Service helps parents, caregivers and professionals get a break using respite services in their local area. **www.archrespite.org**

National Caregivers Library is large source of free information for caregivers. **www.caregiverslibrary.org**

Shepherd's Centers of America (SCA) is an interfaith organization that coordinates nearly 100 independent Shepherd's Centers across the United States to help older adults remain independent. **www.shepherdcenters.org**

Hiring and Management of Personal Care Assistants for Individuals with SCI is a downloadable, 26-page booklet in PDF format from the SCI Project at Santa Clara Valley Medical Center. Covers everything from locating and hiring to training and paying personal assistants. Includes forms, checklists and resources. See **www.tbi-sci.org/pdf/pas.pdf**

Paralysis Community, a resource of the Christopher & Dana Reeve Foundation, is a safe and secure online social networking site with a robust discussion area on many areas of paralysis, including caregiving; please see **www.spinalcordinjury-paralysis.org/discussions**

CareCure Forum for caregivers. Active and helpful message board for loved ones and caregivers of people living with paralysis. See "Caregiving" at **http://sci.rutgers.edu**

Spinal Cord Injury Caregivers is a Yahoo Internet forum, a place to share information and to support other caregivers who are caring for people with SCI. Visit **http://groups.yahoo.com/group/scic**

Nursing Home Compare, sponsored by Medicare, offers information about the past performance of most nursing homes in the U.S. Also features "A Guide to Choosing a Nursing Home" and a nursing home checklist. **www.medicare.gov/NHCompare/home.asp**

Resources

Useful resources for the paralysis community

Advocacy

ADAPT started as American Disabled for Accessible Public Transit, blocking buses in cities across the nation to demonstrate the need for access to public transit. The organization played a major role in gaining passage of the Americans with Disabilities Act and continues to take its message to the streets so people with disabilities can live in the community with real supports instead of being locked away in nursing homes or other institutions. See *www.adapt.org*

American Association of People with Disabilities (AAPD) is the largest national cross-disability member organization in the United States, dedicated to ensuring economic self-sufficiency and political empowerment for 56 million Americans with disabilities. 202-457-0046, toll-free 1-800-840-8844; *www.aapd.com*

National Organization on Disability: Since 1982, NOD has been working to expand the participation of people with disabilities in all aspects of American life. NOD promotes voting, housing, employment, religious access, accessible urban design, statistical surveys, marketing to the disability community. *http://nod.org*

National Council on Disability (NCD) is an independent federal agency making recommendations to the President and Congress regarding policies and programs that empower people with disabilities to achieve economic self-sufficiency, independent living, and inclusion into all aspects of society. *www.ncd.gov*

The Disability History Social Project is a community history project for people with disabilities to set forth and share a rich history and culture. See *www.disabilityhistory.org*

The Disability and History Museum is a virtual collection to chronicle the disability experience and dispel lingering myths, assumptions, and stereotypes. *www.disabilitymuseum.org*

Society for Disability Studies explores issues of disability and chronic illness from scholarly perspectives. SDS membership includes social scientists, health researchers, and humanities scholars, as well as those in the disability rights movement. Publishes Disability Studies Quarterly (DSQ), and hosts an annual conference. *http://disstudies.org*

Association on Higher Education And Disability (AHEAD) is an international organization of professionals committed to full participation in higher education for people with disabilities. *www.ahead.org*

National Council on Independent Living advances the independent living philosophy of self-determination and full integration and participation of people with disabilities in society. 202-207-0334; toll-free: 1-877-525-3400; *www.ncil.org*

Independent Living Research Utilization (ILRU) is a national center for information, training, research, and technical assistance in independent living. *www.ilru.org*

United States International Council on Disabilities (USICD) is a federation of disability-oriented agencies, associations, facilities and consumers dedicated to furthering the full integration into society of people with disabilities. *www.usicd.org*

Disabled People's International advocates for the full participation of all disabled people in the mainstream of life, particularly those in developing countries. *www.dpi.org*

Rehabilitation International is a worldwide network of people with disabilities, service providers and government agencies working together to improve the quality of life for disabled people and their families. *www.riglobal.org*

Media

Abilities is Canada's cross-disability lifestyle magazine. Covers health, active living, disability rights, resources, etc. *www.abilities.ca*

Ability Magazine crosses celebrity journalism with disability awareness. *www.abilitymagazine.com*

Exceptional Parent is a magazine with support, ideas, encouragement and outreach for parents and families of children with every type of disability. *www.eparent.com*

Mouth is about disability rights and empowerment that says this about itself: "This rude little magazine demands answers from the people in charge, laughs at the lying answers, and occasionally bites down, hard, somewhere near the throbbing jugular." *www.mouthmag.com*

New Mobility is a monthly lifestyle magazine for the wheelchair community, created in 1988 by Sam Maddox. Essential reading for the paralysis community. *www.newmobility.com*

PN (Paraplegia News) is a magazine for service veterans with disabilities, and for anyone who uses a wheelchair. Covers healthcare, issues, news and events, sports and recreation. From PVA Publications. *http://pvamag.com/pn*

Ragged Edge, the online successor to The Disability Rag, covers the issues concerning disability: medical rationing, genetic discrimination, assisted suicide, long-term care, attendant services. *www.ragged-edge-mag.com*

Spinal Network: The Total Wheelchair Resource Book (the mother publication of New Mobility magazine) comprises 586 pages of profiles, articles, humor, pathos and bathos. Real world advice and unsentimental role modeling. Created in 1987 by Sam Maddox, this is the original survival manual for paralyzing conditions. "Awesomely complete," said the Los Angeles Times. *www.newmobility.com*

Sports 'N Spokes is a colorful bi-monthly magazine about wheelchair athletics, competitive sports and recreation. *http://pvamag.com/sns*

Online

CareCure Community offers lively Internet forums with news and comment on paralysis care, caregiving, cure, funding, active living, pain treatment, sexuality, research, clinical trials and more. *http://sci.rutgers.edu/*

BrainTalk Communities is a huge collection of Internet message boards covering nearly every known neurological problem and disability social issue. *www.braintalkcommunities.org*

Multiple Sclerosis Complementary and Alternative Medicine (MS-CAM) is an Internet community that shares experiences with complementary and alternative medicine (CAM) therapies. *www.ms-cam.org*

The Stroke Network is a community of web sites designed to help "everyone in the stroke family." Features chats, message boards, survivor profiles, resources, etc. *www.strokenetwork.org*

Paralysis Community: from the Christopher & Dana Reeve Foundation Paralysis Resource Center, a safe and secure online social networking destination. Numerous discussion areas on topics related to spinal cord injury and paralysis, including active living, relationships, caregiving, cure research, clinical care and creature comforts. Topnotch blog squad can be found here. *www.spinalcordinjury-paralysis.org/discussions*

Religion

Joni and Friends is a Christian ministry formed by quadriplegic Joni Eareckson Tada to evangelize people affected by disability. *www.joniandfriends.org*

National Catholic Partnership on Disability (NCPD) was established so Catholics with disabilities can fully participate in the celebrations and obligations of their faith. *www.ncpd.org*

Yachad National Jewish Council for Disabilities insures participation in the full spectrum of Jewish life. *www.njcd.org/*

Lift Disability Network promotes the spiritual well-being of people with disabilities. *www.liftdisability.net/*

The Episcopal Disability Network focuses on the physical, cultural, emotional, and programmatic barriers that prevent persons with disabilities from full participation in church and society. *www.disability99.org*

Glossary

Activities of daily living (ADL): activities involved in self-care, bowel and bladder management and mobility, including bathing, dressing, eating, and other skills necessary for independent living.

Activity-Based Therapy: a rehabilitation modality based on the theory that activity affects neurologic recovery, that patterned activity can stimulate spinal cord plasticity and "reawaken" nerve pathways related to movement. (*See* Locomotor Training).

Acute: the early stages of an injury (as opposed to chronic, which is long-term); in spinal cord injury, better early management of acute trauma may be the reason for an increased number of "incomplete" injuries. Theoretically, early intervention with drugs or cooling will limit functional loss. If the progressive cascade of secondary effects of trauma at the cellular level (e.g., blood flow loss, swelling, calcium toxicity) can be reduced, the severity of the injury will be reduced.

Allodynia: condition in which pain arises from a stimulus that would not normally be experienced as painful.

Alpha blockers: Medications that can relax the urinary sphincter and prostate and therefore allow better bladder emptying.

Ambulation: "walking" with braces or crutches. Some paralyzed people have ambulated using special electrical stimulation. Many find the energy expenditure to "walk" is too much for too little function; they are more functional in their wheelchairs.

Ankylosis: fixation of a joint leading to immobility, due to ossification or bony deposits of calcium at joints.

Anticholinergic: a drug often prescribed for those with indwelling catheters to reduce spasms of smooth muscle, including the bladder. Anticholinergics block certain receptors (acetylcholine), resulting in inhibition of certain nerve impulses (parasympathetic).

Antidepressant: a drug prescribed to treat depression.

Aphasia: change in language function due to injury to cerebral cortex of brain. Language, not understood or not formed, is often restored once swelling is reduced.

Arachnoid membrane: the middle of three membranes protecting the brain and spinal cord.

Arachnoiditis: inflammation and scarring of the membranes covering the spinal cord, sometimes caused by the dye used in a myelogram. Constant burning pain is a common symptom, as is bladder dysfunction. Some cases advance to paralysis. Arachnoiditis is often misdiagnosed as "failed back surgery syndrome," multiple sclerosis or chronic fatigue syndrome.

ASIA Score: a tool to assess function after SCI, on a scale from A (complete, no motor or sensory function) through E (normal motor and sensory).

Astrocyte: star-shaped glial cells that provide the necessary chemical and physical environment for nerve regeneration. These cells proliferate after injury and are believed to break down toxins such as glutamate. The astrocyte also has a bad side: Reactive astrocytes contribute to the formation of glial scar, which may be a major obstacle to nerve regrowth following trauma.

Atelectasis: loss of breathing function characterized by collapsed lung tissue. Can be a problem for high tetraplegics who are unable to clear lung secretions. This, in turn, can lead to pneumonia.

Augmentation cystoplasty: A surgery that enlarges the bladder by sewing a piece of intestine onto the top of the bladder.

Augmentative and Alternative Communication (AAC): forms of communication that supplement or enhance speech or writing, including electronic devices, picture boards and sign language.

Autoimmune response: Normally, the immune system recognizes foreign substances; the system produces antibodies against the invader to eliminate it. In an autoimmune response, the body creates an antibody against itself. Multiple sclerosis is thought to be an autoimmune disease.

Autonomic dysreflexia: a potentially dangerous reaction that includes high blood pressure, sweating, chills, headache, which may occur in persons with SCI above the sixth thoracic level (T6). Often caused by bladder or bowel issues. Untreated, autonomic dysreflexia can lead to stroke or even death.

Autonomic nervous system: the part of the nervous system that controls involuntary activities, including heart muscle, glands and smooth muscle tissue. The autonomic system is subdivided into the sympathetic and parasympathetic systems. Sympathetic activities are marked by the "flight or fight" emergency response; parasympathetic activities are marked by lowered blood pressure, pupil contraction and slowing of the heart.

Axon: the nerve fiber that carries an impulse from the nerve cell to a target, and also carries materials from the nerve terminals (e.g., on muscles) back to the nerve cell. When an axon is cut, proteins required for its regeneration are made available by the nerve cell body. A growth cone forms at the tip of the axon. In the spinal cord, a damaged axon is often prepared to regrow, and often has available a supply of material to do so. Scientists believe it is the toxic environment surrounding the axon, and not the genetic programming of the axon itself, that prevents regeneration.

Biofeedback: a process that provides sight or sound information about functions of the body, including blood pressure and muscle tension. By trial and error, one can learn to consciously control these functions. Useful in some paralyzed people to retrain certain muscles.

BiPAP: a type of non-invasive mechanical breathing assistance for treating sleep apnea.

Bladder augmentation: Another term for augmentation cystoplasty.

Bladder outlet obstruction: any type of blockage that restricts urine from flowing freely from the bladder. In SCI this may be related to detrusor sphincter dyssynergia, or from scar tissue.

Botulinum Toxin: better known as Botox, a neurotoxin used clinically to treat crossed eyes, wrinkles, and other muscle related issues, including overactive bladder and spasticity in people with paralysis.

Bowel program: the establishment of a "habit pattern" or a specific time to empty the bowel so that regularity can be achieved.

Brown-Sequard Syndrome: a partial spinal cord injury resulting in hemiplegia, affecting only one side of the body.

Calculi: calcium deposits form stones in either kidney or bladder. Bladder stones are easily removed; kidney stones may require lithotripsy (shock wave shattering) or surgery.

Carpal tunnel syndrome: painful disorder in the hand caused by inflammation of the median nerve in the wrist bone; commonly caused by repetitive motion, including pushing a wheelchair. Splints might help; surgery is sometimes indicated to relieve pressure on the nerve. When it hurts, give it a rest.

Catheter: a rubber or plastic tube for withdrawing or introducing fluids into a cavity of the body, usually the bladder. Some catheters are enclosed in sterile packaging and are used but once. Some catheters remain in place in the bladder, continuously draining.

Cauda equina: the collection of spinal roots descending from the lower part of the spinal cord (conus medullaris, T11 to L2), occupying the vertebral canal below the spinal cord. These roots have some recovery potential.

CAT Scan: computerized axial tomography is a cross-sectional X-ray enhancement technique that benefits diagnosis with high-resolution video images, some in three dimensions.

Central nervous system (CNS): the brain and spinal cord. Prevailing dogma has been that CNS cells won't repair themselves. Experiments show, however, that CNS nerves are "plastic" and thus can regrow and reconnect to appropriate targets.

Cerebrospinal fluid (CSF): colorless solution similar to plasma protecting the brain and spinal cord from shock. Circulates through the subarachnoid space. For diagnostic purposes, a lumbar puncture (spinal tap) is used to draw the fluid.

Cervical: the upper spine (neck) area of the vertebral column. Cervical injuries often result in tetraplegia.

Clinical Trial: a human research program usually involving both experimental and control subjects to examine the safety and effectiveness of a therapy.

Clonus: a deep tendon reflex characterized by rhythmic contractions of a muscle when attempting to hold it in a stretched state.

Colostomy: surgical procedure to allow elimination of feces from a stoma that is formed by connecting part of the large intestine to the wall of the abdomen. People with paralysis sometimes get colostomies because of bowel care issues or skin care hygiene.

Complete Lesion: injury with no motor or sensory function below the zone of cord destruction, at the site of primary trauma.

Constraint-Induced Movement Therapy: also called forced use. In hemiplegia, half the body is affected. By immobilizing the "good" limb a patient is forced to use the affected limb, leading in some cases to improved function.

Continent urinary diversion: A surgical procedure to bypass the bladder. This is made possible by using a section of the stomach or intestine to create an internal pouch. The ureters are sewn into the pouch, which is drained by catheter from a stoma.

Contracture: a body joint which has become stiffened to the point it can no longer be moved through its normal range.

Conus medullaris: the terminal end of the spinal cord. It occurs near the first lumbar vertebrae (L1). After the spinal cord terminates, the lumbar and sacral spinal nerves continue as a "freely moving" bundle of nerves within the vertebral canal and are called the cauda equina (literally, horse tail).

Credé maneuver: Pushing into the lower abdomen directly over the bladder to squeeze out urine.

Cutaneous ileovesicostomy: A surgical procedure in which a piece of the intestine (ileum) is attached to form a tube from the bladder to an opening in the skin (called a stoma) on the lower abdomen. Urine is thus able to drain from the bladder, avoiding the urethra.

Cyst (post traumatic cystic myelopathy): a collection of fluid within the spinal cord; may increase pressure and lead to increased neurological deterioration, loss of sensation, pain, dysreflexia. Cysts can form in months or years after an injury. Their cause is not known. Surgery is sometimes indicated to drain the cavity or to untether the cord. (*See* Syringomyelia.)

Cystogram (CG): X-ray taken after injecting dye into bladder; shows reflux.

Cystometric examination: an exam measuring pressure of forces to empty or resisting to empty the bladder. Used to evaluate catheterization program.

Cystoscopy: An examination of the urethra and bladder using a small, circular instrument called a cystoscope. It is used to check for inflammation, bladder stones, tumors or foreign bodies.

Decubitus ulcer (*See* Pressure sore).

Deep vein thrombosis: the formation of a blood clot (thrombus) in a deep vein. It commonly affects the leg veins, such as the femoral vein. The risk for DVT is greatest in the first three months after injury. The primary concern for clotting is pulmonary embolism. Most patients get an anticoagulant drug to prevent clotting.

Demyelination: loss of nerve fiber "insulation" due to trauma or disease; reduces ability of nerves to conduct impulses (as in multiple sclerosis and some cases of SCI). Some intact but non-working nerve fibers might be coaxed into remyelinating, perhaps restoring function. (*See* Myelin.)

Dendrite: microscopic tree-like fibers extending from a nerve cell (neuron). Receptors of electrochemical nervous impulse transmissions. The total length of dendrites within the human brain exceeds several hundred thousand miles.

Depression: a mental health disorder characterized by low mood, low self esteem and loss of interest or pleasure in activities that were typically enjoyable. Causes of depression may include psychological, psychosocial, hereditary and biological factors. Patients are often treated with antidepressant medications as well as psychotherapy.

Dermatome: map of the body that shows typical function for various levels of spinal cord injury.

Detrusor: The muscle that forms the bladder.

Detrusor sphincter dyssynergia: A loss of coordination between the urinary sphincter and the bladder.

Diaphragmatic pacing: also known as phrenic nerve pacing; the rhythmic application of electrical impulses to the diaphragm, resulting in respiration for patients who would otherwise require a mechanical ventilator.

Dorsal root: the collection of nerves entering the dorsal section (on the back) of a spinal cord segment. These roots share central and peripheral nerve connections, and enter the spinal cord in an area called the dorsal root entry zone (DREZ).

Double blind studies: neither the participating trial subject nor the investigators, institutional staff or sponsoring company are aware of the treatment each subject has received during the trial.

DREZ surgery: dorsal root entry zone microcoagulation, a procedure used to relieve severe pain by cutting specific nerves at the point they enter the spinal cord. Less effective for pain arising from midthoracic and cervical areas; better suited for lower thoracic, upper lumbar pain in legs.

Dura mater: outermost of three membranes protecting the brain and spinal cord. Tough, leatherlike; from Latin, "hard mother."

Edema: swelling.

Electro-ejaculation: a means of producing sperm from men with erectile dysfunction. Uses an electrical probe in the rectum. The sperm can be used to fertilize eggs in the uterus, or in a test tube.

Epididymitis: an infection of the tubes that surround the testicles. If the testicle also becomes infected the condition is called epididymo-orchitis.

Ergometer: exercise machine, equipped with an apparatus for measuring the work performed during exercise.

Exacerbation: in multiple sclerosis, a recurrence or worsening of symptoms.

Flaccid: muscles are soft and limp.

Foley: a catheter that remains inserted in the bladder, continuously draining to a storage bag.

Frankel Scale: a scale for classifying severity of spinal cord injury that was modified in 1992 to create the ASIA Impairment Scale (*see above*).

Functional Electric Stimulation (FES): the application of low-level computer-controlled electric current to the neuromuscular system, including paralyzed muscles, to enhance or produce function (e.g., walking and bike exercise). FES is commercially available for exercise and for ambulation in paraplegics. Other uses include correction of scoliosis, bladder control, electro-ejaculation, phrenic nerve stimulation, stimulation of cough.

Functional Independence Measure (FIM): records the severity of disability based on 18 items. Thirteen items define disability in motor functions. Five items define disability in cognitive functions.

Gait training: instruction in walking, with or without equipment.

Genetic engineering (recombinant DNA technology): the manipulation of the gene codes for biologic processes. Genes are units of hereditary material located on a chromosome which, as a blueprint, determine a specific characteristic of an organism. Gene transfers have been shown to control processes of nerve regeneration.

Gizmo: condom catheter external device for collecting urine in males without bladder control. (Also called Texan.)

Glial cells: from the Greek for "glue," supportive cells associated with neurons. Astrocytes and oligodendrocytes are central nervous system glial cells; in the peripheral nervous system, the main glial cells are called Schwann cells. Glial cells are not involved in impulses (they are not "excitable"), but play a very significant role in maintaining the proper environment for neural growth and survival.

Glossopharyngeal breathing (GPB): a means of forcing extra air into the lungs to expand the chest and achieve a functional cough. (Also called "frog breathing.")

Harrington rods: metal braces fixed along the spinal column for support and stabilization.

Heterotopic ossification (HO): the formation of bone deposits in connective tissue surrounding the major joints, primarily hip and knee. Incidence of 20 percent and as high as 50 percent has been reported in SCI patients, more commonly in higher level injuries. Cause is unknown. Treatment prescribes range-of-motion exercises and weight-bearing activity, can involve surgical removal if severe loss of function occurs.

Hydronephrosis: a kidney distended with urine to the point that its function is impaired. Can cause uremia, the toxic retention of blood nitrogen. Long-term catheterization often prescribed.

Hypothermia: a technique to cool the spinal cord after injury; may reduce metabolic and oxygen requirements of the injured tissue; may reduce edema (swelling), which may reduce secondary nerve fiber damage.

Hypoxia: lack of blood oxygen due to impaired lung function. Important issue in emergency treatment and also for those with limited pulmonary function. Hypoxia can further damage oxygen-sensitive nerve tissue.

Immune response: the body's defense function that produces antibodies to foreign antigens. Important in tissue and cell transplantation: the body is likely to reject new tissues.

Incomplete injury: some sensation or motor control preserved below a spinal cord lesion.

Incontinence: lack of bladder or bowel control.

Indwelling catheter: a flexible tube retained in the bladder, used for continuous urinary drainage to a leg bag or other device. The catheter can enter the bladder via urethra or through an opening in the lower abdomen (suprapubic ostomy).

Informed consent: a patient's right to know the risks and benefits of a medical procedure or clinical trial.

Intermittent catheterization: using a catheter for emptying the bladder on a regular schedule. (*See* Self-catheterization).

Intermittent positive pressure breathing: a short-term breathing treatment where increased breathing pressures are delivered via ventilator to help treat atelectasis, clear secretions or deliver aerosolized medications.

Intrathecal baclofen: administration of the anti-spasm drug baclofen directly to the spinal cord by way of a surgically implanted pump. More effective than oral dosage without side effects of systemic dosage.

Intravenous pyelogram: A test to determine kidney anatomy and function. It involves an injection of a liquid contrast followed by an x-ray.

Ischemia: a reduction in blood flow; thought to be major cause of secondary injury to brain or spinal cord after trauma.

KUB: an X-ray of the abdomen, showing the kidneys, ureters and bladder

Laminectomy: an operation sometimes used to relieve pressure on the spinal cord. Also used to examine the extent of damage to the cord.

Late anterior decompression: surgical procedure to reduce pressure on spinal cord by removing bone fragments.

Lesion: an injury or wound, any pathologic or traumatic injury to the spinal cord.

Lithotripsy: ("litho" for stone, "tripter" for fragmentation) is a noninvasive treatment for kidney stones. Shock waves, generated under water, crumble stones into pieces that will pass with urine.

Locomotor training: an activity-based therapy to retrain the spinal cord to "remember" the pattern of walking. There are two versions: manual-assisted and robotic-assisted. Both consist of supporting part of the patient's body weight with a harness suspended over a moving treadmill. Benefits include, for some, better walking, lower blood pressure, better fitness.

Lower motor neurons: these nerve fibers originate in the spinal cord and travel out of the central nervous system to muscles in the body. An injury to these nerve cells can destroy reflexes and may also affect bowel, bladder and sexual functions. (*See* Upper Motor Neurons).

Lumbar: pertaining to the lower back area immediately below the thoracic spine; the strongest part of the spine.

Metabolic syndrome: highly prevalent in the SCI community, characterized by risk factors including abdominal obesity, high blood pressure, insulin resistance and cholesterol issues. People with the metabolic syndrome are at increased risk of coronary heart disease, stroke and type 2 diabetes.

Mitrofanoff procedure: surgery to place a stoma, or alternative outlet in the abdominal area, for bladder drainage.

Modified Ashworth Scale: a qualitative scale for the assessment of spasticity; measures resistance to passive stretch.

Motoneuron (motor neuron): a nerve cell whose cell body is located in the brain or spinal cord, and whose axons leave the central nervous system by way of cranial nerves or spinal roots. Motoneurons supply information to muscle. A motor unit is the combination of the motoneuron and the set of muscle fibers it innervates.

MRI (magnetic resonance imaging): a diagnostic tool to display tissues unseen in X-rays or other techniques.

Multiple sclerosis: a chronic disease of the central nervous system wherein myelin, the insulation on nerve fibers, is lost. MS is thought to be an autoimmune dysfunction; the body turns on itself.

Myelin: a white, fatty insulating material for axons; produced in the peripheral nervous system by Schwann cells and in the central nervous system by oligodendrocytes. Myelin is necessary for rapid signal transmission along nerve fibers. Loss of myelin accompanies many central nervous system injuries, and is the principal cause of multiple sclerosis. The process of remyelination is an important line of research in spinal cord injury.

Myelomeningocele: a neural tube birth defect in which a portion of the spinal cord protrudes through the vertebral column. A form of spina bifida, usually accompanied by paralysis of the lower extremities and by hydrocephalus.

Nerve Growth Factor (NGF): A protein that supports survival of embryonic neurons and regulates neurotransmitters; one of several growth factors identified in the central nervous system. These factors, including BDNF (brain-derived neurotrophic factor) and CNTF (ciliary neurotrophic factor), have important roles in regeneration.

Neurogenic bladder: A bladder that does not function normally due to nerve damage related to spinal cord injury, multiple sclerosis or a stroke.

Neurogenic shock: can be a complication of injury to the brain or spinal cord; a type of shock caused by the sudden loss of signals from the sympathetic nervous system that maintain the normal muscle tone in blood vessel walls. The blood vessels relax and become dilated, resulting in pooling of the blood in the venous system and an overall decrease in blood pressure.

Neurolysis: destruction of peripheral nerve by radio-frequency heat or by chemical injection. Used to treat spasticity.

Neuron: a nerve cell that can receive and send information by way of synaptic connections.

Neuropathic pain: a type of pain (sometimes referred to as central pain) that cannot be traced to a simple stimulus, rather, it is a complex pathology related to spinal cord nerves that may have sprouted new, inappropriate connections, may have lost myelin, or may operate in an altered biochemical environment.

Neuroprosthesis: a device using electrical stimulation to facilitate such activities as standing, bladder voiding, hand grasp, etc.

Neurotransmitter: a chemical released from a neuron ending, at a synapse, to either excite or inhibit the adjacent neuron or muscle cell. Stored in vesicles near the synapse, released when an impulse arrives.

Nitroglycerine: vasodilator used in paste form for treatment of autonomic dysreflexia.

Occupational therapist: the member of the rehabilitation team who helps maximize a person's independence; OTs teach daily living activities, health maintenance and self-care, and consult on equipment choices.

Off-label: the prescription of a drug for conditions other than what it was approved for.

Oligodendrocyte: a central nervous system glial cell; the site of myelin manufacture for central nervous system neurons (the job of Schwann cells in the peripheral nervous system). A myelin protein from oligodendrocytes (called Nogo) is known to be a potent inhibitor of nerve growth.

Orthostatic hypotension: related to pooling of blood in lower extremities in combination with lower blood pressure in people with SCI. Elastic binders and compression hosiery often used to avoid lightheadedness.

Osteoporosis: loss of bone density, common in immobile bones after SCI

Ostomy: an opening in the skin to allow for a suprapubic catheter drainage (cystostomy), for elimination of intestinal contents (colostomy or ileostomy), or for passage of air (tracheostomy).

Overactive bladder (detrusor): a bladder with uninhibited (involuntary) bladder contractions. These may cause leakage (urinary incontinence). An uninhibited contraction may cause autonomic dysreflexia in a person with SCI at T6 or above.

Oxybutinine: an anticholinergic drug with an antispasmodic effect on smooth muscle, often used to calm overactive bladder.

Paraplegia: loss of function below the cervical spinal cord segments; upper body usually retains full function and sensation.

Parasympathetic system: one of the two divisions of the autonomic nervous system, responsible for regulation of internal organs and glands, which occurs unconsciously. (*See* Sympathetic nervous system).

Passive standing: getting on one's feet, propped up in a standing frame or other device; said to benefit bone strength, skin integrity, bowel and bladder function.

PCA: personal care assistant or attendant.

Percussion: forceful tapping on congested parts of chest to facilitate postural drainage in persons with high tetraplegia unable to cough.

Peripheral nervous system: nerves outside the spinal cord and brain of the central nervous system. Damaged peripheral nerves can regenerate.

Phrenic nerve stimulation: electrical stimulation of the nerve that fires the diaphragm muscle, facilitating breathing in high tetraplegics.

Physiatrist: a doctor whose specialty is physical medicine and rehabilitation.

Physical therapist (PT): a key member of the rehabilitation team; PTs examine, test and treat people to enhance their maximum physical ability.

Placebo: an inactive substance or dummy treatment, e.g., a sugar pill, that has the same appearance as an experimental treatment but does not confer a physiological benefit. The placebo effect reflects the expectations of the participant.

Plasticity: long-term adaptive mechanisms by which the nervous system restores or modifies itself toward normal levels of function. The peripheral nervous system is quite plastic; the central nervous system, long thought to be "wired" permanently, reorganizes or forms new synapses in response to injury.

Pluripotency: refers to a stem cell that has the potential to differentiate into any of the three germ layers: endoderm (interior stomach lining, gastrointestinal tract, the lungs), mesoderm (muscle, bone, blood, urogenital), or ectoderm (epidermal tissues and nervous system).

Polytrauma: a clinical syndrome with severe injuries involving two or more major organs or physiological systems which will initiate an amplified metabolic and physiological response.

Post-Polio syndrome: signs of accelerated aging and decline in people who long ago had polio. Fatigue, pain and loss of function.

Postural drainage: using gravity to help clear lungs of mucus; head is lower than chest.

Postural hypotension: lowered blood pressure resulting in light-headedness. Blood pools up in legs or pelvic region. A common remedy is elastic hose. (*see also* Orthostatic hypotension).

Pressure sore: also known as decubitus ulcer; potentially dangerous skin breakdown due to pressure on skin resulting in infection, tissue death. Skin sores are preventable.

Prosthesis: replacement device for a body part; e.g., an artificial limb.

Quad-coughing: also known as assisted coughing; a caregiver assists the person with SCI to clear his or her airways by applying pressure below the ribs over the diaphragm while pushing upward.

Quadriplegia: loss of function of any injured or diseased cervical spinal cord segment, affecting all four body limbs. (The term "tetraplegia" is etymologically more accurate, combining "tetra" and "plegia," both from the Greek, rather than "quadri" and "plegia," a Latin-Greek amalgam.)

Randomized Control Trial (RCT): a clinical trial in which the subjects enrolled are randomly assigned to either the experimental treatment arm (group) or control study arm of the trial. It is the preferred clinical trial protocol to be used in all pivotal clinical trial phases (e.g. Phase 3 trials). Well-designed RCTs minimize the influence of variables other than the intervention that might affect trial outcomes. For this reason, they provide the best evidence of efficacy and safety. The most rigorous RCTs utilize a placebo (inactive) control group and blinding (conceal from trial examiners which participants have received active vs. control treatment) to minimize bias in interpretation of results.

Range of motion (ROM): the normal range of movement of any body joint; also refers to exercises designed to maintain this range and prevent contractures.

Reciprocating Gait Orthosis (RGO): a type of long leg brace used for ambulation by paralyzed people. Uses cables across the back to transfer energy from leg to leg to simulate a more natural gait.

Reflex: an involuntary response to a stimulus involving nerves not under control of the brain. In some types of paralysis, reflexes cannot be inhibited by the brain; they become exaggerated and thereby cause spasms.

Reflux: the backflow of urine from the bladder into the ureters and kidneys, caused by high bladder pressure (too full, or sphincter won't relax). Reflux can lead to serious kidney problems, including total kidney failure.

Regeneration: in brain or spinal cord injury, the regrowth of nerve fiber tissue by way of a biologic process. In the peripheral system, nerves do regenerate after damage and re-form functional connections. Central nerves can be induced to regrow, provided the proper environment is created; the challenge remains to restore connections to effectively restore function, especially in long tracts necessary for major motor recovery.

Renal scan: A test to determine kidney function. It involves the injection of liquid into the vein that then passes through the kidneys and down into the bladder. If the kidneys are weak or there is a lot of backpressure from the bladder, the liquid will not pass down to the bladder with its normal speed.

Residual urine: urine that remains in bladder after voiding; too much can lead to a bladder infection.

Retrograde pyelogram (RP): insertion of contrast material directly into kidney through an instrument. Used to study kidney function.

Rhizotomy: a procedure that cuts or interrupts spinal nerve roots; sometimes used to treat spasticity.

Sacral: refers to fused segments of lower vertebrae or lowest spinal cord segments below lumbar level.

Schwann cell: responsible in the peripheral nervous system for myelinating axons; provides trophic support in injury environment. Schwann cells transplanted to the spinal cord are being studied to see if they restore function.

Secondary injury: the biochemical and physiological changes that occur in the injured spinal cord after the initial trauma has done its damage. Among the suspected pathologies are swelling, loss of blood flow, lipid peroxidation. Drug treatments have been used both in the lab and in clinical trials to reduce these secondary effects.

Self-Catheterization: intermittent cathing, the goal of which is to empty the bladder as needed, on one's own, minimizing risk of infection. Some may need assistance if hand function is impaired.

Septicemia: local infection that spreads to affect multiple body systems.

Shunt: a tube to drain a cavity; in the spinal cord, used to treat a syrinx by equalizing pressures between the syrinx and the spinal fluids. In spina bifida, used to reduce pressure of hydrocephalus.

Sleep apnea: irregular breathing during sleep resulting in fatigue, drowsiness during the day. Higher incidence in tetraplegics. (*See* BiPAP).

Spasticity: hyperactive muscles that move or jerk involuntarily. Spasms may be triggered by bladder infections, skin ulcers and any other sensory stimulus. Such uncontrolled muscle activity is caused by excessive reflex activity below the level of lesion.

Sphincterotomy: a permanent surgery that involves cutting the urinary sphincter so that urine can more easily flow out of the bladder. This surgery may be used when the sphincter does not relax at the same time the bladder is contracting (*see* Detrusor sphincter dyssynergia).

Spinal shock: similar to a concussion in the brain. After spinal cord injury, shock causes immediate flaccid paralysis, which lasts about three weeks.

Stem cell: a type of cell that can become any cell in the body. These cells have been found in adult animals. There are great hopes, and many great claims yet to be validated, that stem cells will treat paralysis, diabetes, heart disease, etc.

Stoma: a surgical opening that provides an alternative path for urine to exit the body (*see* Cutaneous ileovesicostomy).

Suctioning: removal of mucus and secretions from lungs; important for high tetraplegics who lack ability to cough.

Suprapubic cystostomy: a small opening made in the bladder and through the abdomen, sometimes to remove large stones, more commonly to establish a catheter urinary drain.

Synapse: the specialized junction between a neuron and another neuron or muscle cell for transfer of information (e.g., brain signals, sensory inputs) along the nervous system; usually involves release and reception of a chemical transmitter.

Syringomyelia: formation of fluid-filled cavity (a syrinx) in injured area of spinal cord, a result of nerve fiber degradation and necrosis; sometimes the result of tethered cord. The cyst often extends upwards, extending also the neurological deficit. Treatment may include surgery to insert a shunt for drainage of the cavity, or to untether the cord.

Syringomyelocele: a congenital neural tube defect, a cause of spina bifida; spinal fluid fills a sac of spinal membrane.

Syrinx: a cyst; a cavity.

Tenodesis (hand splint): metal or plastic support for hand, wrist or fingers. Used to facilitate greater function by transferring wrist extension into grip and finger control.

Tethered cord: tendency of membranes surrounding spinal cord to scar or stick together and thus impede flow of spinal fluid; the result is often a cyst that can in turn lead to functional loss. Can be treated surgically.

Thoracic: pertaining to the chest, vertebrae or spinal cord segments between the cervical and lumbar areas.

Tracheostomy: opening in neck (windpipe) to facilitate air flow.

Transurethral resection (TUR): a surgical procedure to reduce bladder neck resistance.

Upper motor neurons: long nerve cells that originate in the brain and travel in tracts through the spinal cord. Injury to these nerves cuts off contact between brain and muscle.

Urethral diverticulum: a small pocket in the urethra that can interfere with insertion of a catheter.

Urethral stent: A tubular device made of wire mesh; placed in the urethra to hold the external sphincter open.

Urinary sphincter: The muscles that relax when urinating and tighten to prevent leakage.

Urinary tract infection (UTI): Bacteria that cause symptoms (cloudy, strong smelling urine, blood in the urine or sudden increase in spasticity) in the urethra (urethritis), bladder (cystitis) or kidney (pyelonephritis). Bacteria that does not cause symptoms usually does not need treatment.

Urodynamics: a test that involves filling the bladder through a catheter to determine how well the bladder and sphincter are working.

Valsalva maneuver: Bearing down with abdominal muscles in order to push urine out of the bladder.

Ventilator: mechanical device to facilitate breathing in persons with impaired diaphragm function.

Vertebrae: the bones that make up the spinal column.

Vesicoureteral reflux: urine flows backward from the bladder up to the kidneys. This can cause a bladder infection to spread up to the kidneys or cause stretching of the kidneys (hydronephrosis).

Voiding: eliminating urine through the bladder.

Weaning: gradual removal of mechanical ventilation, as a person's lung strength and vital capacity increase.

Index

Sam Maddox is Knowledge Manager for the Reeve Foundation Paralysis Resource Center. He is the author of the books *Spinal Network* and *The Quest for Cure*, and is the founder of *New Mobility* magazine. He writes and produces the newsletters *Progress in Research* and the *Reeve Report*, and writes a blog about biomedical research for *www.ChristopherReeve.org*

Christopher Voelker was a highly regarded professional in the entertainment community and has worked with top record labels, networks and studios. He has shot the likes of Mick Fleetwood, Ringo Starr, David Lynch, Beyonce, Lauryn Hill, Billy Zane, Carmen Electra, Christina Applegate, Bow Wow, and Brandy. As an artist and poet of light, Voelker has been an integral part of the evolving disability community; he has photographed covers of *New Mobility* for over 20 years. Mr. Voelker passed away on September 11, 2014.